FLAMES OF RETRIBUTION

A Queens Of Destruction Novel

Katlin Pruitt

The characters and events portrayed in this book are fictitious. Any similarity to real persons, living or dead, is coincidental and not intended by the author.

ISBN-13: 9798873249619

Cover design by: crimsonsdesigns

Printed in the United States of America

For everyone whose darkness has threatened to consume them. Keep fucking going.

PLAYLIST

Hope - We Came as Romans
Can you Feel My Heart - Bring Me The Horizon
Bow Down - I Prevail
You Won't Be Missed - Like Moths to Flames
Riptide - Beartooth
From Darkness - Upon A Burning Body
Estella - KennyHoopla and Travis Barker
Fuck You - The Used
Just Pretend - Bad Omens
Sick of it All - Magnolia Park
All Fucked Up - The Amity Affliction
I'm Made Of Wax Larry, What Are You Made Of - A Day To Remember
Thought It Was - Iann Dior ft Machine Gun Kelly
Have Faith In Me - A Day To Remember
A Match Into Water - Pierce The Veil
Times like this - Fit For a King
Disguise - Motionless In White
Rescue Me - Marshmello ft. A Day To Remember
The Sinner - Memphis May Fire
Sleepwalking - Bring Me The Horizon
Roger Rabbit - Sleeping With Sirens

CONTENTS

AUTHOR'S NOTE

Trigger Warning:

This book contains themes and content that may be distressing or triggering for some readers. We believe in providing a safe reading experience, and we want you to be aware of the following potential triggers:

- **Violence:** This book may contain scenes of physical, emotional, or psychological violence, including but not limited to, abuse, assault, and combat.

- **Sexual Content:** There may be explicit sexual content, including scenes of a sexual nature, discussions of sexual violence, and non-consensual situations.

- **Self-Harm and Suicidal Themes**:The book may explore topics related to self-harm, suicide, or suicidal ideation, which could be distressing for some readers.

- **Substance Abuse:** Characters in this book may engage in substance abuse or addiction, and these themes may be depicted graphically.

- **Mental Health Issues:** The story may delve into mental health issues, such as depression, anxiety, or other psychological disorders, which may be triggering for some readers.

- **Loss and Grief:** Themes of loss, grief, and mourning may be present, potentially evoking emotional responses.

- **Abuse and Trauma:** The book might address themes of abuse, trauma, or post-traumatic stress, which may be upsetting to some readers.

- **Strong Language:** The book may include strong language, offensive slurs, or derogatory terms.

We encourage readers to prioritize their emotional well-being and make an informed choice regarding whether to read this book. If you find yourself feeling distressed or triggered while reading, we recommend reaching out to a mental health professional or a trusted individual for support. Your well-being is of utmost importance to us, and we want your reading experience to be a positive one.

BLURB

In the twisted world of dark desires and forbidden vendettas, two souls collide, igniting a passion that burns hotter than revenge.

Lorelei has spent a lifetime plotting, her heart consumed by one relentless desire: vengeance. With patience as her closest ally, she waits for the perfect moment to strike. But her meticulous plans are thrown into chaos when he enters her life—the enigmatic man with a bleeding pupil. She's the Queen of Fire, a force to be reckoned with, and she'll incinerate anyone who dares to stand in her way.

Dash is a man on a mission, determined to eradicate the worst of humanity. But a deadly encounter with a bewitching siren ensnares him in a web of forbidden temptation. Despite his strength, he finds himself powerless against her mesmerizing green eyes. But Dash harbors a perilous secret, one that, once revealed, could make him a target on her hit list as well.

In a world where danger and desire entwine, "Flames of Retribution" is a seductive and thrilling tale of two souls locked in a dance of dark romance, where the lines between love and vengeance blur, and only the strongest will survive. Will they succumb to their darkest desires or find a way to conquer the darkness that threatens to consume them both?

PROLOGUE

Thirteen years ago

Lorelei

Standing here with my knees shaking, clad in nothing but my tattered old shirt and worn-out underwear, I can't help but wonder how I've allowed this to persist for so long. I barely have time to contemplate that before I feel another searing pain in my thigh, as though it's about to hit bone. I clench my teeth so tightly that I fear a molar might crack.

Judging by the intensity of the pain, he has gone too deep once again. I glance down at my thighs, which are now smeared with crimson blood flowing down my legs like a rain-swollen creek, pooling in the stained bathroom tub beneath my grimy feet. My father's knife dangles in his hand, but his gaze is fixed on my bleeding legs, his brows draw together in concern. However, his concern doesn't stem from the fear of harming me but rather from the dread of potential consequences if I don't survive.

"We just need to purge all the bad from you; you'll understand someday," he mutters in a distant voice. Without another word, he drops the knife onto the linoleum floor and exits the bathroom, leaving me alone. I've learned the hard way not to resist him during these episodes, when I do I pay the price in flesh. When he's in this state, he's so detached from reality that it's almost as though it's not him at all, but an evil twin he summons to torment me.

As the bathroom door slams shut with a heavy thud, I collapse in the tub, unable to support my own weight any longer. There's far too much blood in the tub for this to end well. I came to terms with the fact that I would die at his hands years ago, but I never thought that tonight would be the night.

I curl up on the cold tub floor as the sticky blood envelops me. Maybe I can remain like this; soon, I'll run out of blood, and it will all be over. It will be just like falling asleep, at least that's what I've read.

Is death my only way out? I lay there for minutes or hours; I can't tell. I silently beg for the end to claim me soon.

Then something dark blossoms in my chest—twisted, ugly, and growing by the second. Why should I be the one to die? He deserves to rot for everything he's put me through especially when all I've ever done is seek his love. I'm not the one in the wrong.

With shaky hands, I slowly push myself up, attempting to focus my eyes after the considerable blood loss has left me weak and dizzy. I carefully climb out of the tub and manage to grab a few towels, pressing them against the wounds in an attempt to staunch the bleeding. I can't die here. I won’t die here.

I'll never try to get help for my dad again. His time in the behavioral health unit did nothing to improve his mental state; if anything, it seems to have worsened. It's not worth sacrificing my life.

When I regain my strength, I stand and face my reflection in the grimy mirror. My eyes burn with a hatred I've never witnessed before, but I grasp onto it with both hands, using it as a lifeline. This one last time, I’ll stitch myself back together.

I'm getting out of here, and when I return, it will be to seek justice for the girl who once lay in that bathtub.

CHAPTER 1

"I can't drown my demons they know how to swim"
-Bring Me The Horizon

Lorelei

I've always enjoyed my solitude. In those moments of isolation, my inner darkness is unshackled, flowing naturally, like a wild creature tasting freedom after years of captivity. It feels like an unburdening of the soul. If anyone were to truly glimpse the depth of my inner chaos, they might recoil in terror, their very core shaken by fear. But that's perfectly acceptable to me; after all, people inevitably depart at some juncture in my life.

I wear my darkness as a badge of honor. Most are too weak to face the demons that live in the dark, or they just ignore them as if they don't exist entirely; living in constant denial, what amateurs. I embrace it. We all have it wandering around inside, I'm just not deluded like the majority. I've honed the skill of playing a role when I need to blend in with the crowd, donning a mask pleasant enough to navigate the world, all the while knowing my true self. I'm aware of what simmers beneath the surface. Most never have the privilege of glimpsing those facets of my being, because I guard my darkness closely.

I stand before the bathroom mirror fixing my long dark brown hair in a braid so it won't get in my way at work later tonight. As I meet my own reflection, I pause for a moment. It's my eyes that always draw people in, not my high cheekbones, not my petite nose, not even my full lips. It's those piercing green eyes.

I've carried these comments with me throughout my life, the hushed conversations of people remarking on how unsettling they can be. If the eyes indeed serve as a gateway to the soul, it's as if they hint at something sinister residing within me.

I may appear average in size, but beneath that unassuming exterior, I've cultivated more strength and muscle than most would anticipate. I get satisfaction from being underestimated. I've dedicated countless hours training, driven by a solemn vow: never again would I allow anyone to hurt me through my weakness. No, the next time, I swore I would fight back with every ounce of my being, even if it meant pushing myself to the brink of destruction. Every action I take now is a conscious choice, a testament to my unwavering determination to never be stripped of the freedom I deserve.

"We just have to bleed out the bad, Lor. Once we do that, you'll be all better," his voice slurs, and the scent of whiskey burns my nose, making my eyes water.

A sharp, searing pain courses through my skin, and I glance down at my right thigh, where a long cut now runs down the center. It appears I won't be wearing shorts to school tomorrow.

I hold onto the hope that once he removes all the bad from me, we can put an end to this torment. Will the bad ever truly leave, or am I destined to forever carry it with me? I try to be good; I swear I do. But he never cares.

Maybe once I'm not bad anymore mom and dad will love me.

I tear my gaze away from my haunted reflection, realizing I was sinking into memories I'd rather not relive at this moment. Stepping out of my bathroom, I enter the living room of my apartment. I've called this place home for a while now, and I draw comfort in this haven I've crafted because, after living without safety for so long, it's a small glimmer of peace. However, I remind myself that nothing in life is permanent.

I must prepare for the day when this place will no longer be home. It's an inevitable reality.

A quick look at my black couch tells me that the guy I brought home last night isn't smart enough to pick up on the cues that he should leave before I'm done in the bathroom. It's like this one isn't in tune with "fuck boy" behaviors. I only bring hookups to my territory, to an environment that I can control and where I know I will get out alive. I stayed in the bathroom longer than normal, hoping he'd get the hint. I'm trying to be nice, but now my patience is wearing thin.

He stands up shirtless, his dark skin chiseled with muscle, slowly making his way over to me with what I'm assuming is supposed to be a seductive face. All men are the same, thinking women will crumble for a nice pair of abs and a stupid fucking smile.

I struggle to keep from rolling my eyes. I didn't bring him home because I liked him. I just needed a release, and he wasn't bad to look at. This is pretty common for me, and I've been told many times, by many different people, how fucked up it is. But what I find amusing is that if I were a man, no one would dare question my behavior. I'd probably get a pat on the back and an 'atta boy.'

Before he can reach me, I raise my hand and say, "You should go; I need to get to work." Bending down, I snatch his shirt from the floor and toss it at him. Then, I walk to my front door, holding it open for him, making my intentions clear. What I told him was somewhat untrue – I don't have to be at work for a while. But he's lingering, and his presence is grating on me, and I have somewhere to be.

He's staring at me with his mouth open, looking like an absolute fool. Most guys don't anticipate this assertiveness from a girl, but they have no idea who I am.

He bends over aggressively, snatching up the rest of his belongings without making eye contact. He storms over to me, clearly furious, and invades my personal space, towering over me in an attempt to assert dominance. But I refuse to cower. Men who use their size to establish dominance make me sick, and I will never yield to them again.

"I wish I had known you were such a bitch last night,I would have chosen someone more attractive," he snarls at me.

It takes everything in me to stifle my laugh, but I fix a gaze on him, knowing my inner darkness is right at the surface, ready to engage, and his time is running out. A small smirk tugs at my lips, subtly signaling that I'm prepared to play if he's game, and I hope he is. I got a release, maybe my demons can too, I laugh to myself.

He falters and retreats, walking through my door and nearly tripping over his own feet. It's the eyes. Always the eyes that ensnare them. It's like a siren's call at first, drawing them in, leading them to believe it will be a good time, until I'm through with them. They're nothing to me and I cast them aside when I'm done.

I close my door, and head into the kitchen to retrieve my phone from the island. I pick it up and swipe my finger to unlock it, noticing a message from Bex, probably a reminder that I'm not at brunch where I was supposed to be ten minutes ago. It shouldn't be a surprise to her.

I quickly press the call button and scramble around my apartment until I spot my purse on a chair. Grabbing my shoes, I rush out the door, locking it behind me.

"Where the heck are you?" her voice is loud and blares through my phone. I can hear chatter in the background, along with what sounds like music.

"I know, I know, I'm sorry. I'm on my way. It took me a minute to throw out uh...," I say breathlessly trying to put a name to the face but come up empty as I run toward my apartment's elevator.

"Lor... You don't even know his name, do you?" she's loosened up now, and I can hear the laughter in her voice. Bex always finds my nonchalant attitude toward men amusing. She's the complete opposite; she loves and loves intensely. The last guy she loved ended up hurting her, and she's been single since. It's often the people with hearts of gold who get mistreated. It's a good thing mine is black, charred, and devoid of emotion.

Bex scoffs at my response, "Girl, just get here now; people are starting to look at me funny." At this point, I'm already in the parking garage, climbing into my black truck. This truck has been a dream of mine for years, and after putting in what felt like an eternity of hard work, I finally made it happen. After growing up constantly struggling, I find that I become attached to things I'm now able to provide myself.

"I'll be there in five," I huff and promptly hang up on her.

Saturdays always mean brunch before heading to the club for work. We've maintained this tradition for four years now, ever since I hired Bex as my head bartender. I first met Bex when I was working at the club. Some obnoxious guy was getting aggressive with her, and I stepped in, threatening to kick his ass before throwing him out. I wasn't about to let that kind of behavior slide in my club. From that night on, we became friends, and shortly after, I brought her on board.

I've been running Club Sin for six years now, and I genuinely love it. The owners are hardly ever around, and who knows what they do, but their absence doesn't bother me. It makes the club feel like it's truly mine. They don't seem to care much about what I do since I generate significant profits for them, and that's all that matters in their eyes.

The air conditioner is blasting in my truck as I pray for a reprieve from the already intense heat. It's only April, and it's already a scorching 92 degrees here in Phoenix, but I'm accustomed to it. I also appreciate the fact that I never have to worry about harsh winters; I'm simply not built for the cold. I pull into the parking lot of the breakfast restaurant she chose and hurry inside, fully aware that if I take longer than I quoted, Bex will be fuming, she hates waiting alone.

Walking through the front doors, I pay no attention to the host and spot Bex at a small table, sipping what I assume is a mimosa. I can't help but roll my eyes, yet I feel a smile tugging at my lips as I make my way over to her. I give my jean shorts and black tank top a quick adjustment, feeling like a bit of a mess after the rush out of the door earlier this morning.

"It's about time; you're picking up the tab for making me wait" she says, lifting the glass to her lips once more.

All I can do is stare at her for a moment; she can be a firecracker now and then. That's one of the things I love about her, but her default setting is genuinely sweet. She stands a few inches taller than me, her light cinnamon-brown hair falling to shoulder length, with dark brown eyes to match, along with a sprinkling of freckles decorating her nose. She's undeniably gorgeous, and it's no wonder men flock to her.

Yet, the best part about her is that she carries this positive outlook on life, and she refuses to let anyone forget it. At times, I'm a tad envious of that, but having her around feels like I've stolen a bit of that goodness for myself. There's a gentleness about her that I lack, and over time, a small part of me has warmed to it. I imagine that having a sister might feel something like this.

I look up and lock eyes with a staff member, waving them

down as I take my seat across from Bex.

"Can I help you ladies?" our waiter, a young guy chirps with far too much enthusiasm.

"Can you bring us both a bloody mary? I'll have the meat lover's omelet, and she'll take the French toast," I state firmly, then look away, indicating that I'm finished with the conversation. After the morning I've had, I'm in no mood for small talk with strangers.

I can sense that he's a bit taken aback by my straightforwardness, and he glances at Bex for reassurance. She nods, and he meanders off.

“What if I wanted something different for breakfast this week?” She’s staring at me with one eyebrow raised almost like a challenge, and I smirk and reply “well then I'll wave him down again.”

As I'm turning away, she grabs my hand and playfully chokes out, "No, I'm kidding you know that's what I wanted." Bex despises making a fuss and would gladly eat the wrong meal to avoid confrontation, but if our roles were reversed, she'd make a scene for someone she cares about. And then, she'd promptly apologize.

She orders the same thing every time, and I can predict her order at any restaurant. I think that might drive her a bit crazy, but Bex is predictable, and I love that about her. I'm not a fan of surprises, and her consistency provides me with a comfort I cherish that I didn’t have growing up.

We spend the next hour sipping our drink and laughing until we both realize it's time to head to the club to stock the bar and get the club ready for a busy night. After I settle the bill, we make our way to my truck and drive just one mile north to Sin. We rarely use her little white car, a choice I've made intentionally, as her driving skills are far from stellar.

We arrive at the back of the club, where employees park, which will be overflowing with cars later, but being here to set up ensures my parking doesn’t create havoc trying to leave. Walking up to the back door of our imposing brick building, which grants staff access, we find it already unlocked. Kellan, our bar back must be inside already.

I hired Kellan around a year ago, and he's been nothing short of amazing. It's clear he has a little crush on Bex, but she hasn't acted on it, despite my strong suspicion that they would make a great couple. After having your heart broken like she did, it takes time to open up again, or so she tells me. I have no firsthand experience in that department.

"And there they are, the ladies of the afternoon," his husky voice booms over the loud music blaring through the speakers.

"Are we fully stocked for tonight?" I ask, turning down the music so I don't have to yell.

"Yes, we're all set on my front," he smiles while looking at Bex. This poor guy has it bad, but he's been patient with her.

Kellan is only a year or so younger than us, but his innocence makes him seem much younger to me. He has light brown skin and closely shaved dark hair. Tall and lean, his blue eyes always seem to be smiling. He represents everything hopeful in this world, and I genuinely hope nothing changes that for him.

I nod and make my way to my office while they finish up out there. Sin's decor is precisely as you'd imagine. It's adorned in dark reds and blacks, with a sadistic gothic vibe that I adore. If the devil himself were to run a club, it would look like this. But I’m a close second.

Sitting in my office, I make sure to get the cash drawers ready and, lastly, start dressing in our "uniforms." I shouldn't really call them uniforms since it's a rather loose term. We wear all black and make sure to look as devious as our name suggests. Apart from these guidelines, we're free to wear whatever we choose as long as it doesn't inhibit doing our jobs. We have a reputation to maintain.

In the privacy of my office, I slide off my jean shorts and tank, replacing them with a skin-tight, black, floor-length dress. It features a long slit up the right leg, stopping just at the top of my thigh; any higher, and it would be indecent. I slide into my usual strappy black heels and keep my hair in the braid from earlier. Now that I manage the club, wearing a dress is more manageable for moving around. However, if I were still bartending, I'd have opted for something else.
Not to sound conceited, but I know I look stunning. I step out of my office and make my way to the main club area, prepared to call our staff meeting before the doors open. At this point, all the staff members are present, and they start to gather around me, eager to receive their briefings for the upcoming night.

"Alright, everyone, doors open in ten minutes. The club is fully stocked, and there's already a line around the building. We have a few VIP members on the list tonight, including politicians and small caliber celebrities, so be on your worst behavior and squeeze every tip you can out of them. Lastly, remember to keep your mics on tonight so we can communicate effectively. Kellan, I'm looking at you," I say, looking around at all my staff before settling on Kellan. He smiles, his light brown skin gleaming under the red lights overhead.

Kellan often forgets to charge his mic after each shift, resulting in it dying every time. Normally, something like that would irritate me, but I have a soft spot for him. I may have a tough exterior, but I won't be the one to snuff out his brightness. There's so little of it left in the world.

Everyone smiles, knowing that if they do their job well, they'll leave tonight with heavy pockets. This is a busy club, well-known throughout the area. We're only open from Thursday through Saturday, which makes us more exclusive. Not to mention, the lines are always so long that it's a gamble whether you'll make it in or not. You need to know someone important to end up on a VIP list.

The night becomes a blur, like always. My staff excels at their jobs, making it a smooth night for me aside from the usual duties. I pay well on top of the generous tips they receive, and as a result, they bust their asses. I only hire the best, and in that regard, they have yet to let me down. If they aren't the best, they don't work here; it's as simple as that.

As I'm making my rounds, checking on guests and ensuring my staff is handling the crowd, I come to a sudden stop. I can feel something, or someone, although I'm not quite sure. Slowly, I turn my head toward one of the VIP booths and notice a man staring at me from his seat in a red velvet booth.

I learned at a young age to hone in on my gut feelings and trust them. It's probably a trauma response. I notice every little detail, every movement, every change in tone. It's as if I'm constantly preparing to protect myself. It might seem as if I have a background in law enforcement, by the way I etch every detail into my memory, just in case it's needed later when something goes down.

The dim lighting makes it difficult to discern many details, but he appears relaxed in his seat, one ankle crossed over the opposite knee, holding a glass of amber liquid that rests on the back of the booth. His unwavering gaze continues to feel like it's drilling into me.

I turn and walk toward him, exuding confidence in every stride. Whatever this guy is up to, he needs to know that I won't tolerate any nonsense.

Walking up to the booth, I look at him directly and say, "Is there anything I can get for you?" I leave open space for him to fill in his name, he's not a VIP I recognize, but he doesn't. I take a quick glance around and notice he's alone, which is rather unusual. People usually reserve a booth to show off and flaunt money they often don't have, a pathetic status symbol that they mistakenly believe holds meaning.

He leans forward, placing his drink on the napkin laid out on his table, and slowly stands up, buttoning his finely tailored suit jacket. As he straightens, I realize he's quite tall, with shoulders so broad that I wonder if he struggles to get through doorways. His presence is imposing, the kind of man you can't ignore when he enters a room.

His suit drapes over him impeccably, accentuating a physique chiseled with lean muscle. As my gaze rises to meet his eyes, I become ensnared by their beauty, even in the subdued lighting. A mesmerizing shade of green, not as vibrant as mine, yet one of his eyes features a sizable brown spot at the base of his iris, creating a captivating illusion of a bleeding pupil. It's a distinctive and strangely alluring detail.

His jawline is defined, adorned with a subtle shadow of facial hair. Dark brown strands of hair are meticulously combed, tempting my hand to run through them, curious to discover if they're as soft as they appear.

There's a heavy pause as we both continue to lock eyes. He extends his hand as if he's about to brush a strand of hair behind my ear but then stops himself, apparently having second thoughts. Instead, he says, "I'm perfect now that you're here." I can feel knots forming low in my stomach, which is unusual; no one has ever elicited such a reaction from me. Almost as a reflex, I take a small step back, and he frowns for a moment but quickly wipes it from his face almost unnoticeable. His ability to mask his emotions becomes evident as his expression shifts.

"Can I get you another drink?" I inquire, glancing toward his half-empty glass.

"No, I was just about to leave, but it was a pleasure meeting you," he smirks, running his thumb along his lower lip. The simple gesture takes me by surprise for a fleeting moment as my eyes are drawn to his lips.

I give him a small smile, nod, and turn to walk out of the circular booth, still feeling his eyes drilling into my back. I make a conscious effort to walk with confidence to the club bar, where I see Bex staring at me with her jaw hanging open.

As I approach where Bex is, I turn and look back toward the booth just in time to see him toss something down next to his drink and walk out without another glance. Curiosity gnaws at me, so when I notice he's left through the main door, I return to the table to investigate. Lying next to his glass is a paper sailboat, cleverly folded from a black bar napkin. I pick it up and take it back over to the bar area with me, ensuring it's out of Bex's line of vision.

"What the heck was that?" Bex gushes like we're in high school and the captain of the football team just asked me to homecoming.

"I was just asking him if he wanted another drink," I reply, pretending to check her bar for any needs, even though we close in an hour and it doesn't really matter. But I need to appear busy and unfazed.

"Are you kidding me?" Bex exclaims while mixing a drink, her gaze unwavering as she looks at me. "He was eyeing you so hard I felt dirty just watching."

She's being a bit dramatic, but there might be some truth to what she's saying. No one has ever looked at me with such intensity, and I can't deny that something deep inside me responded to it. Nonetheless, I push the man out of my mind and focus on finishing up my night.

We finally lock the doors after the staff has quickly cleaned the club, allowing us all to go home. Everyone is tired but content from the generous tips they earned tonight.

Bex and I, as usual, are the last to leave. We've changed back into our casual clothes from earlier, and we're walking toward my truck to head home when something catches our attention on the hood. We notice it simultaneously.

We're hesitant, but I reach into my purse and grab the knife I always keep in there, my instincts on high alert. The knife feels heavy in my hand as I inspect our surroundings, and I grip it tightly, prepared for anything.

On the hood of my truck lies a single paper sailboat.

I grab the paper sailboat and signal for Bex to get into the truck, glancing around to see if anyone is watching us. Once we're inside the truck, I lock the doors behind us and scan the back seat. After confirming that we're clear, I turn the paper sailboat over in my hand, but there's no note or any other clue as to why this was left for me. Again.

This seems like a private game between just the two of us, and an instinct tells me to keep it that way. So, I don't mention the one he left me earlier on his table before he walked out.

"What the... What is that, a boat? Who leaves a folded boat on someone's car?" Bex asks, clearly puzzled, but I just shrug in response, "probably some drunk guest playing a prank."

We pull out of the parking lot, not wanting to linger, especially since I can sense Bex's unease with the situation. However, I don't share her discomfort. Instead, my body feels like a live wire tingling with excitement at the thought that maybe someone is able to rise to the task of playing with my demons.

Bex usually stays with me on Saturdays after work, as we're both off until Thursday rolls around again. I still have managerial tasks to handle, but I usually take care of them from home. On Wednesdays, I do a final check of the club before we open again on Thursdays, it's become our routine.

This job works well for those who need an open schedule. Some of my staff are students, some are parents wanting more time with their kids during the week, and others have second jobs for reasons only they need to know. I appreciate that I can provide a work environment that gives them flexibility for other aspects of their lives.

As I see my high-rise coming into view, I feel relief knowing I'm almost home. I love living downtown, but even amidst the city, you can still see the mountains. The view of the mountains surrounding me is breathtaking from my apartment. To be honest, it was the primary reason I picked this place initially. There's something about the vast mountain ranges that make me feel protected, like a barrier between me and the outside world that lives beyond my bubble.

Just as we finish parking and head to the elevator, my phone dings. It's a bit odd since it's almost three in the morning. I pull out my phone to see a text from my mom, and a sense of dread starts pooling in my gut.

MOM: ur dad is in the psych ward again. Not that you care but thought u should know.

The manipulative tone in her text makes me smile, and the fact that she still calls it a psych ward rather than a behavioral health unit shows just how out of touch she really is.

I sigh and tuck my phone away without responding. I unlock my door, and Bex throws herself inside before I can even turn on the lights.

My entire living room has big windows that offer a stunning view. When I first moved in, Bex said it looked like Hades's bachelor pad, and to me, that was endearing. Her apartment is the complete opposite of mine, just like she is my opposite, but somehow it works.

We spend the remaining dark hours drinking and laughing, only going to bed when the sun starts to peek around the mountains. Bex heads to the guest bedroom just down the hall. There's really no point in calling it a guest bedroom since she's the only person who has ever slept there.

I climb into my bed and think about the text from my mom. It's almost a ritual at this point, my dad having an 'accident,' and me going to visit to see if this time he finally succeeded. My eyes finally close, and for a while, I forget how fucked up they truly are. Maybe I'm more like them than I think.

CHAPTER 2

"You will never know, it's the price I pay
Look into my eyes, we are not the same"
- I Prevail

Dash

It takes a lot to catch my attention. I've seen many things, both good and bad, in my lifetime, so it means something when my interest is piqued. When I saw those green eyes across the bar, peering into my soul, I couldn't help but stare.

I watched her from my booth for far longer than I should have, but I couldn't force myself to look away. I was there for another reason but she was distracting. The way she moved in the shadows, like she owned the darkness, was entrancing. She kept herself hidden, observing her surroundings from the dark and only emerging when necessary.

I have to shake my head to push away the image of her walking towards me, unwavering and exuding confidence as if she owns the very ground she walks on. I intimidate most people, but she was unfazed, as if she's faced things far worse. I put my other hand on the steering wheel, forcing myself to pay attention to the road ahead before I crash my car.

My phone rings over my car's Bluetooth, and James is talking before I can fully process it. I need to get this girl out of my head. Nothing good can come from this much distraction.

"Alright, boss, what did we learn?" James has been my right-hand guy in my personal business for years now and never fails to deliver. I found him on a wanted list because of his extraordinary hacking skills, which he was using to expose corrupt business leaders. When I saw that, I knew I needed him on my team, so I tracked him down, and we've worked together ever since. While he has the hacking skills, I have the resources to make his reach even wider and inflict maximum damage. He is the hacker above all hackers, and he knows it. Although I hate to remind him and watch his massive ego inflate further.

"Your intel was right, Senator Jenkins definitely goes to Sin, and uses the private booths to entice young girls into going home with him for further entertainment," I inform James, my voice laced with disgust. James knows exactly what sort of entertainment I'm referring to. The VIP booths at Sin provide relative privacy, and with the dim lighting in the club, people can easily conceal their identities. The unfortunate girls who leave with him have no idea he's an old piece of shit who will turn their world upside down in the worst way. The worst part is he uses his power to silence them, allowing him to escape punishment. But not this time.

The election is looming, and Jenkins has used his wealth to rise in the polls. I intend to expose him before he can be elected into office again.

"Let's release everything we have, all the concrete proof, on the 8 o'clock news tomorrow morning, and run it all day," I suggest. It's a thrilling part of what I do. Once I've meticulously gathered all the evidence, I unleash it to expose the corrupt individuals in positions of power. It's my way of leveling the playing field.

"While I have you, James, I need you to do some digging into the club Sin. There's someone I want you to look at in particular—her name is Lorelei," I say quickly, hoping he won't detect my intrigue. On my way out last night I asked the bouncer her name, and he gave it without question.

This request is for my personal interest, and it's unusual for him to investigate something that doesn't relate to my business. But there are some things he doesn't need to know. I've already done a preliminary search on her when I was leaving the club and left her a little surprise on her truck.

“Lorelei Hart, I'm assuming,” he quips, and I can hear the rapid tapping of keys on his end. "She is the general manager of the club and has been in that role for a few years. She has generated a significant amount of revenue since her hire. The club is owned by the D'Santos family, and I can't find much on them at first glance, which is unusual but I'll dig into that more later. It appears Lorelei Hart's history only goes back about 10 years; there's nothing on her before that," he continues, his voice tinged with frustration. He dislikes it when he can't figure something out immediately.

“Send me what you have on Lorelei and dig deeper into the club. You've certainly piqued my interest," I say and hang up before he can respond. I pull into my driveway, my thoughts consumed by Lorelei Hart.

Despite my wealth, I don't flaunt it. While I live comfortably, I could certainly afford more if I wished. When I founded Ash Media Group, I never expected it to grow so extensively. But that's what transpires when you establish a media company committed to exposing the unseemly truths that other media organizations attempt to conceal. Most media companies I know are deeply entwined with politicians, except for us. Stories can be manipulated in favor of the highest bidder, but we stand firm with our integrity.

Some people thirst for the truth, while those with weaker minds prefer to run from it, avoiding the sight of the real monsters. Our company is comprised of truth seekers, individuals with the courage to unveil the world's true face, but the risks are real.

I suppose I owe my wretched father some gratitude for the inheritance that I cleverly invested to launch AMG. After all, he was my source of inspiration. With the initial inheritance alone, the company could have operated for years without turning a profit. Yet, through investments and strategic advertising deals with like-minded businesses, we never had to fret about money. We could wholeheartedly focus on our mission.

Throughout my adult life, every choice I've made has been a deliberate contrast to my father. While I may possess a slightly distorted moral compass, I take solace in the fact that I am nothing like him.

While my father was unrelenting in his ruthless pursuit of power, I channel my ruthlessness into exposing and ending people like him. My mother, a saint trapped in a loveless marriage, ultimately succumbed to an early death. They labeled it as cancer, but I suspect it was her body's way of liberating her from her torment. My father was a deadlier disease than cancer could ever be.

I'm relieved to have concluded the Senator Jenkins project. It demanded countless hours of investigation, and my visit to Sin to catch him in the act provided the final piece of evidence I required. It was a gripping case for me to tackle through my company.

My day job, as I like to call it, is a contractor for the FBI specializing in interrogation techniques. I consult on the unsavory aspects of the job, which affords me access to individuals who could be described as the scum of the earth. It's partially through this role that I have access to people like Senator Jenkins, who were previously operating beneath the radar, at least until I got wind of their activities and decided to take matters into my own hands.

Entering my home, a rare smile graces my lips. It's a smile born of the knowledge that even those who believe themselves too powerful or too clever to be caught will eventually find themselves ensnared by the devil himself. While I work for the government, my position provides me with the ideal cover to allow me to get the real job done.

Once I'm inside my large, open foyer, I make my way to my office, my shoes clicking softly on the darkly stained concrete floors. My house is located in a secluded spot on the outskirts of town, surrounded by dense shrubbery that provide both privacy and a barrier against prying eyes. It's an industrial-looking home with large windows and a sleek black exterior. Inside, it's sparsely decorated, as I've never been one for clutter, or excessive personal effects.

My office features brick walls, and a large wooden desk sits prominently in the center of the room, commanding attention. I appreciate the poetic symbolism. I take a seat and switch on my black desk lamp, opting to keep the room dimly lit. I slowly open my laptop, allowing it to power on, and then make my way to the bar cart in the corner of the room. I pour myself two fingers of whiskey before returning to my desk. I don't drink often, but it's a small indulgence I allow myself after successfully closing one of my cases. AMG handles a wide range of cases, but I prefer to be as hands-on as possible when it comes to pursuing the biggest pieces of human garbage.

Sitting in my office chair with the drink in my hand, I focus on the laptop screen, reading through the email from James that contains the information he uncovered about Lorelei. As I delve into her life, I experience an inexplicable pull toward her. Who is this woman, and why is she captivating my attention? There's not a wealth of information available, and the scarcity of details prior to a decade ago only heightens my curiosity.

An unsettling obsession is slowly taking root in my dark soul, and I'm aware that if I let it fester, she won't survive the storm that's brewing within me.

Over the years, I've had my share of casual encounters with women, but my connections have always been devoid of any emotional involvement. My partners understood the boundaries and expectations right from the beginning. I've never held any interest in the fleeting and fragile realm of emotions. My life revolves around much greater concerns, and I won't allow anyone or anything to jeopardize that for something as insubstantial as feelings.

With resolve, I know I need to stop these thoughts and put an end to the growing infatuation. My work is my life, and I am determined to keep it that way. There's no room for anything else. I can't allow this fixation to persist. My role in this world is to eliminate as many horrible individuals as possible, and in the end, I'm prepared to face the same fiery fate as those I pursue.

I swiftly close my laptop and rise from my chair, downing the last of my drink and placing the glass back on the bar cart. I need to head to bed and prepare for the unveiling of Senator Jenkins' story when it airs tomorrow. It's another step in holding lowlifes accountable for their actions.

As I make my way upstairs and down the hall, I enter my bedroom, a spacious haven that surpasses the typical master bedroom's size. The centerpiece is a substantial four-poster bed, adorned with luxurious black silk sheets and my cherished down comforter. Much like the rest of my residence, the room follows a simplistic and modern design. A brick accent wall behind the bed connects seamlessly to two other walls, painted in a neutral beige. In the center of the room hangs a black light fixture from the ceiling.

I quickly shed my clothing and slide under the silk sheets,

ready to rest for a few hours. Soon, Senator Jenkins' story will unfold across my media channels. However, my thoughts can't help but return to those damn compelling green eyes that have captured my attention. There's an unexplainable pull, like a siren to a ship captain. I won't let her pull me down. I have bigger priorities and no one has that control over me.

CHAPTER 3

"So let your fire burn
Oh, your flame will be lit"
-We Came As Romans

Lorelei

"Girl wake up you have to see this, hurry!" With Bex's urgent interruption, I reluctantly stir from my sleep, only managing to crack one eye open. Squinting against the sudden burst of light from the television, I groan and roll over to see what she's so anxious to show me.

The blonde reporter is broadcasting the news of Senator Jenkins, who portrays himself as a family man, being caught in a scandal involving multiple young women throughout Arizona. Allegations suggest that he has engaged in violent behavior towards them. He lures them in on a guise of a date, but when they're alone he mutilates them, and threatens them with blackmail if they dare speak against him. Disturbing images flash on the screen, revealing young girls bearing the horrifying marks of physical abuse, their identities carefully concealed. My heart aches for them. I empathize with the profound sense of powerlessness one experiences when in the clutches of a sadistic man who views you as nothing more than a disposable object.

My attention is drawn to the bottom right of the screen, where I notice that Ash Media Group is the source behind this story. This doesn't come as a shock to me. Some may label them as vigilante media, but I believe that they are performing a valuable service by unveiling those individuals, both small and influential, who have become corrupted by power. I also admire the fact that they are providing a platform for these women to share their testimonies while safeguarding their identities, ensuring their safety in the wake of their courageous decision to speak out.

Ash Media Group's reach extends far beyond Arizona; it has a national presence, although it seems to focus more keenly on the residents of this state. The nature of the media company adds an air of mystery to their operations. With a faceless owner and no discernible headquarters, it appears that they are deliberately hidden in secrecy, likely to protect themselves from potential retaliation or backlash.

"I served that man at the club last night, Lor," I finally turn my attention to Bex, recalling her presence in my bed. I look at her, her appearance disheveled, and I stifle a laugh.

"The senator was at Sin last night? I don't remember seeing him on the VIP list," I say, my words somewhat muffled by a yawn.

"Well, duh. He probably used a fake name, but that man was definitely in a VIP booth last night, right next to where Mr. Hot, dark and mysterious was sitting."

The mention of him catches my attention, and I quickly turn my head in the opposite direction, pretending to gaze out the window at the bright, sunny day outside. I can feel my cheeks warming in the gentle morning sunlight.

Hastily, I divert the conversation, saying, "My dad is back in. Want to come with me?" There's no need for any further explanation, and Bex immediately understands the invitation.

It's not the first time she's joined me on a visit to check in on my parents. I never go to their house; I usually only see them when my father is back in the behavioral health unit. I'm not entirely sure why I keep showing up. Maybe some part of me is waiting for the call that one of them is gone. It's a bitter thought, I know, but after everything they've put me through, it might be seen as a blessing. Although, if it were up to me, I'd prefer their death to come at my own hands.

"Yeah, I'll come with you. I enjoy getting under your mama's skin," Bex quips, fully aware that her comment will make me laugh. Bex doesn't know the full extent of my story, only that I'm here today because I fought hard to escape my past. There's not a single soul on this planet who knows the full depth of my history, except for dear old mom and dad.

My mom doesn't seem to like anyone, myself included. She's always said I ruined her life, getting pregnant with me at such a young age. I've never quite understood how that's my fault; after all, I didn't have much say in the matter. If I did, I would've probably chosen not to be born. Anything would've been better than the perpetual hell I was born into.

I climb out of my warm bed and make my way to the bathroom. I leave the door open while I undress and start the shower. There's no room for modesty between us anymore, and, frankly, I'm too exhausted to care at this point.

Once I'm undressed I step into my shower letting the hot water burn into my lightly tanned and tattooed skin. It's nearly impossible to live in Arizona without acquiring at least a hint of a tan. As I mindlessly wash my long, dark hair and scrub away last night's work, my hands run along the scars on my skin, adorned with tattoos. These scars serve as an ever-present reminder, a testament to the past I refuse to forgive. Someday, I'm determined to exact the vengeance I'm owed.

Emerging from the shower, feeling refreshed, I wipe off the steam-covered mirror and observe that my eyes seem unusually bright today. It's a sign I need to be vigilant. My emotions surface when I visit my parents, a situation that always demands caution.

Wrapped in a large black towel, I re-enter my room. Bex is in the process of undressing to take her turn in the shower. I raise an eyebrow, questioning why she isn’t using the other bathroom.

"What? I prefer the water pressure in your shower over the guest bathroom," she explains as she moves past me to start the shower. I shrug one shoulder, conceding that she has a point, and let her carry on.

I peer into my closet, surveying the array of clothes, each seemingly a variation of the same thing. After a moment of contemplation, I decide on a pair of denim jean shorts that accentuate my figure and a black v-neck t-shirt to complete the look.

Once I'm dressed, I return to the bathroom where Bex is still in the shower. The mirror is entirely fogged up, so I grab a hand towel to clear it enough to get ready. "Could you at least turn on the fan while you shower?" I say and flip the switch to activate the ventilation.

I grab my hairbrush and run it through my thick brown hair, opting for a more low-maintenance look today. Fortunately, I inherited effortlessly wavy hair once it dries. A quick swipe of mascara and I deem myself ready enough.

By the time I'm finished, Bex is stepping out of the shower, wrapped in a matching black towel.

"How do you always look so good?" Bex grumbles in my direction. My only response is a playful wink. She's one to talk – a natural beauty that no one can ignore when she enters a room. However, she doesn't seem to recognize it herself. Where I have hard edges, she exudes smooth grace, and she's the light to my dark. A slight pang of sadness washes over me, knowing that one day, I won't have her by my side anymore.

She won't stick around if she really knows me.

With that reminder in mind, I quickly rebuild my emotional walls and steel myself against the thought.

Less than thirty minutes later, we're pulling up to the behavioral health hospital, a place I've grown all too familiar with.

As we step through the doors, Dolores, the older lady at the reception desk, immediately notices me through her thick glasses. She smiles, but behind that smile, I can see the pity in her eyes, along with the countless wrinkles that time has etched around them.

I fucking despise pity with a burning passion. I managed to break free from my abusers, where they can't hurt me anymore, and I certainly don't need anyone's pity. I return to this place by my own volition, not out of obligation, but as a stark reminder to them that I'm still here, despite their best efforts.

"Your dad is back in room 3, dear. I'll buzz you both in, but I must warn you this episode has been one of the more challenging ones I've seen him go through," Dolores cautions with concern in her voice.

I can't help but scoff slightly under my breath, well aware that Dolores has no idea just how harrowing these episodes can be. But I know, and so do my demons, after all, he created them. Parents are supposed to be the two people in the world programmed to love you, but mine? They must have harbored some deep hatred to inflict the things they did.

As I arrive at the room, I pause, and I notice a change in Bex's demeanor. This is the one place where she sheds her usual bright and sunny self. She becomes quiet, present only for support and perhaps to get under my mom's skin if the opportunity arises. This is the only time when I see Bex harden, even if just a bit.

Inside the somber room, my father lies in his bed, his gaze fixated on the window with his head turned away. My mother occupies a corner, seated in a chair, and she startles when she notices me. Visiting hours are short, so I anticipated that she'd be here as well.

"It's about time you came to check on your father," she remarks. It takes every ounce of self-restraint not to lash out at her. I remind myself that I don't owe them anything.

"Mom, you literally told me just a few hours ago, in the middle of the night, which was clearly outside of visiting hours," I deadpan, my gaze unwavering as I challenge her. I can feel the shadows lurking behind my eyes, poised to be unleashed if she pushes me any further.

She averts her gaze without further argument, fully aware that she lacks any valid point in this situation. In this place, there are witnesses, and they tend to maintain a facade of civility.

I turn my attention back to my father. He shares my dark brown hair, but his is now dull and lifeless. His eyes resemble dark pits, and his leathered skin bears the marks of age. I wonder if, back in the day, he was a handsome man, before succumbing to his own darkness and letting it consume him.

The big gauze bandage on his wrist serves as a reminder that he was doing the same thing he always does. This scenario has repeated itself more times than I can tally. Despite my lack of affection for my father, I'm aware that he isn't entirely to blame. Instead of confronting and overcoming his inner darkness as I did, he allowed it to devour him whole. Seeking help isn't something he does, and my past attempts to get him help only led to my own pain. He only ends up here when he goes too far, and my mother can't piece him back together on her own, so he gets put on a mandatory hold.

Finally, he turns to look at me and says, "I wasn't trying to kill myself like the doctors always think. I was just bleeding out the bad stuff. You know that, Lorelei." When my dad is in a bad state, he often rambles about "bleeding out the bad stuff." I never truly grasped what he meant, he thinks that if he severs flesh it will bleed out the bad. I should know; my scars are a tangible testament to his belief.

I choose to disregard his statement but ask, "Is there anything you need?" We all understand that I won't be getting them a goddamn thing.

Before my dad can even respond, my mother's snide voice chimes in from behind me. She claims, "Yeah, this wouldn't have happened if you loaned us the money like we asked. Your dad did this over not being able to pay the bills again." Both of us know this is a blatant lie, and her inability to meet my gaze only confirms it. She has a knack for manipulating situations, no matter what they may be.

"Well, if either of you could hold down a job, paying the bills wouldn't be an issue," I snap back, aware that I'm teetering on the edge of losing control. I take a deep breath through my nose and exhale once my lungs start to burn. The pain serves as a stark reminder that I'm still alive, regardless of what they have put me through it's a challenge to separate past and present when I'm around them.

How many times did we go through this when I was growing up? The times when I couldn't shower before school because the water was shut off, and I got teased for having greasy hair. Or when we nearly suffered from heatstroke because the power was shut off all summer, leaving us without air conditioning. Or how many times we went without food because we couldn't afford it.

Every day, I'm grateful that I was the only accidental

pregnancy they ever had.

"You know how hard it is for us to work, Lorelei. I thought you would want to take care of us. We took care of you all of your life, and this is how you repay us," my mother retorts. It's a familiar guilt-tripping tactic she often employs.

I've reached my limit. "How hard it is for you to work?" I'm laughing now, feeling the venom on my tongue. "No, Mom, it's not hard for you. You choose not to do it because you're lazy, and employers won't put up with it. And Dad won't work because that would cut into all the ESPN he watches at the bar down the street, drinking away his disability check. Don't get it twisted." I spit at her.

I realize how far I've allowed myself to slip. I'm in her face now, and I have no recollection of how I got here, her dull brown eyes staring back at me with fear.

I've often wondered about the origins of my eyes. But given that we had no family around when I was young, I never knew if they came from some long-forgotten relative. I've always had this inkling that they weren't my true parents, but I could never find any concrete evidence. Plus, they must hate me for them to be able to hurt me as they have. If I weren't their child, I imagine I would've been abandoned at a fire station the moment I was born.

I stand there, glaring at them both, and then turn and walk out without looking back. This encounter is over. It's a reminder that no matter what they did to me in the past, I will never break, and I'd sooner watch them die than give in to their attempts to make me crack.

Bex is right on my heels, and I can sense the tension emanating from her. She despises confrontation and does everything in her power to avoid it at all costs.

Back in my truck, I turn on the engine and crank up the air

conditioning to cool us down. I still don't fully understand why I subject myself to these visits, but I do it every time. I need to know they're still alive, at least until I'm ready to take matters into my own hands and witness the life drain from their eyes.

"Nothing quite like a family reunion on this fine Sunday," She comments, and at that, I start to laugh. Bex has a way of bringing me back from the depths of darkness. Maybe that's why I always invite her to come with me, to help pull me back into the light.

"Let's grab some coffee and head back to my place to watch movies," I suggest as I turn onto the main street. I could really use a day of doing absolutely nothing.

I park us back at my building because my favorite coffee shop is just a short walk down the street, and there's never any parking available. Plus, I could use some fresh air and sunshine to dispel my foul mood.

The coffee shop is a quaint little place nestled into the side of an old historic building. Inside, it's bright and cozy, with a small bookshelf in the back. Sometimes, I enjoy coming here to read, using a book as a temporary escape from my thoughts.

"I'll have a hot latte, and whatever she wants, please," I say, offering a friendly smile to the young girl behind the counter. She appears to be around 16, so when I pay, I make sure to leave her a generous tip. I remember what it's like to be her age and working for every dollar, each one feeling like a small victory.

As I receive my coffee from the girl, I can't help but be reminded of my own past. When I was younger, I worked at a pizza place near our house, saving every dollar I earned with the promise to myself that I would run away once I had enough. However, one day, I went to make a purchase and realized that my card had been declined. When I called my bank, they informed me that there was no money left in my account. It was only when I confronted my mom that evening that I discovered she had stolen all the money from my account to cover the bills they were defaulting on.

Shaking off that memory, I turn to head towards the door and accidentally bump into something solid.

Not something, someone. I look up and find myself face to face with the man with the bleeding pupil, the enigmatic stranger from last night. His entire front presses against mine, and I can feel the heat emanating from him.

"You," I stammer. When did I start sounding like this?

"Mmm, Lorelei, what a pleasure to see you again so soon," he purrs in a way that makes it sound like I'm a delectable treat and he's planning to devour me whole. Still gripping my arms, he glances down at the coffee in my hand and slowly trails his gaze back up until he locks eyes with me once more. He licks his bottom lip and smirks.

Heat is pooling low in my stomach and no words will come out of my mouth. My traitorous body remains oblivious to my disinterest in this arrogant man. I've always thought that anyone who looks like him and exudes such confidence is probably a lousy fuck. After all, it's all about balance, right? But as I gaze at him, I find myself questioning my own theory.

Finally, he releases his grip on me and takes a step back, his eyes still fixed on mine.

A throat clears next to me, and it takes me a moment to remember that we're in a very public place, with Bex standing right beside me.

"O-oh, yeah, this is Bex. She works at the club too," I quickly introduce, my voice a little shaky, hoping he doesn't notice.

He extends his hand toward Bex and says, "It's a pleasure to meet you, Bex," flashing her a charming smile full of straight, white teeth. But then, his eyes snap back to mine, as if he can't bear to keep his gaze off me.

"See you soon, seirína," he adds and wipes his bottom lip with his thumb before smoothly prowling over to the counter. He's dressed in a two-piece navy suit with a white button-up underneath, casually ordering coffee on a Sunday morning. What kind of creature looks that good on a weekend?

The name he called me, "seirína," finally registers in my brain, and I make a mental note to ask him about it if I ever see him again or try to look it up. He somehow knew my actual name, so it's not as though he has it confused. The name sends a flutter through my stomach, and I hope I never have to hear him say it again, for fear of coming unglued.

I grab Bex's hand and pull her out of the coffee shop, practically running back home. I hear her voice getting louder as she says, "Lor, can you not hear me?" When I look up at her, she's smiling wickedly.

"What?" I inquire, playing dumb.

"What do you mean 'what'?" Bex mocks, her eyes wide with disbelief. "What the heck was that?! That man was practically devouring you right where you stood." I know that, and I can still feel the remnants of it deep in my stomach. He intimidates me a little, and no one intimidates me. It's unsettling, but I can't deny that there's a strange allure to it.

A momentary thought of his strong, calloused hands running passionately across my skin, and the taste of fervent, intense kisses teases my thoughts. Yet, with a determined effort, I forcefully toss it aside, finally getting a grip on my thoughts. Who am I right now?

Back at home, I'm doing my best to distract Bex from the stranger in the coffee shop, realizing that I never even asked for his name. I let her pick out the movie, knowing that it will likely involve something related to murders. She has an unusual fascination with serial killers, but I don't mind at all.

Halfway through a documentary about Ted Bundy, someone knocks on my door.

"Were you expecting another booty call?" Bex wiggles her eyebrows suggestively.

Was I? I don't think so. If I was, I certainly don't remember.

I stand up, allowing the fuzzy burgundy blanket that was in my lap to fall to the floor, so I can walk to the door and peer through the peephole. When I look, no one is there. Slowly, I open the door, ready to fight if there's an intruder. But as I look around, there's no one in sight. Before I turn to go back inside, I glance down and spot a single paper sailboat on my black "Fuck Off" welcome mat.

I pick it up, look around once more, and then shut and lock the door behind me. Bex is staring at me with her big brown eyes. I look back at the paper sailboat and realize, once again, there's no note accompanying it. But I know he's leaving these to let me know he's watching. The question is, why?

There's no doubt in my mind that this is from the mystery man with the bleeding pupil. I should probably be scared, right? How the hell does he know my address? Fear should be coursing through me, but instead, I feel my inner demons dancing with excitement. He found me. Twice now.

Bex jumps up and snatches the paper sailboat out of my hand, her eyes fixed on me as if I've lost my mind. "Girl, who's leaving you these?"

Clearly, I know who it is, but I'm not ready to divulge that information just yet.

"No idea, probably just a prank," I respond nonchalantly.

"Yeah, a creepy prank.You should call the cops, this is the second time this has happened." she responds.

I toss the paper sailboat onto the kitchen island and return to the couch, waiting for Bex to join me. She hesitates but eventually takes a seat.

"Or at least file a report with the police. Doesn't this scare you a little?" she suggests.

Sometimes, I forget that Bex isn't like me. The dark and twisted side of the world doesn't excite her the way it does me. She still thinks the monsters only exist in the shadows or under her bed. She doesn't realize they roam the streets with hypnotizing eyes and impeccably tailored suits.

"Of course not," I reply, but he should be.

CHAPTER 4

"Now that you're gone I can finally breathe again"
-Like Moths To Flames

Lorelei

It's Wednesday, and I need to head back to Sin to ensure that everything is in order before the weekend. Even though I work from home the rest of the days, it's still just as hectic. I have to manage orders, handle payroll, make sure the staff's uniforms are cleaned if they need it, and tackle a ton of other responsibilities I never even considered when I took this job. But it's all been worth it for the financial freedom it's granted me.

Yesterday, my mom called and left a message, informing me that my dad is back home and they have a big idea that will soon make them wealthy, so they won't need to ask me for money anymore. I scoffed at that notion.

My entire life has been a rollercoaster. There would be a low depressive point, and they wouldn't get out of bed for a week. Then, the next thing I knew, we'd be jumping in the car in the middle of the night to head to theme park for a day. Of course, we'd never make it there because we were too broke to even leave state.

The highs were exhilarating, and the lows were devastating. That was the reality I had to accept. When I turned 17, I couldn't bear my skin being flayed open any longer, so I fought like hell to get myself out.

I committed myself to the demanding balance of online schooling and work, a relentless pursuit aimed at keeping a roof over my head in a tiny studio apartment situated in a less-than-ideal neighborhood. Faced with the necessity of securing the place, I lied regarding my age to the landlord. This act of deception, although far from ideal, enabled me to maintain a safe living situation while working toward, and ultimately achieving, my high school diploma.

When I hit 21, I started bartending because it paid the bills. And by the time I was 23, I was running circles around the other bartenders, which, of course, just made them hate me even more.

That's when the D'Santos family approached me and asked if I wanted to come work at Sin. At the time, I had never heard of Sin, and it was just opening. After my first shift, Mr. D'Santos told me they had initially approached me because they wanted me to run the club, and that night was essentially a trial run. Not sure why they picked me but it got me further ahead. Stability for my freedom.

It took a while for me to learn the ropes, but after six months, they both stepped back and have let me run the club ever since. I have no idea why they were so kind to me, but now we hardly speak, except for once a quarter for reporting. I don't mind it, even though they were kind and took a chance on a kid to run something so significant it always struck me as a little odd. But it's not worth speaking up about and risking my well-paying job.

After I've put away all the stock behind the bar, I stand up, brush my hands on my shorts, and check to see if there's anything else that needs to be done.

I catch my reflection in the mirror behind the glass and notice my long wavy hair looks decent today. I'm pleased with what

I see. I've put in a lot of hard work at the gym, and if anyone looked closely, they'd be able to tell. My body is lean and well taken care of. Not to mention, I've always had a great rack and a decent ass to go with it. I'm not bragging; it's just a fact.

With that in mind, I take my phone out of my pocket and text my usual hookup, Liam.

Me: Meet me at Sin tomorrow at closing.

That's all I need to say; he knows the rest. Once upon a time, Liam tried to date me, but he quickly learned I wasn't the type and settled for a booty call at my will. Men are typically only after one thing anyway, so I decided to cut out the rest myself.

I hear my phone ding and look down to read his reply.

Liam: I'll be outside at 3.

Of course he will. Why would he say no?

For a Thursday, the club is bustling, which is no surprise; it always is. However, I find it somewhat unexpected that so many people choose to go out on weeknights.

Tonight, I'm dressed in a short black dress with a plunging neckline, and my attire accentuates my figure. The appreciative looks I receive reaffirm my choice of outfit. I've left my long hair down and completed the look with my trusty black heels.

As the night comes to a close, exhaustion sets in. The staff begins to leave, and I call out, "You all were amazing tonight, but you already know that."

A few employees turn and smile, and I hear Kellan's laughter as he races to catch up with Bex. I had informed her that Liam was coming, and she made a hasty exit.

Stepping outside, I spot Liam leaning against his motorcycle, which is parked next to my truck. He's undeniably attractive – tall and lean, with disheveled dirty blonde hair that somehow always manages to look appealing. His light blue eyes sometimes appear almost white. When we're in public together, girls can't help but drool over him. It doesn't bother me; they can have him. He's merely a good fuck which is rare to find in these times.

"Your place?" his husky voice inquires as he sizes me up, his gaze raking over me. I pause, letting him take in my appearance, knowing that the longer I draw this out, the more he'll worship me later. However, my patience is already wearing from a long night at work.

I remain silent, standing there as his eyes slowly travel up my body, locking onto mine.

"Not tonight," I reply with a wicked smile. "I was thinking here."

Usually, we would go back to my place, fuck, and then I'd send him on his way before my bed got too warm. But that wasn't what I wanted tonight. I needed just enough to keep my mind off the mystery man I hadn't seen since the coffee shop.

"Here? Like in the club?"

"No," I reply. "Here, like in my truck." I sometimes forget how dense he can be.

Before he can reply, I unlock my truck and hop into the back, tossing my purse onto the passenger seat. He practically flies into the back next to me, as I swiftly remove my dress and toss it aside, his shirt following suit with equal haste.

He's kissing up my neck with fervor as I unfasten his pants, releasing his cock. I hear a groan escape from his gritted teeth as his lips continue their assault on my skin. Strangely, the imposing man with the bleeding pupil takes center stage in my thoughts rather than the one who's touching me. Still kissing me, he slides his hand between my slick thighs, yet the arousal isn't for him. My mind remains fixated on the enigmatic figure from before as I wrap my hand around his length, coaxing out another enticing sound.

When his hand creeps too close to the tops of my thighs I slap it away to remind him never to touch me there.

I wish he would hurry; I just need a quick release so I can go home and go to sleep. Growing impatient I let go of him and push him back toward the seat so I can straddle him. He reaches into his discarded pants pocket and pulls out a condom, but I snatch it from his hand knowing he'll take too long to do it himself.

I rip off the top of the foil package with my teeth and roll it over his cock.

"Fuck Lor you're not wasting any time" he grumbles at me. I know he wants more, but I don't need the cutesy shit from him.

With that I rise up so the tip of him is at my core, and right as I start to lower myself feeling him at my entrance the fire alarm at Sin starts blaring.

"What the fuck?" I say, climbing off of him and grabbing my dress from the floor of the truck. Before I can process it, I'm jumping out of the truck door, tugging my dress down, and running towards the back door of the club when Liam catches up with me, pulling his shirt over his head.

"You can't run in there, what if there's actually a fire?" he says loudly over the alarm.

Ugh, what a bitch. I want to tell him to grow a pair, but instead, I slide my key into the lock and rush inside once I hear the click. I fumble for the nearest light switch, flick it on, and start scanning everything for a fire. Liam is hot on my heels, and once we comb through the building, we both realize there isn't one. Then the alarm stops.

"Must have been a test alarm?" he guesses, but somehow I know that's not it. My gut is telling me this was intentional, but I have no way to prove it. If I voice this, I know I'll sound crazy, and I don't feel like explaining myself.

When I'm confident there's no fire we head back outside walking towards our vehicles, and I notice him starting to climb into my truck again.

"No, I'm over it. I'm going home to finish myself," I say, not looking back as I climb up into the driver's seat. Without saying a word, he shuts the door, and I pull away. I don't look back, but I know he's watching.

The drive home is a blur, but now that I'm finally walking up to my door, exhaustion hits, and I can't wait to crawl into my bed. But before I get there, I see something on my mat from where I'm at in the hallway.

A few steps away now, I can see it clearly: a single paper sailboat.

CHAPTER 5

"Finally frozen, no more emotion"
-Beartooth

Dash

I have no idea what causes it, but when I see her climbing into the back of her truck with that blonde douchebag, I can't help but feel an intense surge of jealousy. The thought of driving over there and tying him up to the large chandelier in the middle of the club is invading my mind. Maybe I'm just being overly possessive, but seeing her with someone else stirs up these irrational emotions. What self-respecting man is fucking blonde, anyway?

About a week ago, I had James hack into Sin's cameras to begin monitoring the elusive D'Santos family. It was purely for investigative purposes, but I must admit that it was a nice bonus to be able to keep an eye on her as well.

I've never considered myself a stalker before, but there's something intriguing about watching her work. Besides, I'm focused on my own tasks at the same time, so it feels like a win-win situation. I promised myself that I wouldn't intrude on her personal life, aside from observing from a distance, and leaving the paper sailboats. However, the thought of him touching her is unbearable. It triggers something deep inside of me.

"James, activate the fire alarm," I command, my voice unintentionally harsh as I speak to him.

He eyes me with a mix of curiosity and concern, but he follows my command. A moment later, I see her rush out of her truck, hastily adjusting her dress, and making a beeline for the club's entrance without hesitation. This only fuels my frustration. Why would she run towards what could be a potential threat? It's as if she either craves the danger or has no regard for her own safety.

When she re-emerges from the club without giving the guy a second glance, I can't help but smile. She exudes confidence and knows she's captivating. When I saw her at work the other day, I arranged for a delivery guy to leave a single paper sailboat on her doorstep. I anticipated her reaction and ran into her at the coffee shop the next day intentionally. I enjoy watching her squirm, and I've become well-acquainted with her habits, which tend to revolve around her regular places, thanks to her bank records.

In the week that James and I have been delving into the D'Santos family's background, we've uncovered some significant information.

First and foremost, we now know that their names are Carlos and Maria. It's interesting to note that they don't have any children and are involved in various businesses. However, Sin seems to be their most lucrative endeavor. Additionally, I stumbled upon their alarm system logs, which indicate that they consistently show up at the club every Tuesday morning but stay for only a brief 30-minute window before departing. I can't help but wonder if Lorelei is aware of this regular pattern.

James's discovery of their work email communications is certainly intriguing. The fact that they only contact Lorelei when necessary, with most of the communication initiated by Carlos for quarterly financial data, raises more questions. It increasingly appears that something suspicious is happening. I can't shake the feeling that Sin may be a front for a larger operation, and perhaps they never expected it to become as successful as it has. Alternatively, the substantial profits from Sin could be concealing something even more significant.

"Uhm, boss," I hear James meekly interject from his seat, likely curious as to why I'm so preoccupied with these strangers getting laid in a parking lot.

All my staff work remotely and we've been holed up in my home office for hours. A security measure that's necessary given the sensitive nature of our work. All my employees go to great lengths to safeguard their identities, assets, and locations with my assistance. We expose a lot of high-profile individuals, and confidentiality is essential for their safety.

James, with his laid back style and unmatched intelligence, never ceases to amuse me, even though we're polar opposites. It's a combination that shouldn't work but somehow does.

I raise an eyebrow, prompting him to continue.

"I found some old information on Carlos," he says, "It looks like back in the day, he was arrested for smuggling drugs. If you ask me, some habits die hard."

His revelation triggers a cascade of thoughts in my mind. Drug smuggling? Could they possibly be laundering money through Sin? I mentally file this theory away for further investigation once we have more concrete evidence.

I know I need to return to the bar and do some more digging, but I must ensure that I don't get distracted by the green-eyed siren waiting for me. I have an idea, but perfect timing will be crucial.

But first I take out my phone and shoot off a message to have another paper sailboat delivered to her door. I want her to know I'm watching.

As I approach the bar on a Saturday night, I notice Bex behind the counter, but there's no sign of Lorelei. A touch of disappointment washes over me, but part of me realizes that this might be for the best.

"Whiskey straight, please," I instruct Bex, who eagerly responds to my order. I pass her a $20 bill, ensuring she places it in her drawer. Another $20 bill remains on the bar's surface as a tip.

I turn and head toward a vacant seat, allowing the rest of my plan to unfold. Just as I sit down, my phone vibrates in my jacket pocket, signaling a message from James.

James: Tracker is activated and I can see the location of the money.

Part one of the plan is in motion, and now it's time to see where the money leads. The cash-only nature of Sin has raised a red flag in the digital age. Unlike credit card transactions, cash is harder to trace, and James had found minimal information in that regard.

There's a commotion by the front door, catching my attention. Lorelei and a bouncer are escorting a middle-aged man out, who bears a small resemblance to her. A surge of protectiveness washes over me, and I try to attribute it to my training rather than any personal connection to her. My senses are heightened, and I can't help but perceive potential threats to her. I begin to stand and stop myself when I catch a glimpse of her re-entering the club.

She smooths out her dress and locks her bright green eyes onto mine. There's a hint of something mischievous dancing within them and she winks. It takes her a moment, but her eyes seem to lose some of their intensity, and her brow furrows slightly.

In the background, someone announces the last call, signaling the end of the night.

As she approaches me with unwavering determination, I'm momentarily taken aback. My mouth goes dry when I set my eyes on her, dressed in a stunning black floor-length dress. The daringly high slit up to her thigh and the dangerously low neckline leave me speechless.

I want to lay her on the bar right there in the club and claim her as mine so all these slack jawed fucks would stop looking at her. The men around us act as if they have a chance with her, but in reality, she needs someone stronger, someone who can keep up with her rather than hold her back like they would.

She gracefully sways over to me, her beauty outshining anyone in the room. My eyes are locked onto her, and I can't help but watch as the slit in her dress continues to reveal more with each step. I can feel myself harden in my suit pants and it takes me by surprise, I feel like a teenage boy again.

"You," she purrs in a sultry voice, her gaze a mix of fiery intensity and a hint of apprehension.

"Me," I respond, taking another sip of my whiskey, "please, join me for a minute." Before I can fully think, I find myself standing up to pull out a chair for her.

She eyes me with a mixture of curiosity and uncertainty but eventually decides to take the offered seat.

"How did you find out where I live?" She doesn't waste any time, her tone accusatory rather than inquisitive.

"For a man like me, it wasn't difficult to locate Lorelei Hart, but we both know that's not your real last name," I respond with a tight smile. I probably shouldn't be provoking her, but the allure of playing with her is too enticing to resist. James had dug up more information about Lorelei, and I wanted to see how she'd react if I dangled it before her. It's a bit like that old saying about not playing with your food, but I can't help myself – it's just too much fun.

I had anticipated that my statement might catch her off guard, but instead, her expression hardens.

"It's intriguing that you found out that information since court documents were sealed," she responds, her voice cool and steady, "but I can assure you, if this gets out, I know it will be because of you, and I will come after you."

Her threat is delivered with a measure of confidence, leaving no doubt that she means every word she says. Who is she, really?

Fuck I'm so hard right now. What she may not realize is that I've only uncovered her true identity, but I still haven't found the reason behind her name change. The documents that James uncovered merely revealed the change of name without providing any explanation. There's still much I don't know about her and her motives.

"So, what's with the paper sailboats?" she inquires, the steel still present in her voice.

Her tattooed arm crosses over the other in her lap, and her exposed leg, adorned with tattoos that snake up her thigh, is crossed over the one still concealed by her dress. Her skin appears smooth and creamy, and an irresistible urge washes over me to leave my mark. She sits there like a poised goddess of death, while I feel like a mere peasant offering tithings at her feet. Her otherworldly green eyes draw me in, and I'm aware that I could easily become lost in them if I let myself.

"It's strange that you found where I live. Couldn't you have just approached me here?" she asks.

"Seirína, I have a feeling you enjoy a little danger," I reply, my voice low and filled with a hint of allure, "and I would never pass up the opportunity to provide that for you."

"I looked up what that means, you know, you've been calling me 'siren,' right? And again what's with the paper sailboats?" She questions, a hint of curiosity in her eyes.

"Did you know that there's a German legend about a woman named Lorelei?" I respond, "In short, it's a story about a woman whose lover was unfaithful, so she threw herself into the river and was transformed into a siren who lured fishermen to their demise."

She raises an eyebrow, "You said the story's origin is German, but 'seirína' is Greek if my googling was correct."

I nod, "You're right. My mother was from Greece."

I choose not to reveal more about myself and leave it at that. What I won't tell her is that I haven't uttered a word of that language since my mother passed away many years ago, but when I called her "seirína" the other day, it flowed effortlessly.

"So, the sailboats then. What are you, a fisherman I'm luring to his death?" she smirks, as if it were a joke. In response, I lean forward in my chair, invading her personal space, and let a sly grin tug at the corner of my lips.

"You've already lured me, seirína," I whisper, my voice low and filled with intensity, "I've surrendered my boat and willingly dove into the waters after you."

At my words, I see her legs squeeze together a little tighter. It's a subtle reaction that most people wouldn't notice, but I've been trained to observe these nuances. My time in the military and now with the FBI has sharpened my attention to detail, and it's probably the only thing that's kept me alive all these years.

I want to keep her engaged in conversation, so I can continue to observe the way her fascinating mind works. I change the subject before she can shut down, a behavior I've noticed in her when she starts to get uncomfortable.

"Everything okay over there?" I nod my head toward the door.

"Nothing for anyone to worry about but myself," she quips, her spine stiffening even more.

That was a personal response, and I can't help but wonder who that man was. There's a dress code at the club, and he certainly didn't meet the standard.

I stand, closing the button on my suit jacket and look down at her. The desire is palpable, and I can't help but envision her on her knees before me. My pants begin to tighten, and I realize I need to leave soon.

"I have to go on a short work trip, but when I return, I'll send word to you about our date. See you soon, seirína." I reach for her hand from her lap, but ultimately decide against it.

"I don't go anywhere with men whose names I don't know," she states firmly.

This will be my first lie to her. I can't reveal my true identity, so I let the lie roll off my tongue with a charming smile.

"It's Dash, seirína, and I expect you'll be saying it again real soon." I wink, and without waiting to see her reaction, I turn and make my exit.

CHAPTER 6

"I come from a darkness you'll never know
And I smell the fear inside your soul"
-Upon A Burning Body

Lorelei

I had to kick my dad out of the club on Saturday. I was surprised he even knew where I worked, but as long as he doesn't discover where I live or that I changed my name, I'm not too concerned. To ensure my safety, I've added him and my mom to the list of people not allowed inside the establishment, which the bouncers maintain at the front door. Arguably I should have taken this precaution earlier, but until now, I didn't believe they would locate my workplace. It's laughable that I have to be concerned about this. He came in claiming they had a big plan and urged me to quit my job, promising to take care of me, just as they had always intended to do, assuring me that he and my mom would make everything better.

It's good to see that his latest episode is behind him and he's riding a high now. At times, I find myself hoping they might find success, if only to vanish from my life, allowing me to lead a peaceful existence.

Dealing with my parents' mental health challenges is something I can manage, but I can never forgive the abuse they subjected me to. In my younger years, I made many attempts to get them the help they needed, but those efforts always resulted in me bloody. Eventually, I had to stop trying for my own survival.

My skin still bears the scars from his hands, but they're cleverly concealed beneath layers of tattoos. It's not a means of hiding them, I couldn't care less about others knowing about them. Those tattoos represent my way of making a statement, a bolder one, reminding myself that I would always triumph, no matter the battle I faced. I have the strength to prevail in any war waged against me.

It's been three days since I encountered Dash at Sin, and I'm still puzzled as to why it bothered me so much. It was probably the overwhelming arrogance that seemed to emanate from him.

I've just completed my workout at the gym located on the first floor of my building. As I stride down the hallway toward my apartment, my gray leggings and sports bra are drenched in sweat, and some of my hair is plastered to my forehead, a testament to the effort I've put in. For years, the gym has been my go-to mental release, a place to channel the aggression I need to keep at bay.

All of a sudden, I halt in my tracks, sensing a presence around me that wasn't there before. I yank my headphones out of my ears and pause the music on my phone, ensuring no residual sound might give me away. My body tenses, preparing for any situation. As I round the corner, approaching the final stretch of my hallway, I see him leaning against my door, casually twirling a paper sailboat through his fingers.

Dash's dark hair is impeccably groomed, short on the sides and longer on top, styled to the side with precision. He sports light scruff along his jaw, and his attire consists of a perfectly tailored black suit. As he gazes at his phone in one hand, a stark contrast to the paper sailboat in the other, my breath catches in my throat. He looks like an angel of death, his presence commanding, and I want to be closer to him.

His eyes quickly shift from his phone to me, and I realize I've stopped moving. I muster the will to continue walking towards him, straightening my spine. A knowing smile graces his lips, and with effortless grace, he pushes off my door frame, slipping his phone into his pocket.

"I did say I'd be seeing you, seirína, and here I am, ready to claim my date. I told you my work trip would be short."

"You certainly have a knack for finding information on people, so why show up at my doorstep unannounced rather than finding my phone number?" I can't help but wonder what motivated this man to be at my home without warning.

"Remember, I mentioned how danger seems to excite you? Well, I thought this would be an exhilarating surprise." His gaze is wicked, as if he's privy to something I'm not.

"Obviously, I'm not exactly date-ready at the moment," I say, waving my hand to indicate my sweat-drenched attire. "And what if I already have plans?" Despite my disheveled appearance, I can't help but feel an overwhelming desire to press my sticky body against his, just to gauge his reaction.

"I'm not here to claim you right this instant," he replies with a confidence that suggests he's certain I'll agree. "I'm simply extending an invitation for you to join me tonight. I'll pick you up at eight."

I can sense my inner demons stirring beneath the surface. If this arrogant man believes he can just show up unannounced and dictate my schedule for a last-minute date, then I'll have some fun with it. He thinks I enjoy danger? Little does he know, I am danger. I'll make him rip out his heart willingly and hand it to me on a gold platter, all while wearing a smile.

"Fine," I respond curtly, meeting his gaze. "What's the dress code for tonight?" His eyes light up at my question, and his piercing stare remains locked onto mine. He inches closer, the heat from his body mingling with my warmth. I allow myself to move a bit closer as well, letting him think he's sinking his teeth into me.

"Something like the dress you wore the other night," he suggests with a wink, then brushes past me and disappears around the corner, leaving me in a state of heightened tension. My body remains rigid and warm from the contact, while a tumult of emotions stampedes through my chest.

Hours later, I stand in my living room, gazing at my reflection in the long, full-length gold-rimmed mirror adorning the far corner of the room.

If this cocky guy believes he can make demands of me, I hope he's ready to eat his heart out.

I decided on wearing a silk burgundy floor length dress with a daring slit up my right leg showing off loads of bare skin. The neckline sweeps down just above my perky breasts, but the best part is the back, which is completely open.

I've chosen to leave my hair down in loose curls, securing one side over the other to expose the open back of the dress. My makeup highlights my green eyes with a dramatic touch of black winged eyeliner, and I've finished the look with a neutral lip.

As I walk over, I take a seat on the black suede couch and begin putting on my gold heels. Just then, a knock at the door, it must be him. I hastily finish buckling my heels, then dash to the kitchen island to retrieve my matching gold clutch, which holds my phone, some cash, and my trusty knife, a companion that accompanies me everywhere. I've learned long ago to wield the weapon that once threatened to end me.

One last look at my reflection in the mirror, and I see my inner demons grinning back at me from behind my eyes.

It's time to play.

I swing open the door, and there he is, his imposing figure dominating my view as he adjusts a cuff on his impeccably tailored black suit. It appears this man exclusively wears meticulously crafted suits, and he certainly knows how to pull them off. I can't help but wonder what he looks like when he lets go of that impeccable control.

Before uttering a word, he leisurely casts his gaze down my body, examining every inch of me without a trace of hesitation. His thumb grazes his bottom lip, and his eyes lock onto mine, his bleeding pupil noticeably dilated.I do a slow turn, he's not the only one who can play with their prey. He's now mine.

"Fuck you look gorgeous," he growls, his voice thick with desire.

The way he says it stirs something within me. As much as this stranger infuriates me, there's an undeniable and primal attraction between us.

"I know," I assert confidently and take a step towards him, assuming he'd shift to let me turn and lock my door. But he remains right there, our bodies pressed close.

"I hope standing here isn't what you had in mind for our date, or I might be overdressed," I challenge him with a hint of playful defiance.

A deep chuckle resonates in his chest. "Oh, seirína, I have so much more in store for you," he remarks, his words always carrying an air of menace.

With that, he finally shifts, permitting me to turn and lock my door, all the while keeping a watchful eye on me. We walk down the hallway in silence until we reach the parking garage, where a sleek black sports car awaits. At least he has a good taste in cars.

He gracefully circles around to the passenger side, opening the door for me, and I slide into the car. But before he shuts the door, he gazes down at me, licking his lips. It's unclear if he's ready for dinner or if he's planning to devour me. Oddly, I find myself surprisingly open to either possibility.

Everything about his actions seems to awaken some desire deep within me, and I can't seem to resist it, even though it makes me resent him a little more.

He settles into the driver's seat, and the car roars to life beneath me. Fuck this is a beautiful car, I can appreciate his taste in cars and women.

As we peel out of the garage, it's clear that he has little regard for the speed limit, and I can't help but wonder how he feels so impervious to rules. It probably has something to do with his line of work, but I'm not ready to delve into personal questions just yet. My plan for tonight is to make him fall in love, then disappear. Though it might prove challenging considering how he keeps turning up everywhere, including my home.

We've been in the car for about 20 minutes, and I notice we're going even faster now. Glancing over, I see his speedometer hitting 90 mph, and I look up at him. When our eyes meet, I see he's already looking back at me.

"Are you getting nervous?" he inquires.

"No," I assert firmly, because I'm not. I'm not afraid of death; I welcome it when the time comes.

He grins wickedly and begins to accelerate, driving faster and faster down the streets around us. Obviously he's attempting to provoke a reaction from me, but he'll never succeed in scaring me.

Instead I decide to play a little. I let my leg uncross from the other and spread them slightly, barely enough for him to notice and place my hand at the top of the slit in my dress. I catch him glancing down swiftly, believing I wouldn't notice. As I sense his eyes on me, I tilt my head back slightly, offering a sly smile, letting the exhilaration of the car ride take me away as I close my eyes. He effortlessly maneuvers the car, and if the way he drives is any indication I bet he fucks just as good.

As he goes faster I let my hand creep closer up the slit and roll my head a little and crack my eyes open just enough to see his reaction. His eyes dart between my hand, the road, and me, confirming that I've successfully captured his attention. A laugh escapes my lips, and I can sense the car slowing down as it turns into a parking lot.

I straighten up and take a look at our surroundings. It's a restaurant I'm not familiar with, but I can see a charming small brick building adorned with twinkling lights outside.

He skillfully pulls into a parking spot and then turns to face me, his expression hopeful.

"Wicked seirína, not only do you like the danger but I think it turns you on."

As expected, he promptly gets out of the car, and I anticipate that he will come to open my door. It's something I enjoy – the fact that he comes to me.

Sure enough, he opens my door, and I exit gracefully, not faltering in my heels. I slip past him, heading towards the restaurant's entrance without waiting for him to catch up. However, he does so swiftly, his long strides easily matching my pace.

His large hand clasps the door handle, and as we step inside, the restaurant reveals itself. It's dimly lit, small, yet elegantly decorated. I'm not entirely sure what I was expecting from him, but as my eyes adjust to the lighting and I survey the surroundings, I notice that no other tables are currently occupied.

"Are we alone?" I inquire, my gaze fixed on him, curious about the intimate setting.

"Of course we are. I couldn't have you looking like that, knowing you'd steal the attention of every other man here. It would have been rude to gut someone in front of you on a date," he says, and his words leave me a bit stunned.

Before I can think of how to respond, a young woman at the entrance guides us to a table by the large windows, offering a beautiful view of the Phoenix mountains.

We take our seats, and in the soft candlelight, I notice his eyebrows knit together slightly, a barely noticeable sign of inner turmoil. He looks haunted, much like I often feel.

"What demons are you wrestling with at the moment?" I inquire, keeping my tone light, so as not to alarm him but hoping to coax him into opening up a bit.

His bleeding pupil turns to me, and I detect a flicker of amusement in his gaze.

"My demons?" he repeats, seemingly contemplating his response.

"Everyone has them, but I wonder, Dash, do you ever let them out to play?" I inject just enough seductive mystery into my voice to make it seem like a game, but little does he know, I genuinely believe it.

"My demons are dark, seirína, and I don't fight them. I'm a bad man, and bad men have bad demons that accompany them," he replies.

I find his honesty intriguing. Most people deny the darkness that lurks beneath their surface, but we all have a shadowed side.

"What I'm really struggling with is if I've decided what I'm going to do with you," he admits, his tone edged with uncertainty.

"Excuse me?" I retort, my voice louder than intended, but I don't care. I've gone from being the one initiating the game to being an unwilling participant in his.

The waiter is placing appetizers and drinks on our table, items that Dash must have pre-ordered. I consciously avoid acknowledging the waiter, refusing to break my intense gaze with Dash, trying to convey as much fiery determination as possible.

"Truth is, seirína, there are a few reasons you're here tonight, which I had originally planned to address later in the evening. One of them is I can't seem to stop thinking about you, which, for a busy man like me, is quite a nuisance," he casually mentions, eating on one of the oysters the waiter placed before us. I steadfastly refuse to touch the food until he finishes.

"Second," he wipes his mouth slowly with a napkin, placing it in his lap, then fixes his intense gaze on mine. The intensity of his stare might make others recoil, but I'm not like anyone else, and his intensity excites me a little. So, I lean forward, resting my forearms on the table.

"I have it on good authority that something doesn't add up with Sin and the business model in which they operate, and I'm wondering if you're a willing participant," he reveals, his voice holding a note of curiosity.

"What the fuck did you just say?" My shock is evident, and for a moment, I struggle to form an intelligent response. The Sin business model is not flawed; I work tirelessly to ensure we generate substantial profits.

"How filthy that beautiful mouth of yours is," he remarks, and now I'm not just turned on but genuinely infuriated.

"Your claim about Sin is absurd. I've dedicated six years of my life to ensure that Sin is the most renowned club in the Southwest. What precisely doesn't sit right with you? Is it because I'm a successful woman?" I retort, my hand hidden inside my clutch, wrapping my left hand around the hilt of my concealed knife beneath the table.

He's physically larger than me, but that doesn't intimidate me. I've faced more dire circumstances, and I currently hold the element of surprise in my favor. I have no intention of sitting here and allowing myself to be berated by an arrogant jerk.

"Indeed, seirína, what you've achieved with the club over these years is undeniably impressive. What raises suspicion for me is the fact that the money collected by the D'Santos family from the club on Tuesdays when you're not present is then transported to Mexico and deposited into a bank under a shell corporation," he divulges.

I find his claim difficult to believe. I have a business card tied to a major bank here in Arizona, which I use when I need to make any purchases for the club. If the cash were indeed being deposited in Mexico, how would I have access to these funds? I don't vocalize these thoughts because it's not something I feel inclined to share with him. There's a nagging feeling in the back of my mind, telling me to at least hear out his evidence, a notion that I begrudgingly heed.

"Who are you?" I seethe.

"My name is Dash like I said, and I'm an investigator of sorts," he replies.

I abruptly push back from my chair. Just as swiftly, he's on his feet, gripping my arm, which finally unleashes the last vestige of darkness I had been holding at bay.

In a split second, I employ the hand with the concealed knife to break free from his grasp on my right arm and press the blade against his throat. No one touches me without permission.

At that moment, he doesn't make any attempt to resist but rather looks down at me with his eyes filled with desire and what appears to be a hint of pride. As I glance at the blade and see a small trickle of blood coming from his neck, I snap my eyes back up to meet his, trying to gauge his reaction.

"If you wanted to draw blood, all you had to do was ask. I'd gladly bleed for you," he purrs, moving closer, which causes the blade to dig in a bit more.

I can sense my demons stirring within me, reacting to his words, but I force myself to refocus on the immediate situation at hand.

"So, you're investigating me for running a profitable club?" I inquire, my tone laced with disdain.

"No, I'm investigating the D'Santos family and their activities, and I wanted to determine if you were aware of the situation or merely a pretty face concealing their wrongdoings. Judging from your anger, it's clear you had no idea. Yet, you must feel used, don't you? Women like you don't take that lightly."

He's right; we certainly don't.

Could they truly be involved in something illicit and using Sin as a cover? I don't know the D'Santos family well, but why employ Sin as a front, and for what purpose?

"I want proof, and you're going to provide it," I assert firmly.

"Proof, you say?" At that, he gently pushes my arm, freeing it from its position pressed against his throat, and I permit him to do so. The sight of the blood stirs something inside me, but I can't let him see that. Only someone deeply twisted would be aroused by such a sight.

"And what exactly will you do once you have the proof?" he inquires, slipping his hands into his pockets, exuding an air of nonchalance. I can sense him weighing the idea in his mind, and he remains remarkably composed, even with a droplet of blood running down the front of his throat.

"If the claims are true and they're using me as a cover, I'll help you burn the whole operation to the ground." I assert with conviction. It's true; no one uses me. Yet, I'm still not entirely sure I trust this guy.

"Finish your dinner while I contemplate," he commands, and his tone simultaneously irritates me and ignites a spark within me. Few have the audacity to tell me what to do.

"Fine, but only because I'm hungry. You have until the end of dinner to decide, or I'm walking out of here, and I'll take you down along with them."

We both settle back into our seats, but he continues to look at me with a smirk.

CHAPTER 7

"When my sight's on you
You're fucked"
-Upon A Burning Body

Dash

I find her willingness to help surprising and intriguing. To be honest, I wasn't sure what to expect when I confronted her. I sensed her uniqueness from the moment we met, but I was prepared for either her relenting or storming off, not her offer of assistance. It's a valuable proposition; having an inside person could provide a significant advantage.

Throughout dinner, we exchange very few words, and her intense gaze remains fixed on me. Her eyes, now even greener than usual, watch and assess my every move. I can still feel the mark where she nicked my throat, a sensation I've never experienced before. No woman has ever drawn blood from me, not due to a lack of trying on their part, but mainly because of my size and training, which doesn't often afford them the opportunity.

The revelation that all of her lean muscle isn't merely for show, combined with her getting the upper hand, stirs something in me causing my dick to get hard again.

Standing outside her apartment, I've reached a decision. She's positioned herself against the front door, keys in hand, and her gaze is fixed on me, waiting for my response. It's clear she has no intention of inviting me inside, and her eyes convey a hint of resentment, possibly even a touch of hatred. Yet, her emotions do little to dampen the growing intensity of my desire; if anything, they fuel it further.

In one stride I press my large body against hers pinning her to the front door and she doesn't relent. No part of her exhibits fear, but perhaps she should be afraid. There's a significant amount of blood on my hands. In instances where the crimes I uncover are excessively heinous and I'm aware that their wealth will secure them freedom in the court of law, I assume the roles of judge, jury, and, most enjoyably, executioner. I take meticulous care to cover my tracks, ensuring that no one could ever trace these actions back to me or AMG. My experiences during my time at war are a different story, even more gruesome, and those memories are generally revisited only in my nightmares.

"Fine," I huff, allowing my warm breath to caress her jawline. "We'll start stakeouts in three days. In the meantime, I'll continue my investigation, and you should go about your normal routine. We'll conduct a stakeout from Sunday to Wednesday, after which you'll need to return to work. It's crucial that you follow the instructions provided to prevent compromising the case's integrity." I press myself even closer to her, savoring the heat that radiates between us. "And before you inquire, a detail you overlooked until now, yes, I've been closely monitoring the club."

"How long?" she inquires, and I can sense the underlying question. A faint smile tugs at my lips.

"I've been keeping an eye on you for long enough to witness your parking lot encounter, seirína, if that's what you're curious about," I reply, thinking back to the incident involving the stupid blonde fuck.

She doesn't even flinch at my comment, but her eyes ignite with a challenging spark.

"I hope you enjoyed the show," she retorts. With that, she tries to push me off her by bucking her hips, but I counter by shifting my weight against her, determined not to let her escape so easily.

“Either fuck me against my door, or go home and I’ll see you Sunday, but I’ve grown bored of this.” She says grinding her hips against me.

There's a fierce undercurrent of animosity in her eyes, accompanied by something darker and more tantalizing, something I'm eager to explore. However, I know I must maintain my focus on this case. At the moment, we're allies, and I can't deny the thrill of the ongoing exchange between us.

"Well, that's one way for my first date to go," she mutters under her breath, and I almost miss it.

"You mean our first date?" I ask, a little confused by her comment.

"No. I mean my first date. As in the first one I've ever gone on. I don't do dates," she says, no longer hiding her feelings about it.

I'm surprised, and I’m not sure how to respond. I decide to give her some space and say, "Till Sunday, seirína," then turn to leave her hallway. "In the meantime, no more parking lot flings. I don't share what's going to be mine."

It's Sunday morning, and I'm here to pick her up, just as I said I would.

When she emerges from the front doors of her building, I can see it. There's still anger in her eyes, but I don't think it's directed at me. Her gaze seems distant, which makes me believe it's something personal. My mind goes back to the man she had to escort out of Sin the other night.

She looks stunning. Her long, lustrous dark hair is elegantly gathered into a ponytail that gracefully cascades down her back. As I catch a glimpse of her, a fleeting image of me wrapping the ponytail around my fist crosses my mind, and I quickly blink it away. She's dressed in sleek black athletic shorts that perfectly complement her figure, paired with a dark green tank top that accentuates her curves. I had suggested she dress comfortably, and while I adore seeing her in those alluring dresses, I much prefer this look.

I step out of the car, running my fingers through my rich, dark brown hair, and walk around to help her with the single suitcase she's pulling along.

She had been given clear instructions to pack light for the three-night trip, focusing solely on comfortable attire. Most people might feel uneasy about embarking on a three-day journey with a stranger, but she displayed no reservations. Oddly, her trust in me both irks and flatters me. It's either a small part of her that genuinely trusts my intentions, or her self-assuredness is strong enough to handle any precarious situations that may arise.

I appreciate her confidence, and willingness to travel with me. Yet, the protective side of me is simmering with frustration at the thought of her willingly placing herself in potential danger similar to the fire alarm at Sin.

After stowing her suitcase in the trunk and closing it, I notice her waiting by the passenger door, expectant. Her unwavering confidence manages to bring a faint, approving curve to the edge of my mouth.

As I open the door for her, I duck my head inside first. When I turn, I have a paper sailboat in my hand.

"Seirína, it's wonderful to see you again," I say with a warm smile.

She accepts the paper sailboat, and a subtle smile tugs at the corner of her lips, almost imperceptible.

"I'm sure it is," she replies.

Once we're on the highway, I begin to brief her on the details that James had compiled for me.

"When the money is picked up, we've managed to track them crossing into Mexico and heading to what seems to be a small private bank. It's consistently Carlos who deposits the money, and they usually stay in Mexico for a few days before returning. Interestingly, the account isn't registered under Sin as the business name. We're currently running the names of the other customers visiting that bank through James to see if we can uncover anything significant."

She absorbs the information in silence, her expression contemplative, before eventually turning in her seat to face me.

"Did you ever consider the possibility that they actually reside in Mexico and prefer to keep all their money there?" she suggests.

I shake my head, countering, "Don't you find it strange to live in Mexico while running multiple businesses here? It's also peculiar that you're the only cash club in the area. Moreover, it's odd that you don't utilize a local bank, and as the manager, you can't deposit the money; instead, the owners pick it up and leave the country. Even the money you have for your business expenses is managed through a credit card paid off from their personal account in Arizona, not the bank where they deposit the business funds."

She remains silent, her thoughts churning as she contemplates my questions. It's clear she's already considered many of the points I raised.

It's only Sunday, but we're en route to Mexico to stake out the bank before the D'Santos family's expected arrival on Tuesday. I want to observe any changes, if any, during that time and afterward.

The drive passes swiftly, and as the border looms closer, I instruct Lorelei, "In the glove box, there are a few documents. Pull them out; we'll need them up here."

She follows my instructions without resistance, which pleases me. When she retrieves the documents, I notice recognition crossing her face.

"Passports?" she inquires.

"Yes, we need passports to travel into Mexico and back," I confirm.

She examines the passports one by one. "Noah Hanson?" She scoffs at this, as if it's a joke, then glances at the other. "Ava Blanchford." She stiffens at the sight of her false last name, clearly uncomfortable with the situation but unwilling to admit it.

Before she can speak, I attempt to explain, "I—"

"Stop," she interjects, her tone ice-cold. "I warned you that if anyone ever found out information about me, I'd show no mercy. Be cautious with the games you're playing."

I quickly defend myself, "First, the fake passports were necessary. Lorelei Blanchford disappeared from the radar over ten years ago. This weekend, we're just Noah and Ava, a new couple embarking on their first trip together. Second, I've revealed your true last name to no one. And third, do not threaten me. You're treading into a dangerous game that could ruin you as well."

Before she can respond, I roll down my window to hand our passports to the border patrol agent. I had James create fake identities for us with enough backstory to be convincing if anyone grew suspicious. These identities include bank accounts, social media profiles, and even a rental history at a fictitious apartment. We're not entirely sure how deeply involved the D'Santos are in their questionable activities, but I want to cover all my bases in case someone begins to dig into our backgrounds.

The border patrol agent waves us through, and we continue our journey in silence for the last few miles.

As we arrive in the town where the bank is located, I pull up to our resort, and I can see Lorelei's eyes widening in surprise.

The resort is a picturesque paradise, situated right on the beach with all the rooms offering breathtaking views of the pristine white sands. Mexico holds a special place in my heart, as it was one of my favorite vacation destinations during my childhood. These fond memories are a testament to my mother's influence.

I pull up to the front of the resort and hand the car over to the valet. After gathering our bags and tossing the keys to the valet, we head inside, and it's time for me to check us in as Noah.

While we wait, Lorelei, or rather, Ava, remains near the front doors, her eyes scanning the people and surroundings meticulously. She seems to do this as a habit, not just in situations like this. It's as if she's constantly on guard, like her life depends on being hyper-aware of her surroundings and the people in it.

I know precisely where our room is because I had James hack the system to secure a room with a view of the beach and, consequently, the bank through binoculars.

As we walk down the hall toward our room, I hear Lorelei's discontented comment. "I didn't pack for this. You only mentioned comfortable clothes, and none of this looks like we're a couple on a beach vacation."

I chuckle softly in response, sensing her irritation.

Standing in front of our resort room, I go to swipe my key card, but she interrupts with a question. "Is my room the one next door? Where's my key?"

Not wanting to have this conversation within earshot of others, I swiftly pull her inside and close the door, making sure not to create a scene.

"Can you not trust that I have things under control?" I ask, taking a bold step closer, invading her personal space.

"You won't be wearing your own clothes this week," I continue, advancing again. I notice her chest rising slowly, but she maintains our intense eye contact. "The clothing you'll wear will be of my choosing, something no one has seen you in before. You'll also be sharing a room with me. I don't want you in harm's way, and my trust in you is still not absolute. For all I know, you might decide to run off. Besides, it would look suspicious if a supposedly in-love couple had separate rooms on vacation, wouldn't it? I prefer you to be as close as possible," I conclude, emphasizing my last point with the smirk she despises.

She stands her ground, her words laced with venom. "How dare you expect me to just follow suit. You may be used to women bowing to your commands in a prior life, but I am not one of them. I am here as a partner, and I will be treated like one."

I press my growing hardness into her and grind out "I told you before that you will follow my instructions when it comes to this case. If you keep speaking to me in that way I will be forced to fuck that attitude out of you, are we understood?"

"You seem to have forgotten that we're equals in this partnership, best you don't forget again" she clips out and pushes past me. "Since you have things under control, what's the plan? The sun is already starting to go down."

I straighten and walk over to open the long curtains. "Tonight, we'll be going out to eat at a restaurant owned by another D'Santos, who also happens to bank at the same institution."

"That's the plan? Going out to eat? I thought we were watching the bank," she remarks, her tone incredulous.

"We are, but I'd like to keep an eye on what's happening in the restaurant as well to gauge any connections, if they exist. Overworked kitchen staff tend to have loose lips," I explain.

"I'm going to shower. I would like my clothes laid out for when I'm done since I can't wear my own," she states before heading to the bathroom and closing the door behind her.

As she disappears into the bathroom, I can't help but feel a surge of anticipation. The thought of selecting her attire for the evening, with her clinging to my arm, is something that brings a sly grin to my face. I reach into my bag, ready to retrieve the perfect outfit for her.

CHAPTER 8

"I just died, at the thought of being alive"
-kennyhoopla

Lorelei

I realize that he has orchestrated this situation intentionally, and it's clear to me. When I step out of the shower, I find that he has left out only a mid-length light blue dress with a perfect V-neck on the chest, which ties in the back. There are no undergarments in sight, and I quickly discover that he has hidden my bag so I can't retrieve my own. His intentions couldn't be more obvious.

I decide to go along with his plan, and though I'm not typically shy, I hope he squirms inside when he sees everyone's eyes staring at my nipples through the thin material of the dress. On the other hand, I must admit that the dress fits me perfectly, and it feels surprisingly soft against my skin.

I notice that he's left me a toiletry bag in the bathroom as well, which reminds me that he managed to sneak in quietly enough for me not to notice while I was showering. He's thought of every detail, down to the mascara I always use. It makes me wonder just how much this guy knows about me. A strange thrill tingles up my spine, something I've only felt since I met him.

This isn't a color I'd usually choose for myself, but as I examine my reflection in the bathroom mirror, I see my long dark hair cascading down my back in loose waves, with just a touch of mascara on. I look innocent and beautiful, a perfect look for a beach setting.

As I step out of the bathroom, I find him leaning against a wall, meticulously adjusting his gold watch. For a moment, I allow my gaze to roam over him. His wide chest and shoulders are encased in a simple white V-neck t-shirt. I continue my visual journey down, and I'm surprised to see that his legs are no longer hidden beneath pants but are instead clad in tan shorts and plain white sneakers. It's only now that I fully notice the extent of his tattoos. Beautiful designs adorn a significant portion of both his arms, with some scattered across his legs.

For a fleeting moment, I wonder if there are other parts of him still concealed beneath his clothing that bear more.

He eventually shifts, and our eyes lock in a steady gaze. His dark hair is tousled, but it's far from messy. I find myself drawn to that, bleeding pupil of his. The desire between us is obvious.

"I thought I'd give you plenty of time to get a good look at me before we join the masses," he quips with a touch of arrogance. His words irritate me, abruptly halting any hint of admiration I had been feeling before.

"For me to check you out, huh? Well, at least you're wearing underwear. Think about that," I retort, hoping to throw him off balance. But, of course, he takes it all in stride.

"Oh, that's not the only thing I'm thinking about, seirína," he replies with a wink as he pushes off the wall.

I question our outfits, "What's with the outfits? This is the complete opposite of how we normally look."

He grins and explains, "Ah, exactly. Tonight, we are Noah and Ava, a couple blissfully in love, enjoying each other and the beach. Plus, blue is my favorite color." With that, he leads me out the door.

As we step outside, I notice it for the first time—the man has a dimple in one cheek. Something so soft amidst his otherwise sharp features makes my head spin. I can feel myself irresistibly drawn in, and I can't help but admit to myself that I'm in trouble.

He moves closer, seizing my hand in his much larger one. My instincts prompt me to pull away, but he catches it and speaks in a tone that reminds me I should be playing the role of Ava right now.

"Ava, hold my hand, darling," he says, dropping hints that I'm slipping back into my usual self. I can't help but cringe at the idea of Ava, imagining her as some sappy bitch.

Right, happily in love. I remind myself I can do this, even though I have no real experience in such matters.

I make sure to look at him with big, innocent doe eyes, batting my lashes dramatically and flashing a smile just like I've seen other women do.

"Such a good girl," he croons, his voice laced with a hint of seduction. The praise and that smoky quality in his voice make me stumble on the rocky pathway, and I can tell it doesn't go unnoticed by him. Damn it, I need to pull myself together and maintain this facade.

His large hand tightens its grip around mine, and he effortlessly keeps me upright, maintaining our pace.

"I had no idea you have so many tattoos. Why do you hide them?" I can't help but ask. The man I'm seeing now is entirely different from the version I've seen thus far.

"I don't hide them; I've just only seen you while I'm working. I don't only wear suits, although I do most of the time because I'm usually working," he explains.

"Do they mean anything?" I inquire, curious about the significance of his tattoos.

"No, they don't have specific meanings. I acquired them at various points in my life from different artists during my travels. It's more of a collection of artwork," he explains.

"Interesting. Most people tend to have personal reasons behind their tattoos, and you seem rather nonchalant about it," I remark, though I immediately regret the words as they leave my mouth. I can already predict his response.

"Well then, what do yours mean?" he inquires, clearly turning the question back on me.

"Mine are simply trophies, from a war I won," I declare firmly, making it clear I'm not interested in delving into further details. I'm not prepared to open up to a stranger, and the sudden focus on my scars causes an uncomfortable itch on my skin. But I push the discomfort away, determined not to let my façade waver. I've spent too much time building these walls to let them crumble so easily.

We continue down the walkway hand in hand, listening to the waves crashing against the shore. It strikes me that life could be this calm, this serene, if I allowed it. The thing is, I can't. I've grown accustomed to the chaos; it's a part of who I am. Yet, there's something about the hand holding mine that I could get used to.

I snap out of my momentary daze as I feel him tugging on my arm, leading me into the archway of a charming little restaurant. The delightful aromas wafting from it almost knock me to my knees.

"Hanson for two, please," he confidently tells the host.

His voice is consistently assertive and dominant. I can't quite put my finger on why, but I find myself drawn to the sound of it. No one has ever been able to dominate me, and at times, I yearn for it. I long for someone in this complex world who can finally be my equal.

The young host leads us to a cozy table in the back of the restaurant. It's a small, intimate space with not many tables, but the walls are adorned with bright, cheerful colors while the tables are dressed in red tablecloths, each adorned with a vase holding a single candle for ambient lighting.

Despite the lack of natural light, the dim atmosphere creates a mellow, tranquil ambiance that I find rather appealing. The host leaves us with a pair of menus and informs us, "Here are some menus. Your server will be over shortly to take your order," before stepping away.

Dash gallantly pulls out my chair, inviting me to sit, and then takes his seat across from me. Our eyes lock over the crimson-tinted candlelight, and he breaks into a broad, toothy grin, a sight I've never witnessed from him before. That damn dimple is on full display once again.

"So, he does smile," I remark, genuinely surprised to see this softer side of him.

"Like I said before, seirína, you've always seen me in a work capacity. When I'm working, I must be a different man to achieve the results I desire. Right now, we're on vacation," he explains with a wink.

"Will you ever tell me what your job is?" I challenge him, refusing to let the topic go.

"Ava, I've told you, I'm an investigator of sorts," he replies, his choice of my cover name serving as a subtle reminder that now is not the time for such discussions.

"So, what's up with your eye?" I blurt out before I can stop myself.

"Everyone stares at it, but no one ever has the courage to ask," he chuckles, running his thumb across his bottom lip. "But not you. So brave, my little seirína. Very well, it's a birthmark on my iris, and its position and dark coloring can make it look like my pupil is bleeding downward. My mother used to tell me the meaning of the birthmark is that I love being the troublesome one, seeking adventure even if it's bad. I will say that part is true."

Before I have a chance to respond, our waiter appears at our table, a cute waitress with a sweet smile and her dark hair neatly pulled into a tight bun on top of her head.

"What would you two like to drink?" she inquires.

"Soda water with lime for me, please," I order.

"I'll have the same," he requests, and then he adds with a kind smile, "And could you please put in an order of chips and salsa to start?"

His polite request catches me off guard, and I can't help but wonder if that's Noah talking or if it's Dash without his work persona.

An hour later, our plates are empty, and we've thoroughly enjoyed the best Mexican food I've ever tasted. We engage in light small talk, avoiding anything that's too personal, and it feels nice to unwind for a while.

"I need to use the restroom. While I'm gone, if anyone dares to touch you, stab them with the knife I know you're carrying," he instructs, his eyes filled with heat and mischief as he gazes down at me in my seat. His words send a shiver down my spine, and I can feel the heat rushing between my thighs.

It's rare for a man to encourage a woman to defend herself, and even rarer for it to be a turn-on, but that's precisely what it seems to do to Dash. If we were in a different situation, if I were a different person, I might very well find myself attracted to this man. But reality is that people always leave, so there's no point in getting close.

A few minutes pass, and I start to grow anxious. There doesn't appear to be anything suspicious, but just as I'm about to get up to find him, he rounds the hallway where the bathroom door is located.

"Were you getting worried about me, seirína?" he taunts.

"Of course not. I assumed this was all a joke, and you were abandoning me here in Mexico," I retort.

We're both standing now, and I head for the front door, but he stops me with a hand on my bicep and nudges something into my hand. When I look down, I see a dark red rose.

"It's no paper sailboat, but it was the closest I could find on short notice," he says.

"Oh, Noah, aren't you just the sweetest," I reply, lacing my words with just enough sarcasm to earn another one of his big, toothy grins. He truly is a striking figure, dark and dangerous in a way that's undeniably appealing.

"Come on, let's return to our room. We have much to do," he suggests with a wink, and once more, I feel a rush of heat, this time between my thighs.

CHAPTER 9

"Whenever you walk in the room you control me
You take me, you own me"
-The Used

Dash

It appears my hunch was correct. The busboy proved to be loose-lipped after I handed him that $100 bill. I discovered that the owner of this place is indeed a D'Santos, a cousin of Carlos. Similar to Carlos, this cousin is seldom seen by the staff, and he, too, runs a cash-based restaurant, as indicated by the sign on the front door.

In this day and age where credit card payments are the standard, it's intriguing that they stick to cash. I suspect it's because credit card transactions are traceable, and accepting them would require the business to account for all their income and expenses. It's becoming increasingly evident that this family is smarter than I initially gave them credit for.

"Let's take the scenic route, shall we?" I suggest, eager for a change of pace.

Before Lorelei can respond, I grasp her hand and lead her toward the sandy beach. Surprisingly, she doesn't resist. She lets go of my hand to remove her sandals and sinks her black-painted toes into the warm sand. Her smile is radiant, and it causes a peculiar sensation in my chest.

"What has you smiling like that?" I inquire, wondering how I can make that smile a permanent fixture on her face.

"I've never been to the beach before. I always wondered what the sand would feel like on my toes, but this is better than I imagined," Lorelei confesses, her smile remaining firmly in place. It's a rare moment where her mask seems to have slipped entirely in front of me.

"You've never been?" I can't conceal my surprise as I ask the question. Given my research, I know she's 29 years old, which means she's spent nearly three decades without ever experiencing the simple pleasure of a beach visit.

"Growing up, we never had the money. When I moved out on my own, I was always buried in my work, trying to make ends meet. Then, once I had enough money to go, I was so wrapped up in the club, I never took the time," Lorelei explains, her tone casual, but I can sense that it's far from being just another fact.

This woman in front of me, so strong and resilient, willing to do whatever it takes to survive, missed out on the simple joys of feeling her toes in the sand. It's a reminder of how life's struggles can rob us of the small pleasures, and I won't rob her of that now.

"Well, let's not waste any more time then, Ava. Dig your toes in and run free," I encourage her, pleased to see her smiling even brighter now.

She heads towards the direction where we can hear the waves crashing against the shore. Although it's too dark to see much, that's the beauty of the ocean; you don't need to see it to feel its sense of freedom.

As I watch her go, my pocket begins to buzz, indicating an incoming call from James. "You go ahead; I'll catch up with you in just a second," I tell her, gesturing to my phone that's now in my hand.

Lorelei nods and takes off without hesitation, making her way straight for the water. I smile as I watch her go, reluctant to miss seeing her experience the ocean up close for the first time.

I answer James's call, my voice reflecting the smile on my face. "Yes, James?"

"Uh, boss man, are you enjoying yourself?" James asks.

He must have sensed my enjoyment, and I quickly wipe the smile from my face. "What is it, James?" I inquire, correcting my tone back to the business at hand.

"I was checking in to make sure your room had the correct view and to see if the restaurant provided any more information I could dig into. You'll have all day tomorrow to watch the bank before they arrive on Tuesday," James explains.

"Only one thing," I begin to say, but I'm interrupted by a loud grunt and a scream coming from the direction Lorelei had headed. My heart sinks into my stomach, and I quickly end the call with James before we can finish our conversation.

I sprint toward Lorelei, my body moving instinctively over the uneven terrain. Within seconds, I'm standing beside her.

"Lo - are yo -" I start to ask, but I can't complete my sentence because I'm too busy taking in the whole scene. She's standing there, her bright green eyes gleaming in the setting sunlight, with her knife in her hand, hovering over a large man who's lying on his side, crumpled in the sand. In any other circumstance, I might have found this sight amusing.

"The crazy bitch stabbed me!" the man yells at me, clearly in pain.

I watch as Lorelei responds, her voice steady and resolute. "I warned you once not to put a hand on me. You didn't listen and took the liberty of doing it anyway. Plus, that's just a flesh wound, a warning if you will. If I had stabbed you, you wouldn't be talking right now." Her words hold a sense of cold authority, leaving no doubt in my mind that she can take care of herself. Surprised by the unfolding events, the lingering question remains: Who is she?

Before I can even think, I've kicked the man onto his back, and my sneaker-clad foot is pressed firmly against his throat. Anger courses through me, and I can feel the darkness within me threatening to surface. If I let it go too far, she'll witness the demons that lurk deep inside me. But I think I've just seen a glimpse of hers.

"Apologize now, or I will end you," I growl, my voice laced with menace. "No one touches what's mine, and the fact that you're still breathing right now is pissing me off more with every passing second." I press down a little harder, emphasizing my point, and I see fear flare in the man's eyes. I could end him without a second thought. I've shed more blood than most people could ever fathom.

"I - I'm sorry," he chokes out, his voice trembling.

"Seirína, are you satisfied with this apology?" I inquire, turning my head to look at her.

Her response surprises me. "Not entirely, but I've grown bored, and hopefully, he's learned his lesson not to touch anyone without their permission."

Her confidence is astounding and once again I can feel myself growing erect in my shorts. I have to do something about these reactions she elicits from me. I'm not one to mix business with pleasure so I need to get my mind right before I rip a fucking hole in my shorts.

Slowly, I let my foot off the man's throat. "Run, far away from here. If you are seen again touching a woman without consent, I promise it'll be the last thing you do."

I don't even wait for a response from him before I turn to

Lorelei and take her hand. After ensuring our surroundings are clear, I pull out my phone to send a quick text message. We continue down the beach in silence for a while until we eventually return to our hotel room.

Once we're inside, she turns to me. "So do I have pajamas I can wear?"

I smile and walk over to my suitcase, pulling out a set of black silk shorts with a matching short-sleeve button-up shirt, handing them to her.

"Thank you, by the way, for sticking up for me with that stupid ass guy. Most people would have been terrified to see that I cut someone just for touching me," she says, her gaze averted.

Her lack of eye contact angers me. "Lorelei," I growl, gripping her chin to force her to look at me. The anger surges within me as I think about that man's hand on her and how this whole situation has shaken her confidence.

"You defend yourself however you see fit. If I had been the one to see it first hand, that man would be at the bottom of the ocean right now. I meant what I said. No one touches what's mine."

As I speak, my hand moves from her chin to grip her by the shoulders. My anger starts to dissipate, and I find myself in this unexpected position.

"Your eyes are glowing like mine do when I'm angry," she whispers.

"Are you scared?" I inquire.

Her response is unwavering. "No. You're only touching me right now because I've allowed you to, but if you ever do it without my permission, you'll end up like the man on the beach."

“Fuck, I hope I do.” The thought of her drawing my blood again sends electricity straight to my dick and I know my erection is pressing against her stomach.

She inhales sharply and pulls away from my grip. I release her arms, allowing her to go into the bathroom and get dressed. I'm dangerously close to losing control around her, and I'm beginning to doubt the wisdom of this trip. However, it's too late to turn back now.

When she emerges from the bathroom, she's dressed in the pajamas I selected for her. Her face is freshly washed, and her hair is casually pulled up into a bun. At this moment, she is the most beautiful I've ever seen.

This woman was made for me. All that fire and darkness wrapped in the most incredible vessel ever created.

"You'll be sleeping on the couch," she remarks.

Her audacity elicits a hearty laugh from deep within me. "I planned to. I would never force you to be touched, but know this, very soon you'll be begging for it."

I can see her roll her eyes clear to the back of her head before she climbs onto the bed, slides her long legs under the blankets, and starts to snuggle in for sleep. It's late now, and we need to be up early to watch everything surrounding the bank tomorrow. I'll have a feed running to James to do facial recognition on the patrons going in and out.

I go over to Lorelei and hover over her while she looks at me confused. "May I?" She nods her head in response, and I grab the blankets, letting my calloused fingers graze her soft skin that's peeking out between her shorts and her top. Slowly, I work my way up, tugging the blanket along with me. She lets out a shuddered breath with each touch of her skin, and I try so damn hard to ignore it, but I can't.

It's a risk but I go for it anyway watching her face the whole time for any indication that I've gone too far. When I get part way up her arms I extend each thumb and graze her already hard nipples through the thin fabric of her top. I stifle the groan that's threatening to fall from my mouth.

I'm rewarded with a sigh that sounds like it's one brush of my thumbs away from a full on moan. I could spend the rest of my life testing out the different reactions from her and the delicious noises she makes in response.

If I push her too hard I know she will slip that mask back into place and retreat in on herself, so rather than push her farther tonight I file this information away for later. With one more graze of my thumbs across her nipples I finish pulling up her blankets and tuck them around her.

Before I straighten I rub my thumb across her bottom lip and turn to check the locks on the doors. I intentionally strip down to my boxers allowing her to see the erection that's currently tenting my underwear, turn off the lights, and climb onto my makeshift bed.

I meant it before, soon she'll be begging for it.

CHAPTER 10

"I'm not afraid of the war you've come to wage against my sins"
-Bad Omens

Lorelei

Drip.
Drip.

Drip.

It's so cold, always so cold, but the warmth of my blood running down my leg is anchoring me. The edges of my vision are fading to darkness, and I must find a way to bring myself back.

Drip.

Drip.

Drip.

My back presses against the cool shower siding, and as I crack my eye open, I gaze down to witness bright crimson blood dripping from my torn flesh onto the stained tub surround.

I can't die in this bathtub.

As consciousness slowly washes over me, it takes a moment for my brain to realize that I'm no longer in the bathtub. My body is enveloped in warm, soft blankets, where safety embraces me. A faint layer of sweat clings to my skin from the nightmare. I focus on steadying my breathing and regulating my racing heart as swiftly as possible.

Sometimes, I can't help but wonder if, by shooting myself in the head, I could find a moment of quiet. Just a brief respite from the ceaseless battle that rages within my mind, both in my waking hours and during restless sleep.

It's early, and I can see the sun sneaking in through the balcony curtains, which are left slightly ajar, allowing just enough light to pierce through and assault my retinas. As if the sun weren't enough, my nose is greeted with the enticing aroma of coffee, a scent that instantly jolts me awake.

I sit up, and the blankets cascade down to my waist. That's when I notice Dash, perched on the couch at the foot of my bed. His hair is tousled but not messy, and he's shirtless, focused on his laptop. Thank god he at least put on shorts.

Shit, last night. When I almost came from him just touching my nipples. What the hell is wrong with me when I'm in his proximity?

"Good morning, sunshine."

"Mmm," is all I can manage in response.

"I ordered us coffee and had them bring up some parfaits for breakfast."

"How did you know that's my usual breakfast?"

"Seirína, I know a lot more than you think," he says, flicking his eyes from his screen to me, punctuating it with a smirk.

He rises and takes a coffee cup from the small table beside him, then saunters over to me, like a hunter stalking his prey. As he peers down at me, he's only wearing black shorts, giving me my first glimpse of his broad chest. A portion of his chest is adorned with tattoos, much like his arms, and I can't help but wonder if there are more hidden beneath. Seeing him now, it's clear he has far more tattoos than I do, and they seem to add a dangerous edge to this already formidable man.

"I can arrange a different breakfast if you're hungry for something else," He offers, noting the darkening of his eyes and the mischievous glint in them.

"Nope, coffee and a parfait is perfect, thank you," I reply hastily, trying to brush off the innuendo. I realize that I might be in serious trouble with this man, especially if my body responds as readily as it did last night. I'm feeling pathetic. Once I gather the information I need about Sin, I have to sever ties as swiftly as possible. Allowing him any closer could be my undoing.

He chuckles and returns to his computer, donning a pair of black-rimmed glasses. The sight of this impeccably handsome man wearing glasses is unexpected, and a smile tugs at my lips.

"Is something amusing, Seirína?" he inquires.

"I... I suppose I just didn't expect to see you in glasses," I snicker. "How old are you?"

"I'll have you know I've only had to wear them since I came back from my last deployment. This is not due to my age; I typically wear contacts. For your information, I'm 35, not nearly old enough for it to be insinuated that my eyesight is due to my age," he retorts, his tone dripping with mock exasperation.

I can't quite put my finger on it, but 35 feels both too old and too young for him. His physical appearance suggests youth, likely due to his diligent self-care, but there's a certain maturity in his eyes. He's seen and experienced things that have left their mark and aged him beyond his years.

"Whatever you say, old man. So, what's the plan for today?" I ask.

"Today, we watch the bank. I've got all the equipment set up for us to monitor from our balcony window, and my right-hand man, James, has access to the camera feed I set up last night. He'll be running facial recognition software and keeping an eye on things in case we need a break."

The pieces are starting to fall into place, and it dawns on me that this is a highly professional operation. Dash just revealed something personal about his military background, and I'm certain this investigation isn't tied to any government agency. He operates with a certain rogue independence. I need to be cautious and strategic in my approach to learn more about his involvement.

"You have a right-hand man? I thought someone as controlling as you would hate to give someone else that power," I quip.

"I am nothing without the team I surround myself with. I could never pull off the things I do without them," he replies, surprising me with his humility. It takes a big person to recognize and appreciate their team.

"Did you learn that in the military?" I inquire.

"Ah, so you did catch that slip of the tongue," he smirks at me from his screen. "Yes, in the military, I learned that I was only as strong as the team I surrounded myself with. We went in as a unit and came out as a unit."

"Interesting. I can't quite picture you following orders," I remark, finding it almost laughable to imagine this dominant man as a subordinate.

"I didn't listen to orders for long before I was the one giving them, but being the one to give the orders takes a toll on a man," he admits.

A chink in his armor, a glimpse into the complexities of his identity. The deep furrows in his brow and the darkening of his eyes betray the weight of the things he's witnessed and the decisions he's had to make over the years. I couldn't fathom the burden of making choices that might jeopardize someone's life.

"I used to be a good man, Lorelei, but the blood on my hands has transformed that good man into someone tainted by a darkness that can corrupt even the best," he confesses, his beautiful face now etched with haunting shadows. My hand twitches, aching to reach out and touch him, to offer some comfort.

His admission sends a chill down my spine, and though I'm in the presence of a man who has confessed to involvement in something potentially lethal, I feel no fear. It's not because I've trained myself to be unafraid, but rather because I genuinely believe he wouldn't harm me. I can't quite comprehend how I've come to feel this way about a virtual stranger. This realization relaxes something deep inside me, a feeling I haven't experienced in a very long time or ever. My body has been on high alert for so long that I've forgotten how permanently tense my shoulders have become, always bracing for the other shoe to drop or a fist to fly.

I don't respond to him, unsure of what to say. Instead, we both rise and make our way to the chairs positioned in front of the balcony door, where binoculars are set up, ready for our surveillance.

The day drags on slowly, and I discover that stakeouts aren't exactly my forte. It's well past lunch, and we've only observed a handful of people entering the bank. Dash assures me that James is diligently investigating each one of them. So far, nothing suspicious seems to be unfolding, except for the bank's unusual lack of activity.

We spend most of our time in silence, simply enjoying each other's presence without the need for small talk. I've always appreciated people who can just sit quietly, finding comfort in the stillness. In these moments of hushed solitude, my inner demons tend to surface, and I let them play at the edges of my thoughts for a while.

Tuesday has arrived, and I'm practically overflowing with excitement, fully aware that the D'Santos will likely make their appearance today. I've been bouncing in my chair for hours, and I can sense Dash growing increasingly irritated beside me.

"Why don't you take a break and watch TV for a while?" he suggests, his way of indicating that he needs some space. Instead of arguing, I decide to go along with his suggestion.

I leap onto the bed, grabbing the remote resting atop the white comforter, and click on the small TV mounted on the opposite wall.

As I turn on the TV, a news station appears, and a story seems to be filmed in our vicinity. I turn up the volume, and the female reporter's voice fills our room.

"California resident Chad Clark went missing two nights ago near a resort in Mexico. Clark was here on vacation with some friends, and after wandering off while drinking, his friends reported him missing," the reporter narrates. A picture of the victim flashes on the screen, and my limbs go numb when I recognize him as the man I encountered two nights ago on the beach, the one I had to defend myself against.

From the corner of my eye, I notice Dash straighten up a bit, and I quickly turn my head to face him, my dark hair whipping around my face. He must sense my intense scrutiny, as he gradually turns to meet my gaze with an air of absolute nonchalance.

There's no sign of hesitation in his eyes. He stands with unwavering confidence, discreetly slipping his phone from his shorts pocket to fire off a text. After a brief moment, he returns his gaze to mine and approaches the bed.

I should be frightened, and my instincts say I should be wary, but despite it all, as he prowls closer to me, I know deep down that I'm not in any immediate danger.

He positions his hands on either side of my hips, leaning in so close that our faces are mere inches from touching, and his unwavering gaze remains locked with mine.

"I'll make one thing very clear," he begins, his voice low and intense. "When I've marked something as 'mine,' I'll never allow anyone to insult it. First, that man touched you after you warned him not to. Then he called you a bitch. The only reason I left him alive in that moment was because you deserved to stand up for yourself without my interference. And I have to admit, at that moment, I was more turned on than I've ever been in my life." Is he making a joke right now?

“So you killed him?” I ask.

“The news station only says he went missing," he concedes, his hands still on either side of my hips, "There's no evidence to suggest anything else. Plus I’ve been in our room this whole time, and there’s no evidence to prove otherwise." He leans back slightly, creating a bit of space between us, but his eyes continue to hold mine.

The idea that this man, a stranger and protector, is willing to defend me sets my inner demons swooning. I'm aware that alarm bells should be ringing in my head, my fight or flight instinct should be urging me to find a way out of this resort, but instead, I feel the familiar heat rushing between my thighs once more.

I’m seriously fucked up. We are talking about the fact that this man may have committed actual murder and instead all I can think about is how fucking hot it is to know someone would be willing to kill for me.

The revelation leaves me both relieved and disturbed. Dash's words about the man who attacked me bring a mixture of emotions. "I would also like to add that I had James look into him after your encounter and found that he is currently in a court battle because a young woman claims he sexually assaulted her, but his parents were able to pay bail while they wait for his court date, which they conveniently keep getting postponed. She's also not the first to speak up. His disappearance sounds like a good thing in my opinion."

My gratitude for Dash's protection deepens.

He continues to study me closely, seemingly waiting to see if I'm going to flee, but I remain seated. The pressure between my legs is steadily intensifying, and I can't help but rub my thighs together in an attempt to alleviate it. However, this only exacerbates the sensation, causing friction that ignites an even stronger craving within my body.

I can’t have sex with this man. My mixed feelings towards Dash and his secretive nature persist. He won't reveal who he's working for or the full extent of his job. I won't give in to this temptation, refusing to let him think he's won me over completely.

"I'm going to take a shower while you keep watch on the bank," I announce in a detached tone. I move back from the bed and slip into the bathroom.

As I reach to close the door, Dash suddenly appears, his hand on the door, blocking me from shutting it.

"That's it?" Dash says, his tone heavy, his gaze intense.

"What do you want me to say?" I ask in return.

"Are you frightened of me?" he wonders, his voice laced with concern.

"Should I be?" I reply, not sure what to make of his question.

"Never of me, seirína. I would never harm you," he asserts, his words carrying a sincerity that, for some reason, I believe.

I nod in acknowledgment and signal my intention to end the conversation. Dash eventually removes his hand from the door, permitting me to close it. I promptly lock the door behind me, though I realize that someone as resourceful as him could easily bypass a locked door if he wanted to. My effort is largely in vain, but it's a small comfort in this complex situation.

Quickly I start the shower and strip down, barely giving the water enough time to heat up. I step into the shower and immediately lean one hand against the wall and use the other to slide between my legs where I know it's already wet and not from the shower.

The overwhelming sexual tension in the room demands release, making it hard to think straight.

I slip two fingers inside myself to gather some of the wetness and bring it back up to circle my clit. It won't take long for me to come undone, I've been riding the line since we got here. I plunge my fingers back inside myself and settle the palm of my hand on my clit and rock my hips harshly fucking my hand.

A small moan slips from my lips and my body tightens like a rope that's about to snap from too much pressure being applied. I push my palm to my clit harder and with that my orgasm tears through my body and another much louder moan crawls out of my throat escaping before I can stop it.

I'm praying he didn't hear that.

After collecting myself, I make swift work of washing my body in the shower. As I step out of the warm water and onto the cold tile, I wrap myself in an oversized white towel. It's then that I realize I didn't bring a change of clothes with me in my rush to escape Dash.

Fuck.

I finish towel-drying my damp hair and turn the knob on the door, only to find Dash standing on the other side, holding a bundle of fabric that he shoves toward my chest.

I glance down at the fabric and recognize they're clothes for me.

"You didn't take clothes with you," he states, his mouth tightly drawn and his eyes piercing straight through my conscience. It's clear he knows exactly what I was up to in the bathroom.

I reach my hand out to take them but before I can tug them away his other hand is on my throat and he spins us to pin me against the bathroom wall while he rubs his impressive erection against my abdomen.

“You fucked your little hand, didn’t you seirína?”

I maintain my direct gaze, refusing to be embarrassed by something as natural as my actions. I'm unapologetic about my sexuality and won't shy away from it.

“Yes.” I state.

He releases his grip on my throat and the clothes, frustration etched across his face. "I'm jealous of a fucking hand," he snarls, then retreats, giving me space to escape into the bathroom. I don't trust myself to be too close to him at this moment, so instead of facing him head-on any longer, I shut the bathroom door.

My hand unconsciously moves to touch the corner of my mouth, realizing that I'm smiling. Lately, I've been finding reasons to smile more often.

I'm glad I managed to provoke a reaction from Dash. I hope he's just as pent up as I've been. Slowly, I slip into the navy blue athletic shorts and a white tank top, still no panties in sight. I sigh, but in all honesty, I don't care too much. Instead, I take my time combing through my damp hair and braid it, knowing that it will have loose waves when it dries. I don't bother with makeup.

Once I'm content with how I look based on my comfort level, I leave the bathroom and find Dash with his back to me, peering through the binoculars once more. I return to my seat next to him and inquire, "What?"

"James saw the D'Santos enter five minutes ago. Carlos walked in carrying a large black money bag," he informs me, his eyes still fixed on the binoculars, scanning the scene outside.

"Why didn't you come get me?" I question.

"I didn't want to interrupt your fun, and we can only see the entrance and exit of this place. James is monitoring the camera feed from inside the bank as we speak," he explains.
I can't really argue with that, given that I've been aware of the plan all along. Dash's phone rings, and he answers it on speaker.

"Boss man, the transaction hit. Carlos deposited $30,000 into the account," the voice on the phone reports.

"Did you say $30?" I interject.

"Yes, is that not correct?" the voice on the other end inquires.

"No," I retort, my tone clipped. "I count the money at the end of each night. The total from the weekend should be $52,000 and some change."

"First, that is quite the profit. You go, boss babe," James chimes in, causing me to chuckle. "Second, that's a significant difference."

Dash turns to me, his expression inquisitive. "Lorelei, can

you show me the records of your register counts so we can compare the deposits they make each week?" he requests.

"Sure, I'll send them to James tomorrow when we get back so he can analyze them. I've kept the records for my own reference. I don't even know if the D'Santos are aware that I keep track of all this; they've never asked for it before," I explain.

"Perfect, we'll leave before dawn tomorrow so we can get those records and get you to the club in time to do your pre-weekend run-down," Dash replies.

My mouth slightly drops open in surprise, and Dash just nonchalantly shrugs his shoulders, saying, "Like I said, I've been watching."

"Boss man, that sounded far too creepy," James quips, I almost forgot that James is still on the line.

"Good work, James. We're going to call it a night. Keep watching the camera feeds and alert us to anything of interest. Tomorrow, Lorelei will send you her personal spreadsheets, and then we'll figure out our next move," Dash instructs before abruptly ending the call without saying goodbye.

"Well, that's rude to hang up on someone," I comment.

"It's just James, he hates goodbyes," Dash explains, a seemingly trivial observation that oddly amuses me.

"So, now what? We have a few hours before dark," I inquire.

"Now we pack away all the equipment and get some sleep for our early departure," Dash responds.

It might sound boring, but I don't protest. I'm fully aware of the need to maintain a low profile now that the D'Santos are in town. We can't risk drawing their attention and setting off any alarms.

CHAPTER 11

"Dove in the deep end, stuck and I can't swim"
-Beartooth

Dash

I left Lorelei at her apartment less than an hour ago, but my mind is far from focused on the case. It's more like a jumbled mess, like a cage filled with a swarm of frantic mice searching for an escape.

What truly haunts my thoughts is the fact that I essentially confessed to making someone disappear on her behalf, and instead of running from my darkness, she came straight for it. Literally, as she displayed by her actions in the shower.

She was turned on by the demons that reside just beneath the surface of my skin. I crave her so intensely that I can feel my body rebelling, urging me to return to her and fuck her on any available surface until she's undeniably marked as mine.

The memory of the rosy flush on her cheeks after her climax continues to drive me to madness.

I've never experienced such intense desire for a woman before, but there's something oddly familiar about her. My body seems to recognize her on a level that my brain can't quite comprehend yet.

I forcefully push the thought aside and rush back to my house, eager to immerse myself once again in the case and the mounting workload. If I keep myself occupied enough, perhaps I can keep these thoughts at bay. At least, I hope so.

As I step inside my foyer, my phone rings, and I answer to hear James' voice come through the speaker.

"Boss man, I've been examining the spreadsheet Lorelei sent me not long ago, and none of the deposits match her records. We're talking hundreds of thousands of dollars in discrepancies just in the last few months alone," James reports.

I had a feeling this was what he would uncover. Things just weren't adding up. I'm grateful we were able to get Lorelei on our side to provide us with this crucial information, saving James the time and effort of having to hack into her computer.

"I'm also continuing to run backgrounds on all the individuals we spotted at the bank, but the initial results for the first few are showing familial ties to the D'Santos on both Carlos and Maria's sides," James adds.

The odds of such a coincidence are starting to look quite slim.

"James, also run a background check on the bank's owner. Something feels off about them too, and I'd bet money they know something," I instruct, my suspicion hard to ignore.

"Already running, boss. I'll have some information for you shortly," James responds before ending the call, saving me the need to say anything more. James is efficient and thorough; I rarely need to provide explicit instructions.

As I roam around my house, my thoughts drift freely, always going back to my siren. But often, they return to the case, and I can't help but imagine the satisfaction of making these people bleed for her.

I've structured AMG to operate relatively autonomously. For larger-scale decisions, I've assembled a board of individuals I trust to manage the company, allowing me to stay in the field where I believe I belong.

My work with the FBI doesn't demand too much of my time; I have the flexibility to choose any contracts I want. The one I accepted just before going on a date with Lorelei was primarily to maintain the facade and avoid raising any suspicions.

Exposing both my identity as an FBI agent and as the owner of AMG would be catastrophic. If that secret were to ever come out, my life's work would shatter. Therefore, I am meticulous in maintaining this delicate balance.

For a brief moment, the echoes of a gunshot reach my ears, and I instinctively flinch before recalling that I'm no longer at war, no longer in perpetual danger.

It's true, you can take the soldier out of war, but it seems that the echoes of war never truly leave you. I notice my hand shaking slightly by my side and clench it into a fist, hoping to quell the trembling. Every time my mind wanders back to those days of war, I can feel myself slipping back into the darkness of that time.

I sense that another trip to Mexico is looming on the horizon, and I know better than to fully unpack my suitcase. It's as if there's more information waiting for me there than here. Everything revolves around that bank, and I won't rest until I uncover the why behind it all.

My mind is racing, overloaded with thoughts and memories. Lorelei, flashes of war, her piercing green eyes, this case – it's all too much at once. For someone like me, control is everything. I've invested significant effort into mastering my urges, but right now, I feel vulnerable to the chaos within my own head.

Fuck.

Without hesitation, my legs carry me up the stairs, taking them two at a time as I make my way to my bedroom. I swiftly remove my shirt, tossing it carelessly in the direction of the hamper, but missing it completely. Entering my pristine white marble bathroom, I turn the shower on and allow the water to warm while I strip off the remainder of my clothes.

I don't bother to check the water temperature again. I step into the glass shower, and the forceful water pressure bores into my skin, seemingly washing away the darkness that stains both my body and my mind. Yet, even in the sanctuary of the shower, I can't seem to quiet the relentless torrent of thoughts in my head. Before I know it my hand is gripped around the base my cock harshly stroking my hand down its length.

Frustrated and seeking any semblance of peace and quiet, I decide to give in to my urges. I fuck my hand fast and hard thinking of bright green eyes and long brown hair. In an embarrassingly short amount of time I can feel the desire coil deep in my spine. A few more rough strokes I've shot my load down the drain and all the thoughts have quieted.

I efficiently wash myself and promptly exit the shower, wrapping a gray towel around my waist. As I step out, I hear my phone ringing – it must be James, he's the only one who calls me. Still wrapped in my towel, I bend over to retrieve my phone from the pocket of the pants I discarded earlier and answer it without glancing at the caller ID. It's a rookie mistake.

"Yeah?" I reply breathlessly, my mind racing.

"Uh, Dash?" She says my name, her voice dripping with allure and sensuality. It's like a wet dream come to life. Does she even realize how incredibly sexy she sounds?

I can't help but wonder if she does this on purpose. It's inconceivable for anyone to be as effortlessly perfect as she is.

"Yes, Lorelei," I respond, attempting to sound more at ease than I am. But all the peace and composure I managed to regain after my earlier release was instantly shattered the moment I heard her voice.

"Why was there another paper sailboat delivered to my door?" she inquires.

I allow myself to laugh, thoroughly enjoying this little game.

"I thought you liked them?" I tease.

"And I thought you were only giving them to me to get my attention for this case? Now I'm on the case, so..." Lorelei's voice is devoid of challenge for once, and she seems to genuinely seek an answer. Deciding to give her a straight answer this time, I respond, "The sailboats have nothing to do with the case. Those are just for my pleasure."

"How did you even get this number?" I'm notoriously guarded when it comes to my privacy. I never give out my phone number and prefer to maintain control over such communication. When I need to talk to someone outside of my trusted circle, I usually find them myself.

This time, it's Lorelei who laughs, her laughter echoing like a melody designed just for me.

"I got James' contact info when I sent him the spreadsheets," she explains. "I also told him I needed your info to discuss the case, and he handed it over. Does this somehow shatter your enigmatic illusion?" she teases.

Her ability to unravel me with her charm and wit is both disarming and intriguing.

"See you soon, seirína," I say with a smile before ending the call. What she doesn't yet realize is that this isn't an illusion. I've deliberately let her glimpse every dark and twisted part of myself. If I'm going to ensnare her and make her mine, she must see every demented piece of me. I won't allow her to fall for the fantasy of a prince charming when I am the dark, menacing figure who will swoop in, vanquish the prince, and claim her for myself.

Setting my phone down on the dresser in my bedroom, I change into more comfortable lounge clothes: black sweat shorts, a plain black shirt, and socks. Once dressed, I return to my office, fully aware that I won't find peace until I figure out my next move.

As I open my silver laptop, I notice an email from James waiting in my inbox.

****Subject: Backgrounds****

Hey boss man,

Attached is the report on each individual from the bank. The main takeaway is that each person I have looked into is related to the D'Santos, which we already knew but this confirms it. They also (surprise) all run cash-based businesses, and all these businesses are in the border states of Mexico.

Please pay special attention to the documents labeled Santiago Ortiz. He is the owner of the bank. Everything on him looks clean, except for the fact that he owns a bank that deals exclusively with shady individuals. All his records seem clean for the bank itself, which is no surprise given the tight monitoring of banking regulations. The bank has been in his family for decades and is the only one – no chain.

Back to digging.

-James

I spend the next few hours meticulously examining every document I have on these people. I learn everything about their bank history, their extracurricular activities, and even who they fuck on Tuesday nights while their kids are at soccer practice.

This is one of my favorite aspects of warfare: gaining in-depth knowledge about the enemy, understanding their vulnerabilities, and ultimately plotting their utter and complete destruction. I'm not a merciful man, and I don't believe in second chances, especially not for the kind of people I target.

Finally, I pick up my phone, not caring that it's 2 AM, and dial Lorelei's number.

“What in the fuck?!” Lorelei's voice is raspy and tinged with the remnants of sleep. Instead of feeling sympathy for disturbing her slumber, I find myself stiffening in my pants. I need to do something about this.

"We're going back to Mexico as soon as you're off work on Sunday morning," I inform her.

"You had to call me now and say this when there are still three days in between the time we would actually leave?" She's clearly upset, and her voice hardens with anger. I can almost picture the fiery glint in her eyes, and it amuses me.

"Have pleasant dreams. See you soon, seirína," I respond with a smirk before ending the call.

CHAPTER 12

"All the shame feels the same when the pain hits"
-kennyhoopla

Lorelei

Bex is clearly furious, and her flushed crimson cheeks are a dead giveaway. She's not one to hide her emotions, and it's either an intentional choice or simply beyond her control. I'm not entirely sure.

"Rule one of friendship is no freaking secrets, Lor!" She shouts over the music in Sin. Bex's aversion to using curse words sometimes amuses me.

It's a Saturday night, or rather, Sunday morning, and ever since I returned from Mexico, Bex has been relentless about where I was last week. I can't reveal anything about what might be happening with Sin until I have more information, so telling her the truth is out of the question. Besides, I'm leaving with Dash again in just two short hours when the club closes, and I have no idea how to explain that to her either.

"Bex, when I'm ready, I swear I'll tell you," I respond. She spins with a drink in her hand, and instead of delivering it to a patron, she takes a few steps towards me. "Listen, I know you don't trust people, and for good reason, but it's me, Lor." With that, she walks away and resumes her work, putting on a smile for the customers, but the lines on her face reveal the hurt, like a neon sign glaring in my face.

Closing time comes, and I let out a big sigh, knowing that the night is far from over. I'm aware that Dash will be waiting for me at my apartment, and we'll leave as soon as I have a chance to change. The thought of seeing him again makes my heart race a little, and I'm eager to get home.

Bex is still upset, mostly because I canceled our weekly sleepover, something I've never done before. I do care about Bex, to the extent that I'm capable of, but the truth is, one day she will leave me too. I have to keep her at arm's length to minimize the hurt she could face. She represents everything good in this world, and someone like her shouldn't be tainted by the darkness. She's meant to be a source of light, and I can't take that from her. Allowing our friendship to continue for this long is a selfish act on my part. I make a mental note to address this issue as soon as we've resolved the situation with Sin.

Bex and I are the only ones left as we walk out the back door to finish locking up. She's unusually quiet, and I can't help but notice her proximity, her floral perfume wafting through the air. The thought of eventually having to end our friendship makes my stomach churn.

"This has nothing to do with our friendship, Bex. There's just something I'm not fully ready to share yet," I explain, hoping that she'll understand.

When I turn to face Bex, I find that she's not even looking at me but instead at the hood of my truck, which is covered in paper sailboats. My frustration intensifies, and I feel anger creeping up my spine.

"I think I know exactly what this is about," she says, beaming. "You sneaky thing, you're screwing whoever is leaving you these!" She playfully hits me on the shoulder. My initial reaction is to retaliate, but I quickly remember it's meant to be a playful gesture.

"Well, it's more complicated than that," I stammer out, not wanting to continue this conversation and potentially have to create more lies. Moreover, I don't want to reveal that she's met him before.

Bex's expression lightens up, and she asks, "Why didn't you just say so? You should know I'd be thrilled if you found a guy you'd sleep with more than once."

Her words catch me off guard, and I can't help but smile at her genuine enthusiasm. Bex has always been supportive, even when I keep parts of my life hidden.

I retort, "I've fucked Liam more than once," attempting to downplay the situation.

Bex responds, "That doesn't count. We both know you use him as a convenience. That boy runs every time you call." I'm not proud of that fact, but it's a simple arrangement, and he doesn't seem to complain.

I roll my eyes and walk across the parking lot, my black heels clicking beneath me. Bex follows behind and adds, "He's got it bad, baby girl. When do I get to meet him?" I choose to ignore her question, not ready to discuss this aspect of my life yet.

I don't understand why he's doing this. He got what he wanted – I'm helping him investigate whatever is happening here. Yet I look at the black hood of my truck, adorned with at least two dozen paper sailboats, and can't help but wonder what he's playing at.

I can't let this man affect me. I've spent far too long building up my protective walls to let them crumble for someone I still know next to nothing about.

Instead, I stiffen my back, climb into my truck, and start the engine. I roll down my driver's window to talk to Bex. Over the loud muffler, she calls out, "Aren't you going to grab your boats? And you never answered me about when I can meet him, you jerk!"

"Nope and never. See you later!" I yell back to Bex as I pull out of the parking lot, paper sailboats leaving a trail behind me.

Arriving at my apartment building, I park my truck and spot Dash's black car already waiting. He's leaning against the side of his car, typing on his phone as usual. He's so effortlessly sexy it makes me grind my molars. Before getting out of the truck, I steal another look at him. Tonight, he's wearing jeans and a plain black shirt with black sneakers, and he's as devastatingly handsome as always.

I know if I take much longer, he'll give me grief about it the whole ride, so I decide to pick up my pace. Grabbing my purse, I climb out of my truck, my heels echoing through the parking garage as my feet hit the pavement. His eyes snap up to me.

I'm still wearing my work outfit, one of my favorites. It's a black dress that's skin-tight and falls just below my ass. It has small spaghetti straps at the top and a squared-off neckline that my chest bulges out of. Simple and deadly.

I walk toward him, putting as much sway into my hips as I can without looking like I'm trying too hard.

"Seirína, where are your paper sailboats?" he asks, glancing at my hands that only hold my purse.

He pushes himself off his car and slides his phone into his pocket, keeping his gaze intently on me. He's looked me up and down a few times now with hunger in his eyes like a starved beast. My heart skips a beat, and I promise myself I won't falter in my steps.

"They're in the parking lot at Sin where you left them."

"That's not very nice," his tone is darker now, with a dangerous edge. "Since you don't want to play nice tonight, I won't either.

Get in the car. Now."

"I haven't changed, and I still don't have my bag." I firmly plant both feet and place my hands on my hips.

"I had hoped you'd remember from last time that your bag won't do you any good. If you'd shown some kindness tonight, I might have let you change, but now, I need you in the car before I consider leaving you behind." The authority in his voice allows for no negotiation; he's a man accustomed to getting his way.

He jerks open the car door, swiftly slips into the driver's seat, and ignites the engine. Damn, he's seriously considering leaving me behind. There's no way I'm going to miss out on this, but I'm seething with anger that he'd actually leave without me. It's hard to believe that a few scraps of paper could have caused such a reaction.

Enraged, I stomp over to the passenger side, wrench the car door open, and throw myself inside, making a dramatic entrance. My dress rides up with the forceful movements, revealing a bit of my nude lace underwear. When I slam the door shut, I catch him staring at my lap.

He tears his gaze away from me, and in the subdued lighting, I notice his jaw tightening in response.

I'm somewhat relieved to see that he's just as irritated as I am. I glance toward the backseat, hoping to find our bags so I can change into different clothes, but all I see are empty black leather seats, and I let out an exasperated groan. He must have stashed everything in the trunk.

"I did mention I would've let you change if you'd been more pleasant. I had the perfect outfit in mind," he remarks, his voice still tinged with irritation. Part of me wants to laugh, but I remind myself not to add fuel to the fire, considering the long journey ahead of us.

The audacity of this man is infuriating.

He accelerates out of the garage, heading full throttle toward the highway that leads to the Mexican border.

If he wants to see me be uncooperative, well, fine.

I fix my gaze on him, determined to make him uncomfortable, even if he's already on edge. He rarely allows his emotions to show, concealing them behind a mask that's challenging to penetrate. But I've been honing my ability to detect his subtle tells and giveaways.

I maintain my unwavering gaze on the side of his face as I sensually slide my hands down my bare thighs. The scars, concealed beneath my tattoos, still exist on my skin, but instead of making me cringe as they once did, I now find them empowering. The ink in my tattoos helps hide the scars effectively, and with the night's darkness providing concealment, it's unlikely anyone could discern their presence. So far, I've never let a man touch my scars, and it remains a closely guarded secret.

A sly smile tugs at my lips, and with a hint of mischief, I hook both thumbs under the hem of my dress, tugging slightly on the fabric of my underwear. I notice his eyes darting back and forth, repeatedly drawn to where my hands are, and his jaw seems to twitch from the effort of keeping it clenched so tightly.

Gotcha.

I gradually pull my panties down, teasingly, and raise my hips slightly to slip them off. Then, I lift my heeled feet, placing them gently on the dashboard to maneuver my panties over them. With just a slight adjustment of his gaze, I know I'd be fully exposed to him, and the thrill of that possibility sends shivers down my spine.

As I hold my panties in my hand, uncertainty lingers about what to do with them now. Before I need to make a decision, he seizes my hand with the panties hanging from it, swiftly wrestling them from my grasp and shoving them into his pocket.

His assertiveness leaves me breathless, but it's undeniably hot to think that he'll be driving around with my underwear in his pocket for the next few hours.

I don't utter a word, opting instead to curl up on the seat and rest my head against the door, hoping for a dreamless sleep to envelop me quickly.

When I eventually wake up, I'm greeted by the glaring brightness of lights illuminating the car. I straighten up and notice that we're at the border patrol station, with an agent peering into the driver's window, clutching our passports.

I glance down, praying that my dress isn't leaving me entirely exposed, only to discover a small cream-colored blanket carefully draped across me, preserving my modesty.

I realize that he likely brought the blanket for me, anticipating I might need a nap after work. It's not something I would expect from most men, considering I've never seen a car with a blanket stored inside. The notion that he took my comfort into account starts to diminish the irritation I had felt earlier.

The border agent gives us one final glance and then waves us through, allowing us to continue our journey to the resort, which is now just a short drive away.

"This trip won't be like the last one, seirína. This won't be a recon mission. This is war, and we're at the initial stages of the battle. If you decide to stay at the resort, I completely understand. You'll never be forced to participate in anything you're not comfortable with," he states with a grave tone, which is almost unsettling. Normally, there's a hint of playfulness when he speaks to me.

His words make me fidget in my seat. I may not fully comprehend what I've gotten myself into, but I'm resolute. I won't shy away from this. I've invested too much to back down now.

"Thank you, but I'll be there for every step of the way. I'm not afraid of the darkness that comes with battle. I've learned that some of it is necessary to reach the ultimate goal," I respond, drawing from personal experience.

"You shouldn't fear the darkness. Only the monsters that reside within it," he remarks, his gaze fixed on the road ahead, though his knuckles tighten around the steering wheel until they turn white.

I'm left speechless by his statement, but the return to the resort interrupts my thoughts. If this were a vacation, I'd probably enjoy this place. It has a sense of tranquility during the daytime, offering a brief respite where I can truly let go, even if only for a little while.

Surprisingly, he's managed to secure us the same room we had during our previous visit. He casually tosses our bags to the floor as we enter the suite, which does raise a few suspicions, but I attribute it to James' influence.

"I know the sun will be rising soon, but we need to get some sleep. In a few hours, we have somewhere important to be," he says, his demeanor strictly business at this moment.

His demand for sleep doesn't come with any additional explanations. Instead, he tosses a light pink pajama set in my direction. The silk shorts and cute spaghetti strap top look not only comfortable but also very much to my liking. I can't help but appreciate his excellent taste in clothing; everything he's provided so far has been both sexy and comfortable.

Then, a thought crosses my mind. "I'm not, like, wearing your girlfriend's clothes or something, am I?" I ask, half-jokingly, to alleviate any potential awkwardness.

I turn to face him, and he raises an eyebrow, scoffing. "No, I don't have a girlfriend, and these clothes were chosen just for you. If I were committed to someone, you wouldn't be here, and I certainly wouldn't let someone else wear her clothes," he asserts.

I release a breath I hadn't realized I was holding, my shoulders relaxing. I tell myself I don’t care about his relationship status. Once this mission concludes, I'll return to my life, and he'll continue with his usual pursuits. People like us aren’t meant for meaningful relationships.

I can't help but ponder the fact that I know so little about the man I've chosen to travel to another country with—twice now. It feels careless, like the setup for the beginning of a true crime story where someone becomes the victim of an unsolved murder.

"You sound like a very dedicated fake boyfriend," I quip, attempting to inject some levity into the conversation.

"My loyalty is a matter of great importance to me," he responds, his tone still serious. "If I were to let myself be claimed by a woman, she would have my undivided dedication."

I can't help but ask, "Have you never had a girlfriend before?" It's hard to fathom that a man like him, who resembles a Greek god, has never been in a relationship.

"I've had a few casual relationships, but nothing I've ever fully committed to. And don't be so surprised, I have on good authority you’ve never had a serious relationship either. Just a line of broken hearts trailing behind your dainty feet" he replies with a smug smile that makes me want to wipe it off his face.

In my grumbling frustration, I ask, "What don't you know about me?"

He leans back, his tone flat, "I'm not sure but I hope to find out."

His demeanor takes on a hint of sadness, and the conversation has grown too intense for me. I need a breather. Turning swiftly on my heels, I retreat into the bathroom, change into the silky pink pajamas he provided, and savor the sensation of the soft fabric against my skin. It manages to brighten my mood slightly.

As I emerge from the bathroom, my gaze locks onto Dash in the process of shedding his jeans. His shirt already rests haphazardly on the couch, and all that's left on his chiseled body are his black boxers, which leave little to the imagination. He's undeniably beautiful, every inch of him, and an overwhelming desire to touch him wells up inside me. I'm forced to clench my hands into fists around my dirty clothes to keep myself in check.

He turns to face me without making any effort to conceal himself. Instead, he closes the short distance between us, taking my clothes from my hand and throwing them in the corner where we put our dirty laundry. My skin tingles with the close proximity.

The palpable tension between us feels far from healthy.

"Get some sleep, Lor," he advises. "We'll be leaving in three hours."

"Sleep," I repeat to myself internally, though my entire body seems to be vibrating with energy. Without offering a response, I climb into the spacious bed and cocoon myself in the comforter, attempting to will sleep to take hold. However, it remains elusive, and my mind races with thoughts that all seem to return to the man in the room with me.

CHAPTER 13

"Pulling demons from under your basement"
-Magnolia Park

Dash

Today promises to be a particularly challenging day. While I recognize Lorelei's unwavering determination, I can't help but wonder how this might affect her. She carries herself with the weight of past hardships, but the full extent of her experiences remains a mystery to me. For me, situations like these ceased to be distressing a long time ago, thanks to the desensitizing effects of war. I've seen even the toughest of men falter when confronted with the grim tasks ahead of us today.

We park the rental car I secured under an alias name behind the abandoned building on the outskirts of town. I can tell she has a million questions bubbling within her, questions that will all find answers before we leave this place. I turn my body in the car to face her, and when I notice she's not looking at me but instead out the window, I gently grasp her chin and turn her face to meet my gaze.

"I mean it, Lorelei. If at any point you decide you've had enough, just walk out of here and come back to the car," I emphasize, ensuring that she fully comprehends my words as I pass her the car keys. Her eyes betray a mixture of surprise and intrigue.

I nod once, not uttering another word, and step out of the car. I make my way to the other side and open her door. As she stands and secures the keys in the pocket of her black jeans, she straightens her posture and locks eyes with me, a resolute determination shining in her gaze.

"There's nothing left in this world that can frighten me," she asserts, and I have no reason to doubt her. Lorelei possesses an unyielding spirit, and while I may lead her beyond her usual boundaries, I know that any trials I expose her to, she will bravely face.

She patiently awaits my lead, but I take a moment to admire her. Dressed in snug black jeans and a plain black shirt, her long hair pulled into a high ponytail that cascades down her back. Today, she has opted for minimal makeup, yet her beauty is absolutely striking.

"No suit today?" She breaks the silence, her curiosity apparent. "And why do we match?"

"Today, we'll be involved in activities that might get a little messy," I reply, "and I'd rather not ruin a good suit. Besides, black can hide a multitude of sins."

With that explanation, I take her hand and lead her to the entrance of the abandoned building. I've meticulously surveilled this place, so I'm well aware of what we're about to encounter. My body is primed for anything that lies ahead.

Before we proceed through the back door, I halt her to retrieve black gloves from my pocket. I hand her a matching pair and firmly instruct, "You need to put these on and keep them on, do you understand?"

Her gaze meets mine with defiance, a trait I've come to recognize. I'm well aware that my orders tend to make her dig her heels in, even when it's for her own well-being. Yet, there's nothing more gratifying to me than when this strong-willed woman eventually submits.

"Lorelei, what we're about to face today is unlike anything we've encountered so far. This is the gritty side of my work, and I need to be certain that you'll follow my instructions. It's for your own safety," I explain.

"Fine," she replies tersely, sliding on her black gloves.

I nod in approval and hold the door open for her. I'm aware that two of my associates are already on-site, keeping themselves concealed. I don't want to startle Lorelei before we even step inside.

In silence, we walk the hallway, and I guide her toward the staircase leading to the basement.

"I've already warned you, but it's crucial that you understand I'm a very different man inside these walls than the person you know," I confess without meeting her gaze. She'll need to determine for herself how much of this she can handle.

As I open the door, the sight that meets us is gruesome. Dangling from the rafters by thick metal chains is a naked and bloodied Santiago Ortiz. I can hear Lorelei take a sharp breath, but instead of fleeing, she takes a few more steps forward. Her resilience impresses me. The nauseating scent of blood and urine fills the air, and though repulsive, it's a familiar stench I've unfortunately become accustomed to.

"Seirína, I'd like you to meet Santiago Ortiz, the owner of the bank," I introduce, circling the battered man whose head droops between his arms which are secured above his head by metal chains. My associates have been interrogating him for the past two days, but he hasn't revealed much yet. I instructed them not to push the torture too far so that I could be present when he finally decides to share the information.

I move behind Santiago, confident that I can make him talk. Interrogation is my specialty, and I've made far scarier individuals crack before. It won't be long before he caves under the pressure.

I seize his hair, yanking his head up forcefully. "It's impolite not to acknowledge a beautiful lady when she enters a room," I declare. The force of my pull causes a few hairs to tear from his scalp.

"P-p-please, help me," he stammers, his bottom lip quivering. It seems like this may be over sooner than I anticipated.

"Ah, my friend, she won't be of any assistance here. I think we both know there's only one way you're leaving this building, and that involves you telling me what I want to know," I suggest, implying that he will leave the building alive. But that's a lie; he will indeed be leaving the building, but in a body bag.

"I - I have a family, please," he pleads, desperation in his voice.

"Then I strongly suggest you start telling me what I want to know, and I might consider a trade," I respond, continuing with my deceptive ploy. When it comes to people like him, I have no reservations about lying.

"You don't understand, they'll kill me!" he gasps, desperation gripping him.

I've grown annoyed of his defiance, so I swiftly retrieve the blade from my pocket and press it against the vulnerable flesh under his chin. "You should be far more concerned about me killing you," I hiss, "they may show you pity. I won't."

I allow the blade to press into the skin of his neck, watching as a trickle of blood appears. I raise my eyes to meet Lorelei's, finding her closer now, her gaze full of intent, her questions unspoken, yet not a hint of fear in her expression.

Breaking her stare, I shift my focus back to the task at hand, removing the knife and circling Santiago's weakened form. I strategically make incisions in places on his bare flesh, causing pain but being careful not to make him bleed out before I extract the information I need.

Santiago's screams of agony punctuate the room after each cut, and I allow a twisted smile to creep onto my face. Men like him deserve the punishment they receive. Once more, I sneak a glance at Lorelei, half expecting her to have retreated to the car by now. Yet, she remains standing there, her composure unbroken, hands hanging at her sides.

"Is there anything you're willing to discuss yet?" I inquire, my voice cool and composed.

"I-I can't," he sobs, spit dripping down his chin. While I can handle blood and spit, I detest it when they lose control of their bodily functions. Hopefully, that won't happen while I'm in such close proximity.

I move to the table where supplies have been laid out by my men, and I pick up a towel placed there. Next to it, there's a water spigot with a small hose attached. Returning to Santiago, I glance at Lorelei. "Come here, seirína," I beckon. I'm somewhat taken aback by her immediate compliance; had she resisted, I would have allowed her to leave, but I want her to stay. I'm curious to see how far I can push her.

"I want you to hold his head back for me. Do not let go until I tell you to," I instruct. She doesn't utter a word, simply looks at the man and nods once. "Now, seirína."

Without any further prompting, Lorelei firmly takes hold of Santiago's head and tilts it back as I position the towels across his face. Once the towel is in the right place, I grasp the end of the hose and turn on the spigot, allowing the water to flow out.

"Are you absolutely certain you can't tell me, Santiago?" I taunt.

When he remains silent, I direct the water stream directly over his nose and mouth, beginning to slowly drown him, and a small smile tugs at the corners of my mouth.

Santiago's body convulses violently, the sound of his struggles causing the metal chains to echo through the concrete room. Just before I instruct her to cease, Lorelei releases his head.

"What the hell? You're going to kill him!" she exclaims, her voice rising above the sounds of his choking and sputtering.

"I told you not to release his head until you were instructed to," I roar at her, my frustration getting the better of me and my tone sharper than intended. "Don't you want information from him?"

"Of course I do, but for all we know he's innocent in this, just like I am," she retorts defiantly, planting her feet apart and issuing me a challenging look. I can't help but admire her when she challenges me.

"This man is far from innocent. The intelligence we've collected reveals much more than their business dealings. I have personal information about everyone involved, exposing their true natures. The piece of filth you're concerned about hurting has been molesting his own daughter for years, shielded from justice by the D'Santo family," I inform her, my voice heavy with contempt.

I can see the wheels turning in her mind as she contemplates the truth of my words.

"Why didn't you tell me that before we got here?" she challenges.

"I wanted to see how you would react to this," I reply with a nonchalant shrug.

"I'm not an experiment, D. Don't ever try to pull anything past me again. We're partners in this," she asserts firmly before I can respond. The use of "D" is a first, and it sends an unexpected jolt of excitement through me, especially as I watch her take charge with this monstrous man.

She yanks the hose from my hand, moving swiftly back to Santiago, her fingers gripping his dark, curly hair as she shoves the water back in his face. His body writhes as much as his restraints allow, but my focus remains squarely on her. Her eyes, bright green and filled with a wicked determination, ignite something primal within me. I'm overwhelmed by a desire to take her right here, amidst the blood, once we've purged the world of this monster.

"Let go," I instruct her, fully aware that if she continues, this man's life will be forfeit, and any hope of extracting information from him will vanish.

She snaps her head up with a furious intensity, and I'm uncertain whether it's her usual self behind those eyes or something much more sinister that has emerged.

"Now," I demand, and she pulls the water away, allowing his head to slump down as he gasps for air beside us.

I maintain my unwavering gaze when I address Santiago, "Would you like to talk now, Santiago? Or shall I allow my girl to have more fun with you?" I can't help but want to prolong this just to observe her in action.

"Please," Santiago coughs out, "I can't."

This time, it's Lorelei who lets out a small laugh. "You're delusional if you think I'm letting a rapist walk out of here alive, but if you talk, maybe I'll go easy on you. The speed of your death depends entirely on the information you provide."

I can't help but be deeply impressed by her, and my smile, even though it might appear strange in this moment, remains on my face. Yet, a disconcerting feeling washes over me, given her reaction to Santiago. It hints at something in her past, and once I gather the evidence I need, there will be another monster to purge.

Lorelei pulls Santiago back once more, subjecting him to another assault of water, and again, his body goes into a frantic survival mode, but she remains unyielding. After he's had enough, she finally lets his head drop, and we await his response. But he still chooses not to talk.

"Alright then, on to the next," I say with a smile lacing my words.

Interrogation is my forte, and it didn't take the military long to realize my talent for extracting information from anyone they needed. They cared more about the results than the methods I employed. It's also why the FBI recruited me swiftly after I left the military, although they'd never publicly acknowledge it.

I approach Lorelei and offer her my blade, but she declines, shaking her head. I raise an eyebrow, curious. "Are you finished, seirína?"

"No," she replies, bending down to retrieve a blade from her shoe. She straightens her posture, holding her own weapon in her hand. I chuckle at her preparedness. "It's the same one I used to draw your blood."

Her revelation sends a shiver of anticipation down my spine, and I realize I need to carry on before my desire consumes me further.

I take her free hand and guide her to the back of the man dangling lifelessly in front of us. I crouch down behind him, watching her closely, waiting for my instruction. He's already been stripped naked, making this part of the process easier. While I have no doubt that she has the potential to kill, learning the art of torture is a different skill altogether. It involves inflicting pain without causing death too quickly.

"You're going to take your blade and cut through his Achilles tendon," I instruct, my tone calm and measured. "You might feel some resistance, so apply force."

Once again, she nods, her demeanor almost as if she's learning basic mathematics in school rather than engaging in torture methods. With little hesitation, she slashes her blade across his right Achilles, causing his entire body to convulse in pain as his screams fill the room. After the screams subside, she proceeds to cut through the left tendon without faltering.

Once more, his body convulses with pain, and he sobs before us as we continue our gruesome work. I walk back around to the front of his battered body, observing his face, which is now marred with a mixture of blood, snot, sweat, and tears. Men like him, who prey on the weak, deserve this. For me, it's a matter of black and white. Anyone who intentionally harms an innocent person deserves the harshest of punishments, ideally delivered by my hand.

"Okay, I'll tell you, but please let me live," he cries.

"You're going to beg for your pathetic life rather than bargaining to protect your family?" I retort. What he doesn't realize is that I've already helped his wife and daughter escape to the wife's home country, providing them with new identities to keep them safe from this monster and anyone else seeking retribution.

His wife and daughter had already distanced themselves from him as quickly as they could. They were innocent victims in all of this, and I would never let an innocent suffer for the likes of him.

"Yeah, them too," he stammers.

I hear Lorelei scoff behind me, and once more, a smile graces my lips.

"I don't like to be kept waiting, Santiago. Speak before I decide to take the next several days to kill you," I warn.

"Okay, okay," he stammers, his fear palpable. "The D'Santos family seized control of my family's bank years ago. I didn't have a choice. They had me and my family under surveillance and threatened to kill us if I didn't comply. We're a small private bank, and we were on the brink of closure before they came along with their demands."

His explanation aligns with some of the theories James and I had discussed regarding how the D'Santos family managed to gain control of the bank.

"Go on," I prompt, my grin widening, "before I grow bored and decide to start cutting again." I wave my blade menacingly in front of his face.

"It's simple, really," he continues, his voice trembling. "They all operate cash businesses in border states, skimming money off the top of their profits to transport drugs across the borders into those states. The rest of the money is deposited with me to create clean banking records. A larger bank would've flagged such massive cash deposits, but since it's just me, they were able to seize control swiftly."

I can't help but acknowledge the cleverness of their approach. Rather than prompting him to speak further, I let my frustration get the better of me, taking my knife and slicing through his right nipple, cleanly removing it. When I'm irritated, I tend to become quite aggressive.

I can sense Lorelei's gaze on me, but I need to remain focused on the information I'm extracting.

"Jesus, okay!" he chokes out. "Like I said, this keeps suspicions low, so no authorities catch on. It also helps that they've dispersed their companies, making them all appear as basic business owners."

"And how do they manage to get the drugs across the borders?" I press.

"Man, they've got border patrol and local police in their pockets," he reveals. "They allow the drugs to pass through without any questions. They drop their supplies in low-income neighborhoods, away from their businesses, knowing they'll sell quickly."

The revelation of their predatory tactics, running drugs into vulnerable towns, infuriates me. I've witnessed far too many soldiers return from war, only to fall victim to the clutches of drugs as they struggled to reintegrate into civilian life. They lost everything, and some even lost their lives. There's nothing I despise more on this planet than deceit and the drug trade.

"Lorelei, would you like to finish, or should I? There's nothing more this man can say that will be of use to us."

She remains silent, her gaze fixed on me. I'm not certain if she's prepared for a situation like this just yet.

I nod, indicating my understanding, and then redirect my attention to Santiago.

"Come on, man. Just let me go. I won't tell anyone," he pleads.

I maintain my skepticism; a man of his caliber would readily divulge this information to the highest bidder, and I never leave any loose ends.

Swiftly, I approach him and sever a couple of major arteries. I want him to feel the life draining from his body, aware that his imminent death is inevitable, and there's no one out there willing to rescue him.

I step back, observing the blood pooling beneath him, taking a perverse satisfaction in the way his life force seeps away from his face. Growing weary of the scene, I approach once more, drawing my blade against his throat. I listen as he gurgles and chokes on his own blood until his eyes are finally devoid of life.

I had been tasked by high-ranking officials to lead the interrogation. The man restrained before me was an important member of a terrorist organization responsible for a convoy explosion. We needed to extract vital information about their future plans.

I had spent hours in that room, and by now, I was as drenched in his blood as he was. It was strangely exhilarating. I had immersed myself in the grim world of interrogation and torture, experimenting to uncover the techniques that would make someone divulge crucial information. It felt like an eternity, but I eventually succeeded in extracting the information we needed.

Before I reluctantly tore myself away from the scene to report the gathered intel to my superiors, I allowed myself a moment of dark satisfaction, ending the life of this individual who had caused so much harm. The blood pooled around his feet served as a testament to the price he had paid for his actions.

Snapping out of my flashback, I suddenly realize I had been lost in the memory for too long. I wonder if Lorelei is still standing behind me or if she has decided to leave. The darkness in my vision begins to subside, and I turn back to the table where the supplies are, using them to clean my blade so I can safely stow it in my pocket. I'll thoroughly sanitize it later.

As I turn around again, I notice that Lorelei is still in the same spot where she was before, her knife still gripped in her hand, but she remains silent.

I tear off my gloves and walk over to her, forcefully grabbing her face with both of my hands, making her meet my gaze.

"Still not scared, seirína?" I almost wish she were, so she would run, sparing me from dealing with these unsettling emotions that are stirring within me.

"Like I said, I'm not afraid of the dark, plus that asshole deserved it."

I take her knife from her hand and move to the table to clean it, intending to hand it back to her so we can leave together.

With no words left to say, I place my hand on the small of her back and lead her toward the exit of the building. My team will soon be returning to begin the cleanup and disposal, likely receiving the green light from James' surveillance that my task is completed.

Before we reach the final door, I swiftly rip off my shirt and strip down to my boxers, a standard practice for me. I always leave my bloodied clothes behind for my team to dispose of, ensuring that no incriminating evidence ever enters my car or home.

"If we strip down, what will we wear back to the resort?" Lorelei inquires before she starts undressing.

"I have clothes in the car for us. I won't allow you to walk into the resort naked," I assure her.

Lorelei doesn't question her trust in me and willingly strips down to nothing but the bra and panties that I had laid out for her earlier. I had anticipated the need for her to undress, which is why I had prepared for it. She had been surprised earlier in the day when she saw the undergarments neatly laid on top of her clothes, but I can see it's all making sense to her now.

She's undeniably beautiful, but I recognize the importance of giving her the space and time to process everything that has just transpired. So, I push those thoughts aside, focusing on the tasks and plans at hand. Which proves to be harder than I would have ever imagined.

Once we're both stripped down, I lead her back to the car

and reach into the back seat to retrieve the small duffel I had brought. I toss her a white tank top and matching shorts set and begin pulling on the jeans and black shirt I had selected for myself.

I glance at my phone and realize that it's already three in the afternoon. That's the thing about torture, it takes longer than one would think.

Once we're both dressed, we get into the car, but Lorelei is still not speaking.

"How about we go wash up and then hit the town to blow off some steam? It's still only Sunday, so we can keep a low profile before the D'Santos arrive in town," I suggest, trying to break the silence and offer a change of atmosphere.

"Yeah, I'm too wired to go sit in the hotel right now," she responds with a simple acknowledgment.

I understand what she means; after such intense actions, it's challenging to find relaxation or calmness.

"This week, we'll only be here long enough to observe the D'Santos' interactions at the bank, now that Santiago is gone. We'll leave on Tuesday night this time, to ensure you get back home for work" I assure her, outlining our plans for the week ahead.

Once more, she remains silent and simply nods.

I'm eager to witness the confusion and frustration that will undoubtedly ensue when people attempt to enter the bank, only to find it closed. Even more satisfying will be watching their reactions when they discover their money is securely locked away, and the leverage they once had has vanished.

CHAPTER 14

"Yeah we're all fucked up, it's true (all fucked up like you)"
-The Amity Affliction

Lorelei

I should feel remorse for what we did to that man, shouldn't I? But the truth is, I don't. People like him deserve every bit of what's coming to them. Anyone who preys on those who are more vulnerable should face a measure of brutality equal to their own actions. I'll be the one to bring justice to those who created my demons when the time is right. In the meantime, I take some satisfaction in watching life's consequences catch up with them. After all, patience is a virtue.

I've been ready for the past ten minutes, impatiently waiting for Dash to finish cleaning up in the bathroom so we can blow off some steam. Whatever that entails for him. I'm still wired, so I'm grateful that we won't be stuck in the hotel room. I'd rather not sit there, unable to sleep, thinking about the events of the last eight hours, especially the unsettling realization that I wasn't repulsed by it. In fact, I found myself enjoying it.

The bathroom door finally creaks open, and Dash steps out in black jeans and a snug gray shirt, his tattoos on full display. He's undeniably handsome, but I can't quite determine if he's aware of it. Men who look like him usually come off as arrogant, but Dash seems different, as if he doesn't feel the need to flaunt his looks.

I'm dressed in a simple yet chic white t-shirt dress that's

both tight-fitting and incredibly comfortable. The contrast of the white fabric against my tanned, tattooed skin creates a striking look that I wouldn't have imagined would suit me so well.

"Ready?" Dash inquires, his gaze sweeping down my body.

"Just waiting on you, princess," I retort with a smirk.

That comment earns a smile from him, along with a glimpse of his knee-buckling dimple.

"Where are we going?" I ask.

"I thought we'd grab some food and see what else catches our eye," he suggests.

We walk out of our hotel room, and I hear the reassuring click of the door locking behind us. Side by side, we make our way out of the resort and down the pathway that runs along the sandy beach, lined with small shops.

We walk in comfortable silence, when a tantalizing aroma suddenly fills the air, catching my attention. I follow my nose, drawn to the source of the scent. In the beachside parking lot, I discover a small food truck with "tacos" boldly emblazoned in red lettering across the top.

I glance up at Dash and tilt my head in the direction of the food truck, and in response, he merely gives me a nonchalant shrug. It's moments like these when I appreciate that we don't always need words; he just understands what I need.

The scent of the food has my mouth watering, and even though this isn't a high-end restaurant by any means, I have a hunch that their food is going to be incredible.

As I stand before the menu displayed on the side of the truck, I notice that the options are limited. However, it doesn't take much to please me when it comes to food. Years of going hungry have made me grateful for whatever I can get.

"I'll have two beef tacos and two chicken, please," I order from the small, dark-haired woman in the food truck window. She conveys the order to someone behind her in rapid Spanish.

"Same for me, please," Dash chimes in. However, his attention remains on me, not on the food truck or the woman he's speaking to.

Now isn't the right moment to ask why Dash is staring at me so intently, so I make a mental note to bring it up later.

"Is this considered our third date?" Dash inquires, a note of amusement in his voice.

Instead of responding, I simply hold his gaze, letting the silence linger. People often feel compelled to break it, and I'm curious to see how he'll react.

Right on cue, Dash breaks the silence with his comment. "I hope you know I'm not making fun of you. I'm just surprised that someone as successful, intelligent, and gorgeous as you would manage to not date."

His words catch me off guard. While I've received plenty of compliments on my looks throughout my life, I've seldom been complimented for my intelligence, especially not before my appearance is mentioned. I can feel my defenses starting to crumble, and a strange twinge of vulnerability strikes me in the chest.

Thankfully, an arm extends from the food truck, and the lady who took our order hands us our tacos, sparing me from the need to formulate a response.

Without delay, I head over to the beach, not looking back at Dash, and find a spot close to the water, away from the families playing in the sand. I sit down in the warm grains and gaze at the waves crashing. The sun will set soon, and this is where I want to witness it, as it sinks below the horizon and casts its golden hues across the clear water.

To my surprise, Dash joins me in the sand, sitting down beside me as he eats his tacos in silence, his eyes scanning the people around us.

He never fully relaxes, not even here on the beach. Even when he sleeps back at the hotel, it seems like his body remains rigid, waiting for something to happen. I can't help but realize that we're quite similar, him and I, both shaped by our pasts into the weapons we've become.

I take a bite of my first taco, and it's even better than I imagined. Arizona has great Mexican food, but there's no comparison to this. A small, involuntary groan escapes my throat before I can stop it.

He glances over at me and raises an eyebrow.

"I'm hungry," I respond, unashamed of my reaction. "And why do you keep staring at me?"

"I keep staring at you, seirína, because after today's activities, I expected you to be different. You've surprised me, and it's rare that I'm ever surprised," Dash admits.

It's an understandable sentiment. We did just take a man's life, and now we're casually enjoying tacos on the beach within the hour, a surreal contrast to the events of the day.

We spend the next hour engaging in light conversation and savoring our tacos. It's the most carefree I've felt in a long time. I'm not constantly scanning my surroundings or glancing over my shoulder because I know that the man sitting next to me won't allow any harm come to me. It's a luxury I've never had the privilege to experience before.

As the sun begins its descent, I find myself on my feet, instinctively moving to dispose of our trash. After tossing it into the nearest bin, I let my feet carry me aimlessly along the beach. For once, I'm not overthinking or allowing my mind to dictate my actions.

I don't bother to look back to see if Dash is following me, and honestly, I don't care. I'm doing what I want, on my terms.

My toes brush the water, and I watch as the small waves dance around my ankles. But I want more. I keep walking, and before I realize it, I'm fully clothed, wading waist-deep into the ocean.

The clear water rocks gently against my body, and in this moment, I'm genuinely happy. With the sun setting, I have a perfect view from where I stand. If it were possible, I would swim until I could touch the oranges and reds reflected on the water's surface. I let myself wade out even farther, and soon I'm up to my chest in ocean water. It's a feeling I wish I could hold onto forever.

The salty air, the refreshing scent, it's the most invigorating aroma I've ever experienced. I find myself wishing I could bottle this scent and take it home with me.

As I turn to face the shore, I notice Dash standing there, somewhat distant, his hands tucked into his pockets, still watching me. He probably thinks I'm acting a bit crazy, but at the moment, I couldn't care less.

It's only when the sun has set and darkness starts to creep in that I realize I'm in the ocean when there are creatures living beneath the water. This sudden thought prompts me to quickly turn and wade back to the shore. I walk up to Dash, now soaking wet from head to toe.

Dash doesn't say anything but offers me a small, understanding smile, as if he's aware of how much I needed that brief escape.

The warmth of the evening air feels pleasant against my skin, despite being drenched.

"Feeling better?" he inquires, his voice softer than I've ever heard it.

"Much," I reply with a sense of gratitude in my voice.

Dash nods in acknowledgment, and once again, we walk in silence back to our resort. I relish the ability to walk in companionable silence, a rare experience in a world where many people are uncomfortable with their thoughts and fear the solitude of their own minds. I find solace in it.

As Dash opens the heavy hotel room door for me, I catch a glimpse of my reflection in the mirror. My once-white dress is now almost see-through due to being drenched. I've never been one to worry about modesty, but it does make me wonder what kind of spectacle I unwittingly provided for the few families who were playing on the beach during our return.

"No one saw anything. If I had caught someone staring, they'd be beside Santiago right now," Dash states with unwavering conviction.

His confidence and the unflinching manner in which he delivers this statement leave me with a curious mixture of fear and intrigue. Most people would find such a proclamation chilling, but something deep within me stirs, an inexplicable fascination. Just who is this man to carry himself with such unshakable confidence? There are layers upon layers of secrets hidden beneath his exterior, and I can't help but wonder when or if his tight composure will ever give way and reveal what lies beneath.

I brush past Dash and head to the bathroom where my pink pajamas from the previous night are, intending to get myself dried up for bed.

Once I'm in the bathroom, I take a moment to stare at my

reflection in the mirror. I tortured someone today. A man's life came to an end right before my eyes. Yet, as I stood waist-deep in the ocean, I experienced happiness. I can't help but wonder what the fuck is wrong with me.

I nonchalantly shrug off my thoughts and begin to peel my wet clothes from my body, hanging them over the shower rod to dry out before I need to pack them later. Thankfully, I had tied my hair up in a bun before our dinner excursion, so I don't have to worry about wet hair. I reach for one of the makeup wipes Dash packed for me, gently removing the little makeup I had applied.

Once I'm dressed in my cozy pajama set and have released my hair from the bun, I make my way back into the room we share. There, I find Dash sitting on his couch, clad in sweatpants and no shirt, with glasses perched on his nose as he reads something on his laptop.

Dash's composure remains intact even after the intense day we've had. It makes me wonder if he's just as messed up as I am, capable of taking a man's life and then continuing through the evening without a hint of remorse.

I don't utter a word; instead, I crawl into my bed, hoping that sleep will embrace me swiftly. I understand that tomorrow will likely be another monotonous day, so I need to mentally prepare myself for the mundane. However, a thought suddenly strikes me—now that Santiago is gone, who will be left to run the bank?

"D, how will Santiago's disappearance be explained? He surely has business tomorrow," I inquire.

Dash peers at me over his glasses and responds, "It won't be explained. Now, we get to sit back and watch them start to panic, like ants under a microscope. When people get scared, they tend to make mistakes."

He's has answers to every question.

With nothing more to discuss, I rest my head on the soft pillow, and Dash switches off the remaining light, leaving only the glow of his computer screen at the foot of my bed.

My eyes drift closed, and a deep, peaceful sleep overtakes me.

CHAPTER 15

"See, you're a nightmare
A tragic life scare"
-Magnolia Park

Dash

Gunfire echoes in my head, a relentless sound that jolts me awake. I force my eyes open, struggling to discern my surroundings through the haze of pain. Every fiber of my being throbs with agony, each nerve ending screaming for respite, but surrender is not an option.

Groaning, I summon the strength to raise my head, squinting through blurred vision. I find myself confined within a stark concrete chamber. Every movement sends a stark reminder of my limitations, and I can't discern whether it's sheer exhaustion or the unforgiving ropes that bind me to this wooden chair. My uniform clings to my body, a sticky reminder of the blood I've shed.

Time becomes a blurred concept in this windowless abyss. The continuous barrage of gunfire outside feels like an eternity, hinting at a conflict unraveling beyond these concrete walls. Perhaps those responsible for this nightmare are self-destructing, but it offers little solace as I'm left here, too feeble to break free from my restraints.

Suddenly, the room is invaded by an unfamiliar voice, a mix of words in a language I cannot comprehend. Dread washes over me, and I'm acutely aware that the situation is about to intensify.

I brace myself, but it offers no shield from the brutal impact of his assault rifle against my face. I straighten my spine as much as my restraints allow, spitting out a mixture of blood and defiance before me.

Before the next blow can descend upon me, a gunshot tears through the room, bringing an abrupt halt to the torment. All that remains is a persistent ringing in my ears.

"Soldier, are you okay?" The voice reaches me through the disorienting haze. I'm a soldier, but I can't discern the identity of my savior. Could they be addressing me?

"Soldier, what's your name?" I struggle to form words, but all that emerges is a guttural groan. Instead, I gesture towards the patch bearing my last name, signaling my understanding.

"D. Ashford, huh? Well, alright, Dash. Let's get you out of here," the soldier says.

With swift, skillful hands, the soldier drops to his haunches behind me, efficiently cutting through the bindings that have held me captive. As the restraints fall away, my body goes slack with the intoxicating rush of freedom. It feels incredible.

"We have to do this quickly if we want to get out of here alive. You did good, Dash. You held strong, and soldiers are alive because of that," the soldier commends me.

I take a moment to reflect on the ordeal. I've endured torture for an unknown duration, refusing to betray the location of our hidden base. I was prepared to sacrifice my life to protect the others.

The soldier supporting me drapes my arm over his shoulders, and together, we muster the strength to stand. My legs threaten to buckle beneath me, but I've come too far to surrender now. With every ounce of determination I can summon, I place one foot in front of the other. I refuse to meet my end in this wretched place.

"There's a convoy 50 yards south, ready to transport us back to base," he informs me, and the prospect of escape fuels my resolve.

Alright, 50 yards, I can make that. As we step out from the door of my captivity, two more soldiers are there, ready to guide us to safety.

We move with stealth, the soldiers around me taking point to secure all angles. Yet, the ever-persistent sound of gunfire echoes in my ears. The two soldiers escorting us return fire in the direction of the enemy.

Suddenly, my support vanishes, and I'm on the verge of collapsing. I turn to my left, only to witness the soldier who was aiding me, now lifeless on the ground, a gunshot wound right between the eyes. The vacant look in his eyes sends a shiver down my spine.

Mother fucker.

More gunfire pierces the air, and I scramble to find cover when an unseen force sends me tumbling. Gasping for air, I roll onto my back on the unforgiving ground, only to find a colossal man looming over me, his fists poised to strike.

I refuse to accept this fate, teetering on the edge of rescue, only to have it snatched away. Summoning every ounce of determination within me, I launch my right fist at the adversary's face, connecting with a solid blow. The impact sends him sprawling to the side, and I use the momentum to throw my weight onto him, now finding myself on top.

This assailant chose to attack me without a weapon, which offers a glimmer of hope in this hand-to-hand confrontation. My vision clouds with rage, and I unleash a barrage of strikes, targeting anything I can hit, gradually weakening the man beneath me.

The gunfire may have ceased, but a persistent ringing lingers in my ears, a maddening reminder of the chaos that surrounds us.

Suddenly, a hand rests on my shoulder, and I jerk my head in that direction, briefly diverting my attention from the subdued attacker beneath me.

"Soldier, he's gone. You can stop now. We need to get to the rest of the convoy," the friendly soldier advises.

Confusion mingles with relief as I look up further, realizing the presence of an ally. His hand remains on my shoulder, his rifle in the other, offering a lifeline in this moment of turmoil.

"He's gone, we have to keep moving in case there are more hiding. We've neutralized the threat for now, but we don't know if there are others. You've done your part, let's return to base. Carver is waiting to patch you up," the soldier insists.

I'm taken aback by his words, unable to comprehend how he can say this with an enemy still beneath me.

In a moment of clarity, I break away from the soldier's grasp and look down, discovering that my hands are locked around the man's neck like a vice. His lifeless eyes stare up at me, wide and bloodshot. There's no longer a pulse beneath my palm, and the grim realization washes over me—he's dead.

Dead. The weight of that reality bears down on me. I had killed enemies before, but always from a distance, always with a gun. This was different—up close and personal. Someone's life ended by my own hands.

Amidst the disorienting chaos, the shouting continues, but the soldiers around me appear oblivious to it. I frantically scan the surroundings, seeking the source of the commotion, but there's no apparent explanation for where the voices are coming from. The world around me remains shrouded in a fog of confusion and remorse.

Who the fuck is yelling?

"Get the fuck off of me, Dash!" The familiar, yet unexpected, voice of a woman pierces through the haze of confusion. I've heard that voice before, and it's as beautiful as ever.

However, searing pain suddenly tears through my abdomen, and I let out a gruff groan. My hands instinctively reach for the source of the agony, and when I withdraw them, they're coated in blood.

What the hell is happening?

Before I can process what is happening, I'm forcefully thrown onto my back, the impact stealing my breath.

In a matter of seconds, Lorelei, disheveled and brandishing a knife, looms over me. Her wild, untamed hair frames her face, and she's dressed in her pajamas. I'm no longer in a war-torn setting; I find myself in a hotel room in Mexico.

"Dash, what in the fuck were you doing?!" she shouts, her knuckles white as she clutches the knife.

I'm bewildered by the situation. "What are you talking about? You're the one who stabbed me," I protest.

Lorelei's expression turns incredulous. "Are you psychotic? You were on top of me, choking me!"

Choking her? I sit up on my elbows, my gaze shifting to the wound on my abdomen. It appears that, while not too severe, it would require stitching later.

"This is the second time you've drawn blood from me, seirína," I remark, "if you keep this up, I might start to think you like me, but I will need some explanation here."

"Explanation? Are you kidding?" She marches over to the switch and flicks on the lights.

That's when I see it. Two sizable, red marks encircling her neck.

"Lorelei... Did I - did I do that?" I'm stunned by the realization that I could have harmed her. Nightmares like this have been rare for me in recent years, but now I can't tell if they've actually subsided or if I've simply learned to live with them.

Her response is venomous. "Yes, you fucking did this to me. You almost killed me, you asshole!"

I stagger to my feet, my focus drawn to the marks on her neck, a cruel testament to my own actions. They'll surely be bruised by morning. I can't believe I've hurt her, even in my sleep. Dark thoughts cloud my vision, and I instinctively reach up to touch the marks, hoping to somehow alleviate the pain I've caused.

Lorelei steps back, away from my touch. "You have some explaining to do, or I'm out of here. I'll expose everything. I told you from the beginning, I'll bring down the D'Santos, even if it means taking you with them."

"Lorelei, there are some things I can't talk about, things that are darker than you could even imagine," I admit, my voice heavy with the weight of unspoken horrors. My time at war is a subject I've carefully avoided, for good reason. That one kill, the one that haunts my nightmares, was an awakening for me—a moment when I realized I had a dark penchant for eradicating the world of its scum.

She remains resolute, but I can see her fighting through her pain to put on her mask. She's trying so hard to not let me see that emotionally she's wavering. "The marks of your hands are wrapped around my neck. You owe me an explanation for why."

I can feel the blood trickling down my abdomen, the pain becoming increasingly bothersome. I need to address this wound before it becomes problematic, but right now, my primary concern is Lorelei.

"I can't tell you how sorry I am, Lorelei. I genuinely never meant to put you in harm's way, and I had no idea that harm would come from my own hands. Please believe that," I implore, my voice tinged with remorse. If I had known the events from earlier would trigger a nightmare, I would have chosen a different sleeping arrangement.

Something changes in her bright green eyes, and she slowly lowers her knife-wielding hand before walking over to the bedside table to set it down.

"I am insanely impressed that you were able to subdue a man of my size and training, though. Thank God, or I guess you'd be dead," I don't find this funny, but it's my only defense mechanism at the moment.

"You need to see a doctor," she says with a seriousness that cuts through the tension.

I let out a sickening chuckle. "You're worried about my well-being after I almost choked the life out of you?"

Lorelei's expression remains resolute. "I'll get my brain evaluated when we get back home. For now, we need to take you to a hospital."

"No hospitals. I can handle it," I respond with a sense of self-assuredness. I've stitched myself up in the past during battle, and I've accumulated a fair share of jagged scars. One more won't make a significant difference. In a strange way, this wound might become my favorite among them all.

I make my way to the bathroom and request. "In my bag by the couch, there's a first aid kit. Could you bring it here, please?"

Lorelei hesitates for a moment before heading to my bag and rummaging through it. I use the time to prepare the bathroom. Tile is definitely easier to clean than carpet, and I don't want the hotel staff asking questions after we've left.

I gather some towels and place them on the floor, then sit down, applying a wet rag to the wound to staunch the bleeding.

When Lorelei returns, the marks on her neck have darkened, and the sight ignites a surge of anger within me. How could I have allowed myself to lose control to this extent? I'd much rather see those marks under vastly different circumstances, preferably one that involves my dick inside her.

Lorelei kneels beside me, efficiently opening the first aid kit and extracting the needle and sutures as if she's done this many times before.

I steal a glance at her, but she avoids making eye contact with me. I don't blame her, given the circumstances, but I desperately need her to understand that I would never intentionally harm her. I'm left searching for a way to convey that to her.

"Move the rag; this will hurt," she instructs me, and I comply, watching her intently as she takes control of the situation. For all I know, she might decide to stab me again, and if so, I'll gladly accept it.

A sharp, searing pain tears through the wound, and I can't help but inhale sharply through my teeth, the smell of the alcohol swab burning my nose.

"Don't be a baby," she chides, her words delivered without much sympathy. It's surreal to see her cleaning a wound that she inflicted in self-defense.

"You don't have to do this, Lorelei. I can take care of the wound myself," I offer, a tinge of guilt gnawing at me.

"I know I don't have to. I don't have to do anything." she responds.

She remains focused on the task at hand, not meeting my gaze. Her hands are steady and skilled as she works, and after a few minutes, the bleeding has significantly slowed, leaving the wound clean and sterile.

"I'm no professional, so your perfect skin will be pretty jagged and messed up after this. A token from me to you," she comments, her tone laced with a mixture of seriousness and an underlying tension.

The tension in the small bathroom is palpable, and while now isn't the time for any inappropriate thoughts, there's an undeniable undercurrent of attraction that remains between us.

"Do your worst. I deserve it," I say, willing to accept whatever consequences might come my way.

Lorelei, without hesitation, threads the sutures through my abdomen, working methodically. It strikes me that she's perhaps too skilled at this process, and I can't help but inquire, "How do you know how to do this?"

Her entire body stiffens, and her hands cease their precise work. She clears her throat and, in a barely audible whisper, she responds, "I've had practice." The cryptic response only deepens the mysteries surrounding her.

I'm still shocked by her actions, and I struggle to comprehend her intent as she drops the sutures and lifts the hem of her pajama shorts, revealing more of her toned thighs. My mind hasn't quite caught up to what's happening until she guides my left hand, and my fingertips glide over her right thigh, feeling the raised edges of jagged scars underneath her tattoos.

My stomach tightens, and my body heats up as I touch her skin, but my emotions are spiraling into a dark abyss as I realize the extent of her scars. It all starts making sense—the tattoos, the way she concealed her pain. I can see similar scars on other parts of her exposed skin, and I feel a sense of idiocy for not having noticed it before.

My hands begin to tremble, and I can't help but ask, "What

happened to you?" The depth of her suffering becomes painfully clear, and it's a weighty revelation that I feel responsible to remedy.

Lorelei finally meets my gaze, and her eyes hold a fierce determination. "Some people are afraid of the darkness and try to bleed it from you. They just don't seem to realize the darkness is all that's left keeping some of us alive."

As she takes a deep breath and continues stitching me up, she keeps her eyes fixed on her hands. She begins speaking in a hushed tone, "Once when I was young, I tried to get my dad help. He had been sick for a long time, and one day I decided to call the police and ask them to come to help him."

I'm stunned by the quiet vulnerability in her voice. The strong, fearless woman I've known is barely audible, and something inside me tightens. "My dad spent some time in the behavioral health unit, and when he returned, I had to deal with the wrath that came from it. I never made that mistake again."

I give her a moment to continue, but she doesn't offer any more details. "You mean all those scars are from a singular incident?" I can feel the anger vibrating within me, but I know that's not what she needs at this moment, so I struggle to keep my emotions in check.

She lets out a snort, as if my question was amusing. "No, what you see is years' worth of scars, but the deep one you felt first was from that night."

My entire body trembles now, and the encroaching darkness threatens to overtake my vision. "Please tell me he's dead," I implore.

"That's not your concern," she responds flatly.

"It is my concern if I say it is," I retort, the anger pushing through my concern for her.

"I can handle myself, Dash. Now, lean back so I can finish this," she instructs, her voice firm and resolute.

"Let me be clear, no one will ever harm you like that again. The only person to mark your skin will be me. I see how capable you are, but so help me when I find him, he will bleed." I vow, my anger now channeled into a resolute determination to protect her.

Despite my seething anger, I've committed myself to the mission of finding him and ensuring he faces the consequences of his actions tenfold. I will dedicate my life to torturing him to within an inch of his life, just to bring him back from the brink of death and start over again.

After awhile, she has cleaned the wound, stitched me up, and we tidied the bathroom as best we could. The sexual tension in the small space is building, threatening to unravel us both. If we don't find a way to release it soon, we might both come apart at the seams.

"Thank you, Lorelei," I murmur to her as she climbs back into her bed. I approach her, hesitating just before I touch her bedding to ensure it's okay. She remains still, so I gently pull up the blankets and tuck them around her.

"I can't tell you how sorry I am," I continue, my scarred knuckles brushing across her bare skin. An electric jolt courses through my body, as if I could power an entire country. My hands seem unwilling to move from her, and all I can manage to say is, "We're going home first thing tomorrow morning. James and I will finish surveillance through the cameras. I'll get you back home."

I feel like a bumbling fool, but I continue to slide my knuckles across her skin, pretending that I'm simply adjusting her blankets while, in reality, I'm reveling in the softness of her skin and the memory of her scars.

As complex and troubled as my feelings may be, I can't deny the overwhelming surge of desire coursing through me. It's a tumultuous mix of emotions, from anger to guilt to intense attraction. The realization hits me that despite the horrific incident earlier, all I want now is to claim her, to show her how sorry I am in a way that words could never express.

I'm done fighting these feelings and thoughts. She may not have fully accepted it yet, but I'm convinced that she's mine. I'm not a good man, and she knows it. There's no reason to pretend otherwise.

I continue to hold her gaze as I pull the covers down, my silent question hanging in the air. But all she does is look back at me, her eyes filled with their own complicated emotions. It's as if we're both drawn into an unspoken understanding.

Slowly, I bring her to the end of the bed, the tension in the room is suffocating. I pull down her soft shorts, cherishing the sensation of her skin against mine. It's as if our scars were made for eachother, all our broken pieces laid bare for one another to see.

She's an embodiment of defiance, lying there unashamed, her eyes locked onto mine with unwavering intensity. I let my gaze roam over her body, taking in every scar, every tattoo, committing every detail to memory. I know I'll spend the rest of my life engraving into my mind how she feels, and all I need to do now is convince her of this truth.

Our eyes remain locked as I lower to my knees before her, the fire in her gaze matching the intensity in mine. I grab her legs and pull her as close to the edge of the bed as possible, determined to show her how deeply I want her. No need her.

I take my time, savoring the taste of her skin as I kiss every inch of her thighs, my lips and tongue tracing each and every scar. It's a deliberate act, a way of showing her that I'm not turning away from what she's shared with me. Her body begins to arch off the bed, pushing herself closer to me, and I can feel my own control slipping away, and I need her right now.

As I continue my slow ascent, I reach her wet aching pussy, and it's evident that she's as ready as I am. "Is this all for me?" I inquire, but I don't wait for her response. Instead, I dive in, devouring her like a starving man who never thought he'd eat again. In her, I lose all the control I was holding onto, but I don't mind. I could spend a lifetime on my knees before her.

"You taste like heaven, and we both know a man like me doesn't deserve to savor something so pure. But now that I have, I'll drag you to hell with me," I murmur, my voice heavy with desire and a promise of the future we're forging together.

My hands grip her hips tightly, keeping her firmly in place as my mouth continues its assault. She emits the most enchanting sounds, her body on the brink of unraveling, and I can feel it in the way she trembles and tenses. Her fingers plunge into my hair, securing my mouth in place so I couldn't escape even if I wanted to.

With one hand, I slide two fingers into her, and she cries out my name, her voice husky with desire. A tightness grips my chest; this isn't the name I want on her lips. I push the thought aside, focusing on her. As she nears the edge, I suck her clit into my mouth and bite down with just the right amount of pressure before soothing the pain with my tongue, determined to give her the release she craves.

Her body arches off the bed, her thighs squeezing around my head as I continue to lick her, eliciting the most exquisite sounds and reactions. "Mine," I growl at her possessively, thoroughly intoxicated by the sight and sounds of her pleasure. This woman, in the throes of an orgasm, could bring warring countries to peace.

"Such a good girl, coming apart on my tongue," I mumble into her thigh as I stroke her soft skin. As her body finishes its trembling, I stand up and retrieve her shorts from the floor, sliding them back up her legs. The intense release has made her pliant, and I pick her up and lay her back in her spot, tucking her in so she can finally get some sleep.

As I tuck her in, I notice the conflict in her expression. Her brows are slightly furrowed, torn between the intensity of our feelings and her lingering anger from earlier. I gently push a stray strand of hair behind her ear, and she leans into my touch, seeking that connection.

I don't want to push her further tonight. The day's events and the passionate night have left her thoughts muddled, and I want her to make any decisions with a clear head. After turning off the lights, I retreat to the couch and sit in the silence, lost in my own thoughts for what feels like an eternity.

"I mean it, Dash," she whispers, her voice filled with a reluctant determination that wasn't present in her earlier threats. "You owe me an explanation. Either you give me one, or I'm out of here. I'll finish this, and you."

Her words hang in the air like an anvil about to crush me. She's right; I do owe her an explanation. But how much of myself am I willing to share? I've never allowed myself to be vulnerable, to reveal the darkest corners of my past, but I've also never allowed anyone to get this close to me before.

CHAPTER 16

"So, run like hell
Sleep with one eye open, I can't forgive or forget you"
-A Day To Remember

Lorelei

What the fuck is my plan? Dash owes me an explanation. After witnessing everything I've seen in the past few weeks, it's clear that I'm being deceived. "Investigator," my ass. A simple investigator doesn't suffer from nightmares that drive them to choke someone in their sleep. I can only assume that what occurred is a consequence of his time in the military, but that doesn't excuse the secrecy. He can't keep me in the dark any longer. I need to understand the kind of person I'm dealing with, if only for my own safety.

When someone intends to inflict harm, there's a certain emptiness in their eyes as they cause pain. But his eyes revealed genuine remorse once he realized what had happened. Maybe that's why I find myself already inclined to forgive him. Forgiveness is such an unfamiliar concept to me, and I hope these feelings stirring inside me aren't clouding my judgement.

If I hadn't been prepared for an assault like this, would he have killed me? Although I hardly know the person beside me, there's a part of me that believes he never intended to inflict harm, and I've never trusted someone to that extent in my life. It's an unsettling feeling building and I'll be on edge until I get answers.

The sensation of his touch still lingers on me, and I can't seem to shake it. It was as overwhelming as I had anticipated. A man like him doesn't tiptoe; he bulldozes his way through, and that's precisely what he's done to me. He's demolished every wall I had managed to build, and for the first time I feel out of control in my life and with my feelings. None of which I'm willing to give up yet.

We're heading home a day early, and our interactions have been limited to just a couple of words since last night. I've been trapped in my thoughts, trying to make sense of everything. Maybe he's decided I'm not worthy of an explanation, and this partnership has come to an end. That's fine; I can finish this on my own. I despise liars, and the harsh reality of our situation is that he's a liar. And to top it off doesn't trust me enough to be honest.

I allowed myself to be vulnerable, sharing a piece of my past by letting him touch my scars. My mistake.

Hours later, we pull into my parking garage, and to my surprise, instead of dropping me off at the elevator, he parks the car and turns it off.

"I can walk myself to the door," I retort, my frustration mounting due to his continued silence.

He doesn't say anything but exits the car, making his way to the back to retrieve my bag from the trunk. Maybe he's following me to the door to bid farewell and signify the end of our partnership.

I'm fully capable of handling this situation on my own, but he doesn't have the right to be angry with me when I'm the one dealing with bruises around my throat. Explaining this at work will be a challenge. Bex is already frustrated with me, and she won't let this pass without an explanation.

He's just standing there in front of his car with my bags in his hands waiting.

Fine, if he wants to end this like a coward, then so be it. I slam the car door and head towards the elevator without a backward glance. What's the saying? "Hell hath no fury like a woman who's been lied to." Well, that's not the exact phrase, but it holds true in this situation.

As we approach the corridor leading to my apartment, I'm a few feet ahead of him, reaching into my purse to find my keys. I have no intention of prolonging this any further.

However, just as I'm about to grasp my keys, something familiar catches my peripheral vision. I come to an abrupt stop, causing Dash to collide into my back, nearly sending me tumbling over.

Standing in front of my door is Bex, her mouth hanging open as she takes in the sight of me, Dash, and my bag in his hand.

"So this is why I haven't seen or heard from you? I knew you were seeing someone, but couldn't you just be honest with me rather than blowing me off and—" she stops abruptly and fixates her eyes on my neck her anger filling her expression. She lunges to attack Dash, albeit in my honor, but I grab her. There's no way I can talk myself out of this one.

"Bex, it's not what you think," I say. With everything on my plate right now, I can't handle this too.

Dash stands unmoving in his position, despite her earlier attempt to attack him. He is prepared to face whatever she throws his way.

"And what do you suppose I think it is? We are best friends, Lorelei, and you refuse to open up to me! If he's hurting you, I can help. I would be here for you in an instant," Bex insists, using the term "best friends" so casually. But does she realize how little she truly knows about me? Just because I've introduced her to my parents doesn't mean she's aware of my history.

"You know nothing about me, Bex. We work together, and I can tolerate your company at work, but beyond that, you have no real insight into who I am. I can take care of myself; I don't need you mothering me, so why don't you just go."

She recoils from me as if I've struck her, and I realize that I've hit deep enough to make her leave. Not just leave for now, but to leave me for good. I don't deserve her friendship, and it's better for her if she just moves on. The best way to achieve that is to make her hate me.

"Fuck you, Lorelei," she spits out, turning on her heel and heading in the opposite direction down the hall towards the main lobby and the front doors slamming her shoulder into Dash on her way out. I don't say anything as I watch her recede into the distance. I can feel tears welling up in the corners of my eyes, but I'm determined not to let Dash see them fall.

I take a deep breath, sliding my key into the lock and turning it with ease. I spin around to grab my bag from his hand, but before I can touch it, he yanks it back. His eyes are full of pain so I quickly look away not knowing if his pain is from last night's events or what he just witnessed between me and Bex.

"I understand you're pissed at me, but like you said, I owe you an explanation," Dash begins.

"If you're going to end this partnership, just do it and leave me the hell alone." The bag in his hand contains all the items he bought for me, so, truthfully, I don't need it, and I could easily turn and walk into my apartment. However, my feet remain firmly planted. My curiosity is getting the better of me, and after what just happened I want him here. I want to hear what kind of explanation he's about to offer.

"Is that what you want? For me to leave you alone?" Dash asks, his question hanging in the air. Is that what I want? I've been more genuine with this man in the past couple of weeks than I've ever been with anyone else in my entire life. But that doesn't change the fact that we had a job to do, and then we were supposed to go our separate ways. That was always the plan.

I hesitate for a moment, my mind racing, and then I step back to let him inside. "Fine, come in. But make it quick." Dash nods in agreement, and we enter my apartment, closing the door behind us and leaving the curious neighbor to their own business.

Once inside, he places my bag by the door and begins to look around my apartment. His hand moves to his jaw, and I notice a hint of nervousness in his demeanor. It's almost surreal to see a man like him appear nervous. Even in this state, he remains composed, revealing just enough but never too much.

Dash moves slowly to my couch, settling on the far edge of the cushion. He places his elbows on his knees and gazes up at me through his thick, dark lashes. His face remains devoid of emotion, but I catch a fleeting glimpse of pain in his eyes. It's so brief that I might have missed it if I weren't paying such close attention. It's clear that he's tormented, and whatever he's about to reveal might be almost unbearable for him.

I'm having second thoughts about this. I don't want to make him relive whatever pain this brings him, but something deep within me urges me to press forward. I have to know what's going on. He's felt my scars, and now it's time for me to feel his.

I take a seat on the cushion farthest away from him, allowing me to keep him in view without being too close. I'm afraid that if he touches me, any remaining resolve I'm holding onto will evaporate. All that's left to do now is wait.

"Lorelei, the things I'm about to tell you, they're not common knowledge. Anyone else who has ever been told has been bound by an oath and an ironclad non-disclosure agreement. I need to know that I can trust you with information like this. I have enough information on you to blackmail you into exile, but I don't want that. I want to trust you. There's too much and too many people at risk."

He pauses after saying this, and for a moment, it feels as if he's waiting for a response. I've witnessed him kill a man, so whatever he's about to reveal should pale in comparison. Instead, he lets out a deep sigh before dropping the bomb.

"My name is Damien Ashford," he says, taking a deep breath, and then on the exhale, he finishes, "the founder and CEO of Ash Media Group. I'm also an FBI contractor, mainly consulting on interrogation techniques these days."

I can't help it; a chuckle begins to rise in my throat. My body has never been skilled at reading a room, and now I'm on the verge of laughing at this sensitive information I'm entrusted with. How awkward.

"I keep this from people because, as you've seen in person and surely on my media channel, the people we expose are very dangerous, and they have the means to harm my staff, who are only trying to do some good in this world," he explains.

"Hold on, did you say your name is Damien? Who the hell is Dash?" My voice remains steady, but I'm growing increasingly frustrated, but I still see no reaction from him.

"Dash is a nickname I acquired when I was in the military. It was a play on my name, Damien Ashford. When you asked me my name that night, I thought on the fly, because I was unsure of what your role might be going forward. Partner or accomplice." he explains calmly. "Typically I have a unique alias when I'm on a case, but I didn't want to give you a made up name."

I'm speechless, a mix of emotions churning within me. I'm angry that he didn't just tell me this from the start, as he said he has blackmail material on me that could ensure my silence.

"Nothing to say, Lorelei?" he prompts, his voice steady.

"What are you expecting me to say? You went from a simple investigator to a murderer, to nearly killing me, to the CEO of AMG in the span of 24 hours. Not to mention you're a rogue FBI agent and I just found out your real name," I respond, my voice filled with frustration and disbelief.

"What the fuck" I laugh, overwhelmed by it all accidentally saying it outloud. Trying to sort out what I do with this and how I even feel. Betrayed? Confused? Do I admire him?

He leans back and observes me with a calm demeanor. "Yes, and you've handled it all fairly well, except for the fact that you now look like you want to murder me where I sit. You took me killing a man in front of you better than you're taking this bit of news. You should know that only members of my staff know who I am, and they have just as much reason to protect these secrets as I do. My nightmares were the worst when I came back from my last deployment. Sometimes given my work it gets triggered."

I'm struggling to wrap my head around all of this, but his last words make me consider the gravity of the situation. The nightmares I understand and I want to be there for him. But the rest feels like betrayal.

"You lied to me. You could have told me from the beginning who you were. Most people would just make someone sign an NDA, but instead, you chose to lie," I assert, frustration still evident in my voice.

He contemplates this, straightening and removing his elbows

from his knees. He rubs his thumb across his bottom lip, considering his response. "I told you, I keep as much as I can a secret to protect my staff. For all I knew, you were in on everything with the D'Santos. I didn't anticipate that the deal with Santiago would trigger this or I would have taken precautions."

"When you discovered I wasn't part of their operation, you should have told me. You trusted me enough to go to Mexico, not once but twice. Who knows what else you've lied about," I press, my emotions simmering just beneath the surface.

"I've never blatantly lied to you, Lorelei. I have omitted some things from you, but never outright lied. Even my name, to some, I am still Dash, so not technically a lie," He explains.

I sigh in frustration. "That's supposed to make me feel better? A technicality?"

He starts to pace in front of the windows, his eyes fixed on the city below. "I don't know. I started AMG for a sole purpose: to rid the world of as many bad people as possible before they finally end me. That company is all I have in this life, and I couldn't risk it. I go to great lengths to keep the people who trust me safe. I use the information I gather from my access with the FBI to find some of our targets."

"Why?" I ask, my voice softer.

He snaps his head toward me, drawing his eyebrows together. "Why what?"

"Why does AMG mean so much to you?" I repeat, my curiosity pushing me to understand his motivations.

Dash takes a deep breath, and I can see the weight of the secret he's been carrying. "I served my country for 10 years of my life," he begins, breaking eye contact and gazing out of the large windows behind him. "I used it as a way to escape my piece of shit politician dad. It was expected of me from a young age to follow in his footsteps, but the day I graduated, I walked into the recruiter's office and never looked back."

He moves away from the windows and returns to sit on the cushion where he was before.

"He was more pissed than I had ever seen him, and I had seen him pissed plenty of times," Dash begins. "As much as he hated me for what I had done, I was already gone and heading for boot camp, and there was no stopping it. He used the fact that his only son was fighting for our country as a campaign strategy, winning him another term. A piece of trash like him didn't give a damn about his people, just the money that came from his crooked dealings. In my childhood, I saw the absolutely ugliest sides of people who held power, and I swore I would never play a part in it. I joined the military hoping I could right some of the wrongs these assholes were doing."

He rubs his hands together nervously, trying to collect himself before he continues.

"When my dad died, I decided to finally leave the military, but I had no idea what to do with my life," Dash explains. "I was still angry, and I didn't feel like I had done enough good. I had friends coming home, fighting for their lives, dealing with more PTSD than they did in combat. I was struggling too, and as a result, I had nightmares similar to the one you experienced last night. I got off easy compared to some of my fellow soldiers."

“My entire childhood I watched my father lie and manipulate people to gain power, I wanted to use his blood money to stop others who are like him.” Dash lets out a humorless chuckle but the slight tremor in his hands reveals his nerves.

I’m beginning to understand the man behind the secrets and it’s adding to the feelings I have been denying so far.

"My dad left me everything. We had no other family for him to give it to since my mom was already dead," Dash continues. "The clause in the will stated that I had to enter a government field, no doubt hoping it would be in politics. If I did, then everything was mine, no more strings attached. That's when I decided to start AMG. A vigilante media group whose sole purpose was to take down every piece of trash like him and unravel everything he ever worked for. The FBI was working hard to recruit me, so I took the job, using it as my cover to satisfy the clause. After that, all the funds became mine. I used the money to employ some of my fellow soldiers returning home, as they had the skills to pull off the work I wanted to accomplish. It gave us all a purpose, one we all desperately needed to keep going. As you've seen, we don't only go after politicians; we target anyone who is harming innocents."

"My staff is composed of soldiers from various specialties, from hackers to enforcers. The other staff members are like James, misfits who are the absolute best at what they do," Dash explains. "They put their trust in me to take down these people who promise good but only breed evil. My staff looks to me to keep their identities safe. For seven years, I've kept that vow, and I can't risk anything to betray that. I've lost good men to the work that we do, but we all made it our mission to go down taking every last piece of trash with us."

Sitting in front of the owner of AMG, I'm hit by the reality of the situation. He's incredibly wealthy and is actually doing good with his power and wealth, what a surprise. However, the trust I had placed in him is wavering due to his lies. I'd vowed never to let another person hurt me, and yet, he did.

My gut instincts are telling me to understand. Whispering to me that I would do the same thing if I was in his position, but I always knew this would have to come to an end. I can’t risk any attachments so I can stay focused on my own mission.

The need for distance becomes overwhelming. I have to give my mind space to process this new information. His presence in my apartment feels suffocating, and the space that I used to consider big now seems consumed by him. When I feel cornered, my instinct is to run, and when there's no way out, I'm ready to fight. But I don't want to fight him. For the first time in my life, I feel defeated.

Minutes pass in silence, neither of us saying a word. I've been staring at my black and gold rug, trying to find the right words, but I'm grappling with emotions I haven't allowed myself to feel in decades.

"Do you have any questions for me?" Dash's voice is barely audible, drowned out by the blood rushing through my ears.

I take more time, using it to rebuild the walls within me, brick by brick. The emotional turmoil is receding, leaving behind a cold emptiness. I don't have the space to be emotional right now.

I finally look up at him, and his eyes are already fixed on mine, waiting. His bleeding pupil shifts between my eyes, searching for answers I might hold. I have questions, but I'm not sure where to start.

I clear my throat and ensure I maintain unwavering eye contact with Dash. Despite the fact that he killed someone within the last 48 hours, I'm determined not to show any sign of intimidation. I'm hurt by his lack of trust and the vulnerability I'm feeling truly scares me. A few weeks ago, this might not have affected me as deeply, but now I feel exposed, and the pain of the child in me who suffered abuse is begging me to rebuild my defenses.

"I understand why you did these things," I begin, and I notice Dash's shoulders relaxing slightly. "But I refuse to be lied to. I can understand an action, but I don't have to agree with it."

I straighten myself, trying to convey more confidence than I actually feel in this moment.

"When you made the decision to trust me and form our partnership, you should have told me exactly what was going on," I continue. "You've made a lot of dangerous enemies because of AMG, and I deserved the opportunity to decide if I wanted to continue being affiliated with it. I still would have agreed, but you could have put me in danger I wasn't prepared for."

Dash responds, "I would never let anyone hurt you."

"That's not the point," I counter. "I may not have been hurt, but a target could have been placed on my back, and I deserved to know so I could prepare myself. More importantly, you've shown that you don't truly trust me. Because I don't know what else you've chosen to leave out, I can't believe anything you've said to me that I haven't confirmed with my own eyes." My words carry a resolute edge.

Deep down, I do trust Dash, but my gut and my rational mind are warring.

"I need some time to think about this. For now, I trust that you have the means to continue the investigation without me," I declare.

The room falls into silence, and Dash remains seated, his eyes fixed on me, that bleeding pupil giving nothing away. It's as if he's locked away all his emotions in a drawer, leaving him deadly and unreadable—a soldier's demeanor.

"For someone who keeps a lot of their own secrets, you sure get mad when you don't know everyone else's," He retorts, the words carrying a sharp edge. His comment is colder than anything he's ever said to me, and it strikes a nerve.

"My secrets have nothing to do with the case at hand, nor did they put you in any potential danger. Your secrets could have made me enemies that I'm not capable of handling," I explain.

Dash's voice grows colder, and he accuses, "Ever the hypocrite, Lorelei. I don't think you needing time has anything to do with our work at all. I think this has everything to do with the fact that you like my darkness. You saw something in me that lives deep inside you, and you're scared. You're hiding, just like you did when you were 17. You're using this as your excuse to run."

His words hit me like a punch to the gut, and I'm left reeling. The raw truth behind his accusation forces me to confront emotions and fears I've long buried.

"You know nothing about before! You have no idea who I am, no matter what all your digging finds on me!" I yell, my frustration boiling over, and I can only imagine the neighbors are growing increasingly irritated.

Dash, however, laughs. He actually laughs and swiftly rises to his feet, taking a step in my direction.

"Oh, is that so?" he retorts. "I know that you're a fighter, someone who's battled fiercely, and your unyielding determination is what got you there. I know that you guard yourself when others approach, but with me, it's different. I know you force yourself to confront the darker aspects of this world, so that nothing will ever surprise you again. I know that when you start to feel too much you slide that cold mask back in place freezing out the world. And I can know that you're drawn to me just as I am to you."

He's in my face now, the warmth of his presence overwhelming me. A surge of energy tingles between us, and this time, I yearn to feel his strong hands around my neck.

I wish he weren't privy to any of this. I don't require anyone to fight my battles; I've always faced them alone. I never intended for anyone to get close enough to know me. I know that if given the opportunity, he would seek vengeance for all my suffering, but this isn't his battle. It's mine.

"Get out," I say harshly.

"So, running it is, Lorelei Hart? Is it still Hart, or have you already decided to change it again now that someone's getting close?"

"I said get out. You have no right to sit here and judge me for how I chose to protect myself. Now, get. The. Hell. Out. I shared my scars with you last night, and even then, you didn't think to trust me with this. You didn't even trust me with your real name. So get out." The hurt in my voice is impossible to conceal, and I can hear the slight tremble in my words.

I push against him with all the anger I've been holding in, but he barely budges an inch.

"Alright, have it your way. Take all the time you need."

With the finality of his words, he stalks past me, flinging my door open and slamming it harshly behind him. I'll have to check later to make sure the door didn't crack. I stand there in my living room, feeling like someone is squeezing my lungs in a vice grip.

Time. Did I really need more time? I've never been so confused in my life. I'm doing what I need to do to protect myself, but somehow, it feels like I'm doing something wrong. But it doesn't matter. I'll just sit back and wait for this to all blow up on AMG sometime soon. But then what? I hadn't thought about this yet; all of my staff will be out of a job. I have no plan for this. I was so consumed by everything I neglected to think about what everything would look like after the fire settles.

How did I allow things to escalate to this point? I used to have a plan that stayed five steps ahead of everyone else, but now I'm left with nothing.

I can't even alert my staff to what's happening because that would mean exposing the investigation and potentially jeopardizing everything we've worked so hard for.

My phone vibrates in my pocket, and when I pull it out, I see my mom's contact information flashing across the screen. I don't have the time or energy to deal with her. Seconds after I ignore it, she calls again, but I let it go to voicemail. Then, a moment later, my phone vibrates with a new text.

Mom: I need to talk to you now.

Maybe I could use this distraction, but before that, I need a nap. Exhaustion is dragging me down, and I can't handle much else before the dam breaks, and I unleash every bit of darkness within me.

CHAPTER 17

"So will you wait me out
Or will you drown me out?"
-Bad Omens

Damien

I've been pacing my living room ever since I left Lorelei, and I'm pretty sure that if I look down, I'll have worn a hole in my flooring. I pull out my phone and quickly dial James' contact information. The phone barely rings before I hear his skeptical voice come through.

"I saw you guys leave early and decided to give you some space before I called. Is everything okay, boss man?"

"This case should have been wrapped up by now, but instead, I've been distracted. I want this finished."

"Are we sidestepping the real issue here?" He retorts.

He's right; I'm acting like a dick, but he doesn't have to dig into my personal life, even though he's probably my closest friend.

"How soon can you make it to my place, James?"

"Um, I'll be there in just a few minutes."

Before I have to scrape up another topic, I end the call and tuck the phone back into my pocket. James and I need to stay laser-focused on assembling our case file for submission to the DEA. While part of me would love to see each and every one of them eliminated, we've both agreed to let the DEA handle a takedown of this magnitude. With all the evidence James has gathered, they're facing life sentences in a federal penitentiary.

I only get my hands dirty when the means are justifiable for the ends, like in the case of Santiago. His demise served as a means to uncover the truth. Since founding AMG, I've taken more lives than I did during my entire military service. Sometimes, the monsters prowling our hometown streets are deadlier than the ones we combat in war. At least in war, they openly acknowledge the terrible things they do. The real monsters lurking beneath our noses are sly and adept at concealing their treachery in plain sight.

As I wait for James to arrive and join me in building our portfolio, I decide to open my laptop and sift through some emails. Suddenly, I find myself revisiting the original email James sent me weeks ago about Lorelei.

In such a short period, this woman somehow managed to uncover more about me than anyone else alive. Even James, my closest confidant, remains unaware of why AMG came into existence. The truth I shared with her took me by surprise when it spilled from my lips.

It felt strangely effortless to talk to her, to expose that festering wound and commence the process of cleansing the infection. On most days, I tend to forget that the sole reason AMG exists is due to my wretched father.

I hope he's writhing in agony down in the depths of hell, bearing witness to me dismantling his despicable friends and associates. My scope of operations isn't limited to politicians; they're just a small piece of the puzzle. Over time, numerous cases have emerged where our intelligence exposes individuals with malicious actions, and we bring them to justice. Whether they're kidnappers, drug smugglers, or politicians, no one is exempt from our reach, and before my time comes to an end Lorelei's dad will be added to that list.

She may despise me right now, but no one should have to endure the suffering she's gone through. It'll be a form of closure, a reckoning of sorts.

"Boss?" A familiar voice sounds from the doorway.

"James, you're comfortable enough to just walk into my house now?" I remark without glancing up from my computer.

"I know you can see me on the security cameras. I was merely sparing us the hassle of knocking."

Surprisingly, I find myself unbothered by this invasion of privacy, and given that James is already pulling up a chair and booting up his computer, I see no reason to waste time arguing.

For hours, we work in silence, meticulously assembling all the information we've gathered. After uncovering the truth, we manage to construct a compelling paper trail that the DEA can use to easily implicate all those involved. We're essentially handing them a beautifully wrapped package adorned with a pretty bow.

"I think you should talk about it," James suggests interrupting our work. "You've been seething for hours, and the air in here is so thick I might choke."

James has always been outspoken, but lately, he's been a little pushy too. I've never had many friends to confide in. The friends I had while growing up were those whose parents were friends with my dad, so I couldn't trust them with any information, let alone anything personal.

I formed strong bonds with my fellow soldiers during my time in the military, but they all have a lot going on in their personal lives, and I didn't want to burden them with my own problems. I've always considered myself self-reliant and capable of handling my own challenges. However, as I sit here with James, I can see the genuine concern in his eyes. I spend more time with him than probably anyone else in my life, and all things considered, I know he truly is my friend.

For a moment I take a look at James. He's average build for a male which means he's smaller than me, but most people are. He's lean and his pale skin seems to glow due to all the time he spends inside on his computer. His shoulder length brown hair is pulled into its signature ponytail and his glasses rest on his nose. In a world constantly changing, he never does.

"You're a pain in my ass," I say, half-smiling.

"I'm not a pain; you just hate talking about anything. This is how normal people have a conversation. Not all of us can be hot and broody," James quips, trying to lighten the mood. It almost makes me crack a smile, and I can see he's using humor to encourage me to open up.

I pause for a long moment, still contemplating whether I should discuss my personal life with him. However, I realize that maybe he can help me understand why I feel this gaping hole in my chest.

Taking a deep breath, I decide to open up. Might as well, I'm on a role with this whole opening up concept. Over the next few minutes, I explain everything to James, even revealing the origins of AMG. When I finish, I lean back in my chair and run my hand through my hair. For once, I feel like I can breathe a little easier, having to not bear the weight alone anymore

James appears thoughtful, and his eyes hold mine as he responds.

"First, I appreciate the truth behind AMG, and knowing this information makes me even happier to be a part of something like this."

"Second, you have feelings you need to address with Lorelei.

You don't need to discuss it with me, but you definitely need to with her."

"Lastly, Lorelei has very few people in her life, and what appears to be a lot of skeletons in her closet. Despite what you think, I believe she trusts you, and by not giving her the truth, you've broken her trust that she sparingly hands out."

James' words carry a weight of wisdom and concern. I find myself nodding in agreement, realizing that he's right on all counts.

James' straightforwardness is something I truly appreciate in this moment having only my internal thoughts to sort through it until now. As I ponder his words, I can't help but feel that I have to let Lorelei go. A man like me will never truly deserve a woman like her. She's brave, intelligent, and a fighter through and through, while I'm just a man with blood-soaked hands. What right do I have to bring her into my fucked up world. I couldn't even be honest with her.

After some brief consideration, I determine that now may not be the most opportune moment to delve into this matter. If I'm being honest with myself, maybe I'm even being a bit of a coward, by avoiding a deeper look at my own feelings.

Overwhelmed by what this could mean, I make a conscious decision to stay focused on the task at hand. I'm confident that I can complete this job without Lorelei's involvement, and once it's done, I can consider taking on out-of-state cases. Perhaps I'll even contemplate leaving for a while once we wrap up the current case. It seems I might be a runner as well.

I turn to James and express my gratitude, saying, "Thank you, James." With that, I redirect my attention back to my computer, determined to shut down all thoughts except for the work at hand.

CHAPTER 18

"These days here without you are the best that I've ever had"
-Like Moths To Flames

Lorelei

I managed to take a decent nap, but I feel less rested than before. My entire body is aching, and my head has been full of nothing but static.

As I roll over and reach for my phone on the nightstand, I notice an abundance of messages from my mom.

Mom: I need to talk to you

Mom: Don't ignore me please

Mom: There's stuff you need to know

Mom: Where are you??

That grabs my attention. I go to great lengths to ensure my parents never discover where I live. There's no way I'll allow my safe haven to be compromised.

Me: I'll meet you at the old pizza place I used to work at in high school. Be there in 20.

I fire off the message and head to the bathroom to freshen up. As I step through the door, my head jerks to look at the mirror. Two prominent bruises adorn the sides of my neck, serving as a stark reminder of the hands that encircled them less than 24 hours ago. My fingers rise instinctively to gently trace the bruises, and a strange longing washes over me, as if I yearn for his touch on my skin once more.

My legs clench together, the memory of his skilled tongue between them still vivid in my mind. For a brief moment, I find myself missing him, longing to reciprocate the desire I felt that night. However, I knew I couldn't give in to those feelings, not when so many unanswered questions remained.

That man has a powerful effect on me, but I can't forget that he lied. I understand that he doesn't owe me anything, but his deception also reflects a lack of trust in me. I put my job and even my life on the line to assist him, yet he couldn't provide me with something as fundamental as the truth about his name. I jeopardized the well-being of my staff members, but he failed to alert me to any potential risks I might face by collaborating with him. I even lost Bex.

Fuck that.

I realize there's no way I can conceal the bruises, so I decide not to attempt to cover them up.

Swiftly, I run my fingers through the tangle of brown hair and gather it into a bun atop my head, leaving my face bare. My athletic shorts and tank top are still clean from this morning, but they serve as another reminder of Dash. Or Damien, or whatever the hell his name is. This is an outfit he chose and purchased for me. However, I won't let that deter me from wearing comfortable clothes, so I steel myself against the knot in my stomach and carry on.

Exhausted from the effort of getting ready, I slip on my sneakers, which are conveniently placed by the door, and grab my purse from the counter before leaving my apartment.

The drive to the old pizza shop is short, and they still serve the best pizza in town. After a 20-minute drive, I pull up to the restaurant, and to my surprise, my mom is seated at a table inside. Punctuality, or even showing up at all, has never been one of her strong suits. I take a moment to observe her from my truck and notice that she keeps glancing around the room as if she's afraid of something and on edge.

I'd be surprised if my presence could elicit such a reaction from her. I brace myself for what might turn into another heated confrontation. Drawing in a deep breath to summon my courage, I step out of my truck and lock it behind me.

As the bell on the front door chimes, I notice my mom's eyes dart in my direction, and that's when I see it. A massive black eye marring her pale skin. Something deep within me sinks. For years, my dad used me as his personal punching bag, but he never laid a hand on mom.

"Lorelei!" Antonio's voice rings out from the kitchen as he spots me standing in his doorway like an idiot.

"Take a seat, honey. I'll bring you the usual."

"Thanks, zio!" I yell back with gratitude, offering him a small smile. I'd enjoyed my time working here, but Antonio had always known I'd want more. He had taken an interest in me when I was a hungry kid looking to earn some money, and he became the uncle I had always wanted. He insisted I call him "Zio," and I felt special having someone who looked after me as he did. I had spent a few years working here, even as we moved from house to house so frequently. I couldn't bring myself to give up the comfort I found in Antonio and his family.

Turning away from him, I make my way over to the booth where my mom is sitting.

"Lor - what happened?" My mom's voice quivers with concern. Ah, right, the marks.

"Nothing, I'm fine. What happened to your eye?"

Now she looks down at the table, her hands buried in her lap.

I'm truly surprised to see her with a black eye. Dad always seemed to love her so much, and he only ever got violent with me. I had always assumed he blamed me for their accidental pregnancy, but he was never one for hitting. No, he always preferred the edge of a blade, so he could watch the 'bad' trickle out of me.

"It's okay, I made him upset, but don't worry," my mom says. Her tone is different from how she usually talks to me. She's been snarky and petty for as long as I can remember, but the way she's speaking now tells me that something is truly wrong. The fact that I can't remember ever being alone with her strikes me as odd, but I'll have to revisit that later.

"It's not okay. If he's hurting you, then you need to leave," I say, aware that I might sound like a hypocrite given my own visible marks, but she doesn't know what happened, and our situations are different.

"He's just stressed because of everything going on with you. Once you two can talk through your issues, he'll go back to normal," my mom attempts to explain.

"Get past our issues? I'll never forget the things he did to me; this is our relationship, and it's entirely his fault."

For once, she has nothing to say, no defense for my father and no smug expression on her face.

Fuck.

"Lor, I didn't ask you to meet to talk about this. There's something I've been meaning to tell you for a long time, but never had the courage to."

Before I can respond, Antonio emerges from the kitchen, letting the silver door swing behind him. He places a large pepperoni pizza on our table, along with some plates and napkins. Antonio then gives our table a once-over, clearly assessing the uncomfortable situation. He narrows his eyes on my injuries but I give him a small smile to let him know I'm okay, as okay as I can be considering how chaotic things have been. He nods his head and reluctantly walks back to the kitchen.

Antonio always cares deeply about the people around him. He's a small Italian man with gray hair and a matching mustache, but his personality is larger than life. The restaurant may have its share of wear and tear – red fabric on the booths ripping and white paint on the walls peeling in spots – but people come here for the food and the company, not the aesthetics.

Now that he's gone, I turn my attention back to my mom and wait for her to speak. However, all she does is shift her gaze from the pizza to me. I can tell she hasn't eaten in a while. That was the norm in the Blanchford home – there was always enough money for Dad to drink, but never enough for a loaf of bread.

"There's plenty, eat," I insist, my voice edged with impatience. Her trembling hand reaches for a slice of pizza, and her eyes moisten slightly after the first bite. It makes me wonder how long it's been since she last ate.

"You're not getting out of telling me why we're here, but we should eat first."

She nods, and for a moment, there's a flicker of life in her otherwise dull eyes. As much as I resent her for never stopping Dad all those years, I also recall that she was never the one to lay her hands on me. It was always Dad. But there was never any emotion in her eyes when she saw my broken and battered body. No remorse for what they put me through. Instead, I received cold indifference and was shunned in my own home, and I never knew why.

My anger is on the verge of boiling over, but I know that to get through this conversation, I must maintain a level head. I take a deep breath and push everything back into the small mental box I've created, locking it away tightly. Compartmentalizing has always been a survival mechanism for me.

The ability to put all the bad things in a little box allowed me to detach myself from the situation and keep moving forward. It kept me alive and enabled me to stay rational when emotions threatened to take over.

Seconds turn into minutes, and it feels like we've been sitting in this booth for days. My mom keeps fidgeting in her seat, glancing around as though she's out having an affair rather than sharing a meal with her only child.

"He doesn't know you're here with me, does he?" I ask, even though I already know the answer.

She wipes her hands on a napkin and tosses it onto the tabletop. Her bottom lip disappears into her mouth, and for a moment, she looks like a frightened child.

"I told him I was walking to the public library to use the computer," she admits.

"Well, let's get on with what you want to tell me, since it's clearly eating away at you."

"This won't be easy, Lorelei, but when this," she points to her black eye, "happened, I knew it was time for you to know the truth about why everything has happened the way it has."

This should be interesting.

"I blame myself for your dad's mental struggles, and I know that my actions led to the pain you went through as a child."

"How could you have caused him to hurt me? He made those choices on his own. He chose to cut me, to watch me bleed, to starve me, and to waste all our money on drinking."

"He only did those things because I betrayed him," she added, her voice filled with fear and uncertainty.

Betrayed him? My parents have been together for decades, and the only thing they could agree on was they loved each other, no matter how messed up they were. Even as my father hurt me all those years, she slept in bed with him every night, ignoring the fact that I was hoping the next breath I took wouldn't be the last. I cried myself to sleep down the hall from their room. I refused to die in their house or by his hand. Instead, I wanted his life to be in my hands one day. I planned to make him suffer before I'm ready to end his pathetic existence. That's why I stayed close all these years, not too far, so I could watch him wither away.

As I regain my focus, I can only respond with a dry, "Betrayed?"

Tears stream down her face, and her trembling hands rest on the table between us.

My cold indifference may not align with what many consider normal, but there are many aspects of me that defy societal standards, and I refuse to conform to their expectations. Once my parents are out of the picture, I'm planning to leave this state and never look back.

I look around the nearly empty restaurant, catching Antonio's occasional glances from the kitchen window. I'm aware that I don't deserve his kindness. Even though I never disclosed the details of my life with my parents, I suspect he may have drawn some conclusions from the times I showed up to work, quite literally stitched back together.

It always surprised me that during my time in school, a teacher never called Child Protective Services on my parents. We moved around so often, and I never finished a full school year at the same place, so I probably slipped through the cracks, like so many other children. My dad was also careful to keep as much of his abuse hidden where clothing would cover the evidence. It breaks my heart to think about other kids in similar situations or, even worse, still stuck with their abusers.

But that's something to process another day. Today, I have a weeping mom sitting in front of me, dangling the truth like a juicy steak.

"Is it safe to talk here?" She asks.

"Are you confessing to murder?" A chuckle slips through my lips, but all my mom does is give the room another cursory glance.

I notice her bleeding cuticles, a clear sign that she's not doing well mentally. "Do I need to take us somewhere else?" I ask, concern beginning to creep up my neck. I push it down, determined to keep a level head. I've come too close to exacting my revenge to lose myself to rage now.

"P-Please. Somewhere where no people are around," she stammers.

My apartment is the first place that comes to mind, but I couldn't bring my mom there. She doesn't deserve to enter my fortress of safety, not when she and dad are the reasons it had to exist in the first place.

"Let's go for a drive," I suggest instead.

"No, you can't be distracted while driving," she insists.

I rise from my seat, leaving money on the table to pay Antonio, and give him a wave through the kitchen window, knowing he's been watching. I turn to my mom, watching her closely to see what she'll decide.

After glancing around the room once more, she nods slightly and stands up on shaky legs. Her disheveled and dirty clothes make her appear even worse for wear than when I first arrived.

I know exactly where I'll take us, a place I haven't visited since I moved into my current apartment. I no longer need that location for solitude, so it seems fitting to take my mom there now.

We get into my truck, and she looks around at the clean interior, her hands gliding down the fabric of the seats.

"I'm so proud of you for making this yours," she says. Anger spikes through me, but there's also something foreign. I used to crave her acceptance and praise, but when it never came, I learned to live without it.

"Thanks," is all I can manage.

We spend the next thirty minutes driving in silence, and my mom can't seem to stop fidgeting, which is driving me insane. It's either she's back on drugs again or she's scared of someone. Those are the only things I can think of that would force her to act like this. She's always been paranoid, but this is something else.

I turn off the highway onto a hidden road that leads to a dirt path. Navigating the road like I've done hundreds of times in the past, we finally reach the clearing I'm all too familiar with. I back my truck up to the edge and step out, not waiting to see if mom is coming. I put my tailgate down and hop onto the back.

I'm grateful that whatever she has to tell me, we're doing it here. This place has always had a calming effect on me.

Moments later, mom climbs onto the tailgate not far from me, and I hear her take in a sharp breath, indicating that she's finally absorbed the view.

Where I've brought her is an overlook of the city. From here, you can look down on the city with all its bright lights from downtown, but you can also see the twinkle of the stars in the sky. It's the best of both worlds, a place of contrast—

urban chaos and natural beauty coexisting. There's still some daylight, but watching the sun dip behind the mountains is equally stunning.

A stretch of silence lingers between us as I wait for her to find the courage to speak.

"I'm the reason your dad struggles so much," she finally says, her voice quivering. "I think my betrayal broke something in him a long time ago. He didn't try to fight it, though. No, he let the madness win, and I thought it was temporary, but I don't think he's ever coming back from what happened."

"That's awfully cryptic," I respond, feeling my impatience rise. Mom has always talked like this, and it has driven me nuts ever since I was little. I could never get a straight answer from her.

I can't help but remember being around kindergarten age and asking my mom why dad always cut me. Instead of explaining what was happening, or at least coming up with an elaborate lie, she always told me the same things he did. That he had to bleed the bad from me. That was the only answer I ever got. He was bleeding the bad from me.

Suddenly, my scars start to itch again, and my clothes feel far too rough. I'm transported back to all those years living under their roof, night after night of my dad hovering over me with his blade, cutting my innocent skin to bleed out the supposed bad.

What bad could there be in a child? There's not a single memory, as far back as I can go, where he wasn't cutting my skin. Some nights he was concerned and gentle, the cuts superficial. But other nights, he was in a full rage, dragging his knife through my flesh as I lost blood, sometimes too much blood.

"He had to bleed the bad from me," I mutter, feeling the weight of those words pressing down on me.

It was mainly me he would cut. Sometimes he would cut himself when my small body had taken too much. Rarely did he ever raise his voice at mom, let alone lay a hand on her like he did earlier.

I'm losing sight of why I'm sitting out here with her in the first place. The sooner she reveals the truth, the sooner I can go home and escape from the world, or at least try to.

She takes in a deep breath and asks, "Do you know why he always said he needed to bleed the bad from you?" She avoids looking at me, surely aware that this is a dangerous subject for us to discuss.

"Because he's out of his mind?" I respond, my tone laced with bitterness and frustration.

"No, he's only losing his mind because I made him," she says, her voice quivering. "But that's not why. He says that because your blood is tainted."

I can't believe what I'm hearing. I don't know why I trusted that she would give me a single coherent answer. After all these years, I should have known better, but seeing her with bruises on her face made me think that this time was different, that I would be offered some sort of peace, or at least closure.

"How would a child's blood be tainted? I wasn't even old enough to do anything bad?" I'm yelling now, my anger boiling over, but I'm grateful that we're far away from anyone who could possibly hear us.

"You were born with tainted blood," she replies, her words laden with sorrow. "Tainted with my betrayal."

"Mom, you have five seconds to spill before I get in my truck and drive away, leaving you out here all alone. You're wasting my time," I snap, my patience is gone.

"No, no, no, please, Lorelei, please!" she pleads, frantic now, gripping at any piece of my clothing she can to anchor me on the tailgate. Her touching me almost sends me spiraling, but I have to remember to keep my focus on the situation.

“Your dad and I met when we were teenagers. My mom, your grandma was a single mom raising me. She was a sex worker trying to make just enough to buy bread and her drugs.” she says on a shaky breath.

I had never heard this story from mom. Her and dad always refused to talk about our family to me. I had always thought that everyone must be dead to never hear from a grandparent, an aunt or uncle, a cousin, anything. Even at the holidays, it was always just us.

"When I met your dad, he was nice to me and tried to protect me as much as he could. He became my friend. Only I didn't know that to your dad, we were more than friends. He put his claim on me, but never actually said that."

Thoughts of Dash - no, Damien - flash in my mind, and I wish he was here with me. But I quickly shove those thoughts aside and refocus on my mom, who's shaking like a leaf, even though it's still warm outside.

"Your dad had a half-brother who was a year older than us, he was the result of an affair that their mom had. His name was Joshua. I fell in love with Joshua, and I think your dad caught on quickly."

My mind races. Was this some sort of forbidden love triangle? All my life, I had assumed that mom and dad loved each other, even with how messed up things were. I thought their feelings for each other were the one true thing in their relationship.

"Your dad became scary, possessive. He would stalk me and follow me wherever I went. I became afraid of him, and it made it hard for me to sneak away to see Joshua. Joshua had told me that your dad was becoming violent at home and he was questioning if he should tell his parents that they needed to get him help," my mom reveals.

I find it ironic and darkly humorous that Joshua wanted to get my dad help. There were a few times over the years when I tried to get dad help, but each time I did, the cutting became far more brutal. The last time I attempted, he cut me so badly that I can still feel the pain. I remember my mom screaming at my dad, saying he'd gone too far, and that they should take me to the hospital. But he refused, opting to gamble on my life instead.

"A few weeks after I had that talk with Joshua about seeking help, I noticed my period was late," my mom continues, and my attention is now laser-focused.

"That night, I snuck out and met Joshua at the park to show him the positive pregnancy test."

Oh, no. A sinking feeling washes over me as the gravity of her revelation sinks in.

"He was so happy to be a dad," my mom says, her voice quivering. "We held each other in the park and cried tears of joy. Even though we were young, we loved each other and knew we would somehow make a good life together."

My mind is overwhelmed with questions, but I can't form them into coherent thoughts, so I simply let her continue.

"Out of nowhere, your dad burst through the trees and attacked Joshua. He stabbed him so many times that he collapsed next to him afterward. I was so terrified that my feet were rooted to the ground. Before I could think straight, he was back on his feet and grabbing me. He told me that we were going to raise the baby together and that I would help him cover up what he did, or he was going to kill my baby. The last piece of Joshua I had left. Scared out of my mind, I agreed."

"So where is this baby, then?" I ask, my voice uneasy, fearing she's going to tell me the baby is dead too.

The silence between us becomes suffocating, and I can feel my world turning on its axis. I have no idea which way is up now. "Mom... where is this baby?"

"Honey, you are that baby," she finally reveals.

My mind reels in disbelief. Dad isn't my real father? It all feels impossible.

"How could you not tell me after all these years?" I demand.

"He said if I ever told you, he would kill you. I was so scared," she confesses, her voice filled with fear and regret.

"Killing me was far better than being cut and abused every damn night of my life!" I'm screaming in her face, my anger boiling over, and she just sits there with her head in her hands, choking on her tears.

"He promised he would never take it too far. He said he was just bleeding the bad blood from you. The blood that wasn't his. The blood in you that's from Joshua," she continues, her voice heavy with regret and sorrow.

My stomach churns. The bad blood, the blood that belongs to someone else—my real dad, Joshua.

Fleeting thoughts of what life might have been like with Joshua as my dad cross my mind. I wonder if he would have been a loving, caring parent, tucking me into bed at night, rather than forcing me to stand in the bathtub in my underwear while he cut my skin and watched me bleed. If he would have taken me to school in the morning, packed me a lunch, instead of screaming at me about being dirty and scrubbing my open cuts harshly with scalding hot water that he made mom boil on the stove.

But I can't dwell on the "what ifs." He’s dead.

"So you're saying dad killed his half brother and got away with it?" I ask, trying to process the enormity of this.

"After Joshua was dead, your dad made me help him load the body in the back of his car, and he drove him to a really bad part of town and dumped his body in an alley. There was a lot of drugs and gang activity, so the cops ruled it as gang violence, even against the protests of his parents. They knew Joshua was a good kid and had no business being there," my mom reveals through her tears.

I can see just how broken she is for the first time, and I begin to understand the terrible choices she had to make to protect us. She did what she had to do to ensure that my unhinged not-father wouldn't murder us like he did to his brother.

"Your grandparents suspected that your dad had something to do with it. They had been growing scared of him for quite some time and even told the police that during the investigation. They decided to get a restraining order and move as far away as possible, leaving me with him. Your dad had just turned 18, and my mom didn't care where I was, as long as she didn't have to feed me, she didn't care that I left," my mom explains.

My mom has essentially been a captive all these years, but I never saw her make an effort to get us out of there. Even now that I'm out of the house, she's still stayed. I'm beginning to understand that it's likely out of guilt. She thinks her actions are what caused him to lose his mind, but I believe he was sick long before that, and the story confirms this as well.

She looks up at my face, and her hand moves as if she wants to touch me but stops herself. "You have his eyes. Beautiful bright green eyes. I was always so happy you had that piece of him."

CHAPTER 19

"I'll be there just to watch you fall
So, don't push me, I've got nothing to lose"
-A Day To Remember

Lorelei

I drop my mom off at the public library to avoid any suspicion from dad, just in case he comes snooping around. The ride is silent, and my mind is reeling. Everything I grew up believing is changing. My entire world is upside down, and I don't know how to find my way back up again. Dash would know what to do.

She doesn't push me to say goodbye when she jumps out of my truck, and I'm grateful for her unusual silence. A weight is lifting off her chest, and while she looks a little relieved, there is also terror in her eyes. Whether the terror is aimed at me or him, I don't know.

Before she shuts the door, she looks up and says, "I know you will never forgive me. But I do love you. I made myself distant from you because if your dad saw me clinging to you, the abuse would get worse. He wouldn't even leave me alone with you, scared I would take you and run. I thought I was protecting you. You don't owe me anything, but if you can, please warn me if you decide to tell him. I would be grateful."

I haven't decided what to say to this but before I can respond she says "Can you tell me why you finally left us all those years ago?"

She has to know it was because of dad, but I also sense she wants to understand what triggered that final night.

"Dad was coming in more frequently to cut me, and one night he was going way too deep. I knew I was losing too much blood, and when he finally left, my feet automatically started moving towards the first aid kit I kept to clean myself up. But that night, I didn't want to sit alone in the bathroom, crying and stitching myself back together. So I didn't. I crawled back to the tub and let myself bleed, and I prayed that death would come for me fast. As I lay there, I realized I wasn't the one who should have to die. I decided then and there that I would never again allow another person to hold my life in their hands. I would die only by my choice, so I left."

I look back at my mom, who is clutching the door with silent tears running down her cheeks. She nods her head tightly and then shuts the door.

For the first time in my life, I don't want to be alone. I can't. Without thinking, I start to drive. I circle the block a few times, but I finally muster the courage to pull into the little apartment complex that I've been to a few times.

When I park my truck, I don't linger inside because I'm scared to lose the courage I've built up. I walk myself up to the door and place a few quick knocks and wait. To my surprise, a bright face is staring at me, but it's not the one I was expecting.

I look up at Kellan's smiling face, but when he takes stock of my condition, a look of concern quickly replaces his smile. In one swift motion, he draws me into a tight embrace. A small sob escapes my lips, but I muster the strength to keep the rest of my emotions at bay, not yet ready to let that dam burst.

"Who is it?" I hear the voice I had been searching for, but Kellan doesn't release his hold on me. I sense another presence approaching, and I know it's Bex.

"Come on, get inside," she says softly, and Kellan finally lets me go. He walks over to Bex quietly, whispering something in her ear as I take a seat on her couch. Afterward, he looks back at me and offers a small, reassuring smile before walking through the front door and closing it behind him.

"He didn't need to leave. I'm sorry," I say, looking up at her.

"He's fine, we were just hanging out," she reassures me, not pushing me to talk. Instead, she goes to her fridge, grabs a bottle of whiskey from the top shelf, and retrieves two shot glasses from the cabinet. I'm not big on shots, but I must look like I need it.

"You've never come to me like this," she remarks, and I know she's not expecting a response. I'm also just grateful that, considering what happened the last time I saw her, I'm surprised she's even willing to let me into her home.

"You're all I have, and right now," I take a deep breath and attempt to keep my emotions in check, "I need you. I didn't mean what I said to you. I'm so sorry."
"Does all this have anything to do with what's going on with your neck?" Bex asks. I almost laugh at the question, realizing I'd forgotten about the sizable bruise on my neck. Strangely, his betrayal seems smaller to me now. Perhaps because I was never truly angry with him in the first place, just hurt. I can understand why he did what he did; he was protecting his people.

The betrayal stung because somewhere along the way, I thought I became one of his people, but I was wrong. I had developed feelings for him, and his easy deception showed that those feelings didn't go both ways.

"There are some things I'm dealing with in relation to my neck, but that's not what brought me here. I'm lost, Bex, and I don't know how to find my way home." She looks down at the coffee table where the whiskey and shot glasses are, pours us each a shot, and hands one to me without looking at me, keeping the other for herself.

"I don't even know much about finding home. I don't know if it's a place, or a person. But I do know that if anyone can find it, it's you. If you can't, then there's no hope for the rest of us," I carry on, and she throws back her shot. I follow suit, craving the fiery burn.

As I place the shot glass down, I feel something hot and wet rolling down my cheeks. I'm crying. For the first time since I left my parents years ago, tears are streaming down my face. When I left, I vowed that no one would ever make me feel this way again. But sitting here, crying over what my mom told me, I realize I never truly left at all. I've been trapped in the past, wasting my freedom.

The freedom I thought I had was an illusion. I was still allowing them to control my life; I just couldn't see it before. Damien had called me out on it – I was a runner. I didn't face anything; I ran. I hate it when other people are right.

This vulnerability is like a hammer cracking something in my chest wide open, and, unexpectedly, it feels freeing. I need to confront all of this, and my first step will have to be talking to my dad.

"Bex, there's something inside of me that's broken, and it will never be fixed. But I think somehow you see that, and you don't try to fix me; you just accept me for who I am."

"Of course I do, you idiot. You're my best friend," she responds with an eye roll, and that small, familiar gesture helps me relax a little.

Now, more than ever, I realize that I truly don't deserve a friendship like hers. I've kept her at arm's length for so long, and I'm not sure how I'll change that about myself.

"For a minute there, I thought I needed to find a new job," she giggles, lightening the mood and reminding me of the depth of our connection.

Her laughter lightens the mood, and I manage to crack a smile as I wipe the tears from my face. "Even if I meant what I said, I would never fire you. You're the best bartender I have."

Bex bursts into a good laugh, and in that moment, I feel a glimmer of hope that we might be okay, and that I might be okay.

Hours later, I've sobered up and spent enough time shedding tears. I finally muster the strength to pull myself off of Bex's couch and wrap her in the tightest hug I can manage. She's taken aback at first, considering I never really hug anyone, but after a few seconds, she squeezes me back with all her might.

"There's no reason to go through life alone, Lorelei. Please don't push me out," she says with genuine concern, reminding me that I have a lifeline in this world.

I nod at Bex, letting my eyes convey all the emotions I've been holding in. Then, I turn to leave her place.

The drive home is a blur, and when I reach my apartment door, I realize I don't remember any of the journey here. I'm grateful that I didn't endanger anyone by driving while so distracted. My emotions are all over the place, and I need some time to sit and sort through everything.

Taking a deep breath, I unlock my door and step inside. The apartment is pitch-black, and I slide my hand along the wall, searching for the light switch, finally finding the electrical plate.

As I flip the switch, the sudden brightness shocks my eyes. I close them for a moment, needing a second to adjust. But before I can fully open them, a force slams into my side, and I let out a startled gasp as the air is forced from my lungs.

In the blink of an eye, I find myself on the floor with someone on top of me. My instinct kicks in, and I desperately reach for my knife. In the chaos of the tackle, it hits the floor and is now just out of arm's reach. Panic surges through me as I struggle to regain control of the situation. What the fuck is happening?

The person on top of me, wearing a black mask, triggers my darkness to take over. I have to survive. I summon all my strength and push back with a ferocity , channeling my tactical training. I've prepared myself for this. He has size and weight on me, sheer force won't work. I position my legs and maneuver so his weight is off kilter followed fast by a jab to his kidneys. As they momentarily wince in pain, I seize the opportunity, getting out from under them. Point for me, okay tides have turned.

Breathing heavily, I scramble to grab my knife, still within reach. The assailant, now struggling to regain control, lunges for me. I swing my blade defensively, grazing their arm, causing them to recoil.

"You bitch!" the man grunts, clutching his bleeding arm, my counterattack has left him weakened. I don't hesitate and go on the offensive, landing a sharp kick to his chest, sending him sprawling backward.

I quickly snatch my knife and hold it defensively, ready for any further threats. My heart races, and I'm determined not to be a victim again.

The masked assailant regains their footing, clearly not giving up. The dimly lit room becomes a battleground, and we circle each other, each waiting for the other to make a move.

With a sudden burst of aggression, the attacker lunges at me. We're grappling, locked in a fierce struggle. Not realizing he had a weapon of his own he swings a bat hitting me hard. I wasn't prepared for that. Wind knocked out of me, I slowly stand while he keeps swinging, destroying the room. I channel all that I have left in me.

Despite my best efforts, the assailant manages to gain the upper hand, driving me backward until I stumble over an overturned chair. I hit the floor hard, my knife slipping from my grasp. It skitters out of reach, leaving me defenseless.

Panic sets in as I search frantically for an escape route, but before I can react, the attacker produces a needle from their pocket. With a swift motion, they jab it into my neck. A wave of dizziness washes over me, and my vision blurs. I try to resist, but my body betrays me as I slip into unconsciousness, the world around me fading into darkness.

CHAPTER 20

"I can't find home, and I've been to a million places"
-Machine Gun Kelly

Damien

It has been thirty-six hours since I revealed the truth to Lorelei, and I haven't heard from her. I suppose I wasn't expecting to, but it still stings more than I'd like to admit. A terrible feeling is gnawing at my stomach, and I can't shake it.

"Boss, I'm sorry, but I need to tell you something," James' voice is hesitant, and that catches my full attention. "You told me to keep watching the security footage of Lorelei and to alert you if the D'Santos came near her. I've been doing just that, and while it's not the D'Santos specifically, something feels off."

"What do you mean?" I ask impatiently.

"Remember the guy from the... parking lot?" James hesitates, and I can feel my frustration growing. Screw that guy, she better not be fucking him again.

"Please, just carry on with what you need to say," I reply, my irritation clear, though I remind myself that none of this is his fault.

"Okay, well, I've been seeing him. A lot," James finally admits.

My anger surges at the thought of that idiot, but what infuriates me even more is the fact that she ran into his arms after our conversation. "Well, we know that she knows him, so what if he's been around her?"

"That's just the thing," James replies, "I see him on the security tapes from her apartment building, traffic cams around her favorite places, and the club, but he's never actually with her."

I can't help but acknowledge that this is indeed odd.

"Let me put it this way, he's been showing up in places she's just been, as in, I think he's been following her. And before you say anything, I've been noticing this since before the Mexico trip, and since you guys returned, and I'm telling you, he's stalking her," James emphasizes. I trust his judgment, and now I need to figure out the best course of action. But why am I just hearing about this? I'm furious. I should've handled him weeks ago.

"Where is Lorelei now?" I ask, my voice tight with concern. I hate having to do this, but even if she's angry with me, I'm going to protect her.

"The last known location was her apartment building. Due to the limitations in that area, all I can tell you is that she was last location was in her parking garage. But I haven't been able to track her for the past 24 hours. She's not at the club, her favorite coffee place, or anywhere else. Her truck is still in the garage too. Something doesn't feel right, boss," James concludes, growing uneasy.

I'm seething with anger that James is only bringing this to my attention now, but my rational side knows he didn't have a reason to do so earlier. "And where is that blonde jackass now?" I demand.

"He's headed to her apartment," James replies quietly.

Without giving thought to the potential consequences, I jump up and rush to my garage, flinging myself into my car. Once the engine is roaring to life and I'm backing out, I call James back using the Bluetooth. "James, make sure the police stay out of my way," I order, and then hang up on him.

With all the technology at our disposal, James can ensure that the police are diverted away from my location, allowing me to speed to Lorelei as quickly as possible.

My gut was screaming at me earlier that something terrible was about to unfold, and an overwhelming urge to reach Lorelei is consuming me. My car's engine roars, and I press the pedal to the floor, desperately trying to make it go faster.

As I speed into her garage, I notice that James was correct; her truck is in its usual spot. The hairs on the back of my neck stand on end, and my body instinctively shifts into fight mode, just as it was trained to do. Something isn't right.

Silently, I make my way up to her apartment, checking around every corner with my gun gripped tightly in my hand. My firearm has been an extension of myself for years, and I'm itching to use it on this guy.

When I reach her apartment door, I spot the cracked door frame around the area where the lock engages. I know that this is as bad as my gut has been warning me. I sneak into her apartment, clearing each area as I go. Just as I'm about to step into her bedroom, the imposing blonde fucker steps out, and his eyes widen in shock.

Without hesitation, I slam him against the wall, his face pressed against the drywall, and painfully twist his right arm behind his back. My other hand holds my gun pointed aggressively at his temple.

"Where the fuck is she?" I growl.

"I have no idea, man. I just got here," he yells back in a panic. I wrench his arm further, causing him more pain.

"I'm serious, I just got here. She hasn't been responding, so I came to check on her. I saw her truck in the garage, but when I knocked, no one answered, and the door was unlocked.

What's your problem, man, and who the hell are you?" This guy rambles on too much for my liking.

While he's immobilized against the wall, I take a moment to glance at the disarray in the living room. I know Lorelei well, and she never leaves a mess like this. No, there was a struggle here. Furniture is in pieces, and bits of glass are scattered across the floor.

"Why have you been following her? And don't try to deny it. I don't have time to waste," I demand.

"I'm not following her, we're together," he says defiantly.

I can't help but laugh, and I feel him tense in my grip.

"Ah, and does Lorelei know you're together?" I respond, nearly chuckling at his audacity.

"Listen, man, I don't know who you are, but I don't need to explain myself to you. Wait, is she fucking you too?" he taunts.

My vision starts to blur, and he better watch what he says next. "I would be careful with your next words. Now, when was the last time you saw her?"

"I checked on her at the club the other night, but I didn't tell her I was there. When I didn't see her around any of her usual spots for a few days after that, I came here to check that she was okay. When I showed up, her apartment was like this," he explains.

I sigh, realizing he might be telling the truth. The time she was absent likely coincides with our trip to Mexico, and I don't think he's smart enough to concoct such a story. I raise my gun hand and deliver a swift blow to the back of his head, effectively knocking him out. For such a big guy, he certainly doesn't know how to use his size to his advantage.

I secure Liam to a dining chair using spare sheets I found and make sure he's tied up. I don't want him going anywhere until I find Lorelei. It's imperative that I determine his involvement in all of this. After ensuring her apartment is locked up to avoid drawing attention, I call James.

"She's gone. Find her. I swear, if they have her, I'll burn everything down from here to Mexico to get her back," I declare, my voice filled with a mixture of anger and fear.

"We'll find her. Let me go through the cameras again. Get back to your house, and I'll meet you there," James responds with a resolve that provides some reassurance. But I can't accept that I've put Lorelei in harm's way. If the D'Santos have her, they'll regret ever crossing paths with her.

CHAPTER 21

"A world on fire with nowhere to hide"
-For For A King

Lorelei

My head throbs with pain. The agony makes opening my eyes excruciating, but I need to see what's happening.

I'm sitting on something uncomfortable. Why am I sitting and not lying down? A growing sense of worry starts to crawl up my spine. I never put myself in situations I can't control. There's something warm running down my arms, a sensation all too familiar.

"Lor, baby, open your eyes for Mom, please," a voice pleads with desperation. Wait, mom?

"Aargh," I grumble out, hoping that it's comprehensible.

"That's right, honey, open your eyes for me," my mother encourages. I can do this. I'm strong. I can open my eyes.

With every ounce of strength I can muster, I pry my eyes open, and the sight that greets me is something I wish I hadn't seen. We're in a grimy place, possibly a warehouse or factory. The walls are battered, and any paint that once adorned them is now peeling away. It reeks in here, with a stale odor and a hint of something rotting.

My stomach churns, and I fight the urge to throw up. Did the D'Santos figure out that we were snooping? Fear courses through my body, and adrenaline surges. I start trying to move, but my hands are tied behind my back, and the more I struggle, the deeper the bindings dig into my skin.

I can't believe this is happening. How did they find mom? Why is she here? As leverage?

I look ahead and see my mom tied to a chair directly in front of me. Tears streak down her face, and there's dried blood caked to her skin. She's still wearing the same clothes I saw her in last, and they're now completely ruined, stained with sweat, blood, and tears.

"How long have we been here?" I ask her, desperate for some sort of timeline.

"I think a day," she replies. "I think we were both drugged, so I don't really know for sure. I only woke up a little while ago. I've been trying to wake you up. The last thing I remember is going home after I walked back from the library, but everything else is black."

A day. It's not as long as I feared, and I notice some faint light seeping in through the grimy windows around us.

"What's the last thing you remember, Lor?" my mom asks.

I try to piece together my memories. "Uhm, I think I was in my apartment?" I answer, struggling to recall any details that might be helpful. If we were indeed kidnapped, where is everyone else? Surely the D'Santos would have left someone to guard us.

Time feels like an illusion in this place, and we spend the next few hours trying to recollect any additional memories from our minds. My mom, however, doesn't seem to remember anything beyond being at home, and I'm in the same boat.

I can't fathom how they would have tracked down my mom. Our contact is limited, and our last names are different. It's as if they've been keeping tabs on us. Something about this situation doesn't add up, but I can't quite put my finger on it.

Before I can contemplate it further, a loud bang reverberates through the room as a massive metal door is flung open. My body instantly goes on high alert. I swore that I would never allow myself to be in such a situation again, and I am fully prepared to fight our way out of here. My mom is here because of me, and it's my responsibility to get her out.

From the shadows of the warehouse, I spot someone lanky skulking around the perimeter, watching us. "Show yourself, you piece of shit," I seethe out. The shadowy figure pauses and then slowly steps into the light.

My breath catches in my throat. There's no way this can be happening. It can't be. Panic unlike anything I've ever experienced steals away all rational thought.

I can’t fucking die here.

Damien

James reviewed the surveillance cameras, and he discovered that Lorelei had left the parking garage the day before he declared missing, and she wasn't alone. In fact, upon closer examination of the grainy footage, she was with a man much bigger than her. Her arm was draped across his shoulders, and from what they could discern, he was dragging her around a corner of the garage where there were no cameras.

Fortunately, back in Mexico, James hacked her phone and placed a tracker as a precaution. I’ll apologize to Lor for lying about that too, but right now it doesn’t matter. The tracker's signal had been jammed by poor cell service, so it took some time, but he was ultimately able to pick up GPS coordinates.

I know James is taking this hard, but given the quality of the footage and the size of the man, it was challenging to determine what was happening. At first glance, it looked like a woman with her arms around a man, slowly walking somewhere, rather than someone being abducted. The way her feet dragged on the pavement suggests she might have been unconscious. The man hid his face on the side of Lorelei that was away from the camera, providing him cover. It's infuriating that he didn't reveal himself if he wanted to taunt us.

I've gathered a group of soldiers, and we're prepared to storm the building where she's being held on the outskirts of a low-income city. I've been through countless missions in my life, but never has one been as vital as this. Never.

Now isn't the time for me to let emotions guide my actions. If I'm going to rescue her alive, I need to be a soldier. Her soldier.

We haven't been able to confirm the identity of the man or if he's affiliated with the D'Santos family, but there are too many coincidences in play. I've already given my team orders: anyone involved in her capture will not survive today. No survivors, only my girl.

I pray she knows I'm rushing to rescue her. I'm willing to do whatever it takes to ensure her safety. Regret gnaws at me for giving her that space, but I've learned my lesson. I won't let her slip away from my side again.

My emotions are a volatile mix of frustration and anger. No one can protect her like I can, and I'm ready to unleash my fury. If anyone thinks they can hurt her and get away with it, they're in for a brutal awakening. She's mine, and I won't let anything or anyone take her from me.

I'll forever be indebted to James for his foresight. Without his planning, we might not have located her, and even if we did, it might have been too late. We could already be too late.

A small army and I are crammed into two vans, racing toward

the warehouse where James tracked her. I just hope my seirína can hold on long enough for me to get to her.

CHAPTER 22

"All I've ever known was the black hole that I call my soul
This my last hope, before I let go"
-Machine Gun Kelly

Lorelei

Blood. That funny smell, like coins, always reminds me of when dad gets really angry. My whole body feels cold, like when I don't have a jacket to wear in the winter.

I'm so scared, my heart is thumping like a drum, and I'm afraid this time he might do something really, really bad. It's hard to open my eyes. I have to be brave.

After this is over, I need to get out of this place. I don't want my life to end in this bathtub. Do I deserve something better?

Bleed out the bad.

Bleed out the bad.

Bleed out the bad.

Those are the words he tells me over and over, like a broken record. He thinks I'm really bad, but I'm not. I'm good. I hope one day he'll see that and stop hurting me.

Bleed out the bad.

Bleed out the bad.

Bleed out the bad.

No, no, no! I can't bear to find myself back in that tub. My eyes snap open, and there she is – my mom, bound to that dreadful chair in front of me, her head hanging at an unsettling angle.

"Mom?" I call out as loudly as my trembling voice allows, but she remains motionless. There's no way she can be dead. Then a sudden dread sinks in like a lead weight – he's in the room with us. I can sense it.

"Face me, you fucking piece of shit," I demand, scanning the room, searching for any signs of movement in the shadows. Deep down, I knew something like this was bound to happen.

"C'mon fucking face me you coward!" I scream out.

"I never raised you to speak like that," comes the voice from the shadows.

"So, 'dad,' what's the point of this? Or should I say 'uncle'? I'm so confused these days, you know how it is. Are you here to see if you can bleed out the bad from me once more?" I'm poking the bear, a ferocious one at that.

"No, Lorelei, I now know there's too much darkness within you for it to ever truly disappear. Redemption, in your case, can only come through death," he declares as he steps out of the shadows, appearing more disheveled than usual. His clothes are tattered and appear as if they might disintegrate with a single tug. His face is encrusted with grime and sweat, and his hair stands on end as though he's been pulling at it. However, the most alarming aspect is his vacant, distant eyes; he seems to have detached from reality completely.

I don't allow his threat to rattle me; I can't risk provoking his anger further before I've had the chance to think my way out of this situation.

"Well, how did you manage to find me?"

"It was surprising that I couldn't locate you under the name Blanchford, no matter where I looked. That was frustrating, but your boyfriend made it easy. All I had to do was follow him to figure out your usual whereabouts. Once I had you unconscious, I finished destroying your apartment. Everything you hold dear there is now in ruins. There's nothing left for you here."

Boyfriend? He couldn't be referring to Damien, as he's far too cautious, and I haven't seen him in a while, I think. It's difficult to discern the passage of time while trapped here.

"What do you know about my boyfriend?" I can't reveal my confusion to him. I need to play along and remain vigilant.

"I was surprised to see you with a blonde man. That wasn't what I expected your type to be. He was quite obvious in his pursuit of you, though, which made it easy to find your apartment," he explains.

The more he speaks, the more fragments of memory return to me. I recall bits of the attack in my apartment, how he caught me off guard and injected something into me. Then, I woke up here. How did I let my guard down enough for him to capture me? I also need to address the matter of the blonde man following me. The only one who fits that description is Liam. Fantastic. Rolling my eyes to myself.

"Did you kill Mom? She's not moving," I ask, hoping to distract him for as long as possible while I evaluate an escape plan.

"Your mother will get what's coming to her," he replies coldly.

Great. Add "save Mom" to the ever-growing list of problems. I need to find a way to get out of here – fast.

Damien

She's been missing for far too long, and the fury welling up in my chest threatens to consume me from the inside out.

As we approach the warehouse, the soldiers riding in the caravan maintain a deathly silence, fully prepared for the impending battle.

I clear my throat and address them, "I have no idea what we're walking into. I do know the area around the warehouse is clear, but the unknown lies inside. Lorelei is our primary objective for search and rescue. If you come across any women or children, restrain them until we can get the building secure. However, anyone else kill on sight. The caravan following us has the same instructions. Remember, this is a cartel, and they won't hold back. I'm committed to getting all of you back home by sundown. Let's make sure that happens."

Despite the few grunts in response, I can sense the unwavering loyalty and readiness of my soldiers for the impending battle. Still, I hate putting them in such an uncertain situation. I should have prepared for something like this weeks ago, but there was no indication that the cartel even knew about our involvement.

"Five minutes, boss," someone calls from the front of the caravan. Everyone in the caravan is now preparing their weapons and shifting into battle mode.

I'm coming, seirína. I think to myself, determined to rescue Lorelei and bring her back to safety.

Lorelei

Pain pain pain. My legs feel like they're engulfed in flames. I'm curled up in the bathtub, and it seems like I've been here for hours. I can't muster the strength to rise and clean my wounds. He went too deep again this time, and the pain is unbearable.

I long for help, but there's no one to help me.

No one there for the girl, staining the bathtub red. But then I realize, I'm not a little girl anymore, am I? No, I'm grown up now. I never really had the chance to be a little girl. Little girls don't go through things like this. I grew up much too fast, far sooner than anyone should.

I gather my strength; there's no one here to rely on. I have to get out of this situation on my own. I'm my only lifeline.

Fuck. In a sudden jolt, I lift my head, the pain coursing through my body like an electric shock. The warm sensation of blood running down my arms confirms that he's cutting me again. I force my gaze downward, but what I see nearly makes me gag, all while barely registering the condition of my arms. My legs are a gruesome tableau, marred by cuts that crisscross in every conceivable direction, and my thighs are awash in a sea of dark crimson. I can't even distinguish my skin from the tattoos that adorn my body.

The blood loss must be why I keep going unconscious. I try with everything inside of me to stay awake, to make a plan.

My eyes drift from the gruesome sight of my thighs to my mother, her head held high despite the tears streaming down her face. Despite some noticeable bruising, it's clear that I've borne the brunt of the torment.

"I never meant for this to happen, Lorelei," she manages to say, her words choked out amid tears.

"Oh, really? And what exactly did you expect, my dear?" Dad's voice nearly sounds like a twisted kind of laughter, and I can feel my jaw clenching in response. I despise him.

But before anyone else can utter a word, Dad interjects, "Lorelei, I understand your mother decided to enlighten you a bit about our history. I just wanted the chance to share my side of the story. To do that, though, I needed to let out some of the bad so that you can truly hear my truth. You'll soon realize, I was never the villain in this tale."

It's as if this whole situation is some sick joke. If the universe has a sense of humor, it certainly picked an awfully grim punchline.

I see my father approaching, and my entire body tenses with fear. I can't allow him to keep touching me, but showing any sign of weakness would only make things worse. As he nears, I realize that my hands, once tied behind me, are now bound in front of me, most likely so he had better access to my flesh. This unexpected change might work to my advantage.

He kneels before me, the glint of his blade in hand, and moves into my line of sight. He takes the sharp edge of his blade and slowly drags it across my forearm, creating a cut far longer than I can bear. Blood instantly wells up around the wound, dripping down the side of my arm.

I won’t lose it.

I won’t lose it.

I won’t lose it.

I refuse to let this monster continue to torment me, but my eyelids feel impossibly heavy. I just need some rest, and then I can formulate a plan to free myself from this nightmare.

Fatigue washes over me like a tidal wave, making it increasingly challenging to keep fighting. There's a growing temptation to surrender to the seductive embrace of sleep, to escape this torment. But I can't allow myself to meet my end at their hands. If I'm going to leave this world, it must be on my own terms.

I remind myself that I am the darkness that my father fears. I must find a way to show him that, to assert my strength, and to take control of my fate.

Crack.

Startled, I groggily pry my eyes open just enough to glimpse Dad standing in front of Mom, her face streaked with tears, and her cheek red from the impact.

"I warned you," he hisses, his voice dripping with menace. "I told you that if you ever told Lorelei, you'd pay with your life. Are you prepared to face the consequences?"

Through her sobs, I hear Mom whisper, "P-please, we can get you help. I know this isn't you. We can support you. We're your family, me and Lorelei. Please, let us help you."

"I DON'T NEED YOUR HELP!" he bellows, the sound reverberating through the concrete walls of the dilapidated building. It's becoming increasingly clear that we're reaching a point where bringing Dad back to reality may be impossible. In the past, I could navigate his abuse, knowing that he'd return once he'd extracted the pain he craved from me. But now, his secret is laid bare for all to see, and he seems like a man with nothing left to lose. He's utterly unhinged.

"Lorelei, are you ready?" He fixes his gaze on me, and I'm left grappling with a foggy mind, unable to decipher what I should be ready for.

"Ready?" I mumble, my thoughts slogging through the mire in my brain.

"Your mom understood what was at stake. She made her decision. Now she will pay the price. It's only right. Maybe then she can repent for the wickedness she subjected us all to. I loved her more than anything, and she betrayed me," Dad's words twist into an eerie justification.

"What are you even trying to say?" I confront him, my voice laced with a mix of frustration and sadness. "Dad, you're not well. You need help, and there's help available if you'd only acknowledge it. But it doesn't give you a free pass to be abusive.

It doesn't justify the pain you've caused," I assert, my voice quivering as I struggle to hold back tears.

"It's time she goes to see Joshua; they can repent together," he utters, and a chill courses through me. I had a hunch this is where he was heading, but I never imagined Dad could be this violent, even though his past might suggest otherwise.

"You can't kill her. You've already gotten away with murder once; twice would be too big of a gamble," I reason, holding onto the hope that some logic might sway him.

"No, once everyone sees my intentions of keeping the balance of good and evil, they'll understand. Plus, it's hard to claim murder with no witnesses. I left a witness last time, but I won't this time," Dad insists, his movements erratic. He remains a looming, unpredictable presence between us, making it impossible to figure out his next move.

"Lor, honey, it's okay. I'm ready. This isn't your fault; it's mine. But when it's time, get out of here," Mom says, her eyes devoid of tears, as if she has come to terms with the impending tragedy.

"Don't worry, my love," Dad sneers at her, "Lorelei will be following behind you. Once she's gone, all the bad will be purged from her. Her next life will be pure, and you'll all see."

The realization that he has no intention of letting me walk out of here has finally penetrated the fog in my mind. I need to summon all my strength and fight my way out.

I need to think, dammit. There's something I haven't finished, Damien flashes through my mind, and for once, I feel a powerful reason to fight. I'm not going to be another victim in this nightmare. I'm getting out of here. I have to get to him.

BANG

The deafening sound vibrates through my body, and I brace

myself for the inevitable pain, but after a few agonizing seconds, I realize it's not me who has been shot.

"No," is all I can manage to whisper. My eyes dart over to Mom, and between her vacant, brown eyes, I see a bullet hole, glistening with crimson blood.

In that haunting moment, she's the most beautiful I've ever seen her—finally at peace. I hope she's found Joshua, wherever that may be. It doesn't feel right to call him Dad, but there's still an ache in me for the life we could have all shared together.

Dad remains there, motionless, staring at Mom with the gun dangling at his side and the knife in his other hand. If I'm going to have a chance at getting out of here, it's now, while he's gripped by grief. Despite any hatred he might have harbored for her, I believe he loved her too.

"Dad," I say as timidly as possible, "before you kill me, please let me say goodbye. I understand what you're trying to do, to release all the bad. But I need to say goodbye."

He snaps his eyes up at me, his shock evident that I'm not reacting with terror over Mom's death right in front of me. I'll process all of this later, but for now, I need to gain the upper hand.

He moves towards me slowly, a single tear escaping his eye. "I loved her. This is as difficult for me as it is for you, but I need to restore the balance after her betrayal."

I fight back the bile that climbs up my throat and maintain a facade of understanding. "I understand, Dad, but please, just hug me before I go," I say with feigned innocence. It's a gamble, but playing on his emotions is the only card I have left to play. Make him think I'm on his side.

He leans down to wrap his arms around my bound body, and I resist the urge to recoil. Instead, I throw my head forward, colliding with his nose, which starts gushing blood, staining both of us. In his pain, he drops his weapons, the knife landing in my lap and he clutches his injured nose.

It's showtime.

As he cries out in agony, I seize the opportunity to use my hands and deftly maneuver the knife between my clenched knees. With careful determination, I start sawing my bindings against the blade, inching my way toward finally freeing my arms.

"You bitch!" he roars, pivoting back towards me. A memory flashes through my mind of the moment in my apartment when he screamed the same words after I managed to graze his arm with my blade.

I can't afford to be slow.

Bending down, I quickly cut through the bindings tying my ankles together, and as soon as they're free, something solid crashes into me, causing me to collapse onto the floor. In a fit of rage, Dad tackles me, desperate to regain his weapons.

I roll out from under him and kick the gun as far away from us as possible. The fact that he's so detached from reality appears to be working in my favor, but I can't afford to hesitate if I'm going to make it out of here alive.

He won't die from a quick gunshot. He'll die in my hands, where I can watch the blood drain from him.

Once I'm confident that the gun is far enough away from him, I muster the strength to get back on my feet, feeling myself sway from the blood I've lost. Not now, body, I silently urge, I need you to hold it together just a little longer.

Dad is on his feet as well, and I launch myself at him with the knife still gripped tightly in my right hand. Though weakened, I'm far smarter than him so I use that to my advantage. I won't let him gain the upper hand again.

With my hand raised I bring it down stabbing him in his upper chest, I don't want to kill him yet. I savor the drawn-out experience, relishing it solely for my own delight. Yet, in a fleeting instant, a wish flickers within me, for Damien's presence. He would have tied dad up for me and let me take my time exacting the revenge I was owed.

Dad yells from the impact of the stab wound and I rip it from his chest and bring it down again until he's collapsed on the floor in pain clutching his wounds. His shirt and hands are smeared with a vivid, crimson hue, but my focus can't remain on the gruesome sight.

He kneels before me, and a sense of childlike pride surges within me, radiating like an inner beacon. I walk behind him and cut both achilles just as Damien taught me to make sure he can't run if he tried.

The cacophony of screams and the pungent odor of blood envelop the warehouse, but within me, a sinister anticipation takes hold, a malevolent grin forming. Damn it, I've yearned for this moment for an eternity.

"I tried relentlessly to find you help. My love for you was boundless, and all I ever wanted was to help you conquer the demons within. Mom felt the same way, I believe. Yet, you opted for this path of suffering. You made your decision, and now it's time for you to face the consequences," I utter, not anticipating a response, given the torment he's enduring.

I take the next few minutes making cuts all around his body watching his blood stain the concrete floor. This idea, drawn from Damien, fuels my yearning for his presence by my side once more. My father's strength wanes, and he collapses from his kneeling position, now sprawled on the floor, his gaze locked onto me. The color drains from his face, and I sense that his time is drawing to a close.

I settle beside my father, my senses absorbing the stickiness of the blood beneath me. I'm indifferent as to whether it's mine, my mother's, or his. I sit close enough to fix my gaze upon him, witnessing his breaths slowly fade away.

Several minutes pass, and I eventually reach over to check for a pulse, but deep down, I already know the answer. He's gone.

I spot a red gas can tucked away in the corner of the warehouse, no doubt intended for covering up his horrifying deeds. With resolve, I rise and make my way over to it, then return to where I left his lifeless body. I cautiously pat his pocket in search of the lighter I'm sure he has stashed away.

After finding it, I proceed to pour gasoline over his lifeless form and then turn to my mother. This isn't the farewell I'd have wished for her, but the evidence must be destroyed. I reluctantly douse her as well. When the gas can is emptied, I toss it onto his remains and take a few steps back.

After some agonizing moments, I summon the courage to open the zippo lighter, igniting a flame, and then toss it toward his body. The fire swiftly engulfs him before moving towards my mother. The stench of burning flesh nearly makes me gag, but my strength is waning, and I must focus on escaping to safety.

I manage to exit the warehouse, which I now realize is an abandoned plant on the edge of town, and not far off I can see more industrial looking buildings. Fatigue holds me in its grip, and the wounds on my arms and legs, exacerbated by our struggle, continue to bleed. Instead, I sit at a safe distance, watching the fire grow, yearning to muster the strength required to stand and seek safety once again.

CHAPTER 23

"I lost my way to find a home"
-Motionless In White

Damien

We arrive to see a building engulfed in flames, and a chilling fear licks up my body, a fear I've never felt before. I jump out of the back of the vehicle before it comes to a full stop, ready to run into the building to find her.

Before I can make it to the door, I spot something laying in a heap on the ground in the abandoned parking lot, and I run to it, praying that it's her.

"Lorelei?" I inquire, gently lowering my rifle, trusting that my team is vigilant in case anyone is hidden nearby or this is a setup.

She turns her head towards me, her pallid complexion raising concerns that she might have lost too much blood, but her clothes are so drenched in it that I can't be certain where it's coming from yet.

"D?" She utters my name with a sense of vulnerability that tugs at my heart. This isn't the confident and strong Lorelei I've spent so much time with; this is a fragile, shattered facet of her that she rarely reveals to the world.

"I'm here, seiriína. Can you tell me what happened?" I ask, moving closer to kneel beside her, seeking a better understanding of the situation.

"My parents," she whispers. Her parents? What could her parents possibly have to do with the D'Santos?

"Where is everyone else, Lorelei?" I inquire, struggling to comprehend why no one else was found here. "Did the D'Santos kill them?"

She raises her gaze to me, and her eyes seem to glow brighter than I've ever seen. "The D'Santos didn't do this. Dad did. So I killed him."

Lorelei killed her dad, and now isn't the time to delve into the full story. My primary concern is her well-being, and upon closer inspection, I notice deep cuts on her arms and legs. Given her aversion to physical contact, I want to be cautious and not make her situation worse.

"Seirína, we have a lot to talk about, but right now, I need to get you to a doctor. Can I pick you up?" I offer.

"No, I'm walking," she asserts, struggling to rise on unsteady legs. "There's no one else in the building. What's with the army?" Surprisingly, she appears quite alert despite her pallor. I glance up, and some of the soldiers are staring blankly at the bloodied woman in front of them, then back at the building still consumed by flames.

"I thought the D'Santos took you," I admit, my arm wrapped around her waist to support her and reassure myself that she's truly standing beside me, alive. Glancing at her as discreetly as I can, I notice that she's bleeding heavily. Time is running out to address her wounds before the blood loss becomes critical, but I won't deny her the opportunity to walk away from here on her own two feet.

"The devil took me, and my darkness won," she confesses. With her admission, I continue guiding her toward the waiting vehicle. The soldiers who accompanied me have verified that there is no one else here aside from two burning bodies inside, and they are prepared to depart from the scene. The building is isolated, so we'll allow it to burn, erasing all the evidence.

Once she's in the van, she lies on the floor, and I can see the blood slowly pooling around her.

Kneeling beside her, I quickly remove my shirt and apply pressure to any visible wounds, desperately attempting to slow the bleeding. In the driver's seat, one of my men takes charge and accelerates, understanding the urgency of the situation. Time is of the essence, and if Lorelei doesn't receive medical attention soon, she may not make it.

I can't bear the thought of losing her.

In a faint whisper, she shares, "When I was little, I prayed every night for a white knight, or an angel, someone to swoop in and save me. But what I needed was something darker to rid my world of its demon. Someone or something to slay it. But all along, it lived inside of me; I was waiting for the darkness inside me to take over." She lets out a relieved sigh "You came for me."

And then, she slips into unconsciousness.

Fuck.

"Faster, I'm losing her!" I shout to the driver, though I'm aware he's already pushing the limits without endangering us. With trembling fingers, I check her neck for a pulse, and I can still detect a faint, feeble beat. We can't take her to a conventional hospital; it's too risky, as it might lead to her arrest.

We're nearly there. Carver is the only person I trust with anyone I care about.

When we arrive at the building, I burst out of the van, immediately scooping Lorelei into my arms. While I know there's an alarming amount of blood, I can't afford to dwell on that now. The doors are already open, and workers are directing me to the first room on the right, where a bed is prepared for her. Gently, I lay her down, taking a step back to allow the nurses to begin their preparations.

My soldiers must have called ahead to inform them about our arrival.

Carver is already scrubbed and ready for surgery. He addresses me firmly, "You need to leave, Ashford. We have to maintain sterility. You can wait on the other side of the window and observe, but I'll take care of her."

I know he's right. Carver has been with me on several deployments, and I trust him completely. Still, it's a struggle to leave her side. I never want her to be alone again.

"I'm serious, Ashford. Out. Don't risk her," he asserts, and his stern gaze leaves room for no argument. Reluctantly, I step away, watching through the window, my heart heavy with worry.

Carver's directive stirs frustration within me, but I understand the lengths he'd go to in order to save his patients. I walk out of the surgery room and take a seat in front of the window, where I can observe the proceedings.

I purchased this building when I brought Carver on board, allowing him to assist my team whenever necessary. When he's not saving lives on this side of the building, we run a free clinic on the other side. The two sections are completely separate, this side is only accessible through the back, and the public remains unaware of what takes place in this hidden area.

The idea for the free clinic was Carver's, a way for him to give back to a low-income community, and I couldn't have argued against it. It's one way we can make a positive difference beyond our usual operations.

Hours pass, and when I look away from the window, I see a handful of the soldiers who were with me in the warehouse gathered around me, and James makes his way forward.

"What are you all doing here?" I ask.

"We came to make sure she is okay," James says, and everyone around him nods.

Anderson, a small soldier with auburn hair pulled back in a bun and her harsh blue eyes looking at me, moves forward. "We saw the scene, we're all curious about what's happening. But more importantly, we want to see the girl who is strong enough to walk out of that alive."

Rightfully so, the sight that greeted us was gruesome. Some soldiers managed to peer inside through the busted-out windows that the fire hadn't spread to yet and spotted two lifeless bodies, a room drenched in blood, and flames devouring the remnants. I'm eager to hear the full account from Lorelei when she wakes up. Because she will.

Carver and his scrub nurse have been tirelessly working for what feels like hours, and my loyal soldiers remain steadfast by my side. I doubt they'll ever fully comprehend the depth of the camaraderie and mutual trust that this group represents. I refer to it as a brotherhood, although there are many capable women among us who grasp the significance of the term.

The female soldiers among us often exhibit greater ruthlessness and, I must admit, are often more intelligent than most of the men. I've never subscribed to the sexism that sometimes plagues the military; in my ranks, there's simply no room for it. My sole focus is on recruiting and retaining the best, regardless of gender.

We sit in silence for what feels like an eternity when Carver finally emerges. His scrubs are drenched in her blood, the familiar protective rage bubbles up inside of me.

"She has suffered massive blood loss," Carver informs us. "I've managed to stitch her up and administer a blood transfusion, which should help, but her path to recovery will undoubtedly be a tough one. Judging from the scars I've noticed on her body, it's clear that she has endured a lot before. She's truly fortunate to still be among the living. If you had arrived any later, I'm not sure she would have made it. We'll need to be vigilant she's not out of the woods yet."

He glances at me with a look of restraint, clearly harboring numerous questions in his keen mind. However, he understands that now is not the appropriate time to ask them.

She's alive.

"When do you think she'll wake up?" I inquire, my eagerness to see her growing.

"It'll likely be a few hours. We had to sedate her to address all the lacerations, and considering the exhaustion she's enduring from what she's been through, she desperately needs the rest. I suggest you all go clean up, and then you can come sit and wait for her. I'll have a nurse with her while you're away," Carver says, his tone carrying an air of insistence. I realize he's absolutely right. I'm covered in her blood, and that wouldn't be the most reassuring sight for her to wake up to.

"I'll stay with her, boss. You go home and take a quick shower," James offers, a gesture that I'm profoundly grateful for. I nod in his direction, noticing that the other soldiers have already left.

"Should I call Bex?" I ask James, feeling somewhat lost in this unfamiliar situation.

"I think you should let her decide when she wakes up," James wisely suggests, a reminder of Lorelei's fiercely private nature. It's a sound judgment, and I don't want to infringe on her boundaries.

In a rush, I make my way to my house, taking the quickest shower of my life and donning comfortable clothing in anticipation of a lengthy wait. I speed back to Carver's office, relieved to find that she's still asleep, and I haven't missed her waking up.

Pausing in the doorway, I gaze at her. The blood has been cleaned from her, and her arms and legs are swathed in large white bandages. A nurse has combed her dark brown hair, which now flows gracefully against the pristine white pillowcase. Dark purple bags mar her eyes, a sign of her exhaustion, but amidst it all, I've never seen her appear so serene.

James is seated in a chair by her bedside, his gaze fixed upon her. "I'm sorry I didn't catch this fast enough to save you from the pain," he murmurs to her, unaware that I've returned. He holds one of her delicate hands and softly rubs the top of it with his thumb.

"This isn't your fault, James," I assure him from the doorway. "As Carver said, her body bore scars of healed wounds, indicating a violent history. The camera footage was so grainy it was nearly impossible to detect it was her"

Startled, he turns toward me in his chair, nodding, his cheeks damp with tears. I've never been particularly adept at handling emotions, and I find myself in a situation where I'm unsure how to comfort him.

"Oh, fuck," I exclaim, and James shoots me an alarmed look, as if expecting some other crisis to unfold. "I left that blonde guy tied up in her apartment."

For a moment, we sit in silence, and then an outbreak of laughter ensues. I find myself doubled over, struggling to catch my breath, and James is laying his head on Lorelei's bed, his body shaking. I guess I'm better at lifting people's spirits than I realized.

Amidst our laughter, a faint voice cuts through the delirium. James is still chuckling, and I glance at the bed to see Lorelei's eyes moving slowly between the two of us. She appears so delicate and yet so stunning that I have to raise my hand to my chest, attempting to soothe the ache that swells within.

"Seirína, you've come back to me," I say with a smile, my heart swelling with relief and happiness.

"Lorelei, you can't ever put me through that again!" James exclaims, his voice coming out louder than intended from his chair, and I hear a pained but relieved laugh escape from her.

"James? I'd know your loud voice anywhere, it's nice not hearing it blaring over the phone anymore. Next time I'm about to be kidnapped, I'll make sure to tell them you said no," she quips, her personality seemingly intact, despite the pain. She gently pats his hand, causing her to wince a little at the movement.

I pass by James's chair and lean in to whisper in his ear, "Arrange for someone to handle our little problem, please." I'll need that situation resolved before she can return home. He nods and stands, but before he leaves, he looks down at Lorelei.

"A lot of people would have been very sad if we lost you," James says sincerely, but he doesn't press her to respond. With that, he exits the room.

Lorelei looks around, trying to make sense of her surroundings. Waking up in a strange place can be disorienting, and I want to help her acclimate.

"You're in a safe place," I assure her. "A friend of mine, a highly skilled surgeon, patched you up. I did ask him to make you a little less argumentative, but I doubt that particular request stuck," I add, attempting to inject some humor into the conversation to put her at ease. However, I know the time has come to address the question that has lingered in the air for hours.

More than anything, I long to embrace her tightly, to hold her close until the worries in her eyes disappear, but I know that such a gesture would risk Carver's wrath and undo his painstaking work.

"Would you like to tell me what happened?" I ask gently. I don't want to pressure her; I understand that this is her story to share, and she will determine how much she's willing to reveal.

She looks at me with hesitation. "You should sit down," is all she says. I take James's vacated seat and wait giving her the space and time she needs.

CHAPTER 24

"I sold my soul to my disguise
I hid myself to stay alive"
-Motionless In White

Lorelei

I'm in a lot of pain, but it's not as excruciating as before. They must have given me some pain medication. Still, my head feels like it's filled with a dense fog, and I'm struggling to comprehend it all. Both my parents are gone.

I glance over at Damien, who's sitting in the chair next to my bed. He looks so handsome, casually dressed in sweatpants and a shirt, his hair concealed under a black baseball cap. A dark scruff lines his perfectly chiseled jaw. I cherish these moments when I get to see him like this; it feels like I'm witnessing a side of him that he usually keeps hidden from the world, as they only see the polished version. It's like a secret that only we share.

"What do the cops know?" I manage to croak, my tongue feeling like sandpaper in my dry mouth.

He gazes at me, his hands resting in his lap, before responding, "The police are clueless. James has been monitoring all incoming calls about a building fire being reported. By the time anyone arrives, all the evidence will have been incinerated. Judging by what the soldiers reported, it will likely appear as a botched kidnapping." His eyes reflect weariness, clearly assessing my reaction.

I can't believe he's covering up a murder for me. I'm pretty sure that's a felony. I'd be more alarmed about it if I hadn't witnessed him commit murder not too long ago.

There's no way around it; I need to tell him. Then it dawns on me, I don't have to share with him, but I have a genuine want to.

Nobody will ever learn the truth, that my dad was the villain in so many stories. With no family left to care, I will bear the burden of every gruesome detail. But this time, I'm not alone; Damien is here by my side.

"The scars on my body, like I mentioned before, are from my dad," I explain. His body tenses, and I can detect anger smoldering behind his eyes. "But there's more to the story. After our trip to Mexico, my mom confided in me. She revealed that the reason my dad abused me was because I'm not really his child. His half brother was my biological father, and he murdered him when he discovered that my mom was pregnant." I pause, scrutinizing his expression for any sign of hesitation, but he remains silent, patiently waiting to see if I want to continue.

"I was in my apartment when my dad attacked me and brought me to that warehouse. I woke up, and my mom was there with us. He ended up shooting her right in front of me. I knew I was going to die if I didn't find a way to kill him. I managed to get a hold of his knife, and I did just that. Slowly. I sat there and watched the life drain from his body. And, for the first time in my life, I think I found a moment of peace."

I hadn't planned to reveal that last part, but it's the truth. If he found it unusual, then so be it.

"We thought the D'Santos had taken you," he replies, his gruff voice laced with fear, causing a painful twinge in my chest.

"Is that why you were there with an army?" I tried to say this with a smile to lighten the mood, but his face remains somber.

"I was prepared to ignite the world and walk through fire to get you back. I would have sacrificed everything to get to you. But you didn't need me to wage a war for you. You needed someone to stand by your side in this battle."

He says this with unwavering determination, as though he has just uncovered the missing piece of the world's most perplexing puzzle. Leaning forward in his chair, there are only inches between us. He has stayed within a few feet of me ever since he arrived, as if he fears letting me out of his sight.

I wait for him to break the silence, but he remains still. "What's going on in your mind, D?" I'm almost afraid to hear the answer.

"I'm not entirely sure, which, I must admit, is a first for me," he responds.

I realize that he needs some time to process everything. Walking into a situation like that must have been quite a shock. "Dad mentioned that he followed someone to locate me. Have you heard anything about that?"

Damien's lips curl into a knowing smile, as if he's privy to a secret I'm not aware of.

"Yes, it appears that Liam couldn't accept your rejection. James caught him tailing you. I arrived at your apartment when I discovered you were missing and found him there. He confessed to stalking you."

I can't help but wonder, "How did I not realize he was stalking me? He isn't particularly smart." Damien lets out a small chuckle in response.

"You're not wrong there. I've got James taking care of the

cleanup at your apartment," Damien explains.

Unfazed by the possibility, I inquire, "Did you... kill him?"

Damien shakes his head. "No, but I might have left him tied up there and completely forgotten about him in the haste to reach you."

I can't help but burst into laughter at the mental image of Liam, abandoned and bound in my apartment.

A tall man in scrubs strides into the room, and Damien rises to greet him. Their interaction suggests a long-standing familiarity, evident in the warmth exchanged through their eyes.

"Hi, Lorelei. I'm delighted to see you're awake. I'm Dr. Carver, but you can just call me Carver." He offers a warm, inviting smile, and I can't help but notice his striking handsomeness. He runs a hand through his almost black, slightly curly hair, giving it a purposefully disheveled but attractive look. There's a hint of something dark lingering in his gray eyes, a depth that speaks of experiences shared with people like me and Damien, a world hidden from the unaware.

"Okay, stop staring," Damien says from his corner, prompting Carver to release a deep laugh.

"Put your dick away, Ashford; no need to mark your territory," Carver quips amid his laughter, giving Damien a friendly pat on the shoulder. Carver then approaches me to check my vital signs and inspect my bandages. His hands, though calloused and warm, don't elicit the same flutter I experience when Damien touches me, despite Carver's undeniably good looks.

"You're healing well, but I can tell you've endured a lot of pain in the past," Carver remarks, casting me a knowing glance. He must have noticed many of my scars while working on me. "There's a room full of people eager to see you. Would you like to see them?"

Perplexed, I turn to Damien. "Who would be here to see me?" I ask, clearly bewildered.

"The soldiers who accompanied me have been waiting to make sure you're okay," Damien explains. His explanation tugs at my heartstrings, I've never had anyone beyond Bex show genuine concern for my well-being.

"I'd like to tell them thank you," I reply, struggling to keep my voice from breaking. It's been a long time since I've felt such intense, unfiltered emotion, but with my father gone, it seems like all the emotions I've kept buried for years are right at the surface. "Does Bex know?"

"I thought you should be the one to decide if you want her to know. I'll have the team come in so they can see for themselves that you're okay and finally leave me in peace and go home," Damien offers.

As Damien leaves the room to gather everyone, I find myself alone with Carver. Speaking with a warm smile and a wink he says "You know, Lorelei, I've never seen Damien quite like this with anyone. He cares deeply for his team, but I've never seen him this intense. You might have changed the man."

He continues, "I'm going to discharge you into his care to complete your recovery. You'll be on an oral antibiotic, and I'll want to see you every week to check your wounds. I'll also send you home with some pain medication for the first few days. Normally, I wouldn't release a patient so soon, but Damien is more than capable of handling this." As he finishes, Carver places a reassuring hand on my shoulder and looks at me with a deeper understanding. "He needs someone strong like you," he adds before exiting the room, just as Damien returns with a procession of people in tow.

A dozen pairs of eyes fixate on me, and I'm not quite sure

how to express my gratitude or explain the recent events. Any words I muster feel insufficient, but I try, nonetheless.

"Thank you all for being willing to risk your lives to come and rescue me," I begin. "I know you believed it was the D'Santos who took me, which meant you were ready to step into a war to bring me back. I'm forever grateful for that."

From the back, a voice chimes in, "We'd go to war for Damien and his woman, no question. We're a family, he would do the same for us." The entire group nods in unanimous agreement, one after another, and it's at that moment a single tear escapes my eye without my consent. "Family," I think to myself, reflecting on what little I truly know about it.

As the others begin to exit the room, offering me reassuring smiles, one soldier remains behind. She's a petite woman, smaller than me, with striking auburn hair pulled back into a tight bun. Her porcelain skin is adorned with a constellation of freckles, but it's her clear blue eyes that truly capture my attention, almost resembling glass.

"I admire your strength," she acknowledges. "Most people, even trained soldiers, wouldn't have been able to fight their way out of that." She nods respectfully in my direction, and without waiting for a response, she swiftly pivots on her heel and exits the room.

"Sorry about them," Damien says, looking somewhat tentative as he slides his hands into the pockets of his sweatpants. "They can be a bit overwhelming. War changes people, and we form some deep bonds as a unit."

Curious, I inquire, "Is everyone who works for you this loyal?"

Damien nods. "Yes, every person I employ has made a commitment to uphold the objectives of AMG. But it's more than just AMG; we're like a family beyond this organization. I'd trust every single one of them with my life."

"I understand now, why you lied to protect them," I say, finally comprehending his actions. I can't hold it against him any longer. Witnessing the loyalty and support that his team has, makes my chest ache.

Changing the subject to something less emotional, I mention, "Carver said I can go home."

Damien nods, his eyes holding a hint of hope. "Yeah, I talked to him in the hallway. I'd like to see if you're comfortable coming to my house while you heal."

The idea of being at Damien's house raises a myriad of questions in my mind, but before I can process them all, a simple "okay" escapes my lips.

CHAPTER 25

"Nothin' around, far as I could see
You were the current that carried me"
- A Day To Remember/ Marshmello

Lorelei

Damien's house turns out to be beautiful, and the industrial design surprisingly creates a cozy atmosphere. He had a whole room prepared for me even before bringing me here, stocked with clothes suitable for wearing over my bandages and all the essentials I might need. It becomes evident that he's one of the most thoughtful individuals I've ever encountered.

In the spacious room, he sets up a desk in one corner, allowing him to work while keeping a watchful eye on me. Most of my time is spent sleeping as I continue to recover. A few days have passed since I was released, and Carver stops by to check on my healing progress, which is met with satisfaction. I appreciate Carver's visits because they offer a glimpse of a different side of Damien—one filled with jokes, teasing, and shared stories from their time in the military together. It's heartening to see them reminisce and bond in this way.

I look at Damien with a sense of determination. "Would you mind if Bex came over?" I ask. "There are things I need to tell her." Damien had already informed Bex that I was in a car accident and would be temporarily out of work, leaving her in charge. But I realize it's time to reveal the truth—I don't want to keep my past hidden away anymore. I have an opportunity for genuine freedom, and I'm determined not to let it slip away this time.

"You don't need to ask, seirína, this is just as much your home," Damien reassures me. "Home." The word lingers in my mind, an enigma. Strangely, this place already feels more like home than my apartment ever did, and I can't quite fathom what that means. Until now, my apartment had been the closest thing to a home I'd ever known. But what if home isn't merely a place?

Damien adds with a playful wink, "I've already texted Bex and given her the address. She'll be here in a few. Let's get you cleaned up so you don't scare her."

I respond with a feigned indignation, "Are you saying I stink?!"

As Damien chuckles, his smile radiates warmth and extends to his eyes, his mesmerizing dimple appearing. He's utterly captivating. These past few days, I've witnessed a different side of him, one far removed from the business-focused Damien. He's been the disheveled, casually dressed, and intimate Damien, and this version of him is just as perfect as any other I've seen.

He briefly leaves the room, returning with a few damp washcloths to gently clean my skin like he's done multiple times now. With the numerous bandages and Carver's recommendations, getting up and showering has been challenging. This act of care and intimacy is something I've never experienced before. It momentarily takes me back to thoughts of my mother, and how I always wished she would care for me in the aftermath of my father's actions. But I swiftly banish those thoughts from my mind, not ready to confront thoughts of them yet.

After he's finished cleaning my skin, Damien retrieves a brush from the nightstand and tenderly untangles my brown hair. His fingers move with expertise and steadiness, and something inside me tugs at my heart. When he finishes brushing out the tangles, his fingers continue to work, pulling my hair back into a ponytail.

Without turning to look at him, I finally release the last thing I've been holding onto, "I love you, D." I don't feel the need to be embarrassed about admitting this to a man with whom I'm not officially in a relationship. I don't require labels. All I need is to trust my instincts, and my gut is telling me that it's time to pursue everything I want. I've spent so long denying myself happiness, but I can't let this opportunity slip through my fingers. I'm certain I'll never find another man like him.

Damien's fingers freeze, still entangled in my hair, as my declaration hangs in the air. Before he can respond, Bex bursts through the door of my room, evidently letting herself into Damien's house.

"Lorelei, oh my God, are you okay?" Bex exclaims, rushing over to me. Her eyes scan me from head to toe, then land on Damien, who is still frozen with my hair in his hand.

Turning to Damien, she asks, "Do you need help?" Her question finally snaps him out of his stupor, and he silently finishes wrapping the band around my hair, tying it back.

Once Damien has finished with my hair, he retrieves his laptop from the desk. "I'll leave you ladies to catch up," he remarks, shooting me a knowing look that speaks volumes without the need for words. This man, I realize, is my future, whether he fully comprehends it himself yet or not. I'm taking control of my life, beginning with him. I won't be able to change overnight, but bit by bit, I'm determined to claim everything I desire in this life.

It's undeniably true. I love Damien. No one has ever cared for me the way he has. He's my safety, my darkness, and my home.

I think I knew this even in Mexico. He saw every dark corner of my soul, yet nothing in his eyes ever changed when he looked at me.

"I owe you a very big explanation," I admit to Bex. She doesn't press me; instead, she waits patiently for me to gather the courage.

Over the next hour or so, I pour out my life story to her. I reveal my past and the truth about what transpired in the warehouse, holding nothing back. The only details I omit concern AMG and the D'Santos. Damien has entrusted me with this information, and it would have to be his decision if she were to know. I also don't want to jeopardize the case until he's prepared to make his final move. However, I have faith that he will help me keep my staff safe.

After I've finished sharing my story, Bex sits in silence for a moment, gazing at me. "I'm glad you killed him. If you didn't, I would have," she remarks with a hint of steel in her voice. "And I can't believe he showed up to rescue you. That's something out of a fairytale. A really messed up one." I had left out the part about him bringing an army to rescue me, but she seemed to grasp the general idea.

"I love him, Bex," I admit to her without any sense of shame.

Bex's words catch me off guard. "Well, of course you do, you idiot. That man looks at you like you hung the stars in the sky just for him." Her description strikes me as intense, but she seems to sense my doubts. She continues, "I've seen it since you first met at the club. It's undeniable. If there's anyone out there who gets you, it's him."

She's right. We continue talking for the next few hours, and before I know it, we're both asleep on my bed. I feel the comforting weight of a blanket being draped across us. Though I'm too drowsy from the painkillers to respond, I'm aware that it's Damien, still caring for me even when he thinks I don't know.

CHAPTER 26

"Bring her back or take me with her"
-Pierce The Veil

Damien

She loves me. Can that be right? In the days since she shared her feelings with me, I've kept my distance, trying to give her space while remaining close enough to check on her. It's not that I don't share the same feelings, but she's been through a tremendous trauma, and I want her to be absolutely certain about what she is feeling. Carver visits regularly to monitor her progress, and he's reassured me that she's healing remarkably fast.

Originally, the arrangement was for me to accompany her to Carver's office for these check-ups, but it seems he has developed a particular fondness for her. I can't blame him. Carver possesses a sharp wit that most can't match, but he doesn't stand a chance against my seirína.

"Carver," I say as we stand in the foyer, "she seems to be getting around the house uh.. well and staying active. Are her physical restrictions still in place?" I try to mask my true intentions, but Carver, being as astute as ever, sees right through my facade. It's the unfortunate reality of the bonds forged in war - you can't deceive each other, no matter how hard you try.

He chuckles, clearly seeing through my act. "She's doing well for most activities, but we should avoid anything that might risk reopening her wounds. So, no running or heavy lifting, but gentle movements should be just fine," he says with a knowing smile, holding back a laugh.

"Fuck you Carver." With that, he lets out a deep laugh that echoes through the house and strolls out the front door. I can't help but think that one day, a woman will come into his life who will completely sweep him off his feet, and I hope I'm there to witness it.

When I return to the living room, Lorelei is sitting there, engrossed in a movie. She looks up and asks, "What made him laugh so hard?"

"Nothing," I reply nervously. It's astonishing how a woman who has me completely captivated can make me feel so uneasy. She has me firmly under her spell, and I wouldn't have it any other way.

I take a seat next to her on the spacious couch. She's dressed in one of the matching sweat outfits I got her, designed for easy on-and-off with her bandages. Wrapped up in a cozy blanket, the contrast between her soft surroundings and her sharp features makes her appear like a dark angel sent from the depths of hell, meant only for me.

As I stare at her, my heart tightens in my chest. She reaches for the remote and pauses her movie, ensuring no sound interrupts our conversation. "Carver says in the next couple of days, I'll be okay to go back home," she mentions, her eyes nervously flicking to the floor and then back to me. "Are you okay, D?"

"You're not going anywhere," I declare firmly.

She responds, "Well, at some point, I have to go back to my apartment so you can have your home back."

"It's not my home without you in it, Lorelei," I say, and her eyes flash with surprise. I wish I could capture that look and hold onto it forever.

"What?" She asks breathlessly.

"I love you, seirína. You're mine, and I'll never let you out of my sight again," I confess, though my planned speech has utterly deserted me. I should have told her this days ago, but I wanted her to have that time with Bex, and I knew that once I opened up, I wouldn't be able to contain myself.

"It took you long enough," she says with a mischievous smile.

I release a deep, heartfelt laugh, and I swear I love her even more in that moment. "I warned you from the start, I'm not a good man. There's something dark inside me that won't ever leave. You can't fix me. I don't want you to think you can mend what's broken in me, but you don't have a choice – you're mine, and I refuse to accept 'no' as an answer."

She slowly scoots closer, climbing into my lap, and there's no wince of pain when she moves. I'm grateful to see how well she's healing.

"I don't want to fix you, D. I want every broken shard and sharp edge of you," she murmurs. "You saw me soaked in the blood of my abuser and didn't flinch. That's the version of you I want. Someone who sees my darkness and can match it. Someone who can walk through hell with me and watch everyone else cower."

At that moment, I hold her close, knowing that we're bound by something far deeper and more profound than either of us had ever imagined.

She knows she's made for me. Her bright eyes search mine, and I'm not sure what she's looking for, but I can't resist the urge to kiss her.

My kiss isn't gentle; it's intense and consuming. I want to imprint myself on her, make sure she can never leave me or want anyone else.

Her hands grip my hair tightly as if she can't get me close enough. I remind myself to be careful not to hurt her wounds, but my self-control is slipping rapidly. As if she can read my thoughts, she pulls away from my mouth and locks eyes with me.

"Please, D. You won't hurt me," she whispers, and a growl escapes my lips as my only response. I wrap my arms around her, lifting us up from the couch, and carry her up to my room. All the while, she runs her hands across my body and kisses every inch of my skin she can find.

In my room, I gently lay her on the bed, and I find myself utterly captivated by the woman before me. With unwavering eye contact, she lifts herself up and slowly sheds her shorts followed by her shirt, revealing that she's not wearing a bra underneath. Despite the healing bruises and the bandages covering her stitches, none of it diminishes her raw and unfiltered beauty. It only adds to her allure.

Anger surges within me at the reminder that someone had harmed her, but I don't have time to dwell on it because she hooks her thumbs under her waistband and pulls off her underwear leaving her completely bare in front of me.

She's always been confident, but it's as if her wounds have given her even more self-assurance, and I can't help but adore her for it. My fierce little warrior wears her marks with pride.

I hastily strip off my clothes, and I hear her sharply inhale at the sight.

“What’s wrong pretty girl?” I ask her as I grip the base of my cock and stroke it a few times. It dawns on me that despite our previous encounters in Mexico, this is the first time we've truly been together like this.

"I just - fuck you're perfect" she says

Lorelei

He's more perfect than I could have ever imagined. This dark god stands at the foot of his bed, gazing at me with nothing but love and desire in his eyes. And, holy shit, he's huge. I've had my fair share of experiences, but this is on a whole other level, which is a bit intimidating, especially considering it's been months since the last time I was with someone.

He approaches me like a beast who's just found his next prey, and my stomach tightens with anticipation. "I've been told I still need to be gentle with you, but you're testing my self-control," he growls, hovering over my body, being careful not to touch any of my bandages.

Knowing he would be cautious about my wounds, I can't restrain myself any longer. I need him now.

Without giving him a chance to think, I grasp his broad shoulders and pull him down on top of me. His massive frame engulfs my smaller one, and we fit together flawlessly. I kiss him fervently, biting his lip until I taste the metallic tang of blood in my mouth. I use my tongue to swipe over the blood, groaning at the taste of him.

Another growl escapes him, and he murmurs, "Goddamn it, Lorelei."

"Stop being gentle with me. I want to see you lose all that fucking control you hold on to so tightly," I demand.

Without another word, he tears his mouth from mine and travels down my body until his mouth finds my clit, and he devours it just as he did my mouth a moment ago. The sudden sensation causes my back to arch off the bed, and a moan escapes my lips.

The moan motivates him and he licks me with no remorse, he places one hand on my stomach, ensuring it's away from any wounds, to hold me in place while the other hand dives into my pussy.

"That's my good girl, squeeze my fucking fingers."

I moan once more, fully aware that it won't take much for me to come undone under this man's skilled touch. He moves his fingers inside me, curling his fingers to hit the perfect spot, and when he sees my reaction, he presses down on me, increasing the pace of his fingers while his tongue explores every inch of me.

When the orgasm hits my body arches off the bed, and I cry out for him. He continues to lick me through it, then returns to my mouth, allowing me to taste us mixed together on his tongue. "Such a good girl, coming apart on my tongue. Now, lay back I want more." he commands.

I press my hips against his in response to his words, and I feel his hand slide between our bodies as he reaches for his cock.

"You're mine, Lorelei. Do you understand that? You'll never be taken from me again," he utters, his words sounding more like self-assurance than a question directed at me.

"I won't be able to control myself once I'm inside you," he admits, his eyes seeking approval in mine. Without the need for words, he slides into me with an intense thrust.

I inhale sharply, and he remains inside me, unmoving, allowing me to adjust to his size.

"Fuck, you feel better than I could have ever imagined. You're going to make me embarrass myself with how tight you are." His voice quivers as I gently move my hips, signaling to him that I'm comfortable and ready for more.

“Please fuck me, D. Don’t hold back, show me every dark part of you.”

My words seem to ignite him, prompting him to withdraw and thrust back into me with intense force, setting a relentless pace. Despite my lingering soreness, I consider taking control, but his overpowering thrusts make it clear that he's in command, and I wouldn't have the strength to overtake him even if I were at full capacity.

I can feel another orgasm coiling deep in my stomach and before I know it I am clenching around his cock riding out the pure bliss. He pounds into me harder and I hear him utter “say my name.”

“Damien” I yell out as I ride through the orgasm.

“Again” He emits a guttural growl as he pounds into me with even greater intensity. His strong hand encircles the base of my neck while the other firmly grasps my hip.

"Damien!" I scream, taken by surprise as another orgasm washes over me, causing me to clench tightly around him while I cry out his name. I've never experienced multiple orgasms with a man before, always having to put in the effort myself. Experiencing three at his skilled touch is beyond anything I've ever known.

His control shatters as he releases inside me, and any semblance of rational thought I had disappears as he growls possessively in my ear, declaring me as his.

As we both come down from the intense high, he shifts to his side and draws me close, enveloping my body with his. After a brief silence, I tentatively mention, "I should clean up; your cum is running down my thighs."

His arms tighten around me, but then he gently releases me to glance at where I'm dripping. With a possessive grin he uses two fingers to push any escaping cum back inside me. I shudder and blossom under his dominance.

"Good. I plan to fill you so full with cum that anyone who comes near you will know you're mine."

This man's dirty mouth sends shivers down my spine, driving my desire to new heights. After he gets up and heads into his bathroom, he returns a few moments later, now wearing clean black boxers and holding a washcloth.

Kneeling on the bed, he gently spreads my legs and starts the tender task of cleaning me up. His care extends to inspecting my bandages to ensure none of them have come undone due to our roughness. Satisfied that all is well, he retreats to the bathroom to dispose of the used washcloth.

He returns with a large black shirt, gently pulling me up just enough to slide it over my head and down my body. I'm engulfed in his oversized clothing, and the subtle, comforting scent of him lingers on the shirt, making me snuggle into it.

Once he's assured that I'm taken care of, he climbs back onto the bed with me, positioning our bodies perfectly next to each other. Satisfied and content, we both drift off to sleep, wrapped in each other's embrace, as if we were meant to be together. Two imperfect and damaged souls, fitting together like the missing pieces of a twisted puzzle.

CHAPTER 27

"Keep me close, keep me close
Keep my head above water"
-Memphis May Fire

Lorelei

Days have been passing by while we cocoon ourselves within the walls of Damien's house. We've skirted around discussions regarding our future, but this morning, a box truck arrived, bearing the contents of my apartment.

Strangely, I expected to feel a sense of loss at parting with the apartment that had been my sanctuary for so long. Yet, nothing has ever felt as right as it does here with Damien. My apartment no longer carries the same sense of security, tainted by the haunting memories of the recent attack. My future is intertwined with him now.

The morning after our first night together, I awoke to find all my belongings had been moved into his room. It's evident that despite our lack of communication surrounding the matter, he's just as committed to this as I am.

I've talked with Bex everyday since her visit, and she's been handling Sin's affairs like a rockstar, just as I knew she would. While the reality of real life tugs at me, I'm relishing this well-deserved break for the time being.

During our daily phone call, Bex raises an important point. "I emailed the D'Santos to brief them on your accident and my temporary management of Sin, but they haven't responded. Is that normal?"

I take a moment to ponder this. "They weren't exactly known for being overly communicative, but it does strike me as unusual that they haven't acknowledged my absence." I make a mental note to inform Damien about this when I return downstairs. We can't afford to be complacent when it concerns Sin and all its intricacies.

"I know you love your work, but everything seems to be going smoothly here. I think you need more time off," Bex suggests.

Her words resonate with me, and I've been mulling over another matter as well. Despite all that's transpired, we still have to resolve the D'Santos issue. While Damien and James have been diligently working on finalizing the portfolio to send to the DEA, I've been somewhat out of the loop. My personal struggles have consumed me, causing me to overlook the broader implications for my team.

My recovery is progressing well, and Carver's visits have become less frequent. I respond, "You're right. I may need another week or two, but I'll be back soon, as long as you're not feeling overwhelmed."

"Of course not, everything is fine here," Bex reassures me, and her confidence brings me a sense of contentment. I can't help but feel that I've been holding her back by having her work as a bartender. She's capable of so much more, and I'm determined to find a way to make that happen for her.

"I appreciate you, Bex. I know I never said it before, but I do." I genuinely mean it. I'm making an effort to be more open with my feelings towards the people I care about. With my abuser no longer a part of my life, there's nothing holding me back from living the life I fought for. I may still carry scars from the darkness, but the least I can do is express my gratitude when it's deserved.

Bex ends the call with a promise, "I'll swing by in a few days for a movie night. Text me what snacks you want me to bring. I've got to run." She hangs up before I can argue, leaving me with a smile.

The recovery journey has led to me sleeping more, so I quietly leave Damien's - my - bed and slip my feet into the warm, black slippers he had considerately provided for me. Quietly, I make my way downstairs in search of him. There he is, standing in the kitchen, shirtless, with his computer perched on the counter next to the stove where he's diligently cooking. His focus is so absorbed in what he's reading that I think I can sneak up on him. But before I can even reach him, he swiftly spins around, gently grabbing my waist and pulling me close to his strong, muscled chest.

"Don't you know not to sneak up on a man while he's cooking, seirína?" he teases.

My mouth waters at the delicious aroma wafting from his cooking. "What are you making?" I inquire, my hunger intensifying.

"Just some pasta. You need to eat so you can take your afternoon medicine," he replies, his hand still resting on me as he uses his other hand to stir the sauce simmering on the stove. The sight of him tending to the meal is oddly alluring. I lick my lips, suddenly craving something far more than just food. But before I get lost in my desire, I need to ask him what's been on my mind.

"Why haven't you been talking to me about the case?" I ask, my voice muffled against his chest, unwilling to let go of him.

He inhales deeply and then brings his other hand to my waist, effectively enveloping me in his embrace.

"I almost lost you, and while I know it wasn't the D'Santos who took you, the thought of you being in harm's way is paralyzing. I've been working with James to bring this to a close as quietly as possible," he explains.

While I can appreciate his protective instincts, I've already faced and conquered my greatest fear. There's nothing left that frightens me now.

"I understand your desire to protect me, but I think you know I don't seek protection. I want to stand by your side, not be home on the sidelines," I assert, gaining confidence in speaking my truth even if it makes me appear vulnerable.

He leans down and plants a tender kiss on my forehead, his grip on me tightening with a hint of desperation. "Home?" he questions, and I instantly grasp the meaning. I haven't referred to this place as home, but that's exactly what it's become. I hold onto him as tightly as I can, understanding that sometimes, like me, he doesn't need words, just actions.

After a moment, he withdraws and refocuses on the sauce simmering on the stove. "I won't keep you in the dark, but this need to protect you won't go away, Lor," he conveys.

I understand that protection is his innate instinct, and I won't ask him to change that. It's a comforting feeling to be shielded by someone for a change. Damien eventually completes the sauce, serving us two plates of the most tantalizing pasta. We settle down at the barstools and enjoy our meal in silence. I've always cherished the fact that he can be comfortably silent with me.

As I savor the delicious food, I can't help but think that home will be wherever he is.

Damien

"James, I think we're good. Go ahead and send everything over to our contact at the DEA. Once we get confirmation that they're taking action, we'll release it all on AMG," I instruct. It's crucial to inform Lorelei that things are about to heat up so she can give her staff a heads-up on the day I decide to make the information public. This will give them time to stay home and begin their job search, ensuring their safety and preventing the D'Santos from catching wind and attempting retaliation.

"Alright, boss. I'll have everything sent in by this afternoon, which means we'll be releasing the story within the next 48 hours. Something this big will make them react swiftly," James advises. He's correct; with all the evidence we've amassed, the truth is undeniable, and they won't be able to hide from it for long.

"Thanks, James," I reply before ending the call. I lean back in my desk chair, interlace my fingers behind my head, and finally take a deep breath. It's almost over. A smile spreads across my face as I close my laptop and stand up. I need to go find my girl.

I traverse through the house, and when I find her, she's standing before the bathroom mirror, gazing at herself in nothing but her underwear. I inhale sharply; she's always stunning. All her bandages are gone, and the stitches have been removed. What remains are only some faint discolorations from bruises and the healing scars. I lean against the doorframe and watch her, waiting for her to notice my presence beside her.

It appears she senses me now because she glances up, locking eyes with me in the mirror. Yet, what shocks me is the sadness I see in her gaze. I move closer and encircle my arms around her waist. She fits against me perfectly, and I'm convinced she was made for me, forged in fire and blood.

"What's wrong, seirína?" I whisper into her hair. She remains silent for a moment, continuing to stare at her reflection in the mirror.

"How can you love something so broken?" she asks, her voice barely above a whisper. Lately, she's been grappling with the emotions she has kept repressed for so long, and I'm proud of her for showing her vulnerability to me.

This brave woman standing before me believes she's too shattered to be loved. I bury my face in her hair, inhaling her scent before responding. Sometimes, just holding her reminds me that she's here and safe. I gently tilt up her chin, making her meet my gaze again in the mirror.

"You may think you're broken, but what I see is a masterpiece. When I look at you, I see an incredibly strong woman who fought her way through indescribable darkness and is somehow still standing. You're incredible, Lorelei. Your scars are beautiful, and when I look at them, I'm reminded of who you truly are inside. You're mine," I affirm.

As she presses her body back into mine, a deep, primal groan escapes my lips when I feel her rub her ass against my growing hardness. Every time I touch her, it just keeps getting better. She turns in my arms, capturing my lips in a fierce, consuming kiss, and I know she's heard the truth in my words.

With a commanding strength, I bend enough to seize two fistfuls of her thighs and hoist her up. Instinctively, she wraps her legs around my body. I keep one hand on her thigh and intertwine the other through her long, dark hair, gripping it firmly to ensure she can't pull away, holding her captive to my wicked desires.

I've had to be gentle with her for a while due to her healing, but now, I don't have to. I'm going to enjoy breaking her and putting her back together so her jagged little pieces only fit mine.

A soft sigh escapes her lips as I carry her over to the spacious bed in my room – our room. Fuck, I love the sound of that. I lay us down on the bed, positioning myself on top of her, ensuring she's completely caged in. She'll never leave me now; I'm determined to keep her close, even if it means crossing lines I never thought I would. This obsession might be fucked up, but I couldn't care less.

She squirms beneath me, yearning for the friction she desires, and that elicits a small, wicked smile from me. I'll give her everything she craves. I start by trailing kisses down her body, but the intensity grows, and my kisses transform into nips that cause her to arch her body off the bed. After each bite, I gently lick the area to alleviate some of the pain, making slow progress down her body.

Bite. Lick

Bite. Lick

Bite. Lick.

In one swift motion, I rip off her panties,and hear her gasp. I bite the inside of her thigh so close to her pussy that I can smell her. Whenever I'm near her, I'm driven by an insatiable hunger. I lean in and deliver a small bite to her clit, following it with another provocative lick. A loud, uninhibited moan escapes her, and once more, I find myself smiling. My seirína craves the exquisite blend of pleasure and pain, and I'm more than willing to oblige.

Unable to contain myself any longer, I delve into her with relentless desire. I fervently work her clit with my tongue and introduce a finger inside her, causing her to arch her back even further off the bed. She has her legs wrapped around my head, squeezing me like a vice, and the sensation is electric. It's a feeling I could savor for a lifetime.

Placing another delectable bite on her clit, she elicits a scream as she reaches the peak of her desire. She releases my head from between her legs, and I sit back on my haunches, gazing at her in the aftermath of her orgasmic bliss. I lick the remnants of her off my lips, savoring every drop, unwilling to let any go to waste.

Observing the red bite marks adorning her body, I'm satisfied by the sight of my marks on her skin, something fucked and twisted blooms in my chest. I'm determined to mark this beautiful specimen as mine, permanently. Swiftly, I reach to my nightstand, retrieving my blade and hovering over her as I flick it open. When I gaze into her eyes, they're gleaming with a mixture of excitement and anticipation.

"I'm going to mark you as mine forever, seirína. Even in my death, everyone will know who you belong to," I growl at her, fixating on the spot where I want to make my mark. She remains silent, her bright eyes locked onto mine.

I settle on a part of her thigh where plenty of other scars mark her lovely skin, and I lean in with my knife. The scars on her body may be a reminder of her past pain, but I'm determined to leave a bigger mark that signifies my love and ownership for every single one of them. She props herself up on her elbows to watch me, and there's no hint of hesitation in her eyes. I look down to the spot that I chose and dig my knife in enough to draw blood. With a steady hand I mark her delicate skin.

When I'm finished, I use my tongue to clean the blood, revealing the 'D' that's now etched into her skin. I lean back, allowing her to inspect my handiwork. Her eyes lock onto mine, and she offers me a show stopping smile.

She sits up and takes the blade from my hand, uttering a simple "lay down." I comply eagerly, shedding my clothes and resting on the pillow with my hands at my sides, granting her access to do as she pleases. Her eyes roam over my body as she decides where to mark me next.

She takes my large hand into her much smaller one, her eyes locked onto mine, and I can feel the heat radiating from her body as she straddles my hips. With the blade confidently gripped between her fingers, she hovers her hand over mine. Her dark hair spills around her face, so I use my free hand to hold it back, ensuring it won't obstruct her work. My self-control is waning rapidly, and I'm fully erect, tantalizingly close to her warmth.

The blade finally breaches my skin, and I can feel her carving her mark, but the pain seems secondary, especially when my attention is fixated on her. Once she's finished, she straightens herself and flashes me a smile. In blood and flesh, she's carved an 'S' right into the fleshy part of my palm. My seirína. What she may not realize is that I've been marked by her for much longer than I've even admitted to myself.

"You hold my heart in your hands now, D, every jagged piece of it," she declares, and her words hit me like a sledgehammer.

Unable to contain myself any longer, I seize the knife from her and swiftly roll us over so that I'm behind her, while she's on all fours, her pretty little ass in the air. Before she fully comprehends what's happening, I slide myself into her, and she gasps.

I hold still for just a moment, my hands gripping her waist with force, and as I slide my hands down her body, I see the trail of blood I've left behind from where she carved her mark into my skin. This sight drives me fucking wild.

When she's had the time to adjust she rocks her hips against mine, and I pull out and slam back into her with force. "Be careful what you're asking for, seirína, I'm hanging by a thread here."

She gives me a wicked smile over her slender shoulder and rocks her hips into mine harder. Fine. I slap her ass hard and she lets out a little yelp. I start a brutal rhythm and remember the blade in my hand. I reach around, and hold it to her throat and she stills beneath me for a moment then when she peaks over her shoulder again I see her eyes light up and she matches my pace. A small trickle of blood beads at her throat and I groan at the sight.

“I’m going to mark every inch of you as mine. I’ll erase every scar from before and cover your body with my own.’ I growl into her and I can feel the orgasm starting to build at the base of my spine. I use my other hand and reach between us to rub her clit.

“Come with me seirína.” A moan comes from her and she screams out my name so loud it echoes off the walls. While she screams I feel her squeeze around my dick. She throws her head back and yells again and she feels like a vice around me as she comes and it causes the orgasm to hit me violently. I bury myself to the hilt and come inside her. I wasn’t meant it when I said I would mark her every way possible.

"Are you okay?" I inquire gently, aware of my intensity and her ongoing healing process.

With a laugh, she responds, "Never been better." Before I can react, she slides out from beneath me and flips me onto my back.

"You always take care of me afterward. Now, it's my turn," she says with a tone that carries an elusive quality. Yet, the gleam in her eyes assures me that whatever she has in mind will destroy me.

She grabs my cock and starts to lick the length clean of both our orgasms and holy shit it’s the hottest thing I’ve ever seen in my life.

All too quickly another orgasm builds, I should be embarrassed about how quickly I reached this point, but can anyone truly fault me? I look down at this glorious woman when I see her already staring up at me, and that's all it takes for me to cum inside her pretty little mouth.

With confidence, she stands upright and eagerly consumes every last bit I had to offer.

I sit up and run my hands through her hair "such a good fucking girl not wasting a drop."

This cunning woman was going to be my undoing, and there isn't a trace of self-respect left in me to give a single fuck.

CHAPTER 28

"I know the pain that you hide behind the smile on your face"
-Bad Omens

Lorelei

It's been 24 hours since the information was sent to the DEA regarding the D'Santos, and AMG is scheduled to release the story on the news in the morning. There's a sick feeling churning in my gut when all I should feel is relief.

"You should call Bex. Since it's an off day, the other staff won't be there anyways, but you should to warn her," Damien says as we sit on the couch together. His thoughtfulness always surprises me; maybe one day, I'll grow accustomed to it.

"I texted her earlier and asked her to come over tonight so I can tell her, but I haven't heard back," I say. This is out of character for her because she always texts back right away, her phone practically glued to her hand. I've had this weird feeling hanging over my head since I sent the text. I pull out my phone and send a message to Kellan.

Me: Have you talked to Bex?

Kellan: She said she was going to your house today, is she not there?

She had mentioned she might stop by, but nothing was set in stone. Red flags are waving in front of my face, and I try not to let myself jump to a worst-case scenario.

Kellan: Lorelei she isn't answering.

I look at Damien and show him my phone. I can see his instincts kicking in, and if it wasn't for his brows pulling together in concern, I would think he was reading what we were going to eat for dinner later. He picks up his phone and sends off some messages. "I have some of my team heading to her house," he says.

Kellan: What is going on? I'm headed to your house. She told me where it was. Be there in ten.

Me: I'm not sure, I'll see you in a minute.

Minutes pass while we wait for news, and finally, I hear a frustrated "Fuck." I look to Damien beside me and wait for an explanation.

"James has eyes on Sin, and she's not there, but Anderson got to her place, and it's been torn apart, and she's not there," Damien explains. There's a knock on the door, and we both look towards the sound. It's Kellan.

I rush to the door and swing it open to see a disheveled Kellan standing there, looking scared. "It's not like her to disappear," he says. I look behind me to see Damien standing in the foyer, his arms crossed over his chest and his feet apart in an intimidating stance. There's a look of determination in his eyes, and I know his gut instinct is just as strong as mine.

I gesture for Kellan to come inside, and he does so slowly. He's so broken that he doesn't even look at his surroundings; he just stares blankly ahead. Damien and I guide him to the couch, and Kellan sits down. Damien and I share a look, silently deciding to fill him in on what's been happening and why his concern isn't unwarranted.

After some time, we've finished explaining everything about the club and the D'Santos. "So you're saying it's possible that a drug cartel has Bex?" Kellan asks.

"It's very likely," Damien replies. There's a lump in my throat, and I can't answer, so I'm grateful Damien stepped in for me.

Kellan's eyes plead with us, and it breaks my heart. He really cares about her. "How do we get her back? And why the hell are you just sitting here calmly?"

Damien responds for me again because I really don't know what the plan is. He smirks wickedly, and I see the darkness beneath his surface. "My team is already working on finding her and formulating an attack plan, which we will be acting on in the next hour once everything is in place. I'm confident we will find her quickly. That's what they want, to draw us out. The story will be released now on AMG rather than in the morning. I want the world to have eyes on them. The more ways we attack them, the better. From my knowledge, the DEA hasn't made moves yet, so let's force their hand."

Kellan stands from the couch. "I'm coming with," he says with determination.

"You can't; you'll only be a hindrance. If you aren't trained to fight or use weapons, I can't assign someone to babysit you," Damien says coldly. He's acting as a leader, prioritizing logic over emotion right now.

"Is Lorelei going?" Kellan asks, pointing a finger towards me.

"Yes," He replies. "She can fight and knows weapons rather thoroughly. I also know I have no way to stop her." My heart swells in my chest, knowing that he wouldn't ask me to stay behind, especially not for something so important. I can see that Damien isn't trying to belittle Kellan, only to keep him safe while also keeping Bex in mind. Our sole purpose is to get her back, and we can't risk Kellan in the process.

"If she's going, so am I, and you can't stop me," Kellan declares. He's so determined to get her back that I think he might find a way to help.

Without any further words, Damien stands from his sitting position and heads upstairs, with me following him, leaving Kellan to stay in the living room for a moment. Damien starts changing into his tactical clothes from the closet in the bedroom, and I don't speak, still trying to process all of this and get dressed in clothes that will be easy to fight in. I have no idea what we're walking into, but he's wise not to ask me to stay behind.

After we're dressed, Damien turns and grabs me by my shoulders, leaning down to look me in the eyes. "I don't like that you're coming. I will not sugarcoat that. But I respect you, and I understand you need to come. I will not apologize for any actions I take to keep you safe. I will kill anyone in my path, and it may change the way you see me." He lets me go and walks out of our room.

Quickly, I follow him, and when I get downstairs, I see our living room filled with people dressed in tactical clothes like Damien. Some of the faces are familiar, and I recognize them from when they came to rescue me.

I see James on the couch with his computer in his lap, typing away furiously, with Kellan perched next to him, watching intently.

"James, take us through everything," Damien bellows from the front, causing everyone to turn to James.

"Yes, sir. I believe we have a mole in the DEA. The only way the D'Santos could have known what was happening was if they had an inside man. I also have a tap on a lot of their devices, and after I sent in the portfolio, all of their devices started going crazy. One transmission I intercepted had to do with Lorelei's 'accident' and Bex stepping in to work for her at Sin. I believe they put the pieces together," James explains.

The tension in the room rises as we realize just how deep the betrayal goes.

The entire room falls into silence, and all eyes shift their attention to Damien. He stands there, a force of pure power, and I can see his jaw ticking with tension. He blames himself. His primary focus is always the safety of his people, and it's evident that he holds himself responsible for not thinking one step ahead in this regard. But he quickly schools his features and addresses his team.

"If they want war, I'm happy to oblige. Taking an innocent person makes this open season. Are you all ready to have some fun?" He grins darkly at his team, and they all wear similar looks.

"James, you have a list of all their local businesses and residents from our research?" he asks.

"Of course. I know everything they own," James replies.

"How many are we talking locally? And I mean the entire D'Santos family. I'm bringing this down on all of them," Damien demands.

"About a dozen here," James responds.

"Perfect. Call in some backup. Break into your normal teams. James, send coordinates to each team with one to two locations. You guys know the rest," Damien orders.

Kellan jumps to his feet. "What does that mean?" he yells, looking between everyone. Damien nods to his team, and they all scatter to get to work.

"What this means, Kellan, is each team will scope out the buildings they are assigned. Once we know Bex isn't there, the building will be blown up. I need you here with James as a line from my team to him. He is our communication hub, and this mission is too big for him to handle alone. What we're doing is drawing them out and eliminating places Bex could be," Damien explains.

I look at Damien and admire how he can remain so logical about the situation, while also handling Kellan with care and keeping his safety in mind. He's a natural leader. Kellan looks at me with reluctance, and I give him a small, reassuring smile. He nods and sits with James, ready to be instructed on how to help.

Damien walks over to me and says, "Ready?"

"Where are we headed?" I ask.

"We are assigned to Sin," he grins and takes my hand, leading me to the garage where his car is waiting. Before we get in, he goes to the gray cabinets lining the walls. When he opens a door, I notice it's actually a huge safe. He gathers a big bag and tucks it in the back seat of his car, then goes back to the safe and straps some weapons to himself before turning to me.

“How well can you handle a gun? I know blades are covered, and right now I'm regretting not taking you to the range,” he inquires.

“I have my concealed carry permit," I respond with confidence. He grins in approval and secures two handguns to my waist, then returns with something in his hands. He lowers himself to his knees in front of me and fastens something to my thigh.

When he stands back up, I glance down and notice a holster containing two sheathed knives. I meet his gaze, and he grins before nodding toward the car. He's never looked more attractive than when he's decked out in tactical gear, armed and ready for action. Despite my apprehension about the impending battle, I'm reassured by the fact that we're both prepared to sacrifice for one another. He's mobilizing his team to rescue my friend.

We speed through the streets to Sin, silently staking out the building. It's a weekday, so there's nobody around. Kellan had informed us that, according to security footage from both inside and outside, the place is indeed empty. We refrain from inquiring about the others, focusing on our immediate task.

"Kellan, have James cut the power to this block," Damien instructs from the driver's seat.

I'm left wondering how in the world they're capable of cutting power to an entire block. Before I can voice my question, the block plunges into darkness. If I weren't so worried about Bex, I might have found it amusing. Damien hangs up without another word.

"Ready, seirína?" he asks.

"Ready, D," I confirm, though I can tell he's somewhat hesitant about having me here. We exit the car, and I notice he's already holding his bag. With the block covered in darkness and residents in a panic, we manage to sneak around the building without drawing attention. Every few fee Damien attaches something to the building's exterior, all of which is well beyond my knowledge. I keep a watchful eye to ensure no one sneaks up on us while he works his magic.

After we complete our circuit around the building, he straightens and grabs my hand, leading me back to the car.

"That's it?" I inquire, incredulous.

He lets out a deep laugh as we settle into the car, and I stare at him in disbelief.

"Would you like to do the honors?" he asks, extending a small device with a few buttons.

"What about the surrounding businesses?" I ask, concerned about collateral damage.

"The explosives we use are designed to contain the explosion," Damien explains. "Any subsequent fires will be extinguished by the fire department, which James is ready to call the moment the blast is triggered. The buildings are spaced far enough apart that it would take a while for any fire to spread to them."

He really has thought of every detail. Before I can talk myself out of it, I press the button. A deafening blast reverberates through the air, shaking the car. Flames start to lick up the building, and within a minute, I hear the familiar sound of sirens. Damien maneuvers the car back to the street, and I watch as the building grows smaller in the rearview mirror, and the lights on the block flicker back to life. On our way home, multiple firetrucks rush past us toward the explosion site.

I just blew up a building. A smile pulls across my lips.

When we return to the house, almost all of the teams have reported back as well. However, they don't come back here; they're all on standby for further instructions, positioned around town. James and Kellan are working seamlessly side by side, tracking news stories about the explosions in the surrounding areas and monitoring all of the D'Santos devices that we have tapped.

"They're all communicating, just waiting for any omission of coordinates or signs of life," James informs us from the couch.

"Now we wait," Damien says, and we all sit there, watching everything unfold.

CHAPTER 29

"We're way too young to be feelin' this hopeless"
-A Day To Remember and Marshmello

Bex

I'm trembling so violently that it's causing the chains above my head to rattle. I can't recall much about how I ended up in this terrifying place. What could anyone possibly want with me? I've led a quiet, unassuming life and always aimed to be kind to everyone I met. Yet here I am, bound in a small, dark room, my mind racing through every worst-case scenario imaginable.

The stench in this place is unbearable, but more than anything, my entire body aches. These heavy chains have me suspended from the rafters, and it feels like an eternity, even though I'm pretty sure it's only been a matter of hours. The cold gnaws at my skin, and all I long for is to return home.

Maybe they've mistaken me for someone else. It must be a mix-up. I'm just an average person with an unremarkable face; this has to be a simple mistake.

"Hello?" I call out, my voice cracking. I'm doing my best not to cry; no matter what happens, I don't want anyone to see how scared I truly am. I've watched numerous documentaries on serial killers, and I know that some of them derive pleasure from the pain they inflict. So, I refuse to give them that satisfaction.

I hear a door open from behind me. I'm in a tiny, featureless room, facing a blank wall made of stained concrete. There's nothing in the room but me, no windows, no way to escape.

"Hello, Bex," an accented voice says from behind me. "We haven't had the chance to meet. I'm Carlos D'Santos."

No way. A sob escapes me, but I do my best to hold back any tears.

"Mr. D'Santos, I think you have the wrong person. I don't understand what's happening," I say, my voice filled with desperation, hoping that he has some semblance of humanity in him.

"You don't need to know the details, but I appreciate your email that Lorelei was involved in an 'accident.' It prompted me to dig a little deeper into her activities and I discovered she has been poking her nose where it doesn't belong. She was tougher to capture than you, especially now that she has a live-in babysitter. Therefore, you're going to be my bargaining chip. I'll ensure your survival, at least for the time being, but that's the only assurance I can give."

He circles so I can see him out of my peripheral, but doesn't come closer.

"You see, I have a vested interest in your cooperation. Your safety hinges on how valuable you can be to me. So, let's discuss what you can offer, and perhaps we can work out an arrangement that benefits both of us. But remember, time is of the essence, and the clock is ticking."

I don't understand anything he's saying, and I have a sinking feeling he won't be providing any further explanations. I'm left with even more questions than I had before he walked into this room.

"Fine, have it your way," he says.

I hear his footsteps retreating, and panic begins to well up inside me. The thought of being left alone in this confined space for who knows how long sends shivers down my spine. My mind races as I try to formulate a plan to ensure my safety and gather any information that might aid me in gaining my freedom.

"No, no, please don't leave me here!" I scream after him. "Please, I don't know anything. Please, let me go!"

"Don't worry, Bex, I won't leave you alone," he laughs and then shuts the door.

Alone?

A minute later, the door creaks open, and I freeze, straining to hear anything I can. Why would he be back so soon?

I can hear more than one set of footsteps, but it's difficult to make out details. There's just one dim light in the room, and it's located near the door. I'm trembling, drenched in sweat from fear. I imagine Lorelei would be strong right now.

A hand reaches up and touches my face, lingering on my cheek for a moment, sending shivers down my spine.

"Don't worry, chica, we'll be nice. Won't we, hermano?" the heavily accented voice says, and I choke down a sob, realizing that I have no control over the situation.

"P-please, I haven't done anything to hurt anyone. Please, just let me go home. I won't tell anyone!" I beg, my voice trembling.

I hear laughter coming from each side of me, but they remain out of my line of sight, and the chains restrict my movement. "I want your tears, so go on and let me have them," one of them says, and I feel their hands on my body, causing bile to rise in my throat. This is all so wrong; every fiber of my being screams for me to escape, but I can't. I was never prepared for something like this. I thought kidnappings only happened in movies and books.

"But first, how about we all have a little fun?" comes from the second voice, and before I can understand what they mean, one of my nostrils is pinched closed, and something is forced up the other. "Breathe through your nose, now."

I shake my head, trying to get whatever it is away from me, but a fist connects with my cheek, and pain shoots through me. "Do not defy us, or it will only make things worse," the laughing voice warns. I shake my head in response, and another blow lands on my face. The hand that strikes me has a tattoo, but I can't quite make out the design. I need a better visual of it in case I manage to escape.

I've never been hit in my life, and I have no idea how much of this I can endure. I grew up sheltered and quiet, never engaging in fights, not even in grade school. I've always approached the world with kindness, so this is all foreign to me.

I can't help but wonder if anyone even knows that I'm missing.

My nostril is pinched closed again, and this time, I obey, fearing how many blows I can take before losing consciousness. "You get to sample what the real business is. You should feel grateful," one of them says.

Real business? None of this is making sense. What has Lorelei gotten mixed up in?

Whatever they've given me is beginning to affect my head, and I'm overwhelmed by terror, not knowing what will happen next. Rough hands start touching my body, and I thrash against the chains, but it's futile. The restraints won't give way.

"Come on, I love it when they fight!" one of them exclaims. I can't see their faces clearly, and I'm grateful for that. I know they have to keep me alive, as D'Santos said, but I can't help but wonder what kind of person I'll be when this is over. Will there be anything left of me after they break all my pieces?

Hands are all over me, cutting my clothes from my body, and sobs wrack through me. Still, I try to hold back the tears, refusing to give them the satisfaction. I continue to struggle against the unyielding chains. I won't just sit here and take it. The hand with the tattoo comes back up to my face, and I can now clearly see the mark, which had been almost concealed in the shadows before. It’s a coiled snake and I hold onto that image in my mind, hoping that if I manage to escape, I can tell someone about it.

Then my heart sinks. I've heard about that tattoo on the news. It's a symbol associated with the Mexican cartel. Not all of them have it on their hands, but this man seems to be blatant about his involvement.

"You can blame your friends for this. Little do-gooders trying to take us down. We are untouchable," he hisses, his foul breath washing over my face. The stench of poor hygiene and alcohol makes my stomach churn, and I tip my head forward, preparing to vomit, but there's just the taste of acid.

A fist lands against my ribs, and the breath is knocked from me. Pain courses through my body, and I gasp for air, struggling to endure the torment. Another hand reaches between my legs and if there was anything in me I would throw up.

I scream in protest, desperation and terror overwhelming me.

The tattooed hand once again pinches off my nostril and forces me to inhale the powder, and I'm almost desperate for the numbness it could provide, even though I've never had any prior experience with drugs. Sharp fingernails scrape against my breasts, and a searing slice is carved across the middle of my right breast.

God, I just want this nightmare to end.

They continue to handle me roughly, the physical violation punctuated by blows to my body. I can barely stay conscious due to the agony, but I need to know what's happening to me. If I pass out, I'll always wonder what truly transpired, unless they kill me. Something painful shoves its way into my back side and I scream and cry in pain. Never in my life have I experienced an intrusion like this, and I'm desperately trying to convince myself that it's not real, that it's just a horrific nightmare from which I'll soon wake up.

"Stupid bitch. Thinking you can get rid of the big bad cartel. This little thing thinks she can take on the cartel, Luis," one of the voices sneers from behind me as he continues to violate me. I feel like I'm being torn apart, and his rough clothes scrape against my bare skin.

The other man, presumably Luis, stands in front of me, close enough that I can still smell his foul breath, and I hear the sound of his zipper being undone. This can't be real; it has to be a nightmare. Any moment now, I'll wake up in tears, realizing it's all a cruel trick my mind is playing on me.

Again something shoves its way inside me while the other continues to slam painfully into me from behind. Hands tighten around my neck, and darkness starts to encroach upon my vision. My head feels lighter with each passing second as consciousness slips away.

After what feels like an eternity, they finally withdraw from me, grunting out their release. All I hear is their cruel laughter, and gradually, oxygen returns to my lungs as they release their grip on my neck. A sharp object cuts into my skin on the side of my neck, and I can feel something hot trickling down the tender skin. It's my own blood, and I don't need to look to know it.

"Something to remember me by before you die," chuckles the

voice I've come to identify as Luis.

The pain I felt when I first woke up is nothing compared to this. I continue to shake as they exit the room, leaving me hanging naked, suspended by the chains. I make an effort to piece together the fragments of information while I'm still coherent, but now that they're gone, I can't help but let the tears fall.

The D'Santos are part of the cartel, and Lorelei was attempting to expose them.

I lose consciousness again, but I'm roused by another painful blow to my face. I can't bear much more of this before I beg them to finally end my suffering. I've never known violence like this before.

"Your little fucking friends are ruining everything!" The voice sounds like D'Santos, and I try to stifle my crying as much as possible.

"They think they can go around blowing up our businesses and homes?! They think they can plaster my name all over the media to ruin everything I've worked for?!" Another blow lands on my body.

Once again, a hand comes to my face, pinching one of my nostrils closed, while the other shoves the powder toward my nose, forcing me to inhale.

"You're my bargaining chip, so I need you alive, but I'll send you back so ruined that they won't want you anymore!" he screams in my face.

He departs, but an eerie sensation lingers, and I can't shake the feeling that someone else remains in the room with me. A chill of fear courses through my body, causing me to tremble.

"Looks like I'll be the one to ruin you," a cold, sinister laugh resonates through the room.

I recognize him as the man I believe is named Luis. With every ounce of determination, I imprint his features into my memory. I vow to never forget the face of the man who shattered my world.

He moves in front of me and reaches up to my chains, fumbling with the locks. Is he actually going to release me? A false sense of hope starts to well up within me, only to be brutally shattered as the lock finally gives way, and he lets go of my body, causing me to crash to the unforgiving concrete floor.

My naked form lands with a harsh, jolting impact, and I can't help but let out a pained groan. Before I can even attempt to move, he delivers a brutal, merciless kick to my ribs, and an excruciating pain like nothing I've ever experienced engulfs me. It's so intense that I feel like I might retch from the agony.

The next thing I know, he's looming over me, and I desperately fight back. I put every ounce of strength into my struggle, kicking, screaming, and thrashing around. But the drugs coursing through my system make me sluggish and weak, and he easily overpowers me.

He laughs callously, his face leering inches from mine. "Don't you remember how much I love the fight?" he taunts.

The sound of a zipper sends a wave of dread through me, and I know what's about to happen next. I find myself begging, pleading for anyone or anything to come to my rescue, but my desperate cries only echo against the cold, unfeeling concrete.

Bennett. I wish he was here to save me.

I'm consumed by searing agony as he forcefully pushes deep inside me, and I can't help but cry out in excruciating pain. Mercilessly, he continues to slam into me, while I sob and desperately try to avert my gaze from his terrifying presence.

A brutal blow to my face lands with a sickening thud, and his laughter only intensifies, mingling with his repugnant grunts. The relentless assault leaves me feeling utterly helpless and violated.

Overwhelmed by the torment, waves of nausea surge through me, and I can't hold it back any longer. I retch and vomit, some of which lands on his face due to his proximity.

"Fucking nasty bitch!" he screams in rage and lands another vicious blow. In my anguish, I wish for unconsciousness to take me, anything to escape this torment.

He shoves himself away from me, and then he forcibly pulls me up from the ground. Before I can put up a fight, he secures my arms back above my head, locking me in place. With a look of pure disgust, he spits at me, and I feel utterly dehumanized.

Ruined. Used. Disgusting.

Another blow to my face, and darkness claims me once more.

CHAPTER 30

"I need to hear your voice
I can't do this on my own"
-Memphis May Fire

Damien

More time than I'd like to admit has passed, and the tapped devices haven't provided us with enough to work with, but I know it's only a matter of time. They'd only take a hostage if they wanted to lure us out.

Lorelei's phone rings, and she freezes when she sees the caller ID displaying "Carlos D'Santos." She looks to me, James, and Kellan.

"Lor, keep steady. Don't give anything away. Let him do the talking," I instruct her. I know she's capable of handling this. From what she's told me, she has plenty of experience dealing with unhinged men.

"Hello?" she answers, keeping her voice steady. Good girl.

"You've sure caused more trouble than you're worth," Carlos's accented voice seethes through the phone, and I can almost feel Lorelei's restrained anger. She remains silent, letting him talk. The more we can get him to reveal, the better.

"I have something of yours, but I think you know that by now. I'll make you a deal," he offers.

"Go on," Lorelei replies, making him think she's open to a deal.

I know I'll never accept it. I may be a man of my word, but not when it comes to people like this.

"Since you chose to put the feds on our path and alerted the media, you've made it difficult for us to leave. I'll trade your friend's life for our passage out of the country," Carlos offers.

Lorelei counters, "How did you catch on?" She doesn't immediately accept his deal, leaving him hanging. Her uninterested tone is surely infuriating him. Men in power often don't like to be challenged by a woman, especially one they consider beneath them.

"We have a DEA agent in our employ. He alerted us about what was being planned. I have to admit you had us chasing our tails when Santiago went missing. I started getting suspicious after I heard about your supposed accident. I began looking into what you were up to and pieced some things together. We took our remaining money then Bex as collateral. I didn't think you had it in you. Although I suspect you're working with someone, based on how quickly you started burning down our properties," Carlos explains.

Lorelei maintains her composure, allowing him to reveal more information.

"Did it occur to you I'm just crafty?" Lorelei responds, her words calculated to leave her opponent underestimating her. She's brilliant.

"We've considered all options. Anyways, what of our deal?" Carlos asks, a hint of eagerness in his voice. We've managed to get under his skin. Overly eager people are prone to making mistakes, and that's exactly what I was counting on.

"You better hurry, one of my men has taken a liking to your friend, now the others want a taste. I won't be able to hold them off much longer." he adds. His words send a chill down my spine, and I maintain my composure, knowing that revealing our determination could turn the tables in this dangerous game of ours and potentially put Bex in more danger.

"Bex alive, and I will stand out of your way to get out of the country. But you'll never come back here," Lorelei says, and I can tell she's bluffing. She won't let him get away with this. Her clever use of "I will" instead of "we will" fills me with pride. She wants him thinking she's not as big a threat as she truly is. I glance at Kellan on the couch, and his face is red with outrage.

"Deal. I'll send you the coordinates. Be here at midnight," Carlos agrees, and Lorelei hangs up with nothing more to say. Shortly afterward, the coordinates are sent to her phone.

"James, alert the team. Rendezvous here in 30. We leave early to scout the surrounding areas. Then we attack at midnight. Tell them all to prepare for battle. I have a feeling it's a trap," Lorelei instructs.

"You're letting them get away with this?!" Kellan screams, leaping to his feet.

I observe as Lorelei approaches Kellan, taking his hands in hers and locking eyes with him in an attempt to calm his rage. "Of course not, Kell. No one will be walking out of there alive but us," she reassures him. With that, she drops his hands and turns her back to him, unintentionally offering him a degree of comfort with her brutal honesty.

Every available moment is dedicated to preparation, and when the time finally arrives, we have two vans loaded with soldiers en route to the given coordinates. We're all equipped with ear pieces to facilitate communication and ensure we can maneuver efficiently. I relay my message through the mic so the occupants of the second van can hear as well.

"There's a good chance we're walking into a setup. However, they have no idea we're involved. They're assuming Lorelei went vigilante, which works in our favor. We have the element of surprise on our side. Van one takes the front. Van two the back. No survivors," I command.

Kellan is sitting next to Lorelei, and I turn to him, delivering a stern command. "You will stay out of the way until you're given the signal. Once it's safe, you'll find Bex, but not a moment before. I don't care what's happening; you are glued to me. Understand?" He nods and keeps his hands in his lap.

I value Kellan's unwavering commitment to rescuing his loved one, but I'm apprehensive about his lack of experience and his role in this operation. I'm uncertain about what we will encounter when we arrive. My concern is ensuring that everyone makes it back home safely, and I won't settle for anything less.

When we're all in position, I relay the signal through the mic. Lorelei approaches the front door of the building, and my stomach churns as I watch her advance alone, just as she had promised him. All the soldiers are strategically placed, and I know she's well-protected, but the desire to be right by her side is overwhelming. The rest of us remain concealed, vigilant, and prepared for any potential ambush.

The door swings open, and Lorelei raises her gun, firing without a moment's hesitation and swiftly eliminates whoever opened the door. That's the signal for the rest of us to spring into action. We storm the building, and as we enter, Lorelei comes close to my side. We'd agreed she would stick with me until it was clear. I keep Kellan behind me to protect him.

It's chaos inside the building, and it's evident that the cartel had no intention of keeping their end of the deal. This was indeed a set-up. But, we never intended to honor our end of the agreement either, and that works in our favor.

As a short stocky man approaches me from the left, I swiftly turn and fire my rifle without a second thought, hitting him square between the eyes. Blood splatters across my face, and a grin creeps across my lips. At this moment, I'm in my element.

Turning my attention back to Lorelei, a female assailant advances on her. Lorelei reaches for her blade strapped to her thigh instead of her gun and expertly slices it across the woman's throat in a single fluid motion. When she looks back at me, blood now coats her as well.

I can't wait to get everyone home safely. When that's done, I'm going to fuck her until she can't walk without feeling me.

Gunfire continues to echo all around us, and I'm confident that my soldiers are securing the area. Suddenly, a gunshot rings out, and a searing pain lances through my leg.

"Goddamnit. I hate getting shot," I mutter through gritted teeth. Lorelei raises her gun and returns fire at the shooter, landing a deadly shot to his head, dropping him.

"Are you okay?" Lorelei yells over the commotion.

"I'm fine. Carver can patch me up later," I assure her, trying to keep the pain at bay.

"Clear," a voice comes over my mic, signaling that it's safe to proceed. I look at Kellan and give him a nod, indicating that he can go find Bex. He leaves, and Lorelei isn't far behind him. I trust they'll be safe now.

"Boss, come to the back," a voice comes through the mic.

I limp to the back, having tied off my leg with a piece of rope I found to slow down the bleeding. I know Carver is going to be furious with me. When I reach the back, I see Carlos tied to a chair, surrounded by a few of my soldiers.

I lean down, locking eyes with Carlos. "Do you know who I

am?" I inquire.

"Should I?" he chokes out with a venomous tone, spitting as he speaks. I take pleasure in my anonymity.

"Everything you've worked for is about to crumble. My name is Damien, and I own AMG. This entire thing will be written off as an internal struggle within the cartel, and my friend in the FBI is personally handling the dismantling of everyone who's left. How does that feel?" I smile at him.

"You bastard!" he screams. I straighten up and nod to my men. As I turn to walk away, another gunshot sounds from behind me. I revel in the satisfaction of my work.

Bex

I wake up with a jolt, the sound of my chains reminding me of my terrible surroundings, as if the pain wasn't enough of a reminder. But there's another noise, one that becomes clearer with each passing moment. It's gunfire.

What's happening? Are they turning against each other? An internal struggle, maybe?

More gunfire echoes, and a tiny spark of hope kindles within me.

"I'm in here, please help!" I scream, and in that moment, something dark ignites in my chest, a rage unlike anything I've ever felt before.

Then, an explosion rocks the area, drowning everything in a deafening roar of chaos.

The door behind me bursts open, and I hear a familiar voice call, "Bex?"

I sob, not wanting anyone to see me like this, especially not him. "Bex, I'm here. I'm here. We came to get you as fast as we could."

Kellan goes to wrap something around my body, but a sudden fear courses through me, and I start screaming at him.

"Don't touch me, no, stop!" I scream, my voice hoarse with fear.

"Bex, it's me, Kellan. Please, I'm here to take you home," he pleads gently.

"No, don't touch me!" I insist, my voice still strained with fear and mistrust.

"Bex?!" comes another familiar voice.

"In here!" Kellan yells back.

Lorelei rushes into the room, panting and holding a flashlight that finally lets me see both of their faces for the first time in what feels like an eternity. Worry is etched across his face, but I don't detect any signs of disgust. Still, he doesn't know what happened.

"We need to get her to Carver," Lorelei insists. When I look back at her, I see that she's covered in blood. I hear another familiar voice from behind her, saying, "We're clear, but she needs a doctor now."

A man moves in front of me and lowers himself to meet my gaze, his tone gentle. It's the same soothing voice my brother uses. "Hi, Bex. It's good to see you. If it's okay, I'm going to release you so I can pick you up and take you to a waiting van outside. Then, we'll head to Carver, the doctor who helped Lorelei. Is that okay?"

Everyone falls silent, awaiting my agreement. My heart swells, realizing he's asking for my permission to touch me.

I look at him, and he nods in acknowledgement. Slowly he reaches up to release me from the chains, and carefully picks me up and cradles me against his broad chest, while Lorelei lays Kellan's discarded jacket around me. I can feel that he's limping, and although I'm concerned about his well-being, I can't bring myself to ask.

"Bennett, you came for me. You're always there to protect me," I sob into his chest.

A hint of confusion tinges his voice as he replies, "I know this is all confusing right now, and I promise you'll have a full explanation once I know you've been checked out and patched up, okay?" He says this in a voice that doesn't quite sound like Bennett, he climbs into the back of a van, gently setting me on a bench seat. He slides over to make room for Lorelei to sit by me, ensuring I'm well-supported.

The van begins to bump down the road, heading to someone named Carver. Despite knowing that I've been rescued, I can't shake the anger that's building within me. I'm furious that this happened, that I had no knowledge of any of it, that my body is scarred, and that I wish someone was shoving that powder up my nose so I could be numb to all of this.

CHAPTER 31

"I'm at the edge of the world
Where do I go from here? Do I disappear?"
-Bring Me The Horizon

Lorelei

Bex can barely look at any of us, and I wish so badly I could ease her pain. She hasn't spoken to anyone aside from Damien and Carver. Today, she's being released from Carver's office, and I'm hoping she'll agree to stay at Damien's place for a while so I can look after her. She won't talk about what happened, but I can only imagine the horrors she experienced based on the injuries she sustained.

Her physical pain will subside over the coming days, but I know all too well the toll that emotional pain will take on her. Bex is a pure soul, and she doesn't deserve to have to deal with something like this. Nobody does. It's tearing Kellan apart that she's pushing him away, but I can see how patient he's being and how he's trying to understand what she needs from him.

I walk into the room she's been in these last few days, where she's been healing, and I find her sitting on the hospital bed, dressed in some of her regular clothes. I have a feeling Damien brought some of her things from her apartment for her. The bandage on her neck, concealing an X cut into her skin, tears at my heart. She will have a painful reminder of that time for the rest of her life.

I stay by the door, giving her some space. "I have some things I need to explain to you, Bex."

A crude snort escapes her, and I know I've messed up worse than I imagined. "I thought you told me everything after your accident. Seems like you left a lot out, is that safe to say?" She's never spoken to me like this before, and it feels like something cracks in my chest.

"I know you're angry with me, and you have every right to be. I'd like to tell you the rest if you'll let me."

"There's no need. Damien came in and explained everything to me this morning when he brought me clean clothes. I know who he is. I know about AMG. I know about Sin. I know about the D'Santos and their real work."

I hesitate for a moment, realizing that Bex seems to have bonded with Damien during the time we got her out of there. If he's the person she's comfortable talking to right now, I'm just glad that she has someone. He was the only one she allowed to go near her once we got to her. Damien has been checking on her regularly, even with his gunshot wound to deal with. Fortunately, it missed anything major and was a clean through-and-through shot. The fact that he took the time to see her because she's important to me gives me hope in these dark times.

"Before you get mad at him for telling me," she continues, "he explained that he wanted to be the one to tell me who he really is. He felt he owed me that. He explained his true identity and AMG. I made him explain any other missing pieces."

I nod, understanding. AMG is for Damien alone to disclose. " I'm sorry for keeping it from you, and I'm sorry for everything you've been through. I'll keep you safe, I promise nothing will ever happen again."

Her pain is palpable, and it cuts me deeply. I want to reach out to her, to comfort her, but I know she needs time and space right now. The trauma she's experienced won't disappear overnight. We'll be there for her as she heals, no matter how long it takes.

"You should have told me when I visited you after the accident. If I genuinely mean anything to you as your best friend, you should've been honest with me right then and there about the true situation. You should've shown enough concern for my well-being to give me a heads up, so I could safeguard myself instead of walking into work each day completely unaware," she says, her voice growing louder, and I'm certain it's echoing through the corridors.

"You're right, but it wasn't my secret to tell. I was also afraid that by confiding in you, I'd be putting you and others at risk. It was a mistake on my part. I tried to meet with you before everything unraveled to explain, but I was too late. I can't express how deeply sorry I am for that," I admit, feeling a lump in my throat but refusing to let the tears flow. She shouldn't have to bear my emotional burden.

"I understand you're upset with me, but I'd like to see if you'd be willing to come and stay with us while you continue to heal," I suggest.

"No," she replies firmly. "I'm going home to my apartment. Damien already informed me that he's had it restored from the kidnapping, and he's installed a security system for me."

I had no idea Damien did that for her. As she stands from the bed and slings a bag over her arm, she forcefully shoulder checks me as she walks past, making her way through the door.

Without thinking, I follow her into the hallways and ask, "Bex, who's Bennett? Damien carried you out of the building, and you called him Bennett."

Her footsteps freeze a few feet outside the door, and all she mumbles in response is, "Don't worry about it."

I've seriously messed up, and I'm not sure if there's a way back from this with her. But I'm determined to do whatever it takes to make things right.

"Are you okay, Lorelei?" a deep, familiar voice comes from behind me. I turn to see Carver, leaning against the wall with his arms crossed, a discerning look in his eyes. He's unnervingly perceptive.

"No," is all I manage to say, because I'm afraid I'll completely break down. These emotions are still new to me, and I haven't figured out how to navigate them all yet.

"I don't know the extent of what happened between you two, but what I do know are the injuries she sustained. Those injuries tell me she endured a very brutal assault. I won't go into specifics because she's my patient, but I've been to war, and I've seen things like this before. She'll never be the old Bex, but she'll need help finding her way to a newer, stronger version of herself. Don't give up on her just because your feelings are hurt," Carver advises, his voice carrying the weight of experience. "If anyone can help her heal from this trauma, I imagine it's you."

I nod in agreement, still fighting back the tears threatening to spill. He pushes off from the wall and steps in front of me, placing his strong hands on my shoulders to steady me. I gaze into his face, and I can't help but notice the blend of brutality and beauty in the people associated with Damien. Carver's gray eyes hold a deep, knowing sadness.

"I'd like to think we're friends now, Lorelei. If you need some help, I'm here for you," Carver offers, giving my shoulders a reassuring squeeze before walking away. He's been taking such good care of me since I got hurt – not just tending to my physical injuries, but always checking on my emotional healing when he was caring for me. I can't help but wish he had been there when I was younger—a brother, a friend—to help me heal and prevent my mind from falling apart.

The drive back home is a blur, and when I pull into the driveway in my truck, I can't recall a single moment of the journey. As I step out of my truck, I see Damien leaning against the front door, his hands in his pockets, and his injured leg crossed over the other at the ankle.

Damien doesn't speak or move; he simply waits for me to express my needs. I walk up to him and wrap my arms around his waist. He takes his hands out of his pockets, encircling me with his strong arms, resting his head on top of mine, and inhales deeply, absorbing my presence. At last, I allow the tears to flow. Sobs wrack my body, and I let out all the pent-up emotions. I cry for Bex, for my grievous mistakes, and even for the childhood I lost. I have no concept of how long he holds me on our front porch like this, but he doesn't rush me to talk; he simply lets the sadness seep out of me, absorbing it all.

I feel permanently broken, uncertain of what this new version of myself looks like. I spent my life consumed by the pursuit of vengeance, and now that chapter is closed, I'm lost, unsure of my identity, and uncertain if I'm even deserving of forgiveness.

When my tears begin to subside, Damien gently guides me to our room, lays me on the bed, and drapes a soft black blanket around me. He climbs into bed beside me, repositions me so my head rests on his chest, and starts to soothingly run his fingers through my hair.

"Would you like to talk about anything?" Damien asks quietly, his tone filled with understanding, leaving the choice entirely up to me.

"I haven't asked what happened with the D'Santos," I admit, my thoughts consumed by Bex. They've barely crossed my mind until now.

Damien continues to gently stroke my hair, and the sobbing has left me exhausted. I can't recall the last time I had a good night's sleep. "We released a story about the building we infiltrated," he begins to explain. "It's being portrayed as an internal struggle within the cartel, with its members turning against one another. Those who are left in other states are being pursued by a personal friend of mine in the FBI. Given the evidence we provided and the murders, the FBI put together a team to eliminate the rest of them. There won't be much of them left soon. Until we identify the mole in the DEA, it was decided that the FBI would handle this case to prevent any compromise."

Knowing that some good came out of this terrible situation provides me with a sliver of comfort. A cartel family being taken out means they can no longer harm anyone through their criminal enterprises.

"What about their businesses?" I inquire.

"We either destroyed them or they've been seized," Damien informs me.

Sin is no more. I find myself wondering what will happen to my staff.

"I need to work on a solution for all my employees," I mumble, my thoughts drifting.

"It's already been taken care of. I provided them all with a severance package of sorts so they have time to find new jobs. They will also be given a letter of recommendation written by you if they need it," Damien assures me. He's truly handled everything, and I can't help but wonder how he manages to keep it all together so well.

We continue to lie there like that until I notice the sun

beginning to dim through the windows. Eventually, I can no longer resist the pull of sleep, and I allow my world to fade into darkness.

Bex

My apartment feels different, and so do I. I can't help but sink into a pit, questioning if I'll ever find my old self. With every merciless blow I endured, something inside me shattered, leaving me feeling like a mere shadow of my former self. It's painful to witness everyone treating me with such caution. I'm not the same person anymore; any trace of the gentleness I once harbored has now solidified into a cold, unyielding shell.

The only person who doesn't handle me like I'm encased in glass is Damien. He doesn't shield me from the truth because he knows that after what I went through, I can handle it. Everyone else looks at me with pity, and the weight of their stares feels suffocating.

Sitting on my couch, the vibrant colors of my apartment seem to close in around me, and my skin starts to itch. I'm aware of what my body craves, and I despise the desire to give in.

My gaze fixes on the orange pill bottle on my coffee table, the one Carver prescribed me.

Knock. Knock.

My head shoots up, and a shiver runs down my spine. I'm not anticipating any visitors.

"Bex, it's me," Kellan's voice calls out. I'd recognize Kellan's voice anywhere. Before my abduction, we had spent time together, and I had even thought there might be a small spark between us. But Kellan only knows goodness and innocence. He couldn't possibly comprehend that I've lost all of that.

Knock. Knock.

"Please let me in. I brought you dinner," Kellan's voice pleads from the other side of the door. He's undeniably kind and considerate, but deep down, I'm aware that if I open that door, his bright blue eyes will only reflect pity. That's is the last thing I need from anyone right now.

Knock. Knock.

He doesn't say anything this time, and after a few moments, I cautiously approach the door and look through the peephole. He's gone, leaving a white takeout bag on the mat. I'm not hungry, and I haven't been for a while. The mere thought of any strong scent is overwhelming, as it triggers memories of the men who took away my sense of safety.

Flashes of rough hands and guttural grunts rush through my mind, and without thinking, I return to the coffee table and open the pill bottle. I retrieve two opioids, small white circles that promise to drown out the haunting thoughts.

I place the pills in my mouth, tilt my head back, and swallow them dry.

I had believed that returning to my apartment would be an impossible task, haunted by the lingering presence of monsters. But the worst has already occurred, and I have nothing left to be frightened of. My hand instinctively rises to touch the X that marks my neck. I head into my bedroom, not even bothering to change my clothes, and climb onto my bed, waiting for the blissful haze of the medication to envelop me.

CHAPTER 32

"Is there a right way for how this goes
You got your friends and you got your foes"
-Sleeping With Sirens

Damien

I'm filled with worry, not just for Lorelei, but also for Bex and Kellan. With the exception of Lorelei they've never experienced the harsh realities of the world like I have, and I couldn't shield them from it. The guilt of that failure will haunt me forever. I should have been better prepared, but my arrogance got the best of me.

Several days have passed and physically, I've nearly recovered from my gunshot wound, and any remaining discomfort is nothing new to me. What troubles me more are the unseen wounds everyone is carrying, the ones that slowly eat away at your mind until all that's left is a hollow shell of your former self.

Since everything happened with her parents, I've witnessed a different side of Lorelei. Something broke inside her that day, and it allowed some of her warmth to shine through. A light I could never be deserving of, but I'll spend the rest of my life trying to. She's convinced she's nothing but sharp edges and a cold heart, but she doesn't see herself the way the rest of us do. Sometimes, I'm tempted to keep her, like a precious treasure in a gilded cage, selfishly hoarding her warmth for myself and protecting it from the world.

She's been aimlessly wandering the halls of the house like a ghost for days. She hardly eats or talks, but I can see every emotion etched into her heartbreakingly beautiful face.

I decided to have James dig up some information for me, and I'm planning a small surprise for her, hoping it might reignite the spark in her eyes.

Every morning, I check on Bex, taking her breakfast, even though I doubt she's eating much. Currently, I'm the only person she allows to come to her door, and I want to maintain that connection so that when she's ready to rejoin the world, we're all here to support her. I hope she can find her way out of this darkness on her own, but I might need to resort to tough love if it comes to that. I've come to see her as a little sister, and I'd hate to see her lose herself to this trauma.

Every time I visit her, her eyes are distant, and the bags under them continue to darken. I can only imagine the nightmares plaguing her sleep and the toll it's taking on her.

Back home after my visit with Bex, I begin to search the halls for Lorelei. I'm not currently on a case, given that the D'Santos case has closed. I have ample time to focus on helping my people and getting things back in order. AMG can function without me for the most part, and I've even turned down work requests from the FBI. It's a surprising change from my usual habit of working myself to exhaustion.

Eventually, I discover Lorelei sitting on the back patio, curled up in an outdoor chair, lost in her thoughts. I slide the back door open, but she doesn't turn to look at me.

"Alright, seirína, it's time to get up. There are clothes on the bed for you to wear. Go shower and be ready to leave in thirty minutes," I tell her firmly. Bex might not be ready for tough love, but Lorelei is.

I can't bear to see her falling apart like this; it's not the strong woman I know. I refuse to let her deteriorate any further.

Lorelei looks up at me with dull green eyes. I have an overwhelming urge to hold her close, but I've resolved to stop coddling her. I need her to find the fire that I know resides within her; I can't do it for her.

"Now," I repeat, my voice unwavering, and I turn to leave her there. She's far too curious to ignore my command, so I trust that she will eventually do as I've asked.

I sit behind my imposing desk, sifting through emails to ensure there's nothing pressing to worry about for the business. James keeps me updated and checks in on Bex and Lorelei regularly. He's been keeping an eye on Kellan for me as well.

Kellan has been assisting James with work, almost like an apprentice. I believe he found purpose and satisfaction in being useful during the mission to rescue Bex. James and I have discussed the idea of offering him the first-ever AMG intern position. It could be a positive opportunity for Kellan, and if James is willing to make a carbon copy of himself, I won't pass up the chance.

Right now, I've sorted out everyone except for Lorelei; she's proven to be a bit more challenging than the others.

Forty-five minutes later, Lorelei walks into my office, wearing a black lounge set, her long dark hair still damp and cascading down her back, and no makeup on.

"We're back to no underwear?" she remarks, a trace of humor in her voice. I knew that would elicit a reaction and hopefully bring back some of the happier memories I need her to start recalling.

I stand and approach her, cupping her small face in my large hands. The size difference between us can be comical at times. I press a kiss to her forehead, and my body responds with a surge of desire. Now isn't the time for that, though. I'm trying to get her out of the house for a while, but if we linger much longer, I'll find it hard to resist the urge to take her on my desk like a barbarian and lose ourselves in each other.

If today doesn't work, that might become my next plan. Lately, the only time Lorelei comes alive is when I'm balls deep inside of her.

I release her face and grab her hand, leading her to the garage where my car awaits. I've memorized the directions to the address James gave me to keep the destination a secret.

In silence, we drive to our unknown location, and I keep my hand on her thigh to provide some reassurance. She doesn't ask where we're heading, merely allowing me to lead her. I'm desperate to rekindle that fiery side of her.

The drive is relatively short, and we pass the Arizona mountains in the distance. The landscape is one of the reasons I love living here. Mountains surround us in every direction. The heat can be unforgiving, but I'll take it over snow any day. I could never imagine living in the Midwest; I'd sooner eat sand.

As we near our destination, I notice Lorelei's posture straighten, and it won't be long before her keen mind puts the pieces together.

When we pull up at the pizza shop and park, we sit for a moment to let her compose herself.

"The last time I was here, my mom told me the truth about everything. How did you find it?" she asks.

"You still underestimate me, and James, for that matter," I reply, flashing my cheesiest smile.

Lorelei reaches over and squeezes my hand before swiftly

opening her car door and hurrying to the front entrance of the pizza shop. The place appears a bit run-down; the sign on the front of the building is deteriorating, and peering through the large windows, I can tell the inside likely mirrors the exterior.

I've learned never to judge a book by its cover though.

I follow her inside, and as soon as she steps through the door, I hear a voice from the back of the shop call out, "Lorelei!" A small Italian man emerges from the kitchen's swinging door, his hands raised, and a wide, welcoming smile aimed at Lorelei. Based on his gray hair and wrinkled skin, I would guess he's in his sixties.

Antonio wipes his hands on his apron, crosses the front counter, and wraps Lorelei in a tight, enthusiastic hug. I can hear the breath escaping her lungs, but for the first time in weeks, a genuine smile graces her face, and her green eyes seem to regain some of their sparkle. As much as I love her, I resist the urge to break the man's hand for touching what's mine. I have a feeling that would only upset her.

I make a mental note to send something special to James for helping me find this place.

Antonio releases Lorelei and addresses her loudly, "It's been weeks. Why haven't you come to see me?" He raises a thick, gray eyebrow and shifts his gaze between me and Lorelei, anticipating an introduction.

Lorelei directs her smile at me and then back to Antonio as she takes his hand in hers. The thick calluses on his hand are likely a testament to years of hard work.

"Zio, this is my boyfriend Damien," Lorelei introduces us and says the word boyfriend like a question. "Damien, this is Antonio. Can you spare some time to eat with us?" Her affection for this man is evident in her expression, and I'm eager to hear their story. However, the word "boyfriend" coming from her mouth feels inadequate compared to the depth of our relationship. I'll need to address that soon.

I extend my hand for a handshake, but instead, Antonio grabs it and surprisingly, with a strong pull, brings me toward him, wrapping me in a hug similar to the one he gave Lorelei. For a small man, he certainly possesses significant strength. His enthusiasm is contagious, and I find myself chuckling as I hug him back. It's impossible to ignore his spirited nature.

"Yes, yes, sit both of you. I'll be out soon with our food, and we can catch up," Antonio says, his big brown eyes locking onto Lorelei's. He gives her hand one last squeeze before disappearing back into the kitchen through the swinging doors.

Lorelei leads me to a booth with red vinyl seats that are showing signs of wear, and her body visibly relaxes when she takes the spot by the window. I slide in next to her.

"Why do you call him Zio?" I ask, curious about the endearing nickname.

She smiles and turns to me. "Antonio and his family were always kind to me. They never knew my circumstances, but they sensed I needed some love, I think. After about a week of working here, he told me to call him Zio, which means uncle in Italian, and to call his wife Zia, which means aunt. They were inviting me into their family."

I decided at that moment that I will fiercely protect Antonio and his family just as I would anyone else who had offered her a safe haven when she needed it, even if the man did hug her.

While we wait, Lorelei shares amusing stories from her time working with Antonio and his family. I realize that these might be the only happy memories she has from her childhood, and it's heartwarming to see her laugh.

She recounts a story about making their homemade sauce and how, while carrying it to the prep counter, she slipped, causing the entire tub to spill all over her. She explains that Antonio never got mad; instead, he laughed with her and helped her clean up, offering guidance on how to do better next time.

Antonio arrives at our table with a large pepperoni pizza and a plate of garlic knots. He sets them down with plates and then takes a seat across from Lorelei, his smile never fading from his face.

"Antonio, how long have you owned this place?" I inquire, taking a bite of pizza.

"Antonio? This man calls me Antonio?" he exclaims, looking at Lorelei and waving his slice of pizza through the air while speaking animatedly with his hands. "No, no, I am Zio. You call me Zio, just like she does," he insists, emphasizing his point with the enthusiastic pizza slice.

I grin widely, and out of the corner of my eye, I see Lorelei beaming, which warms my heart.

"Zio, my apologies. How long have you owned this place?" I rephrase my question, making sure to address him with a grin.

Antonio's chest swells with pride as he shares, "Russo's pizza shop has been in my family since we came over here from Italy. My nonno, or grandpa as you all say, bought the pizza shop to bring quality pizza to America. My papá took it over after he passed, and then when we lost him far too early, it became mine. Having our family name on the wall is my greatest joy in life, right after my wife and children. However, my children have pursued good careers and aren't interested in taking over when I'm done. I fear what will happen after that."

His eyes gleam with passion as he tells the story, and I can tell that this pizza shop means more to him than anything else in the world. I can't help but imagine how devastating it would be for him to lose it, which makes me empathize with the feeling, as I couldn't bear the thought of losing AMG.

Lorelei turns to me, setting her slice of pizza down on her plate, and we exchange silent glances, unbeknownst to Antonio. She flashes me a wide smile, and I already know her plan before she even speaks.

"Zio, I know I'm not one of your children, but would you let me buy Russo's from you so you can retire? I'll even change my last name if you want me to," Lorelei suggests with a laugh.

The only name she's changing to is Ashford, and I'll have to remind her of that later.

Tears well up in Antonio's eyes as he gazes at her. He sets his pizza down and wipes his hands with a napkin. "Lorelei, my girl, you are just as much my child as the others. Would you really want Russo's?" His voice is filled with hope, and it's so heartwarming that it might just bring tears to my eyes as well.

"It would be an honor if you'd let me," Lorelei replies. "This pizza place is like a home to me. I would even put it in writing that I'll keep all the recipes the same and run everything by you before making any changes." She's rambling, and I can tell she's a bit nervous, which I find incredibly endearing.

Antonio erupts into a hearty, deep laugh, and his entire body shakes with mirth. "You have made me a very happy old man, Lorelei. Come by later this week, and we can discuss the details. I believe Isabella would be delighted to pass Russo's on to you and happy for us to work a bit less. I owe her a lot of time off. But for now, we eat."

We spend hours with Antonio, sharing food, laughter, and stories of his business successes and failures. The love between him and Lorelei is palpable, and it's impossible not to be charmed by a man as full of life as he is.

When we finally prepare to leave, Antonio enfolds me in another bear-hug. In a hushed tone, he tells me, "She deserves the world. Thank you for bringing that smile to her face." We break apart, and he gazes into my eyes. I'm certain Lorelei made the right choice in deciding to buy this place. I squeeze his shoulder, then make my way to the door to give them a moment to say their goodbyes and discuss plans for her to return and talk about purchasing the shop.

I open the car door for her and walk over to the driver's side, sliding behind the wheel. Just as I'm about to start the car, she grabs my jaw and turns my face toward her, planting a passionate kiss on my lips. She pulls away but keeps her eyes locked onto mine, and for the first time in weeks, those green eyes are glowing with life.

"Can life really be this good?" she asks, her tone carrying a hint of hesitation. She's spent her life focused on survival, never really getting to enjoy the simple pleasures that life has to offer.

"I'm going to make sure it keeps getting better. You have my word," I assure her with unwavering sincerity. I would go to great lengths to give her the world, even if it meant sacrificing everything. It's a jarring thought, but I know it's the undeniable truth.

I throw the car into drive and accelerate onto the road, eliciting a small yelp from her. "D, you're going to kill us driving so fast," she exclaims, but she's laughing, so I know she's not genuinely upset. Lorelei craves both the thrill and safety, a healthy balance of both in her life and I'll be the only bastard to give it to her.

"I need to be buried in you as soon as possible; there's no time for the speed limit," I retort, pushing the accelerator even harder.

CHAPTER 33

"Can you hear the silence?
Can you see the dark?
Can you fix the broken?
Can you feel, can you feel my heart?"
-Bring Me The Horizon

Lorelei

My life feels good in many ways right now, but there's a profound absence that leaves a gaping hole in my chest—Bex.

It's been weeks since I last saw her, and Damien assured me that she would contact me when she's ready. But I can't help the growing worry that's taken hold of me. Kellan hasn't seen her either, and Damien's reports during his visits to her have been disheartening. He brings her coffee and pastries every other morning, which I appreciate, but he's noted that she doesn't look good.

Every day without Bex feels like an eternity, and I'm not sure how much longer I can let her pull away. The longing to reconnect with her, to make sure she's okay, and to mend our friendship has become overwhelming. So, today, I'm setting out to find her, to knock on her apartment door, and to somehow bridge the gap that's grown between us.

With Damien temporarily away at James' house, the restlessness inside me becomes unbearable. I can't stand the thought of waiting any longer, not knowing how Bex is doing. I grab my truck keys and drive to her apartment like a woman possessed, my gut telling me I need to reach her before it's too late.

As I stand before her apartment door, my fist poised to knock, hesitation grips me. I'm unsure about what I should say to Bex. Will the right words come to me? And more importantly, will she even let me in?

Knock knock knock

My hand seems to act independently, and the rustling I heard behind the door suddenly ceases. I'm certain she's here. Damien believes she hasn't left her house since she returned. He arranges for essential groceries to be delivered once a week, and it seems like no one else comes or goes.

No response. She won't avoid me so easily.

Knock knock knock

"I know you're in there, Bex. If you don't answer, I'll have to use the key you gave me for emergencies. I won't leave without seeing you in person."

Knock knock knock

"You have thirty seconds, or I'm coming in," I assert. After a brief wait, I hear movement behind the door, and it slowly opens a crack.

"Go away. If I wanted to see you, I would have invited you," her voice sounds off, not quite like herself. There's a subtle slur in her speech, as if her tongue is too heavy to move properly.

I place my hand on the door and gently push it open, forcing her back. When the outside light spills into the room, I notice she's lost weight; her cheeks are sunken, and there are dark bags under her eyes, just as Damien had mentioned. But as I gaze into her distant and glassy eyes, I recognize that look all too well.

"What the hell are you taking?" I demand, my concern giving way to anger. I stride into her apartment, and she tries to stop me, but she's too frail. I begin searching the place for anything unfamiliar. Surprisingly, everything looks clean for someone on drugs. I scrutinize every corner for paraphernalia but come up empty-handed.

I get right in her face, and she doesn't flinch. "What are you on, Bex? And how the hell has Damien not realized?" My anger intensifies. If he knew, he would have told me.

"Why do you care, Lorelei?" She remains emotionless, her eyes growing even more distant.

"Because you're my best friend!" I shout at her, losing my temper. "I don't know what happened when they took you, but there are so many ways to seek help. Drugs can't be the solution. I won't stand by and watch you slowly kill yourself in this apartment. I don't care if you end up hating me for it."

I grip her shoulders and gently shake her, trying to bring her attention back to reality. Her glassy eyes finally focus on me, and large tears well up in them. "Please, just let me die," she whispers.

I'm at a loss for words. Instead, I hold her as tightly as I can in my arms, and a sob wracks through her small frame. We stay like that for a while, letting her cry out whatever she needs to.

Gradually, I pull back a bit, still holding her at arm's length. I look into her familiar eyes and ask, "Can you tell me what you've been taking?"

Hesitation and fear are evident in her eyes, but I can see the sadness. The yearning for help.

I guide us over to her couch so we can sit down together, taking her hands in mine and looking into her eyes. "When they had me, they kept forcing me to take their drugs. I started to crave the escape so I could distance myself from the pain. When we got home, the pain was too much, not from the injuries but from everything else.

Carver gave me a prescription to use while I was healing, so I started taking them whenever it all started to feel overwhelming. When I ran out of what he gave me, I reached out to an old acquaintance from high school, and he dropped it off in a bag disguised as food delivery. I made sure to only take them after Damien left on the days he visited, so he wouldn't know."

Her voice is so timid and broken as she shares this with me, and I can feel my own emotions welling up. But I know I need to stay strong for her. "Why didn't you talk to him about it?" I ask, seeking to understand.

"I couldn't. You all seem to have gone through so much, and you're all fine. But I fall apart after one traumatic thing? It's pathetic. I'm pathetic. Disgusting. Ruined," she says, her self-esteem shattered.

I take a slow, calming breath to contain my frustration for the fact that she has been placed in this horrible situation. "Please, do not compare your trauma to anyone else's. Your journey to healing is uniquely yours, and every emotion you're going through is not only completely understandable but also entirely valid. You are so much more than your trauma; it doesn't determine your worth or define your identity."

As my phone rings with D's name on the caller ID, I know I need to let him know I'm safe; otherwise, he'll start to worry. Before I answer, I glance back at Bex.

"I think you need help navigating some of this, and I'd like to take you to someone who can help. Are you okay with that? I'll never force you to go anywhere, but I want to get you the help that you deserve," I say, hoping she won't push me away.

Her eyes search mine, and to my relief, she nods her head slightly. I wrap her in another tight hug. "Can Damien come with us?" she asks. It's clear that their bond has grown stronger in the past few weeks, and I'm grateful that she has someone to lean on, even if it's only a little.

"If you want him to come, then of course he will be there."

She opens up, "I know it might seem odd, but when you guys came to rescue me, he didn't look at me with pity in his eyes. He looked at me like I was strong. I think I would have fallen apart completely right then if it wasn't for that." She speaks quietly and takes a deep breath before continuing.

"Did I ever tell you about my brother?" I shake my head, indicating she can continue if she wishes. After a long pause, I see her eyes misting with unshed tears, and her voice barely comes out as a whisper.

"His name is Bennett. Or was Bennett, I guess. He was tall and stocky even at a young age. He was my best friend. His hair was a shade or two darker than mine, and everyone always told us we had the same hazel eyes," she says, her voice quivering with emotion. I wish I could take this pain from her.

"We were almost exactly three years apart, so we did everything together. He was my protector and my best friend. He made me feel strong. When he was 15, and I was 12, he went off with some friends to play in a creek not far from our house. But my parents made me stay home so he could hang out with his friends without his annoying little sister bugging him. They were goofing around in some rough spots of water, and since it was monsoon season, the water was higher than normal and unpredictable. He got swept under the water, and his foot got stuck. No one could get to him in time to save him."

Tears continue to roll down her cheeks silently, and I maintain my comforting presence by squeezing her leg, allowing her the space to speak freely. "He drowned, Lor. My best friend never came home to me."

My heart aches for her, I had no idea she was holding so much pain inside her. I watch her take another steadying breath. "When Damien carried me out, it felt like Bennett was protecting me again. The look I used to see in Bennett's eyes was in Damien's, it felt like my brother was back."

I don't respond, but I make a mental note to never let Damien go, not just for what he does for me but for the comfort and strength he offers to those around him.

I envelop Bex in a tight hug, allowing her to cry until she starts to pull away. After composing myself, I pick up my phone and call D back. After one ring, his gravelly voice comes through the speaker, laced with panic, "Are you okay?" he asks. I realize I should have told him where I was going, but it slipped my mind.

"I'm fine. I'm here with Bex. Can you come to her apartment?" I inform Damien over the phone.

"Be there in ten," he replies before hanging up.

As we wait for Damien, we sit in silence. I let Bex take the lead in the conversation, giving her space to share at her own pace. When Damien arrives and walks through the front door, he takes in the situation. He first checks to see if I'm okay, and once he's satisfied, he turns his attention to Bex.

In his black shirt and denim jeans, Damien looks imposing in her small apartment. If the circumstances weren't so serious, I might have found it amusing.

"D, can you hang out with Bex while I go pack her a bag?" I ask Damien, and he nods, taking my place on the couch as I get up. He squeezes my hand as we pass each other, providing much-needed support.

"This is the help I wish my dad would have taken," I think to myself.

"Lor, it's between my mattress," Bex calls out on a shaky breath as I enter her room. I find a duffle bag in her closet and fill it with comfortable clothes, then head to her bathroom to gather toiletries. When I'm finished with her bag, I stare at her mattress.

I lift up the side she sleeps on and discover a little orange pill bottle tucked between the mattress and the box spring. I grab it and walk back to the living room with it and her bag. Both Damien and Bex look up at me when they hear me reenter the room. Bex's eyes lock onto the bottle, and I can see the longing in her gaze. This journey to recovery is bound to be just as challenging as the trauma itself.

I can see confusion in Damien's eyes as he attempts to make sense of it all. I'm aware that he holds himself responsible for not ensuring her safety and for not reaching her in time.

"I'm going to give these to the doctor when we get there so they can help you get rid of them. Is that okay?" I ask Bex. I understand that all of this has to be her decision. She will only recover if it's her choice.

She nods in agreement, and together, we all get up to leave, heading toward the help and support that she desperately needs.

As we pull up to the detox and behavioral health center, we take a moment to sit in the truck. I remember the research I did on this place when I still held hope for my dad. It had received excellent reviews and boasted a high success rate, offering comprehensive help for addiction, mental health, and trauma therapy.

I turn to Bex in the backseat and ask, "Are you ready?"

She looks between me and Damien before softly uttering, "I'm sorry."

In this pivotal moment, emotions run deep, and I can't help but feel a sense of hope for her recovery, mixed with the profound understanding that we are here to support her through this challenging journey.

Damien speaks before I can, leaning over the passenger seat he occupies and taking Bex's hand in his. "No, Bex, I'm sorry. For not keeping you safe. For not seeing how much you were hurting. For not getting you help sooner. For not protecting you from all of this."

He doesn't wait for her response, instead, he gets out of the truck and opens her door to assist her. I exit the truck as well and walk over to their side. Damien already has all her belongings in his hands, and he reaches out to me, offering support. I take his hand in one of mine and grasp one of Bex's in the other.

Together, we walk inside, ready to help Bex take the first steps on her path to recovery.

CHAPTER 34

"I kissed the scars on her skin"
-Pierce The Veil

Damien

"Boss," James says, his tone immediately alerting me that something is amiss on the other end of the phone.

"What's wrong, James?" I respond, bracing myself for yet another complication in the ongoing situation.

"Something isn't adding up. There's one body we haven't recovered, and who hasn't been arrested yet. Carlos' right-hand man was his cousin, Luis, also known as the Xterminator. Somehow, he's completely under the radar. I have good reason to believe he was at the warehouse when they had Bex. He was known as their enforcer and was anywhere Carlos was. His reputation is brutal, and he is known to leave a specific mark on his victims." James pauses to take a deep breath, and I exchange a concerned look with Lorelei, who's across the living room. "He's known to leave an X carved into his victims."

The revelation sends a shiver down my spine, and I realize that our ordeal is far from over.

"Fucking damn it. How could he have gotten away?" I mutter in frustration. My anger escalates, and I lose my composure, hurling my phone at the nearest wall, watching it shatter into pieces on the living room floor. Luis, the Xterminator, was at the top of the list of people who deserved to pay for what happened to Bex. She never disclosed all the details, but the aftermath was clear to anyone who saw her.

Lorelei is right behind me, wrapping her arms around my middle. I allow myself a moment to breathe deeply, feeling her comforting presence. I know I need to admit that I messed up.

Turning in her arms, I gaze down at her, her bright green eyes patiently waiting. I hold her shoulders, savoring the warmth of her skin against mine.

"He got away," I finally admit, closing my eyes to avoid seeing her disappointment. I feel her body stiffen under my arms, and when she doesn't respond, I look back at her. There's no disappointment in her eyes, just pure rage.

"Who? How?" Lorelei whispers, her brilliant mind quickly piecing together the missing information. I provide her with the details James shared, emphasizing that Bex is a victim of Luis and then make a vow, "I promise you, my seirína, I will scour the Earth until I find him."

She nods with absolute determination and says, "We can't tell Bex until he's dead. She can't live in fear. We will work with our team until we have him captured, and then we'll give her the option to end him. Killing my dad brought me some peace, and you've found solace in your revenge; she deserves that too."

Hearing her use the term "we" never fails to affect me. My heart clenches in my chest, as her words resonate like a song meant only for me.

Lorelei's logical approach in the midst of this situation never ceases to amaze me. She remains level-headed and composed, and I find myself grateful for her presence. I used to believe that having a partner could be a weakness, as it potentially makes me vulnerable, but she has made me stronger, almost invincible. With her at my side, I feel like I could take on the world, and that's exactly what I plan to do.

Lorelei releases me, and I already miss the comforting sensation of her arms around me. She pulls out her phone and puts it on speaker, dialing James. After one ring, James's voice comes through, "Hey Lor."

"Hey James, I need you and Kellan on the hunt for this asshole, Luis, or Xterminator, or whatever the fuck he calls himself," she tells him.

"We're already on it. Kellan and I are compiling everything we have and tracking what we know about him. As soon as we have anything, I'll let you guys know," James assures us.

"Thanks, guys. We need to go get D a new phone, so in the meantime, call us on mine," Lorelei says before ending the call. She then turns her attention back to me, and I can't help but feel incredibly fortunate to have her look at me the way she does.

"In the meantime, we have work to do on the pizza shop to get it ready to reopen," she tells me with a smile, her fingers gripping my shirt. But I can't focus on repairing walls in a pizza shop when she's wearing those tiny jean shorts and the black ripped crop top that drives me wild.

"Okay, but first there's something else on the agenda," I reply, curling my body around her even more. Her expression momentarily shows confusion as her brows knit together. Then, I see the moment she realizes what I'm suggesting, and her eyes light up. Even in these dark times, she's a small light that I desperately cling to.

I wrap one hand around the back of her neck, holding her hair in a possessive grip, and use my other arm to lift her thigh, causing her legs to wrap around my waist. I growl softly against her neck, taking in her scent, a blend of sin and salvation that drives me wild.

I lead us over to the large sectional couch in the living room and gently lay Lorelei down before caging her in, making sure she can't move. I can sense her instincts flicker each time I put her in this situation, but I'll continue to do it until she understands that she's safe now. If I could bring her dad back from the dead and torture him slowly, I would do it without hesitation. He didn't suffer nearly enough.

Lorelei's mouth starts its ascent up my neck, and all my previous thoughts vanish as I become entirely focused on her.

"We have a lot to do today, seirína, so this has to be quick and dirty," I tell her, and she responds with a wicked smile that tells me she's on the same page.

I slip a hand between us and unbutton her shorts, pushing them down and making sure I don't pull too far away so her mouth can continue its assault on my neck. Once her shorts are discarded, I get my own shorts off and use my hand to line up my erection with her, ready to give in to the heat between us.

My heart races, knowing that I'll sink into heaven any second. I smile down at Lorelei, savoring the anticipation. With a single thrust, I seat myself entirely inside her, and she lets out a delicious noise that blends pain and pleasure. She's already soaked, and I need to hold back for a moment to avoid finishing too quickly.

After gathering myself, I establish a relentless pace, with one hand braced on her hip and the other wrapped around her neck like jewelry. I relish it when she bruises, considering it a reminder to the world that she's mine. A growl rises in my throat, "Reach down and play with your clit, seirína. We're coming together."

Without hesitation, she reaches between us, her fingers circling her clit. I can already feel her pulsating around me, her grip on my erection growing tighter. I know I won't last much longer if she keeps this up.

Leaning down to kiss her, our lips meet, and my tongue slips into her mouth. I don't relent in the punishing pace I'm maintaining, thrusting into her. Suddenly, a sharp pain pierces my lip, and I can taste the coppery tang of blood in my mouth, letting me know she drew blood. I smile at her through the blood coating my teeth, and her eyes start to flutter closed, indicating she's close.

"Open your eyes, look at me when you come," I demand. Her eyes snap back open, bright green searing into my soul, and her perfect pussy tightens around me like a vice. She cries out my name, and the sound echoes around the walls of our home. At that moment, I come undone and release myself inside her, growling against her neck.

After we come back down from the intense pleasure, I push off of her. "Stay," I instruct, and I walk to the guest bathroom down the hall. I return with a wet washcloth, and she lets her knees fall open, allowing me to clean her up. The trust she has in me brings a smile to my face.

Even when my world is dark, she's the only thing that can bring me back.

Lorelei

The next few weeks are consumed by Damien and me working on the pizza shop and diligently following leads provided by James and Kellan. So far, we've made no headway in tracking down Luis, and the lack of progress is a constant source of concern.

In the meantime, Bex has been making significant strides in rehab, and the facility is preparing to release her to go back home. She's determined to return to her apartment. I've always admired Bex, but witnessing her strength after everything she's been through has me seeing her through a whole new light.

There's a constant concern that's been gnawing at my mind: the dilemma of when and how to tell Bex about Luis still being free. While her addiction recovery has progressed well, I'm worried about the emotional toll it's taking on her. She attends therapy sessions, and she'll continue to do so even after her release, but there's a noticeable shift in her demeanor. Her smile doesn't shine as brightly, and it fails to reach her eyes.

I yearn to track down Luis, bind him up like meat in a butcher shop, and let Bex reclaim her peace. However, I'm uncertain if that's what she would want, and I'm torn about whether not telling her about Luis being free will ultimately upset her.

"Where are you, seirína?" Damien's voice startles me, coming from behind. In a split second, his large, warm body presses against my back. I pause with the paint roller in my hand, my work on the last wall almost complete. Once it's done, we can move everything back into the pizza shop and proceed with the reopening.

I lean into Damien, letting him support some of my weight, both physically and mentally. He's been a trooper, helping me get the shop ready and temporarily putting aside his own work. It's as if he knows I need him close by my side.

"I'm thinking about Bex, and if we're making the right decision by not telling her about Luis, and once we catch him, how to proceed there too," I confess, dropping the hand holding the paint roller. I pivot in his arms to face him, seeking his guidance.

As I gaze into his eyes, I still find myself captivated by the striking bleeding pupil, the mark of his resilience and strength.

"I don't have the right answer," Damien begins, his voice steady. "But I do think she's in a fragile state of healing, I don't want her to have to look over her shoulder right now. Once we have him captured, we'll offer her a choice. However she needs to continue her healing process, we can give that to her. I won't let you lose another person."

His large hand rises to gently push a rogue strand of hair behind my ear, and I allow myself to melt into his embrace completely. Admittedly, life was simpler when I only cared about myself, but now that I have them near me, I'd go to great lengths to keep them safe.

Damien's phone rings, interrupting our conversation. He picks it up, offering a curt "Yeah" as a greeting, which makes me roll my eyes. He remains in place, listening to the person on the other end of the line, and I wait patiently to see if it's anything significant. He mumbles a quick thanks and ends the call.

Damien relays the message he received from James. "No update on Luis, but James mentioned we should keep a close eye on Kellan. He's wrapped himself up in this case pretty deep, and James is worried he will go down the rabbit hole too far."

I share Damien's concern. Kellan, like Bex, hasn't had much exposure to the darker aspects of life, and I've wished that I could shield them both from the harsh realities of the world.

"We'll get him. We've already killed, deported, and arrested everyone he cares about. Eventually, he'll come out, and when he does, we'll be ready to play," I reply with determination, shooting a smile up at Damien as I complete my paint job.

CHAPTER 35

"Take my hand and give me a reason to start again"
-Bring Me The Horizon

Lorelei

The pizza shop has been open for a few weeks now, and it's been thriving. I made the decision to retain all of the old staff and had plans to hire Bex as the manager once she gets out of rehab, which is scheduled for this afternoon. She's always been a dedicated worker, and when she managed Sin in my absence, she excelled. There's no one I would trust more to run the place, and for the time being, Antonio is staying on to help ensure a smooth transition.

We've maintained the essence of the pizza shop, preserving its character while giving everything a modern update. When Antonio first walked in after the renovations, he had tears in his eyes, but it was the sight of the wall next to the ordering counter that stopped him in his tracks. Damien had come across a picture while we were cleaning out the premises, one that captured the entire staff back when I worked there. We were all smiling, gathered around Antonio, and I distinctly remember feeling genuine happiness at that moment.

Damien had James digitally restore the picture as much as possible, and we had it blown up and framed as a memorial to honor the man who had placed his trust in me to carry on the legacy of Russo's.

I know that Bex has a long road to recovery after her release from rehab, healing from such a traumatic experience is a daily battle. She's a strong and resilient person, though, and if anyone can overcome it, it's her. She's requested that Damien and I pick her up, and while I wanted her to stay with us, I understand her need to return to her own place.

I recently took the time to clean her apartment and stocked it up with groceries to ensure everything is ready for her. I'm not sure if it's me being a good friend or the guilt I carry from not revealing that one of her attackers is still alive, and every lead we've pursued so far has hit a dead end.

Damien is taking the situation particularly hard, assuming responsibility for it, and I wish I could convince him otherwise. "You ready?" His voice breaks through my thoughts, and I've been sitting on the patio swing, gazing out into our backyard. Damien's touch on my shoulder is grounding, and when I look up at him standing beside me, that piercing bleeding pupil captivates me, momentarily pushing all other thoughts aside.

He gently withdraws his hand from my shoulder and extends it to help me rise from the swing. As I regain my footing, he envelops me in the warmth of his broad chest. I take a moment to inhale his presence, letting it anchor me.

"Don't bear the weight of the world on your own, seirína. That's why I'm here." My heart swells with gratitude, even though I know he'd go to great lengths for me. I'm still adjusting to the idea of sharing my burdens with someone else after being independent for so long. This is a new chapter in my life.

I nod in acknowledgment and gently separate from him. However, I keep hold of his hand and invite him to come with me. He had offered to let me go alone to pick up Bex, but I need him by my side, and I'm certain Bex would appreciate his presence as well.

The next thing I know, we're parked in the lot of the rehab facility in my truck, and neither of us has made a move. I can't recall the drive here because my thoughts have consumed me, and I'm not sure how long he's allowed us to sit in silence.

Without looking at him, I turn off my truck and swiftly exit the driver's seat. I don't need to look to know that he's already out of the truck as well. When I shut the door, I see him leaning against the hood before me, observing my every move. He steps off the truck and closes the short distance between us. He gently cradles my small face in his large hands, planting a passionate kiss on my lips, then pulls away, taking my hand and guiding me inside.

As we step into the building, I spot Bex at the front desk, engaged in conversation with one of her doctors. Her bags are neatly arranged by her feet. I come to a sudden halt as I witness her throw her head back in laughter. It's a sight I haven't seen in what feels like an eternity, and it tugs at my heart.

She didn't deserve the pain and suffering she endured, but somehow, she's found a way to smile again. Finally, she notices us standing in the doorway, and her big brown eyes light up when they meet mine. "Lor!" Even though I've seen her during her time here, this moment feels different, and I believe we both sense it.

She lunges towards me, wrapping her arms tightly around my neck and squeezing with all her might. Damien has left my side to converse with her doctor and collect her bags, while we sit there in silence, her embrace unwavering.

I'm not sure if hugging will ever feel normal to me, but I'm trying my best. After a moment, I reciprocate by wrapping my arms around her. It feels like an eternity before we finally pull away, and I notice the damp streaks on her cheeks.

Damien has already loaded up the truck, and I know he's acquired all the necessary information from her doctor to provide her with the support she needs during her recovery.

"I'm ready to go home now, Lor," she says, using the back of her hand to wipe away the tears from her face, her eyes gleaming with a newfound glimmer of hope.

"Then let's get you home," I respond with a warm smile. We make our way to the running truck, where Damien is patiently waiting behind the wheel, giving us the space to proceed at our own pace. I'm not quite sure how he always seems to know what people need, but I silently resolve to ask him one day if he possesses some mind-reading ability.

As we settle into the truck and begin our journey to her apartment, I update Bex on everything she's missed, from the renovations at the pizza shop to various other developments.

"I'm so proud of you for renovating the pizza shop. After I get settled back at home, I'd love to come by and check it out. Maybe I can swing by tomorrow when I start my job search?" she suggests from the backseat, and I turn in my seat to face her.

"Actually, since you brought it up, there's something I'd like to discuss with you. If you're up for it, I'd like you to be the general manager and run the pizza shop."

Her eyes widen, and for a moment, I half-expect them to pop right out of her head. "But the shop is yours, Lor. I don't know anything about running a pizza shop. I'm just a bartender."

I reassure her, "Bex, don't sell yourself short. If I didn't believe you were capable of it, I wouldn't ask. Antonio, Damien, and I all came to the same conclusion – you're the most logical choice, and there's no one we trust more. I'll still oversee the business, but when Damien returns to work, I'll be involved in some cases with him. So, I need someone who will treat the shop as if it's their own."

Bex's eyes begin to well up with unshed tears, and she stammers, "I... I don't know what to say."

"I think the word you're looking for is 'yes,'" Damien finally chimes in after remaining silent for a while. Bex's gaze shifts to him in the rearview mirror, their eyes meeting. Whatever unspoken understanding passes between them, she then turns her eyes back to mine, and a broad, toothy smile spreads across her face.

"Well, then, my answer is yes," Bex responds with a newfound determination.

"Please, don't feel like you're doing this out of obligation," I express sincerely. "If you genuinely don't want to, I completely respect that. But if you're willing, I believe you'll love it. Zio has agreed to stay on and train you in everything you need to know, and he'll introduce you to the staff."

Bex reassures me, "No, I really want this. I'm just nervous."

I chuckle and say, "I find it amusing that after all this time, you'd think I'd consider anyone else to oversee something so special to me." Damien smiles from his seat, and as he leaves one hand on the wheel, he rests his other on my thigh. It's a moment when things are finally looking up again.

Damien

Once Bex is comfortably settled in her apartment, and I've returned home with Lorelei, it's time to break the news to her. Lorelei is wrapped in a big, fuzzy blanket on the couch, eagerly waiting for me to join her and watch a movie.

As I sit down next to her, she instinctively leans into me, still scrolling through movie options. Her perceptive nature doesn't miss the change in my behavior.

"Are you going to tell me what's wrong?" she asks, and I curse myself for underestimating her intuition. All those years of watching her back have made her keenly observant.

I look down at her, her dark hair pulled into a messy bun, and she gazes up at me, waiting. "I need to leave in the morning to follow up on a lead from James and Kellan, but you need to stay so you can help get Bex started at the pizza shop," I explain, bracing for the expected resistance.

"Fine, but if I can't be there, then take Anderson with you, please," Lorelei insists. She's developed a friendship with Anderson, one of my soldiers, particularly after the incident involving her father. Anderson is a resourceful and cunning soldier, often called upon when things get tough.

"Alright, I'll take her with me," I agree, though Anderson is already lined up for the trip. I want Lorelei to feel like she's had a say in the matter, to help ease her concern.

Lorelei, now curious about the lead, asks, "What's the lead?" as she continues to browse through movie options. "James picked up on a body found in Phoenix with the 'X' carved into the victim's neck. I have a friend working the case on the force, and he offered to drive us out to the scene and let us know what they've gathered."

She stiffens in my arms and abruptly stops her scrolling. "He's in Phoenix? He hasn't set foot here since we got her back. Why now?" She poses the question with a hint of worry in her voice.

I bury my face in her hair and inhale her scent before answering, "I'm not sure, but James believes there might be answers at the crime scene, and I agree. Someone as adept at disposing of bodies as Luis is wouldn't make such a blatant mistake. This time, the body was left out to be discovered. I think he's well aware that we're on his trail."

Lorelei remains silent for a while, and then she asks, "What kind of surveillance do we have on Bex?"

Her intelligence never fails to impress me. I chuckle softly into her hair as I respond, "She wouldn't agree to have cameras inside her apartment, and I can't say I blame her. However, we do have a camera across the street that points directly at her front door – it's the only way in or out since she's on a higher floor. She also has a security system installed and knows what to do if she leaves her home. We're trying to strike a balance between preserving her privacy and ensuring her safety. It's a delicate line to walk."

With her reassured by the preparations made for Bex's safety, Lorelei nestles into my chest to watch the movie. About ten minutes into it, she drifts off to sleep. Once her breathing becomes steady, and her body relaxes, I turn off the TV and gently scoop up her small form in my arms, carrying her up to our bed.

I place her carefully on her side of the bed, tucking the blankets around her. Then, I climb into my own side of the bed. After a while, I feel her body curl up next to mine, even in her sleep. It brings a smile to my face, knowing that subconsciously, she seeks my comfort, even at her most vulnerable moments.

Life is far from peaceful right now, but I would kill everyone in my path to bring absolute peace to this woman. No one is more deserving of this than her.

At the precinct, Anderson and I are greeted by my old friend Keene, who's been waiting for us. Keene had served as a soldier like the rest of us, and I had offered him a job at AMG when he got out. However, he had a different calling – he wanted to follow in his father's footsteps and become a detective.

"Ashford, is that a smile on your face?" Keene remarks as he vigorously shakes my hand and then pulls Anderson into a hug.

"Easy on him, Keene, he's in love," Anderson quips, her voice tinged with humor. It's a rare moment when they all realize that I'm indeed capable of the full range of human emotion.

"Will you both back off?" I retort, but Keene's focus is locked on me, and I know I'm about to be bombarded with questions. This is precisely why I'm so private.

"Holy shit," Keene exclaims and rushes over to a large window behind us, peering outside at the sky. Anderson and I both tense, waiting to see what's happening, but Keene eventually turns to us with a smile. "Pigs aren't flying, but they must be close if you've shown enough emotion to be in a relationship."

Anderson's laughter fills the room, and when she composes herself, she says to Keene, "Just wait until you meet her. She'd terrify even you." Keene raises his eyebrows in surprise. "Looks like I need to come for a visit, then."

I interrupt their banter with a hint of irritation. "Can you two focus so we can get back?"

"Eager to get back to your girl, huh? Alright, I'll ease up. Let's go. The crime scene isn't far, and we'll take my car," Keene says as he leads us through the precinct and out the back door to his undercover vehicle. We all climb in while he briefs us on the crime scene.

There doesn't seem to be anything particularly special about the location, nothing that stands out. The only connection we have to this case is the mark on the victim.

Upon arriving at the scene, it's still taped off. The body has already been removed, but Keene offers to take us to the morgue if we want to inspect it. There's nothing remarkable about the alley; it's located behind some abandoned buildings in a rougher part of town where drugs are a common presence, and a random body doesn't often draw much attention.

Something in my peripheral vision catches my attention, but I avoid looking at it directly, fearing it might be what I suspect.

"Hey, Keene, bring me those crime scene photos, would you?" I request, my instincts on high alert as the hairs on the back of my neck stand on end. A sense of unease washes over me, and when Keene brings me the photos, I quickly flip to the ones that show the area I'm concerned about.

Sure enough, the small camera in my peripheral vision wasn't present when the crime scene was initially investigated by the police. It's apparent now that someone knew I was coming, and this was a setup to lure us out.

Without creating a scene, I maintain a façade of casualness and instruct, "To the car now, no questions asked." Anderson and Keene go rigid but obey my orders, walking towards the vehicle. In the meantime, I pull out my phone and send a message to James to hack into the camera.

As Keene and Anderson enter the car, just as I'm about to grasp the handle to get in myself, a massive explosion erupts, causing my ears to ring. The force of the blast propels me headfirst into the car, and I can only hope that my friends inside the vehicle have been spared from injury.

Disoriented and having hit my head during the explosion, my surroundings are a blur. The building in front of us, closest to where the body was, is now engulfed in flames. If we were standing in the area near the body, we would likely have been killed in the blast.

I feel hands on me, and I'm pulled back into the car. I think we're in motion, but my vision keeps flickering in and out. However, small voices keep bringing me back. One of them,

I believe, is Keene, instructing police and fire personnel to the area. Another voice belongs to Anderson, speaking on the phone with someone.

"Carver is set up and ready, we need to get him there fast. I can't assess his injuries back here, but I'm thinking a severe concussion at the minimum," Anderson says into the phone.

Yup, I was right. Anderson is ensuring that I'm prepared for whatever comes next.

The darkness keeps encroaching on my vision, but I'm determined not to surrender to sleep just yet. I’m going to kill that mother fucker, but before I can do anything else, everything turns black.

CHAPTER 36

"I said I'd never let you fall and I always meant it"
-A Day To Remember

Lorelei

I've never felt fear as intense as the moment I received the call from Anderson, informing me about the explosion and Damien's injury.

I find myself at Carver's office faster than I'd like to admit, and as I burst through the doors, Carver is there, waiting for me.

"You got here fast," he remarks and takes hold of my arms to steady me, forcing me to look at him.

"He's going to be okay, Lorelei. He suffered a concussion and he'll be pretty bruised up for a while, but I've patched him up from worse. Everyone else is unharmed. I've got him on some mild pain meds to help him rest, but when he wakes up, you can take him home to finish healing," Carver assures me in a soothing voice.

My breathing begins to slow, and I can hear more than just the rapid thumping of my heart in my ears. Carver's reassuring presence has a calming effect on me, and I'm grateful for it in this moment of anxiety and relief.

"I need to see him," I reply, desperation evident in my voice.

Carver reassures me, "He's going to look rough, but I promise it looks worse than it is." He releases my arms and places a reassuring hand on my back, guiding me into the room where Damien's large form appears small in the hospital bed.

I go over to him and sit at the edge of his bed, placing my hand on his, and I breathe a sigh of relief as I feel the warmth and familiarity of his touch. He's still alive. He hasn't left me.

Anderson enters the room a moment later with an unfamiliar man. He's tall and lean, with black curly hair and dark brown eyes.

"Do you want the debrief?" Anderson inquires, always getting right to the point. I glance at the unfamiliar man, and she seems to understand the unspoken question.

"This is Keene. He's our friend in the precinct who took us to the scene," she explains.

I turn my anger towards Keene, my fury coursing through my veins. "Your officers are responsible for neglecting to spot the setup?" That's all I can muster at the moment. Keene's expression flickers with surprise, but Anderson interjects.

She spends what feels like an eternity explaining everything to me: how Luis must have revisited the crime scene after the initial police investigation to set up the camera and explosives, and how Damien had spotted it and managed to get them all to safety. Without Damien's quick thinking, they'd all either be dead or critically injured.

I'm still furious at Keene for not having officers protecting the crime scene, and for allowing this to happen. My anger also burns for Luis, who is still out there. His blood will soon be on my hands.

"What has James found?" I finally manage to ask. I should probably apologize to Keene for snapping at him, but I can't bring myself to care about his feelings.

"James is working on it," Anderson explains. "The camera's IP address was bouncing around towers, so we couldn't get a GPS fix on him. This all looks like a setup to get Damien out of the way, which tells me we must be getting too close."

"Tell James and Kellan I want everything they've gathered, and I want both of them at my house when I get home with Damien. We're going to look through everything. I want him found and tied up in a fucking basement. Now," I command, my tone seething with determination.

Keene leans in towards Anderson and mutters, "You were right; she is terrifying." I let an icy stare fixate on him for a moment, then my attention is drawn to Damien, whose eyes are starting to crack open.

"It's about time someone scared you, Keene," Damien rasps, his voice rough. Pain is evident in his eyes, but he's trying to conceal it to avoid worrying me.

I look over Damien, giving his hand a reassuring squeeze. Anderson fills him in on everything that transpired after they got him into the car and that we haven't been able to gather any information from the cameras yet.

"Carver said I can take you home when you're ready. James and Kellan are meeting me there to go through everything while you sleep. We already have eyes on Bex, and she's safe at the shop, training with Antonio," I inform Damien.

He chuckles, though the pain is visible on his face. "You're cute when you're pissed, seirína," he remarks with a hint of humor. He raises his hand and runs his thumb along my jaw, bringing me back to reality. We momentarily forget that Anderson and Keene are still in the room, but frankly, I couldn't care less.

I need to get my man home and kill the stupid mother fucker that threatened to take him from me.

CHAPTER 37

"Is there a right way for being strong?
Feels like I'm doing things all wrong"
-Sleeping With Sirens

Bex

I'm consumed by anger most of the time now. It's been a long journey from the sadness and fear I once felt, and it's become a constant, festering black stain in my chest.

Spending my days at the pizza shop with Zio is a welcome distraction. It's hard not to smile around him; he's so full of life and blissfully ignorant of the darkness that lurks in the world. When I'm not at the shop, I stew in my anger at home, which only seems to make it grow. I was so helpless when I was taken, but I refuse to be helpless again.

A few times a week, Damien trains Lorelei and me at their house, teaching us basics like hand-to-hand combat and how to wield a weapon. Lorelei is far more advanced than I am, but I've always known she's been prepared for a battle. You can see it in her eyes.

When I'm with them, it's impossible not to notice how deeply in love they are. There's no one else in the world who deserves that love more than them. Yet, it makes my heart ache for something similar, someone who can pick up my broken pieces and not flinch when the jagged edges cut them.

Kellan continues to try to rekindle what once existed between us before I was taken, but I don't believe I can ever look at him in the same way again. He's too pure, and I fear that my own darkness would taint his soul.

A shuffling noise outside my apartment door sends a shiver down my spine. Living in an apartment building, it's not uncommon to hear people moving about in the hallway, but the knowledge doesn't ease my anxiety. After a few seconds, the noise ceases, and I assume it's just someone walking to a nearby apartment.

I push myself up from my couch and walk to the refrigerator to grab a drink. However, my gaze keeps returning to my front door. Something is telling me to go and look. While I know my apartment is under surveillance by security cameras, I'm not naive enough to believe there's no way around that.

I retrieve a knife from the butcher block on the counter, fitting the hilt into my hand and ensuring I hold it correctly. I find that I prefer knives to guns, perhaps because Lorelei has a fondness for them, and she's the one who trained me to wield them.

Summoning every ounce of courage I can muster, I cautiously peek through the hole in the door. Unsurprisingly, there's no one there. I decide to crack the door open, slipping my head out to examine the walkway in both directions, but it remains empty.

As I'm about to close the door, I notice a Chinese takeout container on my doormat. I hadn't ordered any food. My hands tremble, but I refuse to let my fear show. I've had enough of that. I lean down to pick up the container and realize that the bottom is unexpectedly heavy. Quickly, I close and lock my door, securing all the deadbolts and adding the chain at the top. I double-check that the security system is armed before feeling a bit safer.

With my apartment securely locked, I set the container on

the kitchen counter and stare at it. Perhaps it's just a mix-up with a delivery person who got the apartment numbers wrong. It wouldn't be the first time. Gently, I open the top of the container, and bile rises in my throat. It takes every ounce of my willpower to choke it down.

What looks to be a chunk of flesh is lying at the bottom of the container. The box was warm when I was holding it a moment ago so I know this has to be fresh. The coppery smell of blood fills my nostrils and I have to keep fighting to not throw up.

Against my better judgment, I look back into the container and there it is—a big X cut into the skin, just like the one I bear. Also in the box is a small pouch of white powder. Tears threaten to well up behind my eyes, and my body quivers with anger. Is this some kind of sick joke? Unconsciously, my hand rises to touch the raised skin of the scar that marks my neck.

In black ink, on the inside of one of the container's flaps, a message is scrawled in terrible handwriting:

"Did you miss me, Chica?"

The memories of my time in the warehouse come rushing back, threatening to knock me off my feet.

"Don't worry, chicha, we'll be nice. Won't we, hermano?" His voice echoes in my head, and I swear I can smell his rancid breath on me again.

Does anyone else know he's somehow still alive? I closely followed the case to the best of my ability, and as far as I know, everyone associated with it is either deceased or incarcerated.

I want to kill him. No - death would be too easy, but I'm uncertain if I'm capable of pursuing this alone. Damien and Lorelei have invested considerable time in teaching me self-defense, yet confronting a killer like him presents a whole new set of challenges.

Would they give me the opportunity to kill him? Their stance on murder is obviously in the gray area considering everything they've done. Would they grant me the opportunity to do this? To find closure?

CHAPTER 38

"So cling to what you know and never let go"
-A Day To Remember

Lorelei

Something is clearly amiss with Bex. It's written all over her face, though she attempts to conceal it with a forced smile as she goes about her tasks at the pizza shop. I've become an expert at detecting that kind of insincerity, having employed it myself countless times.

There's a saying, isn't there? "You can't bullshit a bullshitter?"

However, I must be cautious and keep my cards close to my chest. Bex is in a vulnerable state, and the very thought of her pain infuriates me. The asshole responsible for her suffering is still out there, and I haven't taken a break to rest in days, much to Damien's irritation. He's hardly any better, though.

After pursuing yet another dead end lead, we're finally back home, and the air is heavy with tension. Both of us shoulder the blame for what Bex endured, and neither of us will find peace until we see that fucker in a helpless, agonizing state in some dimly lit basement.

The mental image of that scenario briefly crosses my mind, and a faint, wicked smile creeps onto my lips.

"What's got you grinning over there?" Damien inquires from across the bedroom. I'm still standing in the doorway, observing as he removes his shirt, preparing for a shower after the long, trying day we've had.

His imposing, muscular shoulders ripple as he deftly removes his shirt, and the mere sight of him still has the power to leave me almost breathless. I'm sure he senses my admiring gaze, as his penetrating eyes lock onto mine, ensnaring my attention.

With the knowledge that I'm watching, he deliberately undoes the belt of his pants and eases out of them, all while maintaining unbroken eye contact. I make a valiant effort not to divert my eyes, but I'm utterly defenseless against his allure.

Unable to resist any longer, my gaze briefly dips to his sculpted thighs, and nestled between them is his hard cock, eagerly awaiting my attention. When I lift my eyes back to his face, he's still looking at me with patience, his hand gently grazing the stubble that's sprouted on his jawline.

With no hesitation, I peel off my clothes and let them cascade to the floor, acutely aware that he's already gripping whatever morsel of restraint he has left. We're both wound so tightly due to the events that have unfolded, and the sole means of preserving our sanity is to unleash our pent-up emotions upon each other. Not that I'm complaining; I welcome the unpolished pieces of him, they align seamlessly with my own.

His large hand is fisting his cock and slowly stroking himself and the sight of that is my undoing.

In a mad dash, I sprint toward him, and at the last possible moment, I leap into his arms, wrapping my legs around his broad waist. My shorter limbs struggle to lock behind his back, but it doesn't matter for long. With effortless strength, he cradles me with one arm while the other grips the back of my hair and forcefully joins our mouths in a searing kiss.

His kiss is ferocious, and I'm scarcely aware that we're in motion. The sound of running water catches my attention, prompting me to break our kiss just slightly. I notice that the hand that was entangled in my hair has shifted to test the water temperature in our shower. Even in the throes of passion, he's always attentive to my well-being.

Evidently, the water is at the perfect temperature, in the blink of an eye, my hair is coiled around his fist again, and he's guiding us into the shower, the warm spray enveloping us.

The soothing warmth of the water assaults my senses, and it begins to wash away some of the dark thoughts that have clouded my mind. Or perhaps, it's the man who's ravishing me, helping to dispel the shadows.

He lowers me down along his muscled frame, his arousal pressing into my stomach due to our height difference. Instead of stopping there, I sink to my knees before him, watching as his eyes dilate with desire, so intense they seem to turn black.

I put my tongue out and slowly lick the tip where precum has already started to bead then lick the underside of him and a low growl vibrates through his chest. Without warning I take him in my mouth and breathe deeply through my nose so I don't gag on his massive size. Tears spring in my eyes and I look up to see him staring down at me.

The last of his control snaps and he shoves himself to the back of my throat and pulls out before slamming back in again. His thrusts are brutal and I let him take out whatever he needs on me. I would fight all of his demons and come out soaked in their blood.

I feel his cock twitch in my mouth and I know he's close, before I can take him deeper he pulls out of my mouth and bends to lift me at my waist and spins to slam my back against the smooth tile of our shower. A breath leaves me from the impact but before I can move again he slides me up the wall farther and hooks my legs over his shoulders so I'm on full display for him.

“Mine” he growls out before he dives down and licks me from end to end. My entire body shivers, and I'm aware that I'll unravel before too long. His hold on me might be considered unhealthy, but for someone who has never felt valued by anyone, I find solace in his ownership.

The assault on my clit has my eyes rolling in the back of my head and just when I think it can’t feel any better he shoves two fingers inside of me rubbing my inner walls that makes stars explode behind my eyes.

I ride his face and fingers while I slowly come back to Earth and when I open my eyes again he’s still locked on me with hunger. He must have chosen to forgo the remainder of our shower, because he gently places me back on my feet and turns off the water behind us.

I hurriedly grab a towel for both of us, but he pays no heed to my gesture. Instead, he sweeps me up into his arms and strides through the bathroom door, returning to our bedroom. All traces of tenderness have vanished as he tosses me onto the bed and retrieves his knife from the nightstand.

"This is going to sting a little," he says, climbing on top of me and pinning me in place. I can feel something sharp digging into the inside of my bicep, but I trust him completely and force myself not to fight. After a moment, he tosses his knife on the nightstand and holds something small between his fingers.

My birth control implant. He cut it out.

In one fluid, seemingly impossible movement for a man his size, he slides down my body and fully seats himself inside of me.

He doesn't give me a moment to adjust to his size but continues with the same relentless thrusts as when he was driving into my throat earlier.

I've discovered that when he's grappling with the darkness of the world he faces at work, he needs this roughness to bring him back. Someone to fight alongside him through his darkness and guide him back into the light.

I wrap my legs around his large frame, moving in sync with the rhythm he's set. His thumb presses into my clit, sending me soaring to the stars as I tighten around him. My moans become his undoing, and he buries himself deep within me as he reaches his climax.

As I come down from the orgasm, a sense of panic washes over me when I realize what just transpired. I search his eyes frantically, and with a tender kiss on my lips, he says, "We're going to eliminate this threat, and then I'm going to fill you so full of my cum that it overflows from you. I can't wait to see your belly round with our baby, making my final claim to the world that you are mine."

Speechless, I lay there with him still deeply inside me, our passion seeping onto our shared bed.

"Baby?" I can't fathom becoming a mother. I know nothing about it. I don't even know anyone who is a mother, let alone a good one.

He must have sensed my panic because he withdraws from me, gripping my chin in his hands and reassures me, "You will be an amazing mom, Lorelei. If I didn't believe that, I wouldn't want to have a baby with you." He kisses my mouth once more and heads to our bathroom.

A short while later, he returns with a wet washcloth, gently cleaning me up. No matter how intense our moments get, he always takes care of me.

I lie there, staring at our ceiling, contemplating everything he just shared with me. It occurs to me that he hasn't come to lie down next to me yet. I turn my head toward the bathroom door, where he had disappeared moments ago with the washcloth, and that's when I see it.

He's on one knee, still naked, holding out a black velvet box. The ring inside is breathtaking, with a large black center diamond and small diamonds lining the band. But the most enchanting part is a small folded paper sailboat tucked into the lid of the box, a reminder of our journey together.

My mind races, my heart pounds, and I can't help but exclaim, "What the hell?"

Tears well up in my eyes, and I bring my hand to my mouth to stop my quivering lip.

"My seirína, it's time to get married." he says, and an unexpected laugh bubbles up my throat. Everything I have and everything I am already belongs to him.

I leap off the bed and tackle him to the floor, and his laughter fills the room. There, on our bedroom floor, he slides the ring onto my finger.

I lean on his chest and look up to his eyes that are filled with love and I hear myself whisper "We have to catch him. Luis. Before we can get married I need to close that chapter, for us and for Bex."

An understanding smile pulls at the corner of his mouth as he lifts his head to kiss me on the forehead gently. "I can agree to that, but you will be my wife and soon, so lets make a deal. Three months. That's the deadline. If we haven't caught him by then we tell Bex and go from there."

I nod my head in agreement and rest my head on his chest. Lying beside Damien, I am certain of two things in life.

1. I would burn down the world for the man beside me

and walk through the flames to get to him.

2. I will paint the town red with blood when I capture Luis, with Damien by my side.

I am the Queen of fire, and I will blaze a trail, leaving a path of destruction in my wake.

CHAPTER 39

"Digging a hole that I can't get out of
Deeper and deeper below the surface to find
that there's nothing there"
- Memphis May Fire

Bex

I achieved sobriety from drugs, but that's not my most significant struggle. No, that one still haunts me. It's the battle of being consumed by vengeance and hatred. Every day, I wear a smile to convince everyone that I'm okay, but inside, there's nothing but pure darkness looking to exact revenge on those who captured me.

Exiting the pizza shop after closing, I find myself alone, the last to reach my car. It's then that I notice something on the ground by my feet, right in front of the driver's side door. It's a piece of what appears to be flesh, marked with a jagged X carved into the skin.

This time, the sight doesn't make me nauseous; it's almost becoming a twisted kind of normal for me. I'm aware that he's watching, waiting. I've intentionally made myself bait, ensuring I'm always alone, hoping that his patience will wear thin, leading him to make a mistake, and I can finally seek my revenge.

I cautiously nudge the flesh with my sneaker, revealing a white napkin underneath. Slowly, I bend down to pick it up, careful not to touch any of the blood on it. With a trembling hand, I bring it up and read the scratchy handwriting.

Ready to play chica?

The napkin reveals a print that belongs to a bar just down the road.

Without giving it much thought, I jump into my car and speed to the rundown dive bar. I sit in my car, attempting to summon the courage needed to go inside. What will I do once I see him? The rational part of me says to call for help, but the anger burning inside won't allow any more waiting.

I pat my small purse on my shoulder, feeling the weight of the pistol I've been carrying. Then, I pull out my blade and slip it into my back pocket as I lift myself off the seat. Glancing around, I search for any signs of him hiding nearby.

With one more deep breath for courage, I step out of my car, slam the door, and walk to the front entrance with more confidence than I've ever felt. There are only two cars in the parking lot, an oddity for a late night at a bar. I don't dwell on it for long but it gives me a few minutes of pause trying to trust my gut like Lor does.

I reach out and grab the handle to open the door when suddenly, a loud boom echoes, and I'm thrown from where I was standing at the door. As I hit the hard asphalt on my back, I hear a crack, and all the air rushes out of me. My side is in horrible pain, and I struggle to catch my breath.

When I glance back at the building, it's engulfed in flames. It was a trap. He wanted to see if I would come alone, and unfortunately, I did.But thank god I waited those few moments or I would have been inside.

Tears spring to my eyes, but rather than waiting for him to ambush me, I stumble to my feet and try my hardest to run to my car, all the while gripping my aching ribs.

In a panic, I start my car and peel out of the parking lot. The pain in my side is excruciating, and my vision starts to blur. I realize I need help. Instinctively, I head toward the nearest hospital, but the thought of explaining what happened gives me pause.

Now what?

Then it dawns on me. Carver. I hope he's around and can keep a secret. I make a U-turn and head to his clinic, praying with all my might that he'll be there and won't ask questions.

The drive there is a blur, but finally, I pull into the clinic's parking lot and hastily exit my car, leaving the door ajar. When I reach the front door, I pull hard on the handle, only to find it locked.

In desperation, I cry out and pound on the door with the last bit of strength I have. When nothing happens, I lean against the wall and slide down, unable to maintain my standing position any longer. Vision blurring, closing my eyes, I'll just rest a bit. I'll figure out another option.

Suddenly, the lock clicks, and the door swings open. Carver stands there, his eyes tired, wearing wrinkled scrubs, concern evident in his gray eyes.

"Shit, Bex, what happened?" he asks, leaning down to examine me closely.

"Please, just help me, and don't tell them I'm here," I plead, tears streaming down my face. I can see the hesitation in Carver's eyes, but then a nod of his head, and he scoops me up in his strong arms, carrying me inside while deftly balancing my weight to lock the door behind him.

Moments later, we're in an exam room, and he gently lays me on the table, the paper crinkling under my weight, and I grimace at the movement. It takes him mere seconds to pull on exam gloves and brings his focus back to me.

"Bex, what happened?" he asks again.

"Ugh, my side hurts so bad, please help me, and then I'll tell you," I say, my voice strained with pain. But will I really tell him? I'm not sure.

"You won't get out of telling me," he demands, a determined look in his eyes. "From the way you're grimacing, I'm guessing that's where most of the pain is. Where else are you hurting?" he asks while expertly lifting up my shirt to examine my ribs.

"That's all, the rest of me just aches," I whimper as he grazes his large hands over my ribs. I'm filthy, and my clothes are ripped in a few places. Knowing what I do about his time in the military, I can assume he's piecing together what happened.

After a moment or two of gentle prodding, he straightens and says, "It's safe to say you've broken a rib. Unfortunately, there's nothing we can do about a broken rib other than keep you comfortable with some anti-inflammatory medicine." Before I can respond, he takes a penlight from his scrub pocket and shines it in both of my eyes.

"No concussion, so that's good," he mutters, then settles his gray eyes on mine. Shit. Why have I never noticed his piercing gray eyes before, they're beautiful.

I stare at him for a moment, wondering how much I'll need to reveal to get him off my back without completely revealing what I've been up to.

"Well, thanks for looking me over," I try to say with determination and attempt to sit up. However, the sharp pain cuts through my side, forcing me to lie back down.

"I'll give you the anti-inflammatory, Bex. It has no opioids in it," he says with knowing eyes. I almost look away in embarrassment, but then he adds, "But I'll only give it to you when you tell me what happened. If you don't, Damien will be here in less than ten minutes."

What a jerk.

I let out a frustrated sigh and take a minute to weigh my options. I can tell he's not bluffing. Men like him don't bluff. If he calls Damien, he and Lorelei will be here quicker than I can think, and he'll make me tell them everything.

"Luis has been taunting me, leaving me gifts," I admit, meeting his angry gaze. "Gifts like the one he left me." I reach up to touch the scar that forms an X on my neck, but lower my hand when I see his murderous expression focus on it.

"Tonight, he left one outside the pizza shop with a bar napkin from a place not far from me. I went there, and just as I was about to walk in, the place exploded. I managed to get out of there as fast as I could, but I don't think he wants to kill me," I share, trying to push down the rising lump in my throat.

Carver contemplates for a moment. "He wants you alive to play with you more. Why keep this from Damien and Lorelei?" Do they know he's still alive?

"Because I want to kill him. I need to. I have so much anger inside me it's tearing me apart. What if they don't let me kill him? They might, but their desire to protect me could prevent them from allowing it, and I can't have that. I need to see him die," I admit.

He steps closer to the bed, gently grabbing my hands to help me sit up. Then, he adjusts the bed into a sitting position for me to lean against. Finally, he turns to a cabinet, unlocks it with a key, and retrieves a pill bottle.

He walks out of the room and returns with a bottle of water in one hand and the two pills in the other, extending his hands to give them to me. As I reach for them, our fingers graze, and an electric tingle races up my arm, causing me to shiver. We both hesitate for a moment.

Quickly, I grab the pills and open the bottle of water, swallowing them down, grateful that there are no opioids in them. The silence is unsettling, and I'm nervous, waiting to see what will happen next.

Still standing close to the bed, he continues to stare at me, deep in contemplation. His black hair is disheveled as usual, and his eyes look tired, like he hasn't slept.

"Here's how this will go. I'll be helping you, and if you decide to keep me out of it, I'll tell Damien so fast your head will spin," he declares. I open my mouth to protest, but he holds up a hand and says, "Anything that happens, you call me, and I'll be there to check it out. There will never be a lead that you pursue alone. I may be a doctor, but I'm also a soldier, and you can't be dealing with a murderer alone or the next time you might have more than a broken rib."

I stew in my anger at his brazen attitude, crossing my arms over my chest and huffing. He's left me with no option—it's either this or he rats me out.

"Fine," I say, relenting, "but you have to help, not get in the way. And when it comes to killing him, I get to do it." That's the only thing I truly care about.

"Deal," he replies, extending his large, calloused hand to my much smaller one. I grab it hesitantly, and the shock goes through me once again from our contact. We shake hands, and his lips pull up in a smirk.

"This is going to be fun, sweetheart," he says with a smile. What have I gotten myself into?

EPILOGUE

3 months later…

Lorelei

No one is more surprised that this day has arrived than me. I stand in our bedroom, gazing at my reflection in the full-length mirror, my body draped in a lace, black wedding dress. My long, dark hair cascades in loose curls down my back, and, to my surprise, I feel beautiful.

Tears begin to well in my eyes when a familiar feminine voice breaks my thoughts.

"Lor, you better not mess up that makeup; it took me forever!" Bex's playful scolding forces a smile to cross my face and pushes away the tears.

"Everyone is waiting, and it's my turn to head down. Are you going to be okay?" When I turn to look at her, my smile spreads even wider. She appears much healthier than she did just a few months ago. Bex has gained some lean muscle from the training she undertook with Damien and me, and she's been wearing a brighter smile these days. She looks incredible in her floor-length black silk bridesmaid's dress.

A few weeks ago Damien and I decided to confront Bex about Luis still being alive and that we've been on the hunt for him. Fear flickered across her face, but she didn't seem surprised. She jumped straight to understanding.

When she heard that Damien and I were waiting to get married until we caught him she told us we were stupid and jumped into wedding plan mode. Ever since she has completely consumed herself in planning, and hasn't asked me about Luis once. Something is off and I'll figure out what it is.

"I'm just happy," I reassure her. "Go on before Damien thinks there's a problem and comes up here to get us."

We both know Damien would rush in if he sensed something was amiss, and with an eye roll, Bex heads out of the room, down the stairs, and into our backyard where Damien and some of our friends are gathered.

I take a deep, fortifying breath and pinch my arm to remind myself that today is real. Then, I follow her out the door. The music from the backyard reaches my ears as I approach the sliding glass door I'm meant to walk through.

Struggling to hold back my tears and with a smile that reflects my anticipation, I know that in just a moment, I'll see him.

I step through the door, and a few yards away, I spot everyone I hold dear gathered in one place. I never imagined such a life for myself, one so full with happiness and love.

But then, I see him. At the end of the makeshift aisle, in front of the circular arch, he stands, dressed in an all-black suit. His distinctive, beloved eyes lock onto mine, and my feet continue moving towards him of their own volition. Though I'm aware that others are present, he's all I can see.

Everyone from Damien's company is present, along with Bex and Kellan. I glance to Damien's left and see James with tears glistening on his cheeks; I smile at him. On the other side, Bex awaits to take my bouquet of flowers. But when I look to where Carver should be, it's Anderson standing there. Her and I share a knowing look, but now isn't the moment to ask questions.

I hand my bouquet to Bex, and Damien doesn't hesitate to take my hands and gaze at me with the entrancing intensity I've come to yearn for.

"Are you ready, seirína? You'll be mine even in the afterlife after today. I've dove into the waters after you and I'll do it again in the next lifetime." he says, a wide smile on his face.

"I couldn't be more ready." We both turn our attention to Anderson as she begins the ceremony.

I don't hear a word of what she's saying because my focus is solely on the man standing across from me. After we both say our "I do's," he crashes his mouth against mine in a fervent kiss, uncaring of the onlookers. I hear cheers and laughter from the people gathered to witness our union, and I can't help but join in.

Damien

My wife. Finally. After we came clean to Bex she declared us stupid and planned a wedding as fast as she could.

If it was up to me I would have married her the moment I put my ring on her finger.

As we make our way down to where our friends are waiting, we're enveloped in hugs, handshakes, and smiles. This entire existence feels like a dream I'm unworthy of, but I'm determined to spend my life trying.

Anderson approaches us, and the nagging question looms. Where the hell is Carver? He was excited to officiate our wedding, and his absence doesn't sit right with any of us. Something feels off.

Before I can dwell on it any longer, James hands me my phone, indicating a connected call. "Sorry, boss, but you need to answer this."

I take the phone, and Lorelei is right beside me, watching me with eager anticipation. "Yes?" I answer.

"It's me," Carver's voice says on the phone. "I'm sending you coordinates. I know it's bad timing, but I have a wedding present for you. Get here ASAP and bring Bex."

The call ends, and a moment later, it pings with coordinates from Carver. I quietly relay the message to Lorelei, and she nods before going to get Bex. Fortunately, our guests here will understand the urgency of the situation.

"I'd like to thank you all for coming, but we need to leave," I announce to our guests. "Help yourselves to the food and drinks."

Thankfully, all our guests are soldiers, and they quickly understand the need for our departure. They head to the food and drinks, allowing us to leave in a hurry.

Not twenty minutes later, the three of us, still dressed in our wedding attire, arrive at a rundown warehouse in a rough part of town. I look at my bride and see her lift the hem of her wedding dress, reaching up to retrieve a knife she concealed.

A chuckle escapes me, and from the back seat, I hear Bex laugh too.

"What? I like to be prepared," she says with a smile. I plant a kiss on her lips and then grab my gun before climbing out of the truck, with both ladies following behind me. I take a moment to clear the area. I'm fairly sure it's safe since Carver is here, but one can never be too careful.

As we enter the building, it's one large room. I grip Lorelei's hand, knowing this situation might evoke memories of her past kidnapping with her father. But then, we all come to a sudden halt as we see a man, beaten beyond recognition, tied to a chair. Carver sits in a chair nearby, twirling a knife in his hand.

Lorelei drops my hand, lifts the hem of her dress, and rushes to the edge of the room, where she vomits. I join her and hold her hair back while rubbing small circles on her back. She endures much worse on a daily basis working with me, not to mention what she went through during her childhood, so it can't be the sight of the scene causing this.

Worry etches lines on my forehead as I watch her. She straightens up and wipes her mouth, then looks at me. She grabs my hand, giving it a reassuring squeeze, and guides me back to where everyone else is waiting.

Bex edges up beside me, her eyes fixed on the man in the chair. Carver's gaze is locked on Bex, filled with anticipation. When I see her look at him, there's a moment of silent understanding between them.

The man in the chair struggles to lift his head, but we all hear him mumble, "Miss me, chica?" The realization crashes over all of us like a tidal wave.

WHAT'S NEXT?

Thank you so much for reading my debut novel "Flames of Retribution: A Queens of Destruction Novel" if you're interested in coming along for Bex and Carver's story stay tuned for "Ashen Vengeance: A Queens of Destruction Novel". For updates visit my website https://katlinpruitt.com

Made in the USA
Las Vegas, NV
27 March 2024

87827122R00203